*Indulge in ... ... thrills
from these ... ... authors!*

CHERRY ADAIR

"One of the reigning queens of romantic adventure."
—*Romantic Times*

LEANNE BANKS

"When life gets tough, read a book by Leanne Banks!"
—JANET EVANOVICH, *New York Times* bestselling author

PAMELA BRITTON

"Pamela Britton's engaging, well-defined characters blend with
her storytelling skills for a winning combination."
—*Romantic Times BOOKclub*

KELSEY ROBERTS

"Kelsey Roberts's seamless blend of tender romance and
compelling intrigue will keep you turning pages."
—TESS GERRITSEN, *New York Times* bestselling author

RED HOT SANTA

- CHERRY ADAIR -
- LEANNE BANKS -
- PAMELA BRITTON -
- KELSEY ROBERTS -

BALLANTINE BOOKS • NEW YORK

Red Hot Santa is a work of fiction. Names, characters, places, and incidents are the products of the author's imagination or are used fictitiously. Any resemblance to actual events, locales, or persons, living or dead, is entirely coincidental.

A Ballantine Books Mass Market Original

Copyright © 2005 by Ballantine Books, a division of Random House, Inc.

"Snowball's Chance": Copyright © 2005 by Cherry Adair
"Santa Slave": Copyright © 2005 by Leanne Banks
"Big, Bad Santa": Copyright © 2005 by Pamela Britton
"Killer Christmas": Copyright © 2005 by Rhonda Pollero

All rights reserved.

Published in the United States by Ballantine Books, an imprint of The Random House Publishing Group, a division of Random House, Inc., New York.

BALLANTINE and colophon are registered trademarks of Random House, Inc.

ISBN 0-345-48349-9

Cover design: Royce Becker
Cover photograph: © David Hanover/Getty Images

Printed in the United States of America

www.ballantinebooks.com

OPM   9 8 7 6 5 4 3 2 1

CONTENTS

Prologue   1

"SNOWBALL'S CHANCE"   5
by Cherry Adair

"SANTA SLAVE"   89
by Leanne Banks

"BIG, BAD SANTA"   171
by Pamela Britton

"KILLER CHRISTMAS"   243
by Kelsey Roberts

Prologue

IN DOWNTOWN CHICAGO, ON THE SEVENTH FLOOR OF AN old building refurbished after the big fire, sat an unassuming office two doors from the end of the hall. BROWN AND DONAHUE GENEALOGY RESEARCH was painted on the frosted glass window.

Every day, Monday through Friday, the proprietor of Brown and Donahue, Rosalind Donahue, unlocked the door to the office and entered at precisely nine A.M.

Roz was a dedicated—almost, some thought, obsessed— crusader. Her small one-woman office tirelessly searched, researched, and indexed generations of ancestors for people hungry for something of their pasts, for families lost.

The light glowing through her window seldom went off before midnight.

With an advanced degree in library science and an inheritance that could handle the purchase of the Hope Diamond a few times over, Roz lived and breathed her passion. While helping others, she worked to assuage the pain and rage that had festered inside her since childhood, since the night she went to a sleepover and in her absence her entire family was brutally murdered.

The killer was eventually caught, tried, and convicted,

but the conviction was overturned due to a technicality. The killer was freed and killed again. . . .

Roz knew time couldn't heal all wounds; it just made them . . . different. She also knew convictions didn't provide closure. Only justice brought solace.

From her vantage point, traditional law enforcement needed a little help protecting the innocent from the guilty. Criminal statutes and the justice system were riddled with loopholes that allowed the rats to escape, but kept the innocent trapped.

So Rosalind arose one morning and said to herself, *No more.* With her inheritance and her research skills, she founded the premier agency for victimization prevention. She had operatives all over the world, ready at an instant to tackle dangerous missions. The goal was preemptive—intervene before anyone could be victimized.

Sadly, business was brisk. The never-ending stream of clients ranged from high-profile, distraught parents of kidnapped children to people overlooked and undervalued by society and everyone in between. It didn't matter. Not to Roz. And not to the operatives of the Agency. They had only one goal. One creed. One allegiance.

In return, she asked only two things of her operatives: Protect those in need by any means necessary, and never, ever make it personal.

This morning she didn't bother to return the phone to the cradle after the panicked call from a new client. With a brief glance at the silver-framed photograph of her family on the corner of her desk, Roz depressed the plunger, then hit one of two hundred prerecorded speed dial numbers. All of her operatives had their specialties. She knew exactly which one she needed for this particular job.

"And a good morning to you, too," she told the operative. His photograph flashed in her mind as a smile curled her lips. One of the reasons the Agency had been so successful was the secretive nature of its communications. No direct contact—no face-to-face meetings. The Agency worked because of strictly enforced anonymity. Roz knew more about her operatives than their own mothers did, yet she'd met none of them and planned to keep it that way. "Here is your assignment. . . ."

SNOWBALL'S CHANCE

Cherry Adair

Chapter One

JOE ZORN STAMPED SNOW OFF HIS FROZEN BOOTED FEET as he impatiently jiggled the door handle. Locked. A damn good thing considering that, despite the nation-wide manhunt under way, a serial killer was even now finding his way through the storm to this Nowhere, Montana, ranch.

It wasn't a case of *if* Dwight Treadwell would show. It was a case of *when*.

Although he was standing beneath the deep porch overhang, the howling wind whipped snow down Joe's collar and snuck under the hem of his coat as it flapped around his ankles. He shuddered with cold. Which didn't bother him nearly as much as finding the place lit up like a damned Christmas tree.

Joe glanced around the porch. His new assignment, party planner Kendall Metcalf, must've bought out every Christmas and craft store between Bozeman and Billings.

There was Christmas crap everywhere.

Might as well have a frigging flashing red neon arrow pointing to the house. *Here I am. Come and get me!*

Damn it to hell.

He kept one hand in his left pocket, fingers loosely clasping the grip of his custom-made HK Mark 23. He would rather shoot a hole through his favorite coat than have someone open the door to find a large, armed man standing on the other side.

It worried Joe only marginally that he hadn't been able to reach the Camerons before he left the ski lodge, or that he didn't have their cell numbers. High winds and snow storms frequently messed with the phone lines way the hell and gone out here.

Hunching into his coat, he jabbed at the doorbell. "Get the damn lead out, people." When that didn't elicit an immediate response, he thumped his fist on the door a couple of times, making the oversized Christmas wreath dance. "Open the damn d—"

He heard the faint beeps from inside as the security alarm was deactivated. The door swung open, spilling golden light and the hot, unmistakable fragrance of cookies baking onto the front porch. Joe's heart did a hard *thump-thump* as he got his first look at the Amazon who was his charge.

Kendall Metcalf was luscious. Every curvy, magnificent inch of her. Her hair, the reddest Joe had ever seen, spilled over her shoulders like liquid fire. Her feet were bare, and black leggings accented every incredible inch of her long, long, *long* legs. A red sweater proclaimed, in cursive white script across a mouthwatering chest, HO HO HO Y'ALL.

Before he could get on her case for opening the door without checking to see who was out there first, she grabbed him by the hand, practically dragging him inside. "Lord, am I happy to see *you*."

Joe would have been ecstatic to see Attila the Hun at this point. His freaking nose was numb. He stepped into the warmth, booted the door shut, locked it, and pressed the reactivate button on the alarm before turning around to face her. The smell of Woman overlaid the smell of pine, vanilla candles, and baking. His temperature shot up in response, warming him much faster and more efficiently than a hot shower. But not quite as fast as his anger that she'd opened the door without ascertaining who the hell was knocking. Jesus.

"Lord. You must be a Popsicle," she said cheerfully, oblivious to his stony look. "Let's get you defrosted." She glanced at the control panel, apparently saw the light was on, frowned slightly, then headed across the vast entry hall toward the kitchen. Without turning to see if he was following.

"I just put my millionth pot of coffee on. I'm always addicted when it's this cold, aren't you? Here, can I take your co— No, you're right. Keep it on until you thaw. This way."

She'd taken her sweet time answering the door, but now that he was inside, she moved at the speed of light and hadn't yet paused to take a breath. Which suited Joe just fine. He was a man of action and few words. He suspected she wouldn't like either by the time this was over.

The house was blessedly warm, and smelled mouth-watering. The scent of Christmas was everywhere, but that wasn't the fragrance making him salivate. *She* smelled as clean and fresh as . . . he frowned as he followed her into the kitchen. Some kind of . . . fruit? Yeah. Pears or something. Fresh and clean and—Jesus, he was losing it—*juicy*. She walked over to pour him a huge mug of coffee, bringing it back to the center island where another half-filled mug sat beside a baking sheet of hot-from-the-oven cookies. Joe removed his hat, then unbuttoned his coat. The kitchen was warm, and looking at Miss Metcalf kept his body temperature several degrees above normal.

"Black, I bet." She handed him the mug. The most bizarre current of electricity passed from her fingers to his, shooting directly to his groin. Her eyes widened in surprise. It sure as hell shocked the hell out of *him,* and he almost dropped the mug.

Joe tightened his fingers around the heat of the Christmas mug, which still had a $3.99 price sticker from Ross stuck on the side. He peeled it off and stuck it on Denise's sludge green–black granite counter top. Denise did *not* shop at discount stores. Never had.

"That's what I thought," Kendall said.

He hadn't opened his mouth. He presumed she was still discussing his coffee choice. "Yeah. Thanks. Where—"

"Are Denise and the kids?" she finished for him. Them, too. But he'd been referring to the cops. "She and Adam took them over to Denise's mother's for a couple of days. They'll be back in the morning. It's been *insane* here trying to get ready for the party tomorrow night, and all the guests, et cetera. You know how it is." She laughed, a bright, robust laugh that did ridiculous things to Joe's stomach before moving lower.

Whoa! Back off, pal.

She sat her quite delectable ass half on, half off a stool, then, without looking away from his face, picked up the spatula to slide cookies from the sheet onto a plate painted with some sort of large brown Christmas animal.

Her hands were pale and slender, her nails long and painted Christmas red. Sexy as hell. What wasn't sexy were the defensive wounds marring her smooth skin. The obscene scars were thin and silvery, and there were dozens of them. On the back of her hands, on her palms, on her fingers, and on her wrists. Joe sucked back a black rage.

"Help yourself," she told him, pushing the baking sheet an inch closer to his hand. "I just made them for something to do. The electricity has been iffy with the storm. Good thing they have a generator. I'd go completely apeshi—*nuts* with nothing to do."

He'd thought that if the cops couldn't get to the ranch, he'd at least have Denise's husband here as backup. He and Adam had been in the Marines together, and Joe trusted his friend at his back. He shouldn't have trusted his friend with his *wife*, but that was old news and water under the bridge.

"Are you alone in the house?" he demanded, straining to hear any noise to indicate someone was either upstairs or in any of the other rooms downstairs. All he heard was her sudden indrawn breath over the soft singing of Christmas carols from the battery-operated emergency radio on the counter. "Some of the guests arrived before the storm," Kendall said, a little more cautious now. "The guys are upstairs," she told him without a blink. She might as well have added *Cleaning their guns*.

Since *she'd* let him in instead of one of the local cops he'd spoken to en route, Joe now knew damn well she was alone. Fuck it to hell. So they hadn't been able to make it through before the storm hit. Which meant he and Kendall were alone in the six-thousand-square-foot house with a killer on the loose. Clearly she wasn't aware that Treadwell had escaped. No wonder she'd opened the damn door.

If the local cops couldn't get to the ranch, nobody could, not with the snowstorm raging. But dollars to donuts Treadwell was out there. Somewhere. Storm or no storm. Joe figured they had at least twelve hours before the situation turned to shit.

The fact that Kendall was trying to bluff him into believing she wasn't alone—now, when he was already inside—made Joe's blood boil. Not only wasn't she supposed to be alone. She should be far, far away.

Curling an arm about her waist in an unconsciously protective gesture, she took a sip of her coffee, holding her mug to her mouth as she watched him over the rim. Alone, yet she had on all her warpaint. It was subtle, but . . . there. She didn't need it, Joe thought, almost mesmerized by large sparkling hazel eyes staring at him unblinkingly. Her lips were a pale pink. He wondered if her nipples were the same rosy color. Jesus. He brought his erotic thoughts back in line.

She took another sip of coffee. "I can't *tell* you how great it is that you agreed to do this on such short notice, Don. Really. Thank you. My guy backed out at the last— What?"

The timer went off in a strangely karmic way as he corrected mildly, "Joe."

Her brow wrinkled briefly. "Yeah, I know," she shouted over the noise. "Snow was one of Preston's reasons for not coming. But still, you'd think a guy from New York would know how to drive in a little snow, wouldn't you?" She slid off the stool, slapped a hand on the buzzer, and grabbed a pair of oven gloves. Every vestige of saliva in Joe's mouth turned to dust as she bent over. Hell's frigging bells.

"Not that we get much snow in Seattle—but still, Preston's originally from New York, so you'd think— You don't care, right?" She grinned. "Anyhoo—his rental car went into a ditch on the way in from the airport. Silly guy ended up with a sprained wrist. And while I feel his pain, I really do, it doesn't help me with all the stuff I have to do around here. Not to mention I'll be too busy bossing around the catering people tomorrow night and won't have time to do that and be Santa, now will I?"

He couldn't—not even in his wildest imagination, which he didn't have—envision this woman dressed in a Santa suit. "You'd dress up as Santa?" Now a Santa suit rented from *Playboy* he could imagine without any problem at all.

She scrunched up her face comically. "Well, yes. If you hadn't saved my bacon. I would have," she said quite cheerfully, as she pulled out two sheets of steaming cookies. The fragrance of hot cookies, vanilla, and sweet scented steam filled the kitchen. "I really appreciate that you're willing to come to my rescue like this at a moment's notice so I don't have to. Help yourself to those oven gloves near you. These will be a bit too hot—"

Hot. Definitely hot.

Kendall felt the prickle of sweat beading under her bangs. "I didn't see a car out there." Now that she came to think about it, she hadn't seen a blasted thing. It had been snowing, and the world beyond the lights of the house had been dark. She frowned. "Did Donna drop you off?" Donna was his wife—and Kendall was babbling.

The guy made her incredibly self-conscious as he watched her from steady blue eyes as she moved from oven to counter. He was huge. Tall. Broad. Strong. All of which made her nervous as hell. He was intimidating. His massive shoulders, covered by the bulky, honey-colored shearling coat he still wore, looked a mile wide. She doubted he'd fit into the rented Santa suit she'd brought with her, but she appreciated that he'd come over to at least try it on. Especially in this awful weather.

Which probably wouldn't matter at this point, she acknowledged. She doubted she'd *need* a Santa, since according to the latest weather forecast, this storm would be with them for several days. Poor Denise. She'd been so psyched for this party, but Kendall doubted anyone would be able to make it to the ranch in this storm.

A few of the invitees had arrived several days ago and were staying in the outlying guest cottages. The cabins were well equipped, decorated for the holiday, and self-sufficient. She hadn't seen anyone in two days. So it was nice to have a bit of company. Even if it was only for an hour or so.

Even if the company in question looked like a large caged beast in a too small cage. He was sitting still, yet he gave off waves of leashed energy. And Lord, he was *huge.* Kendall wasn't used to a man towering over her. But Donald Sanders did so, by a good four or five inches. His craggy, unseasonably tanned face was too rugged to be called good-looking, too masculine for her peace of mind. The thick dark hair brushing his collar badly needed a cut, and his lean cheeks could do with a shave.

She had the oddest urge to touch both. One to see if it was as soft as it looked, and the other to see if it was as rough. She curled her fingers into her palm to prevent herself from reaching over to stroke him. He looked to be in his early thirties, which was surprising because his wife, Donna, must be close to sixty. Hell, more power to her. *Lucky* her, her husband had sex appeal in spades. And Kendall certainly wasn't immune.

Just looking at the man made her breath catch and her heart race pleasantly. She was almost preternaturally aware of him. Of the length of his dark lashes shadowing those cool blue eyes. Of the small pale scar beside his lower lip, almost buried in the crease of his smile. Of the way his large, tanned hand cradled, almost gently, the red coffee mug.

She had a vivid Technicolor image of that large hand cradling her breast, and she felt her nipples harden and her knees go weak.

Whew! The guy was *potent.*

Kendall's physical awareness of another woman's husband filled the kitchen like a living entity, making her feel a little guilty. But, hey. What was the harm? It wasn't as though she'd *act* on the attraction she felt. It was a bit like craving a large slice of Black Forest cake when one was on a strict diet. Just because she wasn't going to eat it didn't mean she didn't want it.

Except she'd never experienced this sensation in her stomach over a piece of chocolate cake. This was more like the dangerous excitement she'd felt as kid, standing on tippie-toe on the highest diving board. Looking down at that water miles below. Too scared to jump.

"I came by chopper." His deep voice poured through her like hot buttered rum. He put the Christmas mug down and shrugged out of the heavy coat, revealing a thick off-white wool turtleneck and jeans. Taking off the thick coat didn't make him look any smaller, or any less intimidating. He was still a bear of a man. Masculine in an intriguing way that made Kendall's heart do a little hop, skip, and jump. He looked as solid as a rock, with no appearance of body fat and an impressive physique. Her mouth went dry, and she busied herself with the cookies.

She hadn't felt anything other than fear in so long, it felt wonderful to feel this tug of attraction. Better because she knew there was nothing she could do about it. It just was.

"Set down a half-mile from here," he continued. "Parked back behind the barn." He tossed the coat onto a bar stool beside him.

The scent of him—clean male skin, cold night air, a hint of leather—aroused all her senses with an urgency that surprised her. Perhaps her reaction to him was due to his size, Kendall thought. The man looked as though he could wrestle a grizzly bear. Being tall herself, it was intriguing to meet a good-looking guy who was big enough to make her feel petite.

And they'd been in the middle of a conversation. "You came by helicopter—from next door?" She knew Montana was huge. But people actually *flew* from ranch to ranch?

The corner of his mouth kicked up in a half smile. *Whoa. Down girl.* That small smile was so potent, she wondered what it would be like full strength. Judging from her accelerated heartbeat it was probably a good thing that he'd be leaving soon. To go home to his *wife*.

" 'Next door' is more than twenty miles away," he pointed out, biting into a cookie. "But I didn't—"

The phone rang. Thank goodness. It was working again. It had been out for what seemed like forever, and she'd left her cell phone up at her cottage. As much as she'd like to have made some personal calls, she had no intention of braving this weather to retrieve her own phone.

Kendall held up a hand to stop him as she picked up the receiver. "Cameron residence." As she listened every vestige of warmth she'd felt seconds before drained right out of her, as did most of the blood in her head. "I know. It's been out since this morning. I'm sorry to hear that," she said flatly into the phone as she watched him pick up the mugs she'd bought to brighten up the dark tones of the kitchen. "No, absolutely. I quite under—" The phone went dead. "—stand."

Her heart was beating fast again. But this time it had nothing to do with the proximity of a sexy-looking man. She turned away as she returned the receiver carefully to the instrument on the wall. At the same time she lifted the front of her sweater and surreptitiously withdrew the small LadySmith handgun tucked against her skin.

Given the man's appearance she hadn't mistaken him for a house cat. But she hadn't pegged him as a predatory tiger either. More fool her.

"You're the best so far, ya know that?" She could almost hear Dwight Treadwell's mild voice echoing like a never forgotten nightmare in the here and now. Obscene in this Christmas-scented kitchen a thousand miles away and a dozen months later. Goosebumps rose on her skin. *"Defiant little bitch, ain't ya? You're scared as shit, but your eyes say go to hell. This is gonna be fun. F. U. N."*

Treadwell chipped at the Formica tabletop with the tip of what he'd told her was his second favorite knife. There was nothing but mild interest in his eyes as he observed her.

There was no more room for terror in her mind. It was filled to capacity. It felt like forever since he'd grabbed her at the grocery store and forced her, struggling, into the trunk of his car. Had no one noticed him kidnapping her? Had no one heard her screams before he'd knocked her out?

She'd woken to find herself naked, cut out of her clothes, and him standing, smiling, over her, a large, curved knife in his hand. It was already covered with her blood. She screamed—

Kendall turned around to face the man in *this* kitchen. She knew the six-inch-long gun only weighed about twenty ounces, but it felt as heavy as lead in her hand. "Oh no you don't," she snapped as he started to rise. "You stay right where you are. Keep your hands where I can see them." She motioned at him with the barrel.

"You're not Donald Sanders. So just who the hell *are* you?"

Chapter Two

KENDALL THANKED GOD SHE WASN'T PARALYZED BY HER fear. She'd learned, during her months of therapy, that action cured fear, and inaction created terror. Been there, done that, had the scars to prove it.

She curled her naked body protectively over her bare legs. Her skin was already slippery with her own blood where he'd repeatedly played with her. Short cuts. Long cuts. Shallow. Deep. They all gave Dwight Gus Tread-well pleasure. Each slice made her flinch and cry out. And each flinch caused the bicycle chain he'd used to tether her to the wall to rattle. She could tell that he was growing bored with this. He was going to kill her. Soon.

She shook herself mentally. Back to *now*. This guy didn't have to do anything to appear intimidating. He just *was*. Her stomach did flip-flops, and her heart pounded as she trained the gun dead center on his chest. Big or not, a bullet would make a large hole in him. Her hand had a fine tremor she didn't care if he noticed. She didn't give a damn if he knew he scared her either. He'd know that even a bad shot from this close would kill him.

Watching him, the scar on Kendall's throat seemed to burn, and she struggled to find a balance between the knowledge that she was the one with the gun, and the memory of what a determined, violent man could do.

"Kendall." He said her name softly as he crouched in front of her, stabbing the point of his knife into the floor between her pale, curled toes so he could free his hands to reach for a large roll of canvas. Treadwell wasn't a big man, he didn't look like a monster. He had a soft fleshy face and light brown hair. He looked like a teacher. Or a priest. But oh God, he knew how to inflict the most exquisitely painful kind of torture. . . .

This man was *big.* And scary-looking, now that she came to think about it. She realized too late that this was a man who could use his body as a weapon. Big. Strong. Fast.

She didn't have enough air in her lungs to blow out a birthday candle right now. *Don't show fear. Don't show fear. Don't show fear.* The mental mantra worked fairly well as she tightened her grip on the gun, refusing to blink.

She'd bought the gun after the attack fifteen months ago. She'd wanted a bigger one—a cannon. But found she couldn't hold the weight and settled for the .22. And even though she'd gone through months of rigorous training, she'd hoped never to have to do what she was doing now. Pointing the gun at a human target. But palpable fear made her ready and more than willing to pull the trigger.

"Well?" She spread her feet a little for better balance and adjusted her left hand to cup her right. "Who are you and what do you want?" She'd been expecting the neighbor's husband. He hadn't corrected her—

The Marlboro Man narrowed his eyes. "Prepared to shoot to kill?" His voice was deep and reverberated through her.

"Not just yet," Kendall said through her teeth. "But *hell* yes. I repeat: Who are you, and what are you doing here?" She still didn't bat an eyelid, and now the gun didn't waver in her hands, but her accelerated, sickeningly erratic heartbeats danced behind her eyeballs.

Was he her worst fear? The realization of her nightmares?

God. She'd thought the terror was behind her. What a fool she was to open the door like that. Especially when she was here alone. But damn it, Dwight Gus Treadwell was in jail where he belonged. He'd never get out. And in her own defense, the law of averages wouldn't send her another attacker. Especially not all the way out here in the wilds of Montana, for God's sake.

So much for the law of averages.

The question was: Run or shoot?

She debated a fraction of a second too long.

One second he was sitting at the counter; the next her wrist stung as he moved across the tiled floor, brought the side of his hand down, and yanked the gun from her nerveless fingers.

He turned the barrel to point at the middle of her forehead. The small gun looked ridiculous in his big hand. Ridiculous, but just as lethal as if he'd been holding a machine gun. He was close enough that any one of the five bullets in the chamber would kill her. Dead was dead.

She felt the blast furnace heat of his body, he was that close. His breath smelled of coffee, his eyes were ice cold, his hand dead steady. A shudder of fear rippled down her spine and settled in her stomach.

She had a fleeting thought. At least this would be quick.

She made a small, guttural sound as Dwight revealed an array of sharp, shiny objects inside the unrolled canvas. She shook hard enough that her teeth chattered. Tears, snot, and blood mingled wetly on her face as, completely mesmerized by terror, she watched him slip the first of seven instruments from their custom-made slots. He held up the thin, pointy ice pick for her to see.

Blubbering like a baby, she shrank back against the dirty paneling of the trailer. "Why are you do-doing this to me?"

Treadwell's mouth twitched, the closest he came to a smile. "Because, pretty girl, I can."

If it was a choice between being shot or toyed with for hours at knife point, she'd choose to be shot.

As yet she wasn't having to make that choice. There was a third option. Run like hell. She locked her eyes with his and waited the three terrifying years it took for the first second to pass. The fear crouched in her chest, making it impossible to breathe. Soon he wouldn't have to fire the gun, she'd simply die from lack of oxygen.

"You should've shot me at the front door, Miss Metcalf. You didn't ask for ID, or anything else."

What kind of killer lectures you on safety procedures? she wondered silently. Through the fog of panic, she opted for another strategy. Keep him talking. She figured if he was talking, he wasn't shooting her. If he wasn't shooting her, she had a chance of escaping.

"Give me my gun back. I can rectify that mistake in a flash."

She flinched when he drew her long hair away from her neck with the cold steel barrel of her own gun. If his eyes had been chilly seconds ago, when he saw the still livid scar on her throat they went Arctic. "Son of a bitch."

The scar was red and ugly. But she was alive. While he looked his fill, Kendall brought her knee up in a lightning-swift move perfected in her self-defense classes.

She was quick, but he was a split second quicker. Her knee struck him in the balls, but he shifted just in time to prevent full impact. His shout of pain and his instinctive half crouch gave her just enough time to make a run for it. His hand shot out to grab her arm in passing, but she was too scared, too determined to let that happen. Again.

She flew.

She knew the enormous house pretty well. He didn't. She bolted past him as he gasped for air. Past the counter where their bright red mugs and the coffeepot still sat. Through the dining nook. Through the great room with its thirty-five-foot-high limestone fireplace, soaring cedar trusses, and thirty-foot-tall, half-decorated Christmas tree.

Kendall's bare feet slapped the polished hardwood floors as she ran. *Notagainnotagainnotagain.* She skirted the trio of heavy leather sofas, skidded around two tall ficus trees in their giant terra-cotta pots, almost careened into the ladder she'd left beside the Christmas tree, and hurdled like an Olympian over the last few half-filled boxes of Denise's Christmas ornaments waiting to go up. Although she might not have been as well trained as an athlete, she was a hell of a lot more motivated.

The massive, open-riser cedar staircase rose in front of her. There were eight bedrooms up there. All of them with solid-core doors, and locks. Her breath was rapid and erratic as she started running flat-out up the stairs, her heartbeat in time with the pounding of her bare feet on the hardwood.

PleaseGodpleaseGodpleaseGod—

She was halfway up when his forearm suddenly hooked her around the waist. The world spun dizzily as he lifted her off her feet. At the feel of his viselike grip around her middle, Kendall went apeshit. Twisting and bucking, she screamed bloody murder at the top of her lungs as she tried to kick backward.

There was, of course, no one to hear her except her attacker.

"I'm not going to hurt you," he shouted above her shrieks of fear and rage as he carried her, kicking and struggling, toward the cluster of sofas before the massive fireplace.

But she'd heard that before. The words settled inside

her like bricks. Stay still and suffer. She struggled and bucked as her mind raced with the endless things he could do to cause her pain. Each possibility ratcheted up her anxiety, causing her to fight harder as he moved toward the sofas with her flailing body hooked easily beneath one arm.

Joe dropped her onto the closest one, then held her arm as she tried to shoot to her feet. "Easy. Easy— Damn it, woman, no biting! Sit your pretty ass down. I swear I'm not going to hurt you. We need to talk."

There wasn't a vestige of color in her face. Amber freckles stood out across her ashen cheeks like cinnamon sprinkled on fresh snow. Her pretty hazel eyes were terror-wild as she stared up at him. Joe felt like a heel for scaring her. Feeling like a heel pissed him off. The fact that she could be stone fucking *dead* right now pissed him off even more. He'd handled this wrong. Joe hated being wrong.

"You have five bullets in that peashooter of yours," he said grimly. "You should've *shot* me, for Christ sake. Don't give an attacker a chance to take the gun from you. Didn't they teach you that at— Oh no you don't." He yanked her by the arm as she tried to make a break for it. She sank against the soft, copper-colored leather, her chest heaving beneath the cheerful red sweater.

"You don't think I'm going to sit here passively while you do God only knows what to me, do you?" she demanded through white lips, breath hitching. Her entire body vibrated with tension as she watched him like a mongoose watched a snake.

Joe withdrew his hand from her arm. She rubbed where he'd been holding her with her other hand. Now that he'd seen the obscene scar running across the base of her throat he felt sick to his stomach. He rubbed his hand across his face. "Don't run. Please," he said quietly, dragging his gaze away from the healing gash made by Dwight Treadwell's Ka-Bar knife. The scar was an obscenity across the smooth skin of Kendall Metcalf's lovely throat just above the neckline of her cheerful red sweater.

"I'm not going to sit here and chat with you before—" Her throat moved and she managed thickly. "Before— *anything*."

He felt like a God-damned bull in a china shop. When the hell had this turned from crap to shit? "We got off on the wrong foot—"

"Gee. Ya think?" she interrupted, a little color returning to her cheeks. Sparks made her hazel eyes appear fiery green. "What's the plan here, pal? I'm not going softly into that good night without fighting you tooth and nail, and I sure as hell refuse to have a polite conversation beforehand."

Joe rubbed a hand across his jaw. Shit. What a frigging mess. He gave her a steady look. She shot him a look of pure loathing. Fair enough.

He pulled her little peashooter out of his belt in back. "Here." She took it, flipped the safety off, pointed it at his groin, and glared at him.

"Name's Joe Zorn." He took his wallet out of his hip pocket and flipped it open so she could see the bad photograph on his driver's license.

She frowned. "That expired three weeks ago."

Ah, hell! So it had. "That's not the damn point, lady. It's just ID—" Joe ran his fingers through his hair in frustration. "Look. Your business partner, Rebecca Metzner, hired me to protect you." So much for his first vacation in two years. His boss, Roz, had hauled his ass off the slopes to do so.

And look at the fine damn job he was doing protecting her so far, he thought with disgust. The woman looked ready to have a freaking heart attack.

"But I gotta tell you, getting my nads shot off isn't part of the contract, so could you point that thing someplace else?"

She clicked on the safety, lowered the small barrel, *slightly,* and scooted back into the corner of the sofa. There wasn't an atom of her body that wasn't ready for flight. Even her flaming hair seemed to crackle and lift away from her shoulders as she moved, making a fiery nimbus around her head.

Dragging in a ragged breath, she gave him a flat stare, chin tilted. Which exposed the raised red keloid tissue. "Protect me from what?"

Christ, that scar was going to haunt him into his next lifetime. He felt too damn big. He'd been sent to protect her, and instead he'd scared the poor woman senseless. She needed protection from her protector, for God's sake. "Who," he corrected.

Her pretty pinking-up lips formed the word *who,* but no sound emerged. She knew who. "Wh—" She had to lick her lips before she could get out that much.

He gently took the wavering gun from her hand and laid it on the coffee table between them, before she accidentally on purpose shot him. "Dwight Gus Treadwell."

Even before he'd finished speaking, every vestige of returning color drained from her face. "No!" Her hand flew instinctively to her throat. "He's in Washington State Prison."

Joe shook his head, and the spark went out of her eyes.

She wet her lower lip, clearly trying to marshal her emotions before she whispered, "He won't look for me in Montana." She pulled her bare feet up close to her body, hugging her knees with her arms, and gave him a look that sent shards of ice through Joe's veins. A look that said she knew she wasn't safe. Anywhere.

She crossed one pale, slender foot over the other, curling her toes defensively. Joe frowned at how ridiculously . . . *vulnerable* her feet looked. He dragged his gaze back to her face.

Her large hazel-green eyes glittered. Not with tears, but with fury. "That psycho knows where I am, doesn't he?"

Without a doubt. Joe could practically hear shark music as the son of a bitch got closer. "The guards tossed his room after he escaped early this morning. They found a copy of the *Seattle Post-Intelligencer*. One article had been torn out."

She blanched. " 'Local Designer Returns to Work After Harrowing Ordeal with Serial Killer.' " She quoted as if reading the headline.

He nodded. "Yeah. Which means he knows about the party tomorrow night. Has the location." Sheer, unadulterated terror showed in her expressive eyes. *Shit. Shit and double shit.* "Doesn't mean he'll come after you," Joe added, though even he didn't believe the back-peddling in his addendum.

"He promised at his sentencing that he'd find a way to kill me." Kendall hugged her calves even tighter. From her tone and the haunted look in her eyes, Joe figured she'd replayed that ugly moment in her mind a million times.

Just seeing the photographs from Treadwell's crime scenes were enough to turn Joe's stomach. She was lucky, *damn* lucky, to be alive.

He was here to make sure she stayed that way.

"I'm just here as a precaution. Think about it. Treadwell is on the run with no money, no nothing. He'll be recaptured soon but until then, I'm here to keep you safe."

She met his gaze, her eyes haunted but steady. "I appreciate the sentiment, but seventeen hours—a *lifetime* in Kendall Marie Metcalf years—being taunted and tortured by that lunatic before he slashed my throat taught me there's no such thing as *safe*."

Chapter Three

KENDALL'S MIND SHIED AWAY FROM THE MEMORY OF that hellish eternity spent with Treadwell. Without conscious thought she lay her hand protectively against the base of her throat as she scanned the great room with a professional eye. Mentally she started making a list of what had to be done before she could leave. A coping mechanism she'd perfected in the last few months. She'd discovered that if she kept her body and mind busy enough, she could keep the horrific memories at bay. *Almost.*

She needed to focus on what had to be done now so she didn't lapse into a full-blown panic attack.

She'd been so tired. So terrifyingly debilitated by her terror for those hours with Dwight Treadwell, that she'd almost begged him to end it—

"Beg me."

"Go to hell."

He positioned the paring knife just above her left breast and applied just enough pressure for the tip to pierce her skin.

She gritted her teeth to prevent herself from crying out.

He did it again and again, decorating her torso with a neat pattern of dots. Each dot burned like fire.

"*Beg me now, pretty girl,*" *he whispered, leaning close to her ear.*

"F-fuck you."

Stop. Stop. *Stop!*

The tree. The tree still had to be finished. Three hours. Tops. The bedrooms were ready for the onslaught of guests, the mantels—oh blast it—except for the one in the small downstairs office, were done. That one would take at least an h—

Good God! What the *hell* was she thinking? She jumped to her feet. Ready for action when there was no action to be taken. "We have to tell Denise to cancel the party!" Damn. Damn. Damn. The phone wasn't working, and according to Joe, they couldn't leave until the high winds and this snowstorm abated at least enough to make their trip marginally safer.

She started to pace. It was a nice big room, and she lengthened her stride as her mind raced. "We have to contact the guests in the cottages. They'll come with us when we go, of course, but we should warn them about Treadwell n—"

"No."

"No?" She stopped pacing for a second. Had she taken all the flower arrangements from the mudroom to the bedrooms? She'd better check— She frowned at him. "No, what?"

"No, we are not hauling innocent people with us all over God's creation. When we leave it'll be at a moment's notice. And just the two of us." He rose, withdrawing a large, nasty-looking black gun from the waistband at the small of his back. It looked mean, and powerful, and as if it meant business. Very much like the man carrying it.

Even with Joe and his big gun here with her, her body was taut with fear. Memories of Treadwell and what he'd done to her were as much a part of her now as her distinctive red hair. She counted her own heartbeats as Joe stood.

"Come with me." He picked up her girl gun and handed it to her. He waited while she tucked it into the elastic waist of her leggings, then started walking, clearly expecting her to follow. "I want to check all the windows and doors."

"Sure," she murmured absently, following him across the enormous room. She wasn't much of a follower, but where Joe and that cannon went, so goeth Kendall Metcalf. "There are only two couples—"

"I don't give a damn whether they're crickets I can stick in my back pocket. Nobody goes with us to slow us down. Conversation closed."

Conversation closed, she mimicked silently as she followed him into the dimly lit kitchen. The radio was still playing softly, and she went to turn it off to save the batteries as Joe checked the latches on the bay window overlooking the snow-blanketed front yard.

She didn't give a damn what he said. She had no intention of leaving four unsuspecting people here for that—that monster to find.

Joe pulled the oak shutters closed over the black-and-white scene outside just as the lights flickered. They came on again briefly, then went out, plunging the entire house into pitch darkness.

Treadwell exchanged the small paring knife for a big one, pausing only long enough to wipe the flecks of dried blood from his previous toy on her bare leg. She screamed in earnest when he started taking shallow slashes at her skin as he connected dots in an obscene scarlet geometric pattern.

The lights went out. . . .

Kendall froze beside the center island, a feeling of dread replacing her concern about Denise's guests. "Oh, God. He's here."

"Not possible," Joe assured her. "Hang tight, the

generator—" The lights came back on. "—will kick in. Go and turn—"

"The outside lights off." She was already striding toward the mudroom where that control panel was located. She turned to look at Joe. He'd stopped dead in the middle of the kitchen. "Coming?"

"Yeah." His eyes looked a little glazed.

Kendall shot him a worried glance. "You're not sick are you?"

He swiped a large hand across his jaw. "I'm fine. Hit those lights. I want to get cracking and check upstairs."

He sounded as if he were coming down with a cold. Which was unfortunate. Because just looking at him made *her* feel hot all over.

Odd because she had felt nothing sexually in over a year. Not a flicker. Not even a nanosecond of thought. Yet here was this giant of a man, with his dangerous eyes and his sexy mouth and all she could think of was wanting to climb his body and kiss him.

She shook her head. She was really losing it if she was this tempted to jump the bones of a man she'd just met. She'd had two fairly long-term relationships over the last ten years. She'd dated Jerry for a year, and Andy for more than six months, before sleeping with him.

She just wasn't that spontaneous. She liked to think things through. Weigh the pros and cons. Deliberate. Kendall bit her lip as she pondered this weird anomaly. Part of it, she admitted to herself, was the latent strength and power of Joe Zorn. Not only did he make her feel sexy; more important, he made her feel safe.

Almost—*almost*—back to her previously invincible self. That in itself was a big turn-on to a woman who'd begun to believe her fear was part and parcel of who she'd become.

The scars Dwight Gus Treadwell had inflicted on her weren't all on the outside.

Joe followed her to the door of the mudroom and

waited while she dealt with all the plugs and switches for the outside Christmas lights. That done, she crossed to the counter and started cleaning up the mess she'd made earlier when she'd done the floral arrangements.

"What the hell are you doing?"

Her hands cradling wet newspapers filled with flower stems and stripped leaves, she glanced at Joe over her shoulder. "Cleaning up my mess."

He rolled his eyes. A very male, extremely irritating gesture, that immediately brought back to mind the reason she was racing hither and yon like a florist on speed.

"Leave it," he told her shortly, motioning for her to go through the door ahead of him.

Kendall was so filled with nervous energy, she didn't know what to do with herself. She dumped the armload of cuttings into a nearby pail and busied herself washing and drying her hands. "You're annoyingly bossy, Mr. Zorn." She turned to look at him.

His gaze drifted to her mouth, and something elemental sparked between them. He hadn't moved from the doorway, but Kendall felt crowded, breathlessly so. He lifted his eyes back to hers. "And you're annoyingly . . . busy, Miss Metcalf," Joe drawled.

"Yeah?" He wasn't getting out of the way, and she started to move past him. "Well, there are a billion things to d—" He snagged her arm and her gaze clashed with his. She forgot what she'd been about to say, her breath stopping altogether at the blaze of predatory heat she saw in his eyes. The smell of him—damp wool, woodsy cologne, *male*—was intoxicating, and made her giddy with longing.

She ached to slide her hands under his sweater so she could touch hot, bare skin. She wanted to stand on her toes and press her mouth to his. God. She wanted him to kiss her until she forgot why he was here.

Amusement danced in the smoldering flame of his blue eyes, but he didn't smile back. "We've known each other all of—what? A couple of hours? And I already know a lot about you."

"Oh yeah?" She dragged in a ragged breath. "Like what?" It was almost impossible to have a coherent thought when all her senses were on overload. The smell of him, the strength of his hand on her arm, the radiant heat of his big body so close to hers—all conspired to make Kendall's brain fog up.

"You babble when you're nervous."

Since right now she was pretty much speechless with lust, she blinked. "*Excuse me?* I don't *babble*. . . . Okay, yes, guess I do. Sometimes."

"You make busywork when you're scared."

That too. She narrowed her eyes and glared at Mr. Know It All. "So? I also own my own—very successful I might add—business, make *the* best homemade chili, and knit sweaters to die for. What's your point?"

His gaze moved over her face in a disconcertingly thorough sweep as though he were memorizing each feature, every freckle. Kendall's breath caught in her throat as their bodies seemed to gravitate closer without them actually moving their feet.

"I bet your bras match your panties."

Now *that* came out of left field. It also jump-started her heart as though she'd been resuscitated. Holy cow. "That's an incredibly personal observation for a stranger to make," she told him primly. "And by the way. You'd be wrong. I don't wear panties." A thong, but not panties.

"Ah, Jesus." He choked back a laugh. "No fair." He was still smiling when his big hands framed her face, then he touched a gentle hand to her hair. "Cool, not hot." His voice was husky, thick with desire. A desire Kendall, too, was feeling. He stroked his hand down the glossy curtain, then curled his fingers beneath the strands to cup the back of her head, drawing her toward him.

"You have the most beautiful hair." He brought a handful to his face, rubbing the bright strands against his skin. "So soft. Smells like pears. Delicious." He sifted the filaments through his fingers, watching intently as the red-gold strands drifted to cling to her shoulders and breasts.

He traced her lower lip with his thumb, then bent his head and kissed her as if he were a starving man at a feast. The pleasure of his open mouth on hers was so intense Kendall went deaf and blind with it. His lips were firm, his taste heady, and the unexpected intimacy of his tongue curling against hers was shockingly sweet. Oh, Lord, Kendall thought, that feels *so* good. Wonderful. Amazing.

Fisting his hands in her hair, Joe pushed her back against the doorframe, kissing her with the same urgency she felt. He pressed his knee to the juncture of her thighs. She whimpered with relief. She clutched at his arms for balance as he drew her against the muscled plane of his chest. She needn't have bothered. Joe wrapped his arms around her and held her tightly against him, until their heartbeats echoed one another.

She went up on tiptoe, wrapping her arms around his neck, eagerly pressing her mouth to his. Eyes closed, her senses flooded with the taste of him as he explored her mouth. There was nothing tentative about the kiss. Apparently he'd been as curious about the taste of her as she had been of him.

She made a soft, inarticulate sound of need, of hunger, her soft breasts pinned against the hard plane of his chest.

A phone rang. An old-fashioned sound. *Ring, ring, ring.* Her cell phone played Beethoven's Fifth. She came up out of the kiss like a sleepwalker rudely awakened and blinked back to awareness.

Joe pulled his phone from a back pocket. "What do we have, Roz?" He curled his arm around Kendall's shoulder, pulling her tightly against him as he listened. Including her in the conversation even though she only heard his half.

"Damn, I wish to hell I could get you out of here now," he told Kendall as she accompanied him from room to room as he checked the locks on all the windows and doors upstairs. He'd filled her in on most of what Roz had told him, but there were details, like several more killings, that were—hell, were overkill. She was scared enough knowing Treadwell was on his way. She didn't need the added burden of knowing the man was killing anyone in his path to get to her.

He considered the fact that *he'd* made it here with time to spare. Had Treadwell? He didn't *feel* anyone out there. Not yet. Considering the ferocity of the storm, coupled with numerous roadblocks, it was too soon. But Joe could easily imagine the sleaze hiding out in the dark, biding his time, waiting for just the right moment. This place was a security nightmare. But he didn't intend on hanging around long enough for that to matter. They'd listened to the weather forecast on the emergency radio, confirming what Roz had told him. This part of the state had come to a complete standstill for the duration.

When Roz's call had come earlier that day, he'd closed his suitcase, thrown his coat back on, and hauled ass to the airfield, where he'd rented a chopper. An hour's vacation every two years was apparently sufficient for both of them.

He'd known about the incoming storm and flown in anyway, just making it in the zero visibility. The massive snowstorm swept in quicker than predicted. The full fury of the storm hit about fifteen minutes into his flight, and from the sound of it, was still getting worse.

"I'm willing to take the risk of leaving now," Kendall told him, rubbing her arms as if she were cold. The house was a comfortable seventy degrees. "Of course I wouldn't want you to do anything dangerous—"

Joe smiled, touching a finger to her pale cheek. "Sweetheart, I *live* for danger. If I thought we had a snowball's chance in hell of making it out of here, we'd be long gone. But it would be suicide trying to fly in this; the snow's too heavy, the wind too high."

He'd been damn fortunate he'd been able to land in the high winds and blinding snow swirls earlier. The storm was considerably worse now. He'd known before he arrived that there would be no way to get her out until the storm let up some. Known it, but sure as hell hadn't liked it.

"There's a snowmobile in the garage."

"If I thought we had a shot, believe me, I'd take it." They weren't going anywhere tonight, but somehow, he'd get her out before tomorrow morning. And before Treadwell found his way to the Camerons' ranch.

"As long as we're gone before he shows up," Kendall muttered, reading his mind. Again. "If we can't leave, he can't get here. Right?"

"One would hope." He twisted both locks on an upstairs bathroom window. The room was small, especially with both of them in it. He was becoming addicted to the fresh, crisp fragrance of pears. The kiss downstairs seemed to have happened years ago instead of less than half an hour. He wanted more than to taste her mouth.

Joe wanted to feel her bare skin against his. He wanted to taste her all over. He wanted to feel the weight of her breasts and taste her nipples against his tongue.

It was good to want things, he thought wryly.

"At least your Roz was able to reach Denise and Adam and warn them not to come home even if—when—the storm clears."

Kendall straightened up a basket of luxurious toiletries on the counter as she spoke. "I just wish somebody could get ahold of the guests in the cottages." She refolded two perfectly folded towels, smoothed them flat, then hung them back over the rod.

"Roz and Denise will both keep trying." She was so filled with nervous energy he wondered if he should suggest they go down to the gym in the basement. She could run a few hundred miles on the treadmill. That might tire her out—although Joe had some better ideas on how he could channel some of that frenetic energy.

Biting back a smile as she folded a point in the edge of the toilet paper, he motioned her out of the bathroom. She scanned the small room before exiting, turning left down the wide hallway. A single strand of her long hair clung to his sweater as she passed, and stuck there, tying them together, as he followed her down the hallway.

"Realistically," she said, making Joe speed up to keep pace with her long legs, "how long do you estimate it'll take him to get here?"

Family pictures filled the walls on either side of them. Next to the blissfully happy photograph of Denise and Adam's no-expense-spared wedding was one of himself and Denise at *their* hurry-the-justice-of-the-peace-is-waiting wedding. The fact that they were all good friends hadn't changed with either marriage. For a moment Joe had the foolish urge to share that information with Kendall. Then he remembered that she was an assignment. Strange that she felt like—more.

"We started with nine hundred and three miles between him and us," he told her. "Bellingham to Bozeman. In good weather, thirteen, thirteen and a half hours," he told her, stepping into an unoccupied bedroom. The king-sized bed, draped in red velvet and accented with Christmas-themed pillows, looked decadently inviting.

"He escaped at five this morning." He crossed to the bank of windows on the far wall. Really. He shouldn't be anywhere near a bed with this woman around. Bed? Hell. Who needed a bed? Any fairly flat surface would work.

She glanced at her watch. "Twelve hours."

Joe locked first one window, then the other. "He's encountering the same storm we are. So he won't be moving fast. Plus he has to find transportation." He decided not to tell Kendall that Treadwell had slashed the throats of two prison guards, killing both, before he'd carjacked a guy on his way to work. Took his clothes as well. That guy too was dead.

Three people dead before Treadwell crossed into Mullan, Idaho, at nine this morning. Another when he'd switched vehicles in Foracre, Montana, at noon. All with Treadwell's signature. They'd been brutalized, played with. Sliced and diced, before he'd cut their throats.

At Roz's last update, the authorities knew Treadwell was on Route 90 and headed this way.

The snow must be putting a serious crimp in his travel plans, but Treadwell was determined enough, crazy enough, to persevere.

The son of a bitch was like a heat-seeking missile.

Joe had given serious consideration to taking one of the snowmobiles. Denise and Adam had half a dozen guest cabins on their property. Too close to the house, he'd already decided. But he knew of several holiday cabins on neighboring ranches fairly nearby. Of course *fairly* in these parts was twenty-plus frigging miles. And while no one would find her there, traveling those distances in this weather would be asking for trouble.

He might be able to stand the elements, although honestly Joe knew even he wouldn't make it far or fast. One thing was for sure. Kendall would never make it down the freaking driveway in this weather. It was brutal out there. Even experienced ranchers and locals didn't brave the outdoors when it was this bad.

But the second the snow let up enough to take off,

they'd be gone. If he could get the chopper up, he'd take her to the Andersons' place thirty miles south of here. If the winds were still too high, he'd risk one of the snow-mobiles. But get her away he would.

Treadwell knew to come here, but he'd never find Kendall once Joe whisked her away from the Camerons' ranch. Damn it, he wished to hell they could leave now.

"I'm willing to risk it, if you are," Kendall offered as if she were reading his mind. It was a disconcerting habit she had.

"Too dangerous." Joe brushed aside a strand of hair caught in her lashes, then let his fingers linger on the warmth of her cheek for just a second.

It was a mistake. Because he didn't want to lightly touch this woman with victory scars on her body and fear in her eyes. He wanted to take her to bed and love her all night long. He wanted to wake up beside her in the morning and see her with sunlight on her face.

To paraphrase old Will Shakespeare, Joe thought facetiously, he was melting in his own fire. Too bad. He'd have to burn alone. Because the last thing this woman needed right now was his horny self. "I'm going to take a shower."

Cold.

Chapter Four

Joe told her to pick a room, any room. Kendall chose the last bedroom at the end of the hall. It was beautifully decorated in cream and terra-cotta, and even had its own fragrant Christmas tree in the corner near the fireplace. Not that she cared about the decor at this point. The room was big and had a luxurious en suite bathroom. It also had an interleading door into an adjoining room.

Three exits should they need one. Forget *they*. *She* needed multiple ways out. The ordeal with Treadwell had taught her that—just as he'd taught her the true meaning of terror.

Joe locked the bedroom door, then went around checking windows. "All secure. Stay here while I shower. I won't be long."

Kendall was tempted—more than a little—to ask if she could shower with him or just sit on the floor so she wouldn't be alone. But that would be turning her power over to Treadwell on a silver platter and she refused to do that. She'd worked too hard, come too far to do that again. Instead she asked, "Would you mind if I used your phone?"

He handed it to her, warning her that the charge was

getting low and not to talk too long, then went into the bathroom, leaving the door slightly ajar.

She gave a bemused shake of her head as the shower turned on. She imagined him dragging that thick cream-colored sweater over his head, she imagined him dropping his jeans. God help her, she imagined Joe Zorn buck-naked under the spray. All of which gave her a hot flash.

Her emotions were all over the place. She needed to focus and get her brain in gear. She quickly dialed Becky's home number.

"Call him your early Christmas present," Becky told her as soon as Kendall let her know Joe was with her. His cell phone was crackly, and Becky's voice faded in and out every time Kendall moved her head. "I've been . . . ing to call you since . . . cops called this . . . rning at the crack of," Becky continued. "I even booked a flight out there to come and . . . ind you myself. Damn it. You scared the crap out of me w . . . dn't reach . . . ou."

Kendall wasn't feeling too sanguine herself. Both her body and brain were on sensory overload. She walked over to the window to see if the reception was any better. Worse. She crossed the room to sit on the slipper chair at the dressing table.

"Detect . . . Abrahams r . . . mended the Agency wh . . . lled . . . ell Tre . . . escaped," Rebecca told her. The cell phone was trying to die. Kendall turned her head slightly for better reception. "The manhunt—" Becky's voice was clearer. "—Roadblocks yadda, yadda, yadda are all over the news here. Despite the weather up your way, he's getting past all these damn people hunting for him.

"Every time that monster ditches a car and high-jacks another one, he *kills* someone. The press has been Johnny-on-the-spot with the lurid details. I hate to scare you even more, sweetie, but you do know at last count he's killed seven people today?"

Kendall let out a little murmur of panic. She hadn't known. But she'd bet Joe had. She swallowed down the lump of terror in her throat. *Sound calm. Be calm.* "The house is locked up like Fort Knox, and Joe has the biggest gun I've ever seen." She suspected there were a lot of other very big things about Joe Zorn, and smiled. Really. Fantasizing about him beat to hell being scared out of her mind.

"Don't let him out of your sight," Beck warned unnecessarily. "On the plus side, if the local cops can't get to you, neither can Sick Bastard. But be careful until they have him in custody."

Kendall had no trouble getting Becky to agree to cancel her plane reservation. With the danger of Treadwell looming, and the weather, there obviously wasn't going to be any party tomorrow night.

"I don't give a damn about the commission," her friend said fiercely. "I just want you safe. I'm glad the Agency guy's there with you so you aren't alone. But do *not*," she warned, "do any of that stupid dumb girlie crap you see in movies, like wandering around outside in the dark by yourself. Let this Joe guy stick to you like glue until Treadwell is back in chains. Is back in a cage. Is somewhere far, far away from *you*. Promise me."

"Believe me," Kendall said dryly, "that's an easy promise to make." Joe had proved just how easily someone could take her gun away from her. So much for her false sense of confidence in her ability to protect herself.

She kept an eye on the slightly ajar bathroom door. He was gloriously naked in there. Was he tanned all over? Good God. Stop that, she admonished herself. But *why?* her devil side demanded. It wasn't as though the man was a mind reader for heaven's sake. It was much easier to fixate on Joe's body than it was knowing a killer was rapidly approaching. Both thoughts made her blood pressure throb behind her eyeballs. "I'm not saying I'm not terrified at the prospect of Treadwell showing up, but having Joe here does wonders for my . . . comfort level."

There was a pause on the other end of the line as her voice trailed off. "And? But? If? And then?" Becky tried to finish the thought. "If you don't trust him to keep your ass safe, tell me. I'll call Roz and have her—do something."

"He'll keep me safe from Treadwell," Kendall assured her friend. "But who's going to keep me safe from Joe Zorn?"

While Kendall went in to take a shower, Joe turned off the emergency radio they'd brought upstairs with them. He'd had enough freaking Christmas carols to last a while. He crouched and lit kindling in the fireplace. Probably not such a swift idea. Coupled with the muted glow of the oil lamp, the ambiance was a little too romantic and seductive for his peace of mind. Especially now that he'd kissed her.

If Roz hadn't called when she had, Joe wasn't certain he wouldn't have taken Kendall right there on the floor of the mudroom. He raked a hand through his wet hair.

There was no getting away from the fact that he was attracted to her. God only knew, what man wouldn't be? She was gorgeous, smart, funny, and sexy as hell.

He'd felt this tug of attraction before. Several times, he thought ruefully, as he turned up the wick in the lantern as far as it would go. The room became marginally brighter, and he crossed to sit in one of the extra-wide easy chairs flanking the fireplace.

He liked women. He particularly enjoyed attractive, intelligent women. Which Kendall Metcalf was. In spades. So his heightened physical attraction to her didn't come as a surprise. The woman's sex appeal was off the charts.

Stretching out his long legs toward the fire, Joe absently rested his Heckler & Koch double-action pistol on the chair arm beside him, keeping his hand on the custom tooled grip as he contemplated the flames dancing in the old-fashioned stone fireplace.

He wasn't a guy who spent a hell of a lot of time contemplating his own navel, but his visceral reaction to Kendall Metcalf was as intriguing as it was puzzling. He tried to pinpoint exactly *what* he felt when he was with her. The high lust factor was a given. But it was the strange, unfamiliar feeling in his chest that had him mystified.

A . . . flutter? An extra heartbeat? *Something* that was wholly alien. He hadn't felt this way about Denise. Which was probably why, five months after saying their vows, their marriage had ended with a fizzle in divorce. That had been almost ten years ago. Clearly Denise felt that alien *something* for Adam Cameron.

They had three kids, another on the way, and appeared to be as in love now as they had been when Adam had rushed the ex–Mrs. Zorn to the altar three months after her divorce was final.

Joe was happy for them. He really was. He liked them both. He hadn't even been heartbroken at the end of his marriage. He thought he should have been, but he wasn't. Every now and then he wondered, on a purely academic level, exactly what that elusive *something* factor was that the couple had and he'd never found. Denise called it *spark, magic,* and lots of other girl words that until a few hours ago, he'd pretty much dismissed as the rantings of a romantic.

Spark was a pretty damned good description for the sensations currently annoying him. Why Kendall Metcalf? Why now? When his total focus should be on protecting her from Treadwell. He should be thinking about guns, ammo, close combat, points of entry, etc. Instead his mind conjured all sorts of enticing images of his protectee.

Sparks, he decided, were distracting as hell.

Without making a conscious decision, Joe had created this nomadic lifestyle. Well, not created it so much as fallen into it without much objection.

Every now and then he thought about assessing his choices but then backed off immediately. In his experience, nothing good ever came of that. He shook his head at musings brought on by flickering firelight and thoughts of a wet, naked Kendall in the other room. "Get a grip," he told himself firmly.

From his vantage point he could keep an eye on all the doors in the room. He didn't like sitting here waiting like this. He was a man of action. But Mother Nature wasn't cooperating. If he had backup he'd go outside and check the perimeter. But he wouldn't take Kendall out there, and he sure as hell wasn't leaving her in the house alone.

It would suit him perfectly if that son of a bitch Dwight Treadwell did one right thing in his miserable sick life: walk in right now.

One shot between the bastard's eyes and it would be over.

Roz had faxed Joe the court transcripts while he'd been waiting for the ground crew to ready the chopper. He'd scanned them while standing in the small airport terminal. And he'd been sickened by what Kendall had endured at the hands of that psychopath. He'd also felt the ticking of the time bomb, knowing that while he was en route to her, Treadwell was, too.

At the time Treadwell had kidnapped and tortured Kendall, it was known that he'd brutalized and then killed five other women. At his arraignment that number had jumped horrifically to twenty-three.

Kendall was Treadwell's only living victim, the one

person left to identify the serial killer in court. Which, according to the transcripts Joe had read, she'd done. Clearly and succinctly. Her attention to detail and minutia in her party-planning business had served her well.

She'd recalled in stark, no-nonsense language details that only one of his victims could possibly know. She'd given a specific and succinct physical description of the man. And she'd gone into clinical, precise detail about what she'd endured for seventeen hours at Treadwell's hands, the reading of which had turned Joe's stomach.

What she'd suffered, and the retelling of it, had taken unimaginable guts. Joe had a clear picture of the physical characteristics of the serial killer. He'd also understood the subtext in Kendall's testimony. The sick bastard had played with her like a cat with a half-dead mouse. He'd slashed her deep and he'd slashed her shallow, letting her suffer as he taunted her with death but kept her alive. Barely.

He'd kept her holed up in a trailer deep in the woods south of Seattle for almost two days.

Considering the timeline, the slash across her throat must've still been raw and livid as she sat in court facing her attacker. The jury had deliberated for all of forty-seven minutes before coming back with a guilty verdict on all counts.

Washington was one of thirty-eight states with the death penalty. But Treadwell's attorneys had managed to get a sentencing recommendation of life without parole after the verdict in exchange for the killer's cooperation in finding the bodies of the other eighteen victims he'd confessed to killing.

Dwight Gus Treadwell had received twenty-three consecutive life sentences, plus one concurrent sentence for the attempted first degree on Kendall and another seventy-five years for her torture. He'd also promised, before the court, that he would one day find Kendall Metcalf and finish the job he'd started. And that the next time she wouldn't get away.

Yet despite all that, he'd somehow managed to escape while being transported between the intake center and a more secure facility. Joe cursed the fact that all inmates, and Treadwell in particular, were given a thorough evaluation to determine the right prison for their particular personality and propensity toward violence.

Hell, if it were up to him, Treadwell would be drawn and quartered, dropped down a hole, and left to rot slowly and painfully. An eye for an eye.

The shower turned off and he glanced up just in time to see, through the partially open door, a flash of pale hip and leg as Kendall reached for a towel.

It was going to be a long night. He'd wait for the first lull in the storm and haul ass outta there.

Fully dressed once again, Kendall walked out of the bathroom blotting her hair dry with a towel. She looked deliciously touchable with her still-damp pink cheeks, shining hazel eyes, and dewy velvety skin.

"Let's talk about our sleeping arrangements," she said without preamble. Joe admired her straightforwardness. He admired a hell of a lot of other things, like the fact that he could see she was no longer wearing a bra under that red sweater. He'd like to peel— *Hey! Up here, pal!*

Already disconcerted by his strong physical attraction to her, Joe wasn't about to debate Kendall on the sleeping arrangements. "You're going to offer to sleep in one of these chairs, right?" he said roughly, trying to ignore the gentle sway of her unfettered breasts and the way the firelight painted her in shades of amber.

"No, actually, I wasn't." Her lips twitched.

Joe watched her pace. She smelled delectably of fresh pears. He'd used the same soap and shampoo, but he smelled like—a guy. "Good. Because then you'd be between the door and me," he pointed out, wishing to hell she'd land somewhere. She was making him dizzy pacing like that. Or was it the clean soapy fragrance of her as she passed him? Or her braless state? Or her bare feet—damn it to hell, he was becoming quite attached to her bare, endearingly too large, feet. Joe felt a sharp stab in his belly that was neither pain nor pleasure as she did another circuit of the room.

She went to the armoire and opened the mini refrigerator that no doubt still held its temperature and removed a bottle of wine. She held it up. He shook his head. No drinking on the job. She found a corkscrew, opened the bottle, poured one glass, then resumed pacing, sipping as she walked.

She stopped to run a hand through her wet hair. It was the deep, rich orange-red of an excellent XO cognac. Joe loved a mellow brandy on a cold winter's night. . . .

". . . eep with me."

"Say *what*?"

"I said—" She took another sip of golden wine, her eyes sparkling over the rim. "—you'll have to sleep with me."

Joe nearly choked on his own saliva. "That isn't protocol, Kendall." *Boy howdy it wasn't protocol.* "Besides, I have no intention of sleeping—anywhere. I'm here to protect you, remember? The second this snow lets up, I'll wake you, and we'll be outta here."

She met his gaze with a level look. "Under the circumstances I doubt if I'll sleep either. But to be honest, without a solid five hours' sleep, I tend not to function on all cylinders. So I'd like to at least try to get a few hours in before we leave. I'd feel a hell of a lot safer if you were beside me. I don't mind if you want to leave the lantern on all night. I'd just like— I'd just like . . ."

Protection. "Company?"

Her nod was jerky as, for a few seconds, she concentrated on the wine she was swirling in her glass. Joe wondered if the woman ever relaxed. Hell. If she *could* relax. Filled with nervous energy, she eventually came to perch on the edge of a chair near the fire. Wired and ready to blow she twisted the stem of her glass between her fingers, then looked up to meet his eyes.

"I've worked really hard overcoming this knee-jerk reaction every time I hear something behind me. A creak when the house settles, or when I see the glint of what I pray isn't a knife."

Her gaze was steady as she looked at him. "I don't want Dwight Treadwell to win, Joe. I don't want to live in fear for the rest of my life because of what he did to me. I thought I'd done pretty well up until now. But knowing he's somewhere out there—knowing that I'm no longer a random victim to him, but someone he *specifically* wants to kill—"

"He won't come within shouting distance of you, honey." Joe kept his voice low and soothing, his gaze away from the frightened, erratic pulse of her heartbeat in her slender white throat. And that scar. Hell. "I won't let you out of my sight for the duration. I promise."

Kendall rose and held out her hand. "Then come to bed with me, Joe. Keep me safe."

Chapter Five

HER HEART POUNDED HARD AT HER BOLDNESS. BUT HER heart might as well be flatlining. When he didn't take her outstretched hand she dropped it to her side, arranging her face into a mask of indifference. Her skin went sweaty and hot. Somehow she wasn't surprised by his answer. The tightness in her chest made it hard to draw a normal breath. "Hey, don't worry about it," she told him brightly. "You'll be sitting right there keeping guard while I sleep, right?"

"Kendall—"

She lifted her chin. His gaze flickered to her throat—the scar—then came back up to meet hers. All she read there was pity. An emotion she'd seen more times than she cared to remember. Thanks to Treadwell, she'd forever be the Surviving Victim. Little else seemed to matter to people. She almost remembered a time when people looked upon her with acknowledgment—praise even—for the way she'd picked herself up after her divorce. She'd made a life for herself—defined that life. And now that was gone. For good if that unwelcomed, familiar glint was any indication. "I know it's early," she inserted before he could come up with some lame excuse for not wanting to have sex with her. After all, what man would want to put his mouth anywhere near the red welt of a scar? It was a painful truth, one she wasn't sure she could ever get used to. She added that to her mental list of reasons for wanting Treadwell to burn in hell.

"But I might as well get in a few hours before we leave." She fake-yawned. "Wake me when it's time to go, okay?"

The tremor she'd been battling since Joe had told her about Treadwell's escape, intensified as she walked across the room to the high king-sized bed. Why was she mad at him? They didn't *know* each other. He'd kissed her. So what? Probably just a mercy kiss—until he remembered the scar. She tossed the decorator pillows onto the floor with a little more gusto than was warranted, then pulled back the terra-cotta-colored velvet spread with jittery hands.

She was nothing more than an assignment to him. A ship that passed in the night. A duty. Fully dressed, she climbed under the covers, lay on her side, and curled into a ball. Her fingers went to her neck. The scar always throbbed when she thought about that night.

She usually slept naked, and while the leggings were thin, the sweater wasn't. She was uncomfortable. She also felt antsy, annoyed, and sorry for herself, all of which pissed her off. She didn't know who she was madder at: Treadwell for creeping back into her life like the rodent he was, or Joe for tempting her, but not being tempted enough *by* her, or herself for—she didn't know for what. Which annoyed her even more.

It was too early to sleep. She wasn't even close to sleepy anyway. She lay still. Not moving, not twitching, not showing Joe that she was awake. That lasted, oh, sixty seconds. She had to straighten the uncomfortably riding up sweater. Then her legging twisted. . . .

The room was warm, but she burrowed under the blankets anyway. Blocking out the flickering light. And Joe. She wanted to bury her head like an ostrich. The problem was, when she came up for air, the situation would be exactly the same.

She tried to concentrate on just how damn *freaking* uncomfortable she was, trying to sleep in her clothes. There were only two other subjects to mull over, ponder, dissect, and agonize about. Joe. Or Treadwell.

One aggravated her but made her feel protected. The other downright terrified her and made her painfully aware of how vulnerable she was.

Would she ever believe herself completely safe? God, she hoped so. She'd done every single thing her therapist had told her would help. She'd taken self-defense classes, bought a gun, made sure she knew how to use it and when to use it. She'd faithfully gone to counseling for months afterward.

A violent criminal victimization is a real-life classical conditioning experience in which being attacked is an unconditioned stimulus that produces unconditioned responses of fear, anxiety, terror, helplessness, pain, and other negative emotions. Any stimuli that are present during the attack are paired with the attack and become conditioned stimuli capable of producing conditioned responses of fear, anxiety, terror, helplessness, and other negative emotions.

Intellectually she knew she'd be in a much better position to defend herself. *This* time. But her body was reacting as though she were once again in danger and under siege. Her teeth began chattering. How could she be sweating and cold at the same time? A sob broke through the tight constriction of her throat and tears scalded her cheeks as she curled into a fetal position and hugged herself. Oh, God. She was so *tired* of being afraid.

"Hey now, what's this?" Joe sat down beside her, peeling back the covers from over her head. "Ah, hell, honey. Come here."

She smacked his hand away, when what she really

wanted to do was curl his fingers against her face and draw him to her. "Leave m-me alone."

"I wasn't rejecting you, honey. It was just that—"

Kendall punched him in the arm. Hard. "You egotistical—jerk. If I wanted some guy to sleep with me, I wouldn't have to p-pay him."

In a quick move he hauled her out from under the cavern of blankets and into his lap, wrapping his arms around her and pulling her close. "Pay someone to sleep with you?" He sounded genuinely taken aback by her tear-choked comment. Stroking her hair gently, he whispered against her ear in warm waves of hot, moist breath. "From my vantage point, I'd say you've got the opposite problem. I'm considering demanding a bonus for my self-restraint."

Kendall pressed her face to his shoulder, curling her arms around his neck. Which made her one sad, pathetic puppy. She'd give him another hour or two to comfort her, then she'd tell him to go straight to hell. She neither wanted nor needed pity.

His arms tightened around her. "Shit, sweetheart, you're shaking hard enough to break apart. I promised you I'd keep you safe, didn't I?"

"Your contract probably stipulates that you get paid, no matter what," she said against his throat. The thought didn't exactly fill her with confidence. But the strength of his arms around her did. Joe Zorn was big and solid and his large body seemed to surround her, making her feel very safe indeed.

"Well, yeah. But that would look bad." The smile in his husky voice shimmered through her body like an electrical current, closing the circuit they'd started in the kitchen. Her toes curled.

"On the other hand," he said, pushing damp hair off her face, then raising her chin so they were eye to eye. His expression was dead serious, his steely blue eyes steady as he said, "Did I ever mention what an overachiever I am? Hell, hate to lose at *anything*. Particularly hate to lose when a pretty girl's involved in the equation. And sweetheart, you are *the* prettiest girl I've seen in a lifetime."

His head lowered, and with a small sigh Kendall closed her eyes, parting her lips to welcome him.

She wanted him with a strength and desperation that should have frightened her. Instead she relished the hungry exploration of his mouth on hers. He nibbled and teased, catching lightly at her lower lip with his teeth, then played over the little sting with a hot sweep of his tongue. Her breath hitched, but his lips drifted away to stroke a burning path across her cheek, pause over her closed lids, then return to her eagerly waiting mouth.

She welcomed his tongue, silky-smooth and wet, against hers as he tasted her, the subtle strokes and forays made more thrilling by his control. He didn't plunder. He didn't grab. Instead he savored, which made Kendall feel cherished. It also made her temperature spike and her pulse race with anticipation. Nor was he immune himself; she felt the fine tremor riding through his body as Joe kissed her.

He buried both hands in her long, wet hair, cupping the back of her head in one palm as he gently teased her mouth.

She reciprocated by combing her fingers through the cool, silky strands of his dark hair. She scored her nails gently against his scalp, causing him to draw in an out-of-rhythm breath, but he didn't stop what he was doing.

Suddenly dizzy, she realized Joe had shifted them to a prone position, her head supported by his hand, his body sprawled half over hers. Even through two layers of clothing, his body burned with a furnace heat. His arms were like steel bands surrounding her. Not a cage, but a haven.

"I want you more than my next breath."

And that breath, Kendall noticed, was gratifyingly ragged. A shudder ran through her body as his mouth crushed down on hers. She yanked and pulled at his sweater for what felt like an eternity until she was able to bunch it up, slip her hands underneath and strip it off of him.

His chest was tanned, broad, and lightly furred by crisp dark hair. She rubbed her face against him like a cat. If she'd been capable of purring she would have. She struggled to reach his belt buckle, determined to get his pants off, but kept getting sidetracked by where next he was going to put his mouth on her.

"Hold it. Hold it." He levered his upper body off hers and she reached for him blindly. But he only wanted to pull her sweater over her head. "Did you make this?"

"I'll knit you one just like it if you hurry and get the blasted thing off me." She tried to help, then realized rather muzzily that she was hindering him in her haste to be naked. She relaxed, letting him tug the garment over her head unimpeded. Hurry. Hurry!

His eyes glittered as he stared down. Who knew when she'd dressed this morning that by evening she'd have a strange man staring at her bare breasts.

He drew in a sharp breath.

She'd forgotten the scars. She tried to pull her hair over her chest, but she couldn't lift up her body enough to get it out from under her. Shit! She was lying on it.

Before she could murmur a protest, he trailed a finger down the pale, velvety valley between her breasts and murmured thickly, "Beautiful." And he didn't care about the scars. A wild surge of emotion flooded her, and tears stung behind her eyelids.

Kendall cradled his head in her hands. She brought his mouth down to hers, meeting his tongue thrust for thrust as his warm fingers closed around the cool globe of her breast. His thumb teased her nipple until it was rosy and hard. Gliding his palm down to span her rib cage, Joe lowered his head.

The warm silk of his hair brushed her breasts as he opened his mouth, drawing a peak deep into the hot, wet cavern of his mouth. She let out a cry as he nipped his teeth delicately over the tight bud, then stroked it with his tongue. He paused to look up at her. "Don't hide from me." His voice was soft, thick with desire. "Every part of you turns me on. Every creamy inch of your body makes me hot. There's not a part of you that I don't want to touch. Taste." His hands were everywhere.

"Lift up— God," he said reverently as he pulled her leggings off to expose a small triangle of sheer black lace. He placed his warm mouth on her mound, then lifted his head slightly so he could draw away the final barrier.

"One of us is over . . . dressed," she murmured as he brushed his slightly stubbled jaw across her lower belly. There were scars there, too. Thin white lines that she knew he could see in the dancing light of the lantern.

His skin gleamed and she couldn't resist sinking her fingers into the crisp dark hair that V'd from his chest down to a narrow ribbon to disappear into his jeans.

She reached for his belt buckle again, but he saved her fumblings by standing to practically rip his pants off his body. The firelight behind him limned the dark silhouette of his body in bronze as he kicked off his boots before stripping. It was a spectacular show. He grabbed his pants up off the floor and dug in a pocket for his wallet. Kendall hadn't given a single thought to birth control. He pulled out a small foil square.

"You carry condoms around with you?" Not that she wasn't eternally grateful, but the fact that he was such a Boy Scout gave her pause. Was he always ready for a quick lay? Worse yet—when had she become a quick lay?

"Let me put it this way," he told her stretching out beside her and pulling her back into his arms, the small package in his hand. "Con*dom*. There's no plural about it." He trailed the foil up and over her breast making her nipple ache for a firmer, more personal, touch. "And this damn thing is so old I'm not going to guarantee its reliability. Still game?"

Since he asked the question with his lips against her throat, and his hand sliding purposefully up her inner thigh, Kendall managed only to push out the word, "Now!" He brushed his lips around the curve of her ear, causing every nerve in her skin to come alive, and nudged her knees apart. "Is that an all systems go?"

She wanted to say something clever and witty, but she barely had enough breath to demand, "I want you inside me. *Now.*" And just in case her urgency wasn't coming through loud and clear, she slid her hand down his hip, then wrapped her fingers around his penis. He was hot, silky, and hard. She stroked her thumb over the head until he groaned. "I want to explore every glorious inch of you, Miss Metcalf, but that pleasure will have to—" He groaned as her fingers tightened around him, "—wait."

Like the rest of him, Joe was a big guy. He had big—hands. He slid two fingers inside her, moving them in intense circles, massaging and testing her readiness. Kendall shuddered, moving her hips against his hand in jerky, involuntary motion. She was wet, swollen, and desperate, and several stages beyond ready. "Talk about *chatty*—"

With a huff of laughter, Joe withdrew his hand to settle his narrow hips between her spread knees. She had a moment's pause to feel the sheer size of him—*there*—before he pushed inside.

He hissed out a shuddering breath as he buried himself to the hilt in one powerful thrust, then lay still. And Kendall was grateful. The sensation of Joe inside her was so piercingly sweet, so monumental, that she couldn't move either.

"Okay?" he asked, voice rough against her ear.

She smiled against his throat. "Better than."

"Wrap your legs around me."

"I was getting there," she groused, her voice thick as he pushed himself impossibly deeper. She walked her heels up his back, feeling gloriously invaded, and kissed his jaw as he started to move.

Pinned down by his not inconsiderable weight, her legs tightened as he moved his big, powerful body inside hers. She felt alive, supernaturally so as she ached and burned and shuddered in his arms.

Their lovemaking transcended anything Kendall could ever have imagined even in her wildest dreams. Their bodies were perfectly matched. Yin and yang. The waves of pleasure crashed and churned until she went blind and deaf, her entire being focused on where they were joined. She was being helplessly urged higher and higher, impossibly higher, on a tidal wave of sensation.

The wave broke, huge and powerful, flinging her into sweet oblivion.

Chapter Six

JOE ROSE AND PULLED ON HIS JEANS. HE DIDN'T HAVE TO explain why, and even though she was disappointed, Kendall didn't have to ask. He handed her his sweater. "As much as I'd rather have you warm and naked, put this on. Hang on a sec—" He leaned over to brush a kiss to each breast before she covered them. It was sweet and silly and her heart swelled with emotion as she finished pulling his sweater down over her warm body.

She closed her eyes briefly. The soft merino wool smelled of him. Joe sat beside her on the bed, using both hands to slowly draw her damp hair out from under the neckline.

"Can you come back to bed?" Kendall asked hopefully. He was playing with her hair, lifting and dropping the long strands as if fascinated by the color and texture. Apparently there was a direct route from the hair follicles on her scalp to all her girl parts. She wanted him again with a need that surprised her.

His hesitation was almost negligible before he stretched out beside her on top of the covers, tucking her against his side. Kendall rested her head on his chest and draped her arm over his waist. She snuggled her cheek against the crisp hair underlain by his hot skin. He smelled so incredibly good she wanted to bottle him.

"Will you sleep?" she asked, letting her fingers explore the deep grove of his spine and the bands of taut muscles and satin-smooth skin of his back. Touching him was sheer pleasure.

"Tomorrow. But you go ahead. You said you needed at least five hours to fire on all cylinders. You have time. Get some rest." He reached over and repositioned his gun on the bedside table beside him, then pulled the covers up, tucking them around her back.

Kendall found the perfect spot to rest her cheek in the curve of his shoulder. Joe glided his hand under the sweater to rub her back in slow, lazy circles and her muscles relaxed as she hovered close to sleep.

It seemed as though she'd just closed her eyes, but she woke with a scream and bolted upright in bed. Disorientated and shaking, she looked around the dimly lit bedroom as if she'd never seen it before.

Beside her Joe said softly, "Bad dream?"

Eyes dark and haunted, she nodded, making her hair slide over her shoulders. "He's out there."

"No, he's not," he said with conviction. "Come here, sweetheart." He pulled her back down into his arms. "Roz called to give us an update not an hour ago, remember? He was last seen in Nimrod. That means he's at least five hours away, on a good day. And that's only if he manages to commandeer another vehicle. If the storm lets up. If he isn't stopped by one of the roadblocks between here and there. Everyone is looking for the son of a bitch, honey. He won't get anywhere near you. I promise."

"He doesn't have to be anywhere near me to scare me spitless," Kendall said tightly. She was shivering hard now. Joe tightened his arms around her and rubbed her back in long, soothing strokes. He wished like hell he were touching her bare skin, but this had to be enough. For now.

"How did you get away that night?" he asked, tightening his arms around her. He knew, of course. It had been in the transcripts. But he wanted her to remember taking action. To remember that she hadn't been helpless.

"I'd lost track of time. There was tinfoil over the windows, and I had no idea if it was day or night. Or how long he'd h-had me. He kept me chained to the handle of the oven. There was—b-blood all over me—"

Shit. Bad idea. "But you managed to outsmart the sick fu—bastard and get away, didn't you?" His own stomach lurched at the thought of the cuts on her body and how terrified she must've been.

"He said, 'I've enjoyed our time together, Kendall,' and took a key out of his pocket. I thought— Oh, God. I thought— He's going to kill me with a key. I was so freaked, I believed he could've done it, too." She was breathing fast, and Joe rocked her against his chest, listening to her erratic breathing. Fury blazed in his belly as she talked.

"But he opened the padlock on the chain. He showed me the special knife in one hand and hoisted me up off the floor. He needed me standing. He wanted to add my blood to his wall of s-splatter."

Christ.

"He considered himself an artist," she said bitterly. "I was his medium. He told me . . . told me that I had to be positioned just right so that when he sliced my artery, the spray of blood would add to the mural he'd been creating on the—the wall of the trailer."

The mural that had the blood of more than a dozen other women dried on it. A challenge for the forensic teams to unravel the DNA. "Jesus, sweetheart. I'm sorry. So sorry. But you beat him at his own game. You got away."

Bleeding from dozens of cuts, she'd still had the fortitude to pick up the open padlock from the floor where Treadwell had dropped it. While Treadwell angled her for best effect, then started to cut her throat, Kendall, despite considerable blood loss, had managed to smash him in the face with it. Then she'd run.

When a passing motorist had almost driven over her, he'd called 911 about the dead body sprawled in the middle of the road. The Good Samaritan had, thank God, made the call, but Kendall had almost bled out because the man had stayed in his vehicle until the cops arrived.

"Yes." She burrowed tightly against Joe, shaking hard enough to shatter. "I got away."

At what cost? Joe thought, wrapping her in his arms and holding her tightly. Damn. He hated that he was in a hurry-up-and-wait position. He didn't like not having options. He had a fantasy of getting Kendall to safety, then returning to the house to wait for Treadwell himself. One on one.

Before the cops arrived and made a nice, polite arrest, Joe wanted just half an hour with the son of a bitch. Just long enough to give Dwight Gus Treadwell the punishment he so richly deserved.

He listened to the storm die down beyond the sealed windows and checked the safety on the H&K.

He could tell she was too agitated to remain in bed. She was antsy. Hungry. No, thirsty. They went down to the kitchen, Joe wearing only jeans, Kendall wearing nothing but his white sweater. Her long, pale legs and unfettered breasts did amazing things for his favorite sweater. He found everything about Kendall Metcalf sexy. From her incredible red hair all the way to her slender feet and bright red toenails. And pretty much everything in between.

Carrying the extra oil lamp, they took the radio downstairs with them so they could keep apprised of the weather situation. Dim nightlights, powered by the generator, glowed throughout the house.

They stood at the center island in the semi-darkness

eating cookies washed down with eggnog. Then Kendall decided she needed protein, and ripped off chunks of turkey breast, feeding them to Joe as he leaned a hip against the counter, supporting her body against him.

"Hear that?" She lifted her head. "The wind's dying down. Let's go now."

He felt the same urgency. But going out in that would be suicide. He shook his head, looping a long strand of fiery hair behind her ear. "But it's still blowing hard enough to knock us off our feet if we ventured outside. Sorry, honey. We have a few more hours to wait." He rubbed his hands up and down her arms. "Let's get you back in bed. You're shivering."

She gave him a flirty look under her lashes. "You could warm me."

Where the hell had this woman been all his life? "I could, yes." Joe slid his hands to her hips and started bunching up the sweater. It skimmed up her bare body like some kind of fantasy, making him hard and hot.

With a laugh, she spun out of his hands and dashed across the kitchen. "I don't want to make love on this cold tile floor." She hesitated in the doorway, a silhouette in the darkness. "Race you upstairs."

Joe bit back a smile. "I'll give you a seven-minute head start."

"Show-off." Her voice faded, and he heard the soft thuds of her running footsteps as she sprinted across the great room.

She was easy to catch. She wasn't running very fast.

He caught her by the waist when she was on the fifth step. She giggled, wrapping her arms around his neck as he took her down. He fought to drag his sweater over her head, while she wrestled him for his jeans. Her long hair clung to the white wool as he tossed the sweater aside, leaving her bare and beautiful.

Her mouth curved, and her pretty eyes glittered up at

him as she lay naked on the stairs. She started to laugh. "You know this is physically impossible, don't you?"

His mouth silenced her. Nothing was impossible.

He braced his hands on the riser on either side of her head as her knees came up to hug his hips. Her hips lifted to greet his first thrust.

It was over in minutes, leaving them with ragged breath and sweat-dampened skin.

He sucked in deep, gulping breaths, somehow managing to position himself so that while he was still inside her, he wasn't squishing her against the hard wood of the steps.

"Okay?" he asked, opening his eyes a crack.

Pushing hair off his forehead, she grinned. "Better than. But I think I have bruises on my butt—" She screamed playfully as he turned her over to lavish kisses on her delectable ass.

His jeans rang. He fumbled to reach them, then flipped them to reach his back pocket and the chiming cell, bringing the phone to his ear. "Yeah?"

Cradling her cheek on her folded hands Kendall let herself drift. She was limp as a noodle with a mixture of pleasure and exhaustion. While he talked, she stared through the open risers beneath her at the unfinished Christmas tree below in the great room. Not that it mattered at this point, but still—

And while she was lying here—not that she'd noticed while they were in the throes—but now that she wasn't otherwise occupied, she felt each individual plank of wood across her upper chest, midriff, hips, thighs, and shinbones, just as she'd felt them all the way down her back earlier.

She found just enough energy to turn over, then to clamber over his long, rangy body. Let him take the brunt of the hardwood for a while. He shifted beneath her, getting comfortable, as he talked to Roz. Kendall whiled away the time by kissing his throat, his jaw, his mouth, and wherever else she could reach without expending any more energy than necessary. He moved the open cell phone accordingly. "Yeah. 'Preciate it, thanks, Roz."

He snapped his cell phone closed. "They've managed to clear part of the road up here. The local cops are on their way." Before she could move, Joe scooped her up and carried her upstairs.

"Very manly," she murmured admiringly, looping her arms about his neck and laying her head on his chest. Fortunately, all of *her* clothes were upstairs.

Chapter Seven

THEY DRESSED AND, TAKING THE RADIO WITH THEM TO listen to the weather, went downstairs to wait for the police to arrive. The house was icy, and Joe considered lighting the fire in the great room. But they wouldn't be there long enough to get the benefit.

Kendall had left a pair of bright blue, fur-lined, knee-high boots in the hall closet, and she plopped herself down on the area rug to pull them on.

Joe held out his hand to pull her up when she was done. "Man. I'd give a year's pay to see you in those—and nothing else."

"Yeah?" Her smile didn't quite reach her eyes as she came up beside him in a smooth move he had to admire. "That can be arranged."

"I'll consider that a promise and take a rain check. Here." He took her coat from her. "Let me help you with that." The yellow down coat made her look like a fluffy chick. He took the opportunity to gather her luxurious hair in one hand as she shrugged the garment over her shoulders.

He put his arm around her shoulders and gave her a squeeze. He knew she was scared, and he wasn't going to diminish that emotion by pretending he wasn't aware of her feelings. As much as he sympathized, her fear would keep her on her toes. He should be feeling a mild form of relief at this point. The storm had relented enough for them to leave. He had ample backup and the means to leave quickly, and there had been no reported sightings of Treadwell for almost five hours.

Instead Joe felt a tightening at the back of his neck. There was the sense—the anticipation—of impending danger. Something was off.

Treadwell was close.

Following her into the kitchen, Joe tugged on his own heavy coat, then picked up his hat and gloves from where he'd left them the day before. Hell. Was it only yesterday?

"Want one of these oh-so-stale cookies? Neither do I." She tossed the one she held back onto the animal plate as she passed. She opened the refrigerator. "No coffee," she told him brightly. "But for that all-important caffeine jolt, how about a warm Coke instead?"

She was babbling *and* pacing. "Pass," he told her, buttoning his coat. "The cavalry should be here soon."

He snagged her arm as she passed, drawing her against him to cup her cheek. Her skin was cold, despite the thick coat she wore. "In an hour or less," he promised her, "I'll have you back in a warm bed. With a very hot me." He brushed his mouth over hers. And then because, honest to God, he couldn't keep his body parts off her body parts, he pulled her tightly into his arms and crushed his mouth down on hers.

The kiss was short but filled with promise. Joe lifted his head, then went back in to rub his nose on hers in an Eskimo kiss. "This'll be a hell of a story to tell our grandkids over the campfire, won't it?"

She narrowed her pretty eyes. "I hate camping."

"You're young. Plenty of time to learn to love it. Kids like that sort of thing."

The doorbell rang.

"Easy, sweetheart," he told her calmly as she jumped

at the sound of the chimes echoing through the house. "The cavalry, remember?" It was just after seven, and still dark outside. "Almost over. Got your gun?"

When she patted a pocket, he smiled. "I'll let them in. We'll have our own personal army to accompany us to the chopper. And when he gets here, the local cops and the Feds can grab him."

Kendall wrapped a blue-and-yellow-striped knit scarf around her throat several times. The thing was a mile long. "From your lips to God's ear." She fished a pair of child-sized blue gloves from a pocket and pushed her hands into them. Strangely they fit.

The doorbell rang again, urgently. Impatiently.

"Step back into the kitchen while I let them in," Joe told her briskly. She'd dug a blue hat out of a pocket and was pulling it on over her head with both hands. It covered her ears and forehead. She looked adorable.

He couldn't resist, and dropped another quick, hard kiss to her mouth. "Scoot." He waited until she was well into the kitchen and out of sight.

He wouldn't risk taking a single chance. With the H&K in plain view, he opened the front door. Joe knew several of the officers. He kept the six men on the icy doorstep as he checked the others' IDs. Treadwell was no lightweight; he was doing this by the book. Now, when he got his hands on Treadwell—the book was out the fucking window.

Satisfied, Joe let the guys in, glimpsing the snowplow parked near the steps out front. The door slammed shut with the force of the wind behind the last man. The storm might have died down, but it was far from over. While it wasn't impossible to fly the chopper out, the high winds were going to make it dangerous as hell. And clearly the men hadn't been able to drive a regular vehicle through the snow banks. Damn it to hell.

They spent a few minutes brushing snow off their shoulders. Joe was grateful that he knew some of the officers and also grateful to have them at his back protecting Kendall.

At his all-clear, she came out of the kitchen and introduced herself, glancing around curiously. It was obvious she realized he knew the men, but she didn't ask any questions.

"Your boss lady says y'all are gonna fly a copter outta here?" the chief of police, beefy, red-faced William "Buckeye" Wilder, said to Joe after touching his Stetson briefly to Kendall. Buckeye's son had played football with Joe at the U of Montana way back when. Go, Grizzlies.

"Wouldn't suggest it, son," he said grimly. "Know you've been flyin' since you was yay-tall, but that wind out there'll bring you down before you lift off."

Joe suspected he was right, but he'd done more than fly over the Montana landscape in the last ten years. He had infinite confidence in his own abilities as a pilot, but until he went out there and saw for himself exactly how bad it was, he wasn't going to negate their best, most expedient form of transportation.

"Could be" was all he said. He glanced from man to man. "Is there any other way? All I saw out there was a snowplow. Not exactly my idea of a speedy getaway."

"Better to wait four or five hours, and take a couple of the Camerons' snowmobiles when the wind lets up." Sonny Goodwin, a younger brother of another of Joe's college buddies, suggested, stomping the snow off his boots onto the hall rug. "Don't suppose there's any hot coffee around?" he asked hopefully.

"Sorry, no." Kendall looked at Joe with a frown. "I don't want to wait. But I also don't want to do something stupid and dangerous. What are our options?"

Not many, Joe thought with frustration. A plodding snowmobile a child on a tricycle could follow, or the chopper. Hanging around for another four or five hours wasn't an option. "Stay here. I'll go out, see just how strong the wind is, and come back for you."

She didn't want him to go without her, Joe could tell by the set of her jaw. He touched her cheek with his fingertips. "You're safer here," he answered her unspoken plea. "Light the fire in the great room. Make coffee on the camp stove. It's on the top shelf of the pantry. I'll be back in less than an hour." If the chopper could be flown he'd bring it back and land it on the front lawn.

He headed for the door, pulling on his gloves. He turned around with his hand on the door handle. "Do not," he said to the six men, "I repeat. Do *not* let her out of your sight for even a second. Treadwell is out there. I can feel the son of a bitch breathing down our necks."

With a last glance at Kendall, Joe opened the front door letting in a blast of frigid air.

"Be careful," she told him.

Joe nodded, his eyes holding hers. Then he let the door slam shut behind him.

"Well," Kendall said brightly. "Coffee and a fire it is. Would one of you go in there and light the fire, please? Everything's ready. The matches are—the matches are on the mantel." She felt like a watch that had been wound too tightly. She didn't want to be here without Joe. It didn't matter that she had six men in his place. Six average law enforcement officers didn't equal one Joe Zorn.

Kendall pulled off her hat, then tugged off the gloves, shoving both deep into a pocket. Even with the down coat on she was freezing. She wondered if she'd ever feel warm again. She felt what Joe felt—imminent danger. What if Treadwell was out there waiting, and he hurt Joe— What if— What if. Beneath the scarf wound about her throat, the scar seemed to pulse. Oh, God . . .

While one of the guys went into the other room to tackle the fire, the rest of them trailed her like ants on their way to a picnic into the dimly lit kitchen. The baking sheets of cookies and the two red mugs she and Joe had used yesterday still sat on the center island, along with the glasses they'd used earlier. Kendall carried the dirty dishes to the sink.

"Help yourselves to those cookies. I'll look for that camp stove." She picked up the oil lamp they'd brought down with them.

She paused going into the pantry. "Did you check on the two couples in the cottages?" She hoped that someone had eventually managed to contact them.

"No, ma'am. We came here straightaway."

Heart pounding with dread, Kendall came back into the kitchen on leaden feet, horrified that they hadn't checked that the others were all right. "We have to make *sure* they're okay. My God. He could look for me there first! You have to go and warn them. Please."

The men looked from one to the other. "Joe told us to stick to you like glue, ma'am," the beefy older guy stated firmly. "Those folks won't do nothin' foolish. Not in this weather. 'Sides, Adam Cameron will keep tryin' to contact them, don't you worry."

"Nobody who hasn't felt his knife at their throat really knows about Dwight Gus Treadwell," Kendall told them bitterly. "My God, if you guys made it to the ranch, so can he!"

"I guess a couple of us could go take a look-see. . . ."

They decided which of them should go, and two of the men left—reluctantly, Kendall could tell. It was cold and dark out there, and they didn't think Treadwell was anywhere around yet. But they went, and for that she was grateful.

Coats were removed and guns exposed while Kendall fixed a pot of coffee on the camp stove. "How did Joe know where this was?" she asked out loud as she took down mugs. In fact, now that she came to think about it, Joe had appeared to be quite familiar with the house. He'd known which rooms were where. He'd been familiar with the door and window locks. He also appeared to know these men.

"Oh, this here was Joe and Miss Denise's house before they went and got that divorce."

A mug slipped out of her hand and crashed noisily onto the tiled floor as Kendall spun around. "*What*?"

The man flushed uncomfortably. "You didn't know Joe was married to Denise before she married Adam Cameron?" He glanced nervously to the other two men. "Oh, shit. Was it a secret?"

Kendall bent to pick up the shards scattered around her feet. "I'm sure it wasn't a secret." She tossed the broken crockery into the trash can under the sink. "It's not as though we know each other. He's not obligated to tell me about his past." Especially not when he didn't expect to ever see her again, she thought. There was realistic and there was realistic. Her chest felt as though she'd just taken a body blow. That was pretty frigging realistic.

The radio came on in the other room. "I'm Dreaming of a White Christmas" belted out, filling the quiet, dimly lit kitchen.

"Power's back on," one of the younger officers said.

The older man smacked the back of his head. "Does it look like the power's back on, McKenna?"

"It's the emergency radio," Kendall told them absently. Music. Great. Just what she needed, she thought, pouring coffee into four bright red mugs and leaving the fifth empty until the other cop came back from his fire-lighting expedition.

The men had already polished off most of the stale cookies. She was *so* not in the Christmas spirit. The house smelled of Christmas. It looked like Christmas.

But, oh God, it didn't *feel* like a joyous time of year at all. She was *scared*.

Scared for herself because she knew a killer was close.

Scared out of her mind for Joe who was out there alone.

Scared for the four innocent people whose only thoughts had been to attend a fun, pre-Christmas weekend house party. Was Joe okay? Of course he was, Kendall told herself firmly, drinking the too-strong coffee just to feel the heat of it going down. He knew what he was doing. Apparently he also knew the area very well. Another point he might've brought up at some time in the past twenty-four hours. She gulped down half her coffee before she realized she'd added neither creamer nor Sweet 'n Low.

The annoying song "Grandma Got Run Over by a Reindeer" blasted from the other room, jangling her nerves even more. She set her mug down with a little more force than necessary.

"Getting on your last nerve, is it, ma'am?" the younger, blond officer asked, his eyes twinkling with amusement, or sympathy, or blast it—probably no feelings one way or the other at all. "Want for me to go tell Sonny to turn it off?"

Kendall gave him a smile. "Just *down* would help, thanks." She glanced at her watch. Joe had been gone for less than seven minutes. It felt like an eternity. No, it didn't. She knew what an eternity felt like.

She'd experienced an eternity in that single-wide trailer in the woods fifteen months ago. *That* was eternity.

The officer took a cookie to go and ambled off in the direction of the great room. There was really nothing to say to the two men in the kitchen with her, and the silence stretched, helped only marginally by a rousing rendition of "Jingle Bell Rock."

She had just refilled her mug when a sound reverberated through the house. The retort was as loud as a gunshot. With a scream, she jumped, spilling scalding coffee down her front.

Both men drew their guns in the blink of an eye.

The older man relaxed. "Stand down. Door slammin'."

As the men reholstered their weapons Kendall felt light-headed and sick to her stomach. God, she wanted this to be over.

"You okay, ma'am?"

She nodded jerkily. Her midriff stung from contact with the hot coffee, which had soaked into her sweater. "I'll just go and wash this off me."

"I'll go with you," the blond officer told her. He looked spooked, which didn't fill her with confidence.

She needed just a few minutes to compose herself, give herself a pep talk. Hell. Talk herself off the ceiling. Her heart was still racing. "The bathroom door is right there." She pointed down a short hallway to show the door was visible from where they stood. "There's no window; I'll be safe in there for a few minutes."

She took the oil lamp, went in, and shut the door behind her. The room was decadently large. It had looked charming a couple of days ago when she'd placed red votive candles amid clusters of holly berries and glossy green leaves between the rocks of a small fountain on the counter. Right now it just looked—dark.

She shrugged off her coat, which fortunately hadn't been too splashed, and pulled her sweater over her head. The sting of the faint red mark across her middle was fading. She let herself look at the scars Treadwell had made on her body. Those too were fading. Much faster than those he'd made to her psyche.

She glanced in the mirror over the vanity and gave a choked, semi-hysterical laugh. The way her hair was drying every which way made her look like a wild woman. And even in the flickering light her skin appeared pale. Fear did that to a girl.

She took a deep, shuddering breath, held it, and exhaled slowly. And again.

Better.

She rinsed the coffee out of her sweater, then blotted it with a towel before turning on the wall hairdryer and holding it over the wet spot. After a while she hung the dryer over the towel rack and placed the sweater beneath it.

She closed the lid on the toilet and sat down to wait, rubbing the goosebumps on her arms. The lamp flickered before settling into a steady flame. She felt her sweater, still damp. She glanced at her watch. Joe had been gone for fourteen minutes.

Time stretched. She got up and pulled on her coat. The lining felt icy against her already chilled skin. Tugging the long zipper up to her throat, she paced. From the toilet to the vanity and back. Eleven steps. And back again. He said he'd be back in an hour. She could wait an hour.

How could she possibly feel this deep connection with a man she'd just met? She didn't know the how or the why. She knew only that when this was all over she wanted to explore what they'd started here.

Joe and Denise had been married.

Joe had lived in this house. Loved Denise in the house. Why hadn't he told her?

How long had they been married for goodness' sake? Lord. Were any of the children *his*?

The wick flickered and jumped in the air current every time she passed. Very creepy and atmospheric, she thought, watching the shadows form on the cream-and-gold wallpaper beside her as she paced back and forth.

And now that she came to think of it—why would a door slam? There were no doors or windows open— Oh, God, she really was creeping herself out.

Inhale.

Exhale.

The flame in the lamp leaped, then without warning, died, plunging the bathroom into stygian darkness. "Well, hell!" Kendall stood in the middle of the bathroom for a couple of seconds, waiting for her heart to leave her throat and race back into her chest.

She opened the door. "Hey guys, anyone got a ma—"

Dwight Gus Treadwell was leaning against the wall opposite the bathroom. He smiled. "Hi, honey. I'm home."

Chapter Eight

IT COULD BE ANY ONE OF THE MEN IN THE HOUSE STANDing there in the dark. He was little more than a shadowy figure, but recognition was instantaneous. Kendall knew who he was almost before she heard the voice. His voice.

Heart pounding, throat dry, she jumped back and tried to slam the bathroom door closed with both hands. It was snatched out of her grasp. *OhGodohGodohGod.*

They were close to the same height; in fact, now that she saw him again Kendall was stunned at how weedy he looked. In her nightmares he was always huge and brutish. But the reality was Dwight Gus Treadwell was medium. Medium height. Medium coloring. Medium features.

But his strength was almost superhuman as he grabbed her by the front of her thick coat and yanked her out into the hallway. She fought him wildly, kicking and scratching, screaming at the top of her lungs.

He struck her across the face, a punishing blow that had her sagging in his hold. "Tsk. Tsk. Now is that any way to welcome an old friend?" He jerked her upright, pulling her into the kitchen by her hair. His fine, light brown hair was wet, as were the shoulders of a too-large tan ski jacket. "Know how many *shit* cars I had to drive to get to you?" he demanded, shoving her in front of him. "Know how many *dumbasses* contributed to the cause and gave their lives so I could be here with you? Do you, huh? Do you have any idea how *fucking* cold it was hiding out in the trees waiting for just the right moment for us to be reacquainted?"

He shoved her hard, and she staggered because he was still holding her hair. "Selfish." Shove. "Selfish." Shove. "Bitch."

"Go to hell where you belong." Kendall stumbled before getting her feet under her. Her face throbbed. Her heart skittered, missed several beats, then raced, making her light-headed. Her brain was completely blank with terror. "You won't get away with this. The place is crawling with cops," she whispered through dry lips. Where *were* they?

"Not really." Treadwell smiled, using the blade of the knife in his other hand to indicate something across the room.

She did not want to look. Bile rose in the back of her throat. It took several eternities for Kendall to force her eyes to shift from the faint glimmer of steel to the dark shapes almost lost in the darkness on the floor. "You killed them."

"Ooops. My bad." He shoved her away from him. "Go on. Go. Run. Don't make this easy for me, baby." He slammed his fist into her shoulder. She staggered back a step. His closed fist wasn't meaty or large. She'd been mesmerized, in a horrific way, by his hands before. They were narrow and pale, with fingers like a piano player's—or a knife-wielding lunatic's.

"Go on. Run like the wind, pretty girl. Let old Dwight have a little fun to make up for all the aggravation you caused him."

She was already walking carefully backward, and his next shoulder slam made her totter. Her hip hit the center island with a dull thud. She fumbled to insert her hand into her coat pocket as she righted herself. It crossed her numb mind for all of a nanosecond that she should keep him talking until she could get her gun from her pocket. *Think! Think! Talk! Treadwell likes to talk, to taunt. If he's talking, he isn't killing me.*

Now "It's the Most Wonderful Time of the Year" was playing. The situation was surreal. God. If he'd killed the cops, what about Joe? The image of Joe's body out there in the snow made her physically ill. Her fingers closed around the handle of the LadySmith. She whipped out the .22. The air smelled sweet, unpleasantly so. Nausea rose in her throat at the sickening reek of death.

"There'll be more cops," she told him, keeping her voice steady as she clicked off the safety. "They won't stop until they catch you and put you back in your cage."

He smiled, not acknowledging the small gun in her hand. "Maybe. But I'll kill you first, pretty girl. I'll just kill you dead fir—"

Kendall pulled the trigger.

Pop.

The shot made no impact. He didn't fall back or even flinch, making her doubt she'd hit him. Then slowly dark red bloomed on his upper arm through his coat.

Everything moved in slow motion as though she were underwater, yet images bombarded her. The two dead men at her feet. The flickering lantern on the center island, casting dancing demonic shadows on Treadwell's face as he kept coming, his expression feral, not slowed in the least by the shot. The knife, huge, slick, and already stained with blood—

Pop.

He staggered back with a howl of pain, clutching his ear with his free hand. Blood trickled between his fingers, and his eyes went black with rage. But he kept coming.

"I'm gonna peel your skin off your body real slow, bitch. Run if you can."

Damn it. She hadn't hit him where it would stop him. God, it barely slowed him down, and he kept coming like a psychotic Frankenstein. She didn't waste another shot; she was in motion. Backing away, she felt a total sense of unreality as she fired again. This time she got him in the leg. Not bad. Except that she'd been aiming for his groin. He yelped in outrage, but other than putting a pause in his step, the wound didn't stop him.

Kendall twisted around, running flat-out toward the front door. She noticed a man's body only seconds before she stumbled over him in the entry hall. She jumped at the last fraction of a second, then almost tripped over an askew area rug. Blood made the floor slick, but she skated until she got her balance.

She screamed as Treadwell's fingers tangled in her hair, yanking her toward him. She kicked backward, sending him into the slippery pool of blood. Losing his footing, he almost took her with him, but Kendall risked a few bald spots by jerking her hair out of his grip. He went careening into the opposite wall with an inhuman scream of rage.

She darted out of the front door without looking back. The frigid air stole her breath. The sky had lightened to pewter. The landscape before her looked like a Currier and Ives rendered in black and white. The enormous snowplow loomed in the front yard. Were the keys in it? Did she have time to look? How fast did the damn thing go? Fast enough to outrun Treadwell? She couldn't chance taking the time to find out.

Sticking her gun into her pocket for now, she looked around frantically. Where to hide? Where the hell to hide? The son of a bitch was like the Energizer bunny. He wouldn't stop. Not while he still had a breath in his body.

Chest heaving, she gulped icy, painful air, hard and

fast. The guest cottages were to the left. There were empty cottages and trees behind which she could hide. She hauled ass across the wide porch, knowing he was right behind her.

A flash of silver arced down to her left. She tried to dodge. But his knife ripped through her left sleeve. No pain. Just an ice cold jolt as the blade sliced through fabric and down to skin. But it would hurt later. God, would it hurt later when adrenaline and fear weren't anesthetizing her.

Run. Run. Run.

He tackled her from behind, taking her down. Her head slammed on the wood floor of the porch, hitting hard, but she tucked and rolled as she'd been taught, managing to stagger back to her feet before he could grab hold of her again. She turned to race down the five steps leading away from the house—

He grabbed her arm, swinging her into a support column with teeth-jarring impact. Several of the little fir trees she'd decorated yesterday toppled over. Lights, garland, and faux candied fruit bounced down the steps. He pulled her up by her collar, then clamped her throat in a one-handed vise. "Stupid. Stupid bitch." His voice, as always, was chillingly calm. Which made it more frightening and ominous than if he'd been yelling at the top of his lungs. "You ruined it. You ruined it *all*." He smashed the hilt of the knife into her cheekbone. She screamed with the blinding, white-hot pain. Brilliant dots danced in her vision as she struggled to stay conscious. It was a losing battle. There was a fuzzy buzz in her ears, then she slipped into silence.

Minutes, hours, *days* later, Kendall came to in a rush of cold and bone deep terror. *Oh, God. Oh, God.* Treadwell had her slung over his shoulder like a sack of potatoes.

Déjà vu.

They weren't in the front yard. Her hair hung over

her face, and she surreptitiously parted the strands. She couldn't see the house. Or the snowplow. Or Joe.

Joe.

Her arm was on fire. The pain intense. Nausea choked her. She heard nothing over the blood pounding in her ears, although the trees must be rustling in the wind, and his boots surely must be making a rhythmic sound as he trudged through the virgin snow.

The wind whipped her hair silently about her head as she hung there like a bat, upside down, almost blinded by the dancing, swirling red strands and the blood rushing to her brain. She forced herself to remain limp. But it wasn't easy. Every fight and flight instinct screamed at her to do something. She wanted to ask him about Joe but didn't dare. She focused on that for a second, reasoning that if Treadwell had killed Joe, he'd have told her as much. She'd learned that about him during her captivity. Treadwell liked to regale her with the gory details of past trophies.

She knew she just had to hang on long enough for Joe to realize that Treadwell had her. Just long enough for him to find her. *Please God make it soon. Oh, God. Please* . . . Her arm wasn't totally useless. She might not be able to move it, but hot red blood dripped freely from her fingertips onto the pure white snow. She was leaving a trail of blood in Treadwell's footprints. She could only pray that he didn't look back.

She swallowed convulsively, a blend of bile and terror. She didn't want him to realize she was conscious. She could . . . would . . . as soon as . . . Unfortunately she ruined the element of surprise by puking down his back.

"Jesus! You fucking bitch!" Treadwell growled, flinging her off his shoulder so she landed face first in the snow.

He hauled her to her feet, but somehow she managed to break away. *Run. Run. Run.* She felt as if she was looking through the bottom of a thick glass. Tree branches slapped at her, though she'd stopped feeling pain long ago. Clutching her arm, she ran. Her life depended on it.

He grabbed her around the neck from behind. She bucked and jerked, leaning her weight to counter his, hoping to slow him down. Keeping her completely off balance, Treadwell dragged her through frozen quicksand toward the tree line. Every time she tried to pull away he found another place to cut her. Her bright yellow coat was trailing ribbons of fabric, many of them now tinged red. She kicked and bit, screaming hoarsely as he took her deeper and deeper into the isolated landscape farther and farther from the house.

She saw the snowmobile up ahead between the dark skeletons of the trees, black against the brilliance of the snow.

No! Nonononono!

"This has been fun, Kendall." He spun around, grabbing her by the throat, squeezing hard enough for brilliant stars to explode before her eyes. "But you're boring me now. Time to say b'bye." Her weight was balanced against his chest and he used his knee as a wedge between her legs, freeing his hand to grab her hair at the scalp as he brought the knife to her throat.

Paralyzed, Kendall stared at the knife inches from her face. "Not again. Damn you, not again." Despite the pain in her scalp where he'd fisted her long hair, she wrenched her arm up, the small gun clutched in her bloody hand. She had no idea how many bullets were left. Or God, if *any* bullets were left.

She pointed the barrel over her left shoulder and pulled the trigger.

Chapter Nine

JOE PUSHED THROUGH THE SNOW, FOLLOWING THE
blood trail deeper across the south paddock. *Kendall-
KendallKendall.* An insistent mantra in his brain. Fear
was a new experience for him. But it was real and physical. He'd heard her cries on the way back from the disabled chopper. Heard them, and known immediately
that Treadwell had her. And if Treadwell had her, the
men he'd assigned to protect her were dead. Ah, Jesus.

Every breath was an effort in the icy air. His heart
pounded with helpless frustration at his slow progress in
the fresh, calf-deep snow.

Uncharacteristically bloodthirsty images kept flipping
through his mind as he ran, weapon drawn in his glove-
less hand. He'd learned some interesting techniques with
a knife himself over the years. So far those lessons had
been purely academic. He relished the idea of demon-
strating his skill on Treadwell. Let the son of a bitch feel
the terror of finding *himself* on the other end of a knife
wielded by a madman. A madman who'd been trained
in the art of knife fighting and wasn't afraid to use those
skills to fight dirty.

The wind whipped Joe's hair about his face and
batwinged his coat about his body as he ran. Kendall's
cries, echoing in the isolation of the remote area, pierced

him to the heart. She was alive. At least he had that to
hold on to. He doubled his effort to reach her as fast as
humanly possible as powder skipped and danced across
the surface of the drifting snow, trying to obliterate
Treadwell's footsteps.

He felt the beat of chopper blades overhead before he
heard them. Three coming in fast, spotlights strafing the
snow-covered landscape. The cavalry after all. Snow
whipped up, blinding him. Damn it to hell!—he pointed
in the direction of the tree line. Not that they would be
able to land here. The terrain was hilly, and there were
just too many damn trees. The three beams of light rose;
the choppers moved off, taking their lights with them.

Kendall cried out again.

"I'm coming, sweetheart, hold on. I'm coming." Cor-
recting slightly to the west, he battled across the snow
drifts, chest heaving.

He was close. Two hundred yards and closing.

Go. Go. *Go.*

They were twined as closely as lovers, two indistin-
guishable silhouettes against the stark whiteness of the
snow.

Faster. Faster.

A gunshot cracked through the predawn quiet. Joe's
heart jerked in response. *Kendall . . .*

A hundred and fifty . . . forty . . . thirty . . . twenty . . .
He saw the fiery blaze of her hair, the brilliant yellow of
her coat, as she and Treadwell fell to the ground in a
tangle of arms and legs and started rolling about. Joe
saw the glint of a knife.

Run, faster, damn it, *run.* Ninety feet . . . eighty . . . He
took aim. Treadwell and Kendall rolled just as he was
about to squeeze off the shot. Shit. She was blocking.
They rolled again; this time Treadwell was on top. Joe
fired. The other man jerked with the impact. He tilted.

Sixty feet . . . forty . . .

Kendall took the window of opportunity and shoved

and pushed Treadwell off her. God Almighty! Instead of *running*, she surprised the hell out of Joe by jumping on top of Treadwell with a banshee scream of rage. Straddling the man's waist, she started beating the hell out of his head and shoulders with her fists.

Twenty feet . . . ten . . . *Kendall*— Joe grabbed her arm, flinging her aside just as Treadwell's knife arced toward her chest. He grabbed the killer's wrist, placed his weight on the knee he applied to the man's chest, then dug the muzzle of the H&K *hard* to the underside of the guy's chin. "Play with *me*, dick," Joe said, his voice low and feral as he applied pressure to a tendon in Treadwell's knife hand. The grip should have caused the person's fingers to release whatever he was holding. But Treadwell's fingers, slick with blood, remained fisted around the hilt of the cheap ten-inch kitchen knife. Joe dug his knee into the man's chest and exerted more pressure on his wrist.

"Talk to me, Kendall," he yelled, keeping his eyes fixed on the killer. "Talk to me, sweetheart!"

"I-I'm okay," she replied, out of his line of sight.

"I won't go back there," Dwight Treadwell told Joe vehemently, eyes wild. His brown coat was splotched with blood. It sure as hell better not contain one drop belonging to Kendall. "You can't make me." He attempted to jerk his hand free. Not going to happen. "I won't go back."

Joe kept up the pressure of his thumb on the man's wrist, but the knife remained firmly in Treadwell's bloody but bloodless hand. In one lithe move Joe surged to his feet, dragging Treadwell up with him. The fingers he had around the knife hand remained there like a vise, his weapon stayed put under the weak jaw.

"Oh, you don't have to go back if you don't want to," Joe assured him with silky menace. "In fact I insist that you d—"

"Oh, God! Joe, watch out!"

He felt the sharp jab of pain in his side a second before Kendall's warning. Damn it to hell! Treadwell surprised the hell out of him by producing a second knife—smaller and considerably more effective—and stabbing him right through the hide of his coat. Ah, crap. The other man was also left-handed.

Twisting to deflect the depth of the strike, Joe lifted the H&K. *Pop. Pop.*

Pop.

Treadwell's eyes widened in surprise as he crumpled to his knees, then slowly toppled to his side. His sightless eyes stared at the dawn-flooded sky as bright arterial blood drenched the snow at Joe's feet a satisfying crimson.

Joe plucked both knives from Treadwell's limp fingers. He'd only fired two shots.

Kneeling, he felt for a pulse beneath the other man's jaw. Dead. Perfect. He turned his head to see Kendall, eyes narrowed, still standing in the classic firing stance.

She looked like an avenging angel with her red hair blowing in the breeze, the golden glow of a new day backlighting her. "Is he dead?"

"As the proverbial doornail." Joe assured her as he rose. He kept his gaze on her face as he tossed aside both knives and walked toward her.

"I'm not sure exactly what that *is*," Kendall said with only a small tremor in her voice. "But if it's very dead I'm all for it."

"Very," Joe assured her, touching the blood on her face. Her coat was slashed. He wanted to strip her and check every inch of her skin. "Did he cut you?"

"No."

"Liar. How bad?"

"Bet I won't need one stitch," she assured him, clutching the front of his coat in both hands as she stood in the circle of his arms. Her casual tone was hard won, the terror was still clear in her expressive eyes.

An unfamiliar aching tenderness gathered inside him. He had to clear the thickness from his throat before he could speak. "You won't mind if I play doctor later, and check that out for myself."

"No *playing*. If you want to be my doctor you have to take the job seriously." Kendall's lips curved. "I insist on a complete and thorough physical."

"I concur. Top to bottom and everything in between. Let's get the hell out of Dodge before then. Come on." He wrapped his arm around her, and they started walking across the paddock. In the distance he saw the posse arriving. Dozens of local cops, Feebs, and federal marshals racing across the tinged snow toward them. There'd be questions and more questions—

He veered off and headed in the opposite direction. "How do you like the great outdoors so far?" he asked conversationally.

She pulled a comical face. "Not very."

"Yeah, I can see how the situation would require some rehabilitation." Joe sighed. "The kids would like it out here, though."

She shot him an amused glance as they walked. "Whose?"

"Ours." He rubbed her arm. He was going to have to buy her a new coat. That would take time. "Four, do you think?" he asked.

Her steps, in those sexy blue knee-high boots, faltered, but she laughed. "Don't you think we should go on a couple of dates before we start naming our children?"

They came to the snowmobile Treadwell had left under the trees. "Hop aboard," Joe said, helping her maneuver onto the machine. "Aren't we a couple of stages beyond dating?" he asked politely, starting the engine. The Christophs had a nice, secluded little summer place just over the ridge—

"No," Kendall told him, wrapping her arms about his

waist and resting her chin on his back. "We are not several stages past dating. I want movies, and dinners, and flowers. You can start by calling me."

The snowmobile picked up speed. Anticipation made Joe's heart pick up speed, too. Four miles to a bed. "I don't have your phone number," he shouted as the wind carried them forward.

"I programmed it into your cell phone last night." Kendall laughed, her breath warm against his cheek.

They burst through the trees. Ahead was a pristine expanse of white, pure and fresh and untouched. It held only a few small shadows and was tinged with the promise of sunshine.

Kendall tightened her arms about his waist as he shut off the engine. He turned to take her in his arms. "This looks good, doesn't it?" she said softly.

"Yeah," Joe cupped her face between his hands. "This looks incredibly good."

And it was.

SANTA SLAVE

Leanne Banks

Chapter One

SHE'D DONE HER RESEARCH AND SHE'D LEARNED THEY liked them pretty, stupid, and submissive.

Hilary Winfree had never taken much time with her appearance; she'd been too busy with her studies. So she got a cosmetics counter makeover and dyed her hair blond. Studies indicated people immediately deducted IQ points from a woman who was blond. She mimicked the southern drawl she often heard around campus because people also deducted mental points from those with a southern accent.

Both were erroneous assumptions and irritated the devil out of her, but this once, she used the information to help her. The submissive part was going to bite big time. Her father had always said she'd been a rebel since the day she was born, and he would skin her alive when he found out she'd gone against his recommendation of letting the law handle the task of finding Christine, if the college underclassman even wanted to be found.

Hilary knew better, though. All her instincts told her something wasn't right about the so-called job Christine had been so determined to accept.

Hilary had warned Christine but that hadn't been enough. She should have done more. She'd gone to the police, but they'd been useless. She had no choice except to take things into her own hands.

She climbed the steps to the train. Her stomach twisting with dread, she hesitated on the third step. Was there another way to do this? What if she couldn't pull it off?

She had to pull it off, she told herself. Her heart was racing a mile a minute, but she plastered an expression of controlled enthusiasm on her face. At this point, she was supposed to still believe the story the deceptively polite man had told her at the party in Atlanta.

She was still supposed to believe that in exchange for teaching a six-week course to foreign businessmen about American customs and manners, she would receive free travel to exciting destinations and a bonus of thousands of dollars. The proposition was a dream come true for girls like Christine, whom Hilary had been mentoring through their sorority. Christine had never traveled more than sixty miles from home and always seemed to be scraping the bottom of her bank account.

When Christine had told Hilary about it, Hilary had sensed the position was too good to be true, but she'd been swamped with grading term papers as a function of her teaching assistant position. If only she had taken some extra time with Christine. She'd thought her verbal warning on the phone would be enough to discourage the college sophomore, but it hadn't. When Hilary had realized Christine was gone, she'd done some research on the Internet and her suspicions about the job offer had only escalated. She hadn't found any legitimate, legal listings for the company.

"Miss Winfree?"

Hilary sized up the tall man with the slight Russian accent. He looked about forty-five, but very fit. She wondered if she could outrun him when it became necessary. His gaze took in every inch of her within a few seconds. Checking out the merchandise? she wondered, feeling as if she'd been slimed. She barely resisted wrinkling her nose.

"Yes, I'm Hilary Winfree. You must be Mr. Harris. How did you know it was me?"

His mouth smiled, but his eyes didn't. He took her hand in his and lifted it to his mouth. "Yes, I'm John Harris, pleased to make your acquaintance. I've seen your picture, but it doesn't do you justice."

She wondered how many times he'd said that today. Again, she resisted the urge to pull her hand back and rub away his touch. "Thank you. I'm so excited about this teaching and traveling opportunity. Where are the rest of the teachers?"

"We've reserved a special car for our group. If you'll come with me, I'll take your luggage."

"I don't mind carrying it," she said.

"I insist," he said with a creepy smile, and Hilary allowed him to take her luggage.

He led the way to a car with a table filled with food and wine while Christmas music played from a boombox. Three beefy-looking men in dark suits were positioned at the door and against two walls. Three young women sipped wine and chatted around the food table.

Christine had left two days ago with an earlier group, so Hilary knew she would be playing catch-up.

"Go ahead and join the other candidates," John Harris said. "Have some wine and relax. We'll give an information presentation once the train leaves the station."

Her nerves kicking in again, Hilary offered a small smile and nodded. "Thanks. I'll do that." She walked to the table and introduced herself to the other women and quickly learned that Abigal, Eve, and Katrina lived in small college towns in Georgia. They were all pretty, bright-eyed, and eager to begin their adventure.

"The only bad part is leaving before Christmas," Abigal said.

Hilary's heart twisted when she thought of how worried her parents in California would be when they picked up her voice message. She'd tried to enlist their help, but her father had been adamant. It was none of their business, and no, he absolutely would not foot the bill for a private investigator. That had left her with no choice.

"Not for me," Eve said. "I would have been waitressing on Christmas just like every other day of the year. I'm ready to hit the road and see some of the world."

"Especially when someone else is paying," Katrina added. "Let's toast our new adventure," she added, lifting her glass of wine. "Cheers."

Hilary reluctantly lifted her glass. She just hoped she could get Christine and herself out safely.

The train lurched forward and her stomach took a dip. A woman, dressed in a loose black dress with her gray hair pulled into a puffy bun, entered the room and nodded to the man at the door. He closed the door and locked it. Hilary felt the woman survey the group.

The woman moved toward her. "Hello, I'm Giselle Smith. I'll be serving as the chaperone until your group leaves the country."

Hilary shook Giselle's hand, noticing the woman's voice had an accent similar to John Harris's. "It's nice to meet you. I'm Hilary Winfree. Gosh, I didn't know we would need a chaperone."

The woman gave a slight smile. "An added level of protection for those who participate in our program. We pride ourselves on our security."

"How reassuring," Hilary said. "How often do you sponsor the teaching programs?"

"Oh, it depends on the demand. This year, we've sent almost one hundred women overseas."

"I'm surprised more men aren't interested in the positions," Hilary said.

"We find women are better suited for teaching customs and manners." She smiled in a conspiratorial manner. "No surprise that women see the nuances when men don't."

"Where do we go next? I understand there's some sort of class we take to prepare us for teaching."

"All in due time. You can relax tonight. Tomorrow we reach our destination and you'll have a few training sessions." Giselle crossed her fingers. "Hopefully no one will require additional training, but we have backup plans for that if necessary. We want to make sure everyone succeeds in this program."

"And after that?" Hilary asked.

"After that, we have an informal meet-and-greet with the people who will receive your services. That's when you receive your assignment," Giselle said. "We'll talk more later. I should meet the other candidates."

Hilary switched her wine for water and watched Giselle make her rounds. She gave the impression of warmth and reassuring confidence. After a few moments, she motioned the women toward her. "Welcome to the program, ladies. You can take pride in the fact that we carefully screen all of our applicants and you are absolutely the cream of the crop. As you know, you'll soon be taking an international trip. Your safety is our very first concern. In order to make sure that none of your personal property is stolen or gets into the wrong hands, we're going to collect your purses, passports, and cell phones and store them until you leave the country."

"Oh, but I wanted to call my aunt and tell her where I'm going," Abigal said.

"Of course," Giselle said. "As soon as your assignment is determined, we'll return your cell phones to you so you can contact your families."

Hilary reluctantly surrendered her purse and cell phone. She would have no tool except her brain after this.

The night wore on and Hilary's nerves frayed. Every minute that passed represented another step that Christine took into the unknown. Impatient, she decided to chat up the guards for information. With the first two, she might as well have been talking to rocks. The third, however, responded to flattery.

"You must work out a lot," she said. "You look like you're all muscle."

He shrugged. "I hit the gym when I can."

"Well, it's working," she said, mustering an admiring gaze. "Where are my manners? I'm Hilary," she said, extending her hand.

The man looked surreptitiously across the room and gave her hand a quick shake. "I'm Ivan. I'm not supposed to be talking to you."

"Why not?"

He shrugged. "They're funny about us talking with the girls."

"I wouldn't want to get you in trouble," she ventured.

He paused and gave her a long once-over. "Maybe later," he said.

"Okay," she said, and meandered to the table, feeling the gazes of John Harris and Giselle on her. She felt the walls start to close in and took a few breaths.

"Are you not feeling well?" Giselle asked. "You're not smiling. We like to keep our candidates happy."

"Oh, I'm thrilled. I think I've worn myself out with anticipation. Do you think it would be okay if I went to sleep early?"

"Sure. We have sleeping medication if you need it," Giselle said, studying her.

"Oh, I won't be needing that." She gave a fake yawn. "Just a good night's sleep so I won't wake up with circles under my eyes."

"Good girl," Giselle said. "I'll have Ivan escort you to your cabin."

"Thank you. Good night."

Ivan led her out of the room and down the hall. She deliberately stumbled so he would catch her. "Thank you. What a gentleman," she said and righted herself. "So do you do this all the time?"

"Pretty much," he said.

"How often?"

"It depends. We escorted another group of ladies from your area a couple of days ago."

"I'm surprised they don't use larger groups."

"Security," he said.

"Are we going to the same place as the group who left a couple days ago?" she asked.

"Same place," he said with a nod. "Those girls will ship out with you soon. Nice place. You'll get manicures and facials and the whole VIP treatment."

"It sounds almost like a spa," she said.

He looked at her and his mouth twisted slightly as he chuckled. "Yeah, a spa. Here's your room. I'll be right outside if you need anything."

"Okay, thanks," she said and entered the small cabin. She closed the door behind her and locked it, but she was certain Ivan had a key. She was in and tomorrow she would see Christine. Her task was to find Christine and persuade her to leave. She needed to be just as smart and deceptive as Giselle and John were. It went against her nature to play dumb and to lie. Her intelligence and lack of submissiveness had irritated more than one man she'd dated, but this once she needed to portray herself as eager to please. Her life and Christine's would depend on it.

Sitting down on the small, narrow bed, she felt an ugly sense of foreboding. More than ever, her instincts told her these so-called positions involved prostitution.

Rick Santana signed for a package from the delivery man and heard the sound of "We Need a Little Christmas" blaring from another boat. He thanked the delivery guy but scowled at the holiday music. He hated Christmas. The only thing all the nonstop holiday music and repeated showing of *It's a Wonderful Life* did was remind him that he had no family.

Except for his mistress, and heaven knew he spent most of his nonworking hours and nearly all his money on *Mistress,* his sixty-two-foot yacht. He had his own plan for the holidays: a Caribbean Christmas spent with *Mistress.*

Opening the box, he found cookies and knew his plans had just been changed. He often received cookies at the same time he received a new assignment. He went belowdecks, and within three minutes, he'd munched four cookies and was downloading a file from the Internet.

His cell phone rang and he noticed there was no ID. Probably Roz, but just in case . . . "Rick's Yacht Service," he said.

"Did you get my cookies?" A woman's sultry voice heated up the line.

Rick felt his temperature slide up a degree despite the fact that he suspected Rosalind Donahue was old enough to be his mother and probably wore a girdle. After all, the woman held an advanced degree in library science and, apparently, mothering.

"Thanks, Roz. They're great as usual. I've already downloaded the file for Hilary Winfree. Looks like another college kid who thinks she's Jennifer Garner from *Alias.*" He shook his head, glancing out the porthole of his yacht. "That show has gotten more chicks in trouble."

"Sorta like guys and Vin Diesel or the Rock or Superman or—"

"Okay, okay, I get the message," he said.

"Pull in the reins on the macho attitude if you want Hilary's cooperation. She may have allowed herself to get involved in a human-trafficking ring to find her missing friend, but everything I read about her tells me she's very independent. She's going to college on the opposite coast of where her parents live. She's earned her master's degree and is doing some postgraduate work." Roz paused and sighed. "Just a little too impulsive at times. She tried to persuade her parents to help find Christine, but they told her it wasn't their business, so Hilary took matters into her own hands."

Rick nodded, skimming the e-mail Roz had already sent him. "Hilary's been gone two days, so the clock is ticking."

"All you have to do, Chameleon," she said, calling him by his nickname, "is buy Hilary and get her home for Christmas. I can get a contact name for you within the next few hours."

"Should be cake," he said. "I'll pull out my South American government official ID and accent. I should be able to take care of this within a week and be on my way to the Caribbean."

"Don't underestimate Hilary," Roz warned.

"No worries, Mom," he returned. "I can handle her."

The guard at the iron gate scrutinized Rick's ID while the engine of the chauffeured limousine purred in neutral. The guard gave a nod and waved him on, and Rick took a closer look at the southeast Texas estate that served as a compound for the human-trafficking ring. The ring, headed by a member of the Russian mafia, had escaped government intervention through frequent changes of location. And bribes, Rick thought cynically.

Indicating he could make cash payment immediately and that he preferred utmost discretion, he'd arranged for a semi-private meeting for the purpose of purchasing a pretty, well-educated American woman with eye color, height, and weight identical to Hilary's. Money usually cut through a multitude of barriers, and Rick had learned a long time ago that an opponent's greed could cause him to be careless.

The chauffeur pulled in front of a three-story brick building where a beefy man stood outside smoking a cigarette. Yes, John Harris Slavinsky kept his merchandise well-protected.

Rick clenched his jaw, itching to do more than just free Hilary, but one of the cardinal rules of the Agency was to stick to the case and go no further. His job was to free Hilary.

"When I come back, I'll have the girl with me. Remember, she may fight leaving the compound," he said to Jensen, the agent-in-training/driver. The driver had to be a professional in this situation. Especially if Hilary was a hysterical screamer.

"Got it," Jensen said. "I'll be here."

Rick slid his dark glasses in place and climbed the steps at an easy pace. He offered his ID to the beefy guy at the door, who searched him then pulled a two-way radio from his jacket pocket and announced him as Juan Castillo from South America.

The door opened and a striking woman dressed in emerald green silk greeted him. "You're here for the party. Please come this way," she said and guided him to a room with several women and two men. The women wore provocative dresses with plunging necklines, sheer tops, and short hems.

The air was charged with nerves and fear. Despite the Christmas music playing in the background and the sound of the men's laughter, Rick could almost hear the crackle of unease.

He scanned the room and caught sight of Hilary. Her hair was lighter than her photograph, he noticed, and she had great legs. They looked especially great in those mile-high red heels. She stood in the far corner, her back to the room as she faced a window and tugged on her short red skirt with white fur around the edge. When she wasn't tugging at the skirt, she was pulling at the neckline, trying to cover her shoulders. Even without the information he'd received about her, he would have guessed she came from a privileged background. Something about the set of her chin and her erect posture said it all.

A man approached him. "Mr. Castillo?"

Rick nodded. "*Sí*. Mr. Harris?"

"Yes," the tall man with the laser gaze said. "Welcome to our estate. I'll have one of the girls get you a drink. What would you like?"

"Scotch, neat," he said, though he wouldn't drink more than a sip or two.

Mr. Harris instructed a woman to get Rick's drink.

"I arranged a gathering of some of our candidates for your inspection. We have another buyer tonight, too. Relax. Talk with the girls. They're all beautiful and eager to please."

"*Gracias*. I'll do that."

Rick made casual conversation with two women before he headed toward Hilary.

"*Buenos noches,*" he said to her.

She glanced around in surprise. "Oh, hi."

Her eyes were wide and blue, her lips rosy red with lipstick. She looked him over then dismissed him in three seconds flat.

His lips twitched. "What is your name?"

"Hilary," she said, returning her gaze to the window.

"I'm Juan Castillo. Pleased to make your acquaintance."

She moved her head in a noncommittal response and looked at him suspiciously.

"Tell me about yourself, Hilary," he said, shifting so he could watch her profile.

"What would you like to know?" she asked.

"I'm interested in finding a tutor," he said and took a

small swallow of his drink. "I'd like an attractive, intelligent woman for the position."

Her eyes widened and she glanced away. "There are other more attractive women here."

"Possibly," he said. "But you intrigued me when I walked in the door."

She bit her lip. "I'll tell you the truth," she said in a low voice. "I'm not your best choice. I look terrible without makeup. They had to do a lot of work to make me look this good. You wash all this off and I'm a real dog. And my hair. I'm not a natural blonde. This is out of a bottle and it took forever to fix it tonight."

He resisted the urge to chuckle at her obvious effort to scare him off. "Is that so? Your figure must be beautiful because your dress doesn't conceal much. Nice outfit," he said of the provocative Santa suit.

She frowned. "We were told this was a Christmas costume party. That's why we're wearing these clothes," she said, looking down at her outfit in disgust. "But you're wrong again. No boobs," she told him. "I'm wearing one of those long-line wonder bras and panty hose that suck me in from my waist to my thighs."

"It's working," he said and grinned. "Appearance isn't everything. There's also intelligence and personality."

"I'm very boring," she said. "Terrible at dinner conversation. I have a condition called narcolepsy and I have no control over when I fall asleep. I've been known to fall asleep during dinner, while dancing, and always during sex."

"What a shame. You should try medication. I've heard it can be effective."

She looked at him for a long moment. "I've always considered it rude for people to wear sunglasses indoors."

He nodded. "Unfair advantage. Because I can see your eyes, but you can't see mine."

"Yes," she said and waited. "Are you going to take off your glasses?"

"Not right now," he said.

She frowned and looked out the window again.

"Tell me how a beautiful girl like you ended up here."

"The same way the other women ended up here. We answered an ad to become *teachers* abroad," she said, her voice oozing cynicism.

"Now why do I think that you always knew that ad was too good to be true?"

She glanced at him sideways then shrugged.

Rick knew he needed to work quickly, so he had to scare her with the truth. "You know that the only way you're going to get out of here is to be chosen and bought," he told her.

She blinked. "Bought?" she echoed. "I didn't know—" She broke off and looked away, alarmed.

Rick saw the light dawn on her face. So she hadn't known exactly what she was getting into, he concluded. He considered telling her that he was here to rescue her, but she was still an unknown. Like Roz had said, she could be impulsive. He couldn't allow her to blow his cover. Plus, someone could overhear. He had to persuade her to cooperate with him. He had to make her think going with him was a better risk than staying here. "The place might as well be Fort Knox for all the security it has."

"What do you care about the security?"

"It's just something you might want to think about," he said. "Just as you may want to think about all the different kinds of men who could buy you and how they might treat you."

"What do you mean?"

"I mean some men will treat you well and allow you a great deal of freedom. Other men will keep you locked in the equivalent of a dungeon until they're ready for you to be—" He paused. "Used."

She swallowed audibly and paused for a long moment. "And which are you?" she asked.

"The first," he said. "I have no interest in locking up a woman and treating her like an animal." He touched her hair. "In my social circle, a blond, intelligent American woman is the ultimate sign of prestige."

"So you treat women like objects, too," she said, clearly assessing him.

"Perhaps, but I take care of my objects."

"If you wouldn't want to treat a woman like an animal, why would you feel the need to buy one?"

Rick smiled. "I'm between mistresses and my position demands that I entertain constantly."

She turned to look at him with her arms crossed over her chest, still protective as hell. "I have difficulty believing you have any problem finding a new mistress."

He shrugged. "It's the holidays. I need someone beautiful and well-educated immediately."

"Just to hostess," she said, doubt oozing from her voice.

He allowed himself to look at her for a long moment as if he were considering her physical assets. It was part of the act, he told himself. "Hostess first. Anything else can be negotiated later."

"Negotiation suggests both parties have some say in the final outcome."

"I assure you both parties would. I've never had to force a woman."

Chapter Two

HER ONLY WAY OUT WAS TO BE CHOSEN AND BOUGHT? Hilary's stomach clenched. She'd known the operation was shady, but she'd thought if she could get to Christine before she left the country, everything would be okay. Now she wasn't so sure. She felt as if she was being watched every second, and the security worried her. She'd thought she could find Christine and persuade her to leave, but it looked as if a lot more would be involved.

Hilary studied Juan's clothes. Just how wealthy was he? If he could buy her, could he also buy Christine? He wasn't what she'd expected. Although he was obviously sexist, he had a sense of humor. He presented himself as if he would be reasonable. It could just be an act, though, to gain her willingness.

And why would he choose her? She wasn't the prettiest woman in the room by far. Plus she'd given him a kooky story that should have scared him off and she'd made it clear that she wasn't the submissive type because she didn't want to leave before she learned *something* about Christine.

She was starting to get very nervous about this situation. Christine was nowhere on the estate and Hilary had gone over every inch of the place. She needed information and lots of money to buy Christine if that was the only way out. The only tiny piece of information she'd overheard was when Giselle said that occasionally one of the candidates needed special training that was handled at another location.

Hilary needed to find out where that other location was. Maybe Christine was there. Unless she'd already been sold to some sadistic monster and taken out of the country. The prospect filled her with guilt. She couldn't help thinking that if she'd only taken some extra time with Christine, none of this would have happened.

She took a second look at Juan. Would she be able to persuade him to buy Christine, too? Would she have to trade sex? Her stomach twisted.

No, her instincts told her. She believed he'd told her the truth when he said he'd never forced a woman. He was good-looking in a dark, Latin way. If she weren't in this situation, he would have caught her attention. Just his appearance, she told herself. His height and muscular body, however, made her a little nervous. If he wanted to physically force her, she'd really be screwed.

She gnawed on her bottom lip. She wanted more information. "Who are you, anyway?" she asked.

He tilted his head to one side. "I'm Juan Castillo. I'm a government official in Argentina with private holdings in several companies. Would you like to see my ID?"

"Yes," she said without blinking an eye.

Juan glanced to his side. "We're being watched. Let me get in the corner and you can act like you're leaning into me while you look at it."

"What? But—" She broke off when she glanced over his shoulder and saw creepy John Harris looking at her. "Okay, but if you try anything, I'll do something—" She searched her mind for a threat and couldn't come up with anything. "—awful."

"Such as?" he asked, moving to the corner.

"Spit on you."

His lips twitched as he held up the ID. Hilary studied it, bummed that she wouldn't know a forgery from the real thing. "Okay, I guess. But what if you're a sadistic monster and you're lying to me?" she asked, fighting the loss of her control.

"Unless you have polygraph handy, you'll have to trust me."

Hilary frowned. "Trust a man who would buy a woman from a human-trafficking ring?"

His mouth tightened. "I told you. I'm in a hurry."

She looked at him for a long moment. "Would you take off your glasses?"

He didn't respond.

"Take off your glasses and swear that you've never forced a woman to have sex with you."

He swore in Spanish under his breath but lifted his glasses, so she could see his eyes. He had dark, dark eyes rimmed with sooty black eyelashes. Sexy-looking. In another situation, she reminded herself.

"I swear I've never forced a woman to have sex with me."

His gaze was bold and direct, and he didn't look at all as if he were lying. He didn't look at all as if he would need to force a woman to have sex with him.

But she still needed more information to find Christine. Maybe tonight she could learn something, she thought, struggling with the reality that her freedom of choice could be ripped away from her so easily. "Is there any way you could let me think about this overnight and come back tomorrow?"

"No," he said, irritation bleeding through his tone as he put his glasses back in place. "Someone else could buy you."

She laughed in disbelief. "Trust me. There won't be a stampede for my services."

"You never know. That other buyer keeps looking at

you. You know how men are. If one man wants you, then the others take a second look."

That was true, she supposed, feeling uncomfortable. "I could do something to discourage him."

"And get yourself in trouble with Mr. Harris. What do they do to the troublemakers? Drugs or intimidation?"

Her stomach twisted and she bit her lip. She really didn't want to be drugged. More than anything she needed a clear head. Should she gamble on this man? She didn't have much time. How could she persuade him to help her get Christine?

"Do you have a lot of money?" she asked.

He paused. "Why do you ask?"

"I'm just curious. Do you have a lot of money? Say, enough money to buy more than one woman if you wanted?"

"I'm only buying one," he said firmly. "I only need one."

"But do you have enough to buy another? If you wanted?"

"Yes."

"Do you have a dog?" she asked, trying to get a bead on his personality.

"No," he said. "I have a parrot. What does this have to do with—"

"What about charity? Do you ever donate to charity? Do you buy Girl Scout cookies?"

"We don't have Girl Scouts in my country." His jaw clenched. "But yes, I donate to charity." He glanced over her shoulder. "No more questions. The other buyer is coming this way."

Rick approached John and pressed the note he'd written before entering the compound into the man's hand.

John smiled. "You have found one you like. I'm very happy to serve you." He glanced at the note. "This will do if the other buyer isn't interested. We may need to hold an auction," he said in a sly tone.

"You assured me I would receive a private introduction. I'm not interested in an auction."

"Then perhaps you should choose another girl."

Rick ground his teeth. "I can send other buyers your way. Do you want to jeopardize that?"

John lifted his hands. "Now, now. No need to rush to offense. We don't even know if my other buyer will be interested. Have another drink."

Rick didn't want another drink. He wanted to get the job done and get the hell out of there. He didn't want Hilary to have too much time to think or she might do something crazy in protest. The more he looked around the room, the more he felt the sick oppression in the air. He looked at the other young, naïve women. Who knew what would happen to them? A bitter taste filled his mouth. Would it be that difficult to blow this operation? A few plastic explosives, a call to the FBI . . . Break a few of John Harris Slavinsky's bones . . .

And another man just like him would pop up with the same operation. Human trafficking had a lot in common with roaches. Both had been in existence since the dawn of time.

A woman delivered a drink to him and tried to make conversation, but he cut it short and dismissed her, watching Hilary all the while.

The other buyer finally left her side and ventured over to John. Rick was standing close enough to hear part of the conversation.

"He can have her. She's a nutcase," the buyer said.

Swallowing his amusement, he wandered toward the bar and waited for John to approach him. The tide had turned again.

John clapped him on his shoulder. "Mr. Castillo, you're

a lucky man. You may have the lovely lady for your asking price plus transportation and processing fees."

"Transportation and processing fees?" Rick echoed. "You didn't say anything about transportation and processing fees."

"Mr. Castillo, as a businessman, you know there are always extra costs along the way. Transporting the candidates from their hometowns, arranging for beauty services and clothing. And security, of course."

"I'm paying a prime price. In cash," Rick added. "It's your job to incorporate your fees into your price." He paused. "Perhaps I've been too hasty."

John froze. "You are changing your mind? But you have already given me a written offer."

"And you're changing the fee structure. Maybe I'm overpaying," he said, resenting every penny he was giving this sleazeball even though the pennies weren't his.

"I assure you that you are not overpaying," the Russian man said in a clipped tone, his accent leaking in with his anger. "The woman you've chosen is everything you requested and more."

"I want a cash discount," Rick said, sensing he had an edge. He would return the extra cash, but he liked the idea of decreasing Slavinsky's profit margin.

John's eyes widened. "A cash discount. Everyone pays cash."

"Mine is waiting for you in my limo. You can have it tonight."

John paused, shifting his shoulders. Rick saw when greed took over. "You plan to send other buyers my way?"

Rick nodded. "As long as I'm happy with your service."

Harris wiped his mouth. "I will offer a one-time ten percent discount, but do not tell this to your friends."

"Twenty," Rick countered.

"Fifteen," John countered.

Rick extended his hand. "Done. I want to take the woman with me tonight."

"She may require extra persuasion," John said. "We have pills."

Rick smiled. "I look forward to the challenge of taming her." In actuality, he suspected he was in a no-win situation with Hilary. Something told him she was still trying to find a way to rescue her friend.

"Just make sure you don't hurt her in the state of Texas. That could make things messy for everyone," he cautioned. "I'll give you the pills in case you change your mind." He paused. "We don't accept returns," he said in a low voice. "But in your case, I can offer additional training for her if you should need it."

"I'll take care of her training."

"As you wish," said John Harris Slavinsky, aka Slimeball.

***

Tottering on her high heels, Hilary hustled to keep up with Juan Castillo as he led her out into the winter night to a long black limo waiting in the circular driveway. Still dressed in the blasted slutty Santa suit costume that had been given to her, she shivered in the chilly night. Creepy John Harris wouldn't even let her have a coat. Despite what she'd told Juan boy about her foundation garments, the staff at the estate had only provided her with a thong, garter and stockings, and sheer underwire bra.

She couldn't wait to ditch the slut suit for cotton undies, a pair of jeans, and her Tweety Bird sweatshirt. As soon as she scrubbed the pound of makeup off her face and washed the starchlike hairspray from her hair, she might start to feel human again.

Juan opened the car door for her. "After you."

She looked at him again, with his dark glasses and powerful body, and felt afraid. Glancing around, she wondered if she could bolt.

"There's an electric fence surrounding the property, armed guards, and dogs," he said as if he'd read her mind.

She made a face but got into the limo. It was nice and cozy with a well-stocked bar. As soon as Juan slid beside her, she turned to him. "Could I please have my suitcase and purse?"

"Later," he said, tugging loose his tie. "Jensen, head for Houston. We can stay in an airport hotel and catch a flight in the morning."

Panic roared through her. "Flight?" Hilary echoed. "I'm not ready for a flight."

"You don't have to be," he said, pushing a button to close the window between the chauffeur and the back of the limo. "We're not leaving until tomorrow."

"But I don't want to leave the country," she said.

"Not that it's your choice to make, but we're not leaving the country first. We're visiting some of my friends."

"I don't want to visit your friends."

"You don't set the itinerary, Señorita. I do."

"But I thought you said you would negotiate. That you wouldn't force me."

"I'm not forcing you to have sex," he said.

Hilary frowned. "Listen, I have a much better idea," she said. "I know of another girl John Harris interviewed who would be perfect for you. And since you've already bought me, I bet you could get her at a discount."

"I already negotiated a discount on you."

She opened her mouth and closed it without speaking, uncertain whether she should be relieved or insulted. She cleared her throat. "Which makes my idea even better. I think you would be especially pleased with this other girl. She's prettier than I am and is better at

hostessing. I have to be honest. I flunked charm school."
She could see she was getting nowhere and she wished
he would take off the damn glasses.

She swallowed the metallic taste of desperation in her
mouth. "Plus, I think she actually likes sex, so that could
work out better, too," she offered.

"Then why do I need you if she would be so much
better?" he asked.

"Well, I can offer some extra academic information to
entertain your guests. She and I could work as a team."

Juan leaned back against the seat and stretched out
his long legs. He appeared to consider her proposal.
That was good, she thought hopefully.

He turned toward her. "Are you suggesting a three-
some?"

Hilary was so shocked she couldn't keep her eyes
from bulging in their sockets. She deliberately blinked
and looked away. She bit her lip. A deal with the devil.
Sometimes a girl had to do what a girl had to do. "Well,
that could be part of the negotiation," she lied, knowing
full well that the only bonking that would take place
would be when she bonked Juan boy on the head so she
and Christine could escape. Until then, she would
promise the man the moon.

Hilary spent more than an hour explaining to Juan why
he should talk to John Harris about purchasing Christine. She just knew that if cash was dangled in front of
John Harris, he would somehow produce her friend. If
Christine hadn't been bought yet. She couldn't consider
that, she told herself. She would have continued all night
long, but he told her that if she didn't take a break, then
the answer would be no.

A clock inside her ticked louder with each passing
hour and it had nothing to do with her biological clock.

She had a bad feeling about what might be happening with Christine.

The limo pulled into the parking lot of a hotel with suites and Juan waited in the vehicle while Jensen checked them in. After Jensen returned with keys, Juan escorted Hilary to the elevator and up three floors to a suite. Jensen followed with a carry-on bag and gave it to Juan at the door.

Hilary stepped inside and turned to close the door, expecting to finally get a moment to herself.

"Not so fast," Juan said, stopping the door with his hand. "We share the suite."

Hilary's heart stopped. "But I thought you said you weren't going to force me."

Juan rolled his eyes. "To have sex. But you don't think I'd be foolish enough not to protect my investment, do you?"

She frowned. "What do you mean?"

"I mean, I'll take the couch while you take the bedroom."

She relaxed a millimeter.

"In case you get any ideas about leaving."

Her stomach knotted again. She was at this man's mercy. Swallowing over a surge of panic, she refused to focus on her fear for herself and began to plot and scheme. If she couldn't convince Juan to buy Christine soon, she had to get away.

"I'd really like my clothes."

"I'll get something for you to sleep in," he said.

Irritation prickled at her. "Why can't I have my suitcase? There are other things I need."

"Such as?" he asked.

"Female things," she retorted desperately, hoping to embarrass him.

He didn't blink an eye. "I'll make sure you get what you need."

"I'm hungry, too."

"Room service will deliver club sandwiches in fifteen minutes. Why don't you go ahead and take your shower?"

She crossed her arms over her chest. "I don't want a shower."

"Fine. Be dirty. I have a few things I need to take care of." He turned away from her and walked to the kitchen area, immediately removing a tray of stainless steel flatware and cooking utensils from the drawers. He carried the flatware and cooking utensils to his suitcase and locked them inside.

She stared at him in confusion. "I thought you were well off. Why are you stealing the flatware from the hotel?"

"I'll return them before we leave for the airport in the morning," he said calmly.

"Where are we going?"

"To visit my friends in California."

"I can't," she said. "I have to—"

He lifted a dark eyebrow. "Take a deep breath and accept it. We're going where I say we're going."

Chapter Three

AT THREE A.M., HILARY LAY IN THE KING-SIZED BED AND stared wide-eyed at the ceiling. She'd tried half a dozen different ways to get out of the room. Juan had foiled them all. She was starting to suspect he wasn't from South America. He was watching an American basketball game on television and she'd noticed his accent had begun to fade.

Turning on her side, she frowned. He didn't seem to mind staying on the sofa. If he were truly a wealthy South American government official, wouldn't he demand the best bed? The best food?

Certainly not a club sandwich, she thought.

She wondered if he was just a courier and perhaps she was being taken to someone else. His *friends*.

Her stomach twisted. Who knew what the other people would be like? Rising from the bed, she walked to the window again and looked down. It was a long way to the ground. If she jumped, she hated to think about how many bones she might break, if she even survived.

There had to be a way out. There had to be. For the fiftieth time, she looked around the room for something, anything, that could help her escape. Her gaze landed on a lamp.

Rick heard a high-pitched scream pierce the air as he watched a rerun of *The Man Show* on cable. He glanced at his watch and sighed. When was she going to give it up? It would have been nice to hand Hilary over to her parents at the hotel, but the agency coordinator, Roz, was big on providing a complete mission. In this case, everyone wanted Hilary in California away from the human traffickers, away from the temptation of going after Christine.

He was tempted to tell her that he'd been hired to take her home to her parents, but he wasn't sure that was the best strategy, and, hell, he had only a few more hours before he would be escorting her on the flight to California.

Hilary screamed again and he swore under his breath. The other things she'd done to try to get away had been a nuisance, but the screaming was a problem. He didn't want to have to use his last resort so early in the game.

Hilary screamed again. "Help! A rat! A rat!"

Rick rolled his eyes and rose from the sofa. "A rat, my ass." He wondered what she was going to try to pull this time. Maybe a room change or a hotel change that would give her the opportunity to run.

He stood outside her door. "Your door isn't locked. You can come out here if you want."

"No, I can't," she said. "The rat is right next to the door. I'm afraid of it."

"Yeah, yeah, yeah," he muttered and opened the door. He took one step forward and felt something heavy strike his head and back. Pain shot through him, stunning him. He stumbled.

"Sorry," she whispered as she sprinted past him. "Really sorry."

"Damn," he said, going after her, but his feet felt sluggish and wouldn't move fast enough. "Damn, damn—"

He watched her open the door and disappear down the hall.

Hilary ran down the stairs of the hotel, dressed in a sleepshirt and a pair of cotton undies. She'd had to beg for the underwear. She carried the red high heels, the only shoes she had. They were nearly useless in terms of footwear, but she supposed she could use one of the stiletto heels as a weapon, if she was forced.

Scrambling down the last flight, she rounded the corner and ran toward the lobby. No one was at the desk. She rapped her hand on the desk. "Hello? Hello?"

No one answered. Her nerves jangled in her stomach. Juan might come after her. Or Jensen. She rapped again on the desk and yelled louder.

"Really long potty break," she muttered when, still, no one came.

Her heart pounding with a combination of adrenaline and fear, she went out the door. At least she'd escaped. She was *free*. A burst of exultation lasted three glorious seconds.

Okay, so now what? she asked herself. She'd been so focused on getting free that she hadn't planned what she would do once she accomplished that. She'd thought she could get help in the lobby, but there'd been no one. She had no money, no identification, no charge card, no cell phone.

But there was always collect, she thought, immediately walking across the parking lot in search of a pay phone. She could call her parents—Scratch that. This kind of call would take years off her parents' lives. She could call one of her sorority sisters, preferably one of the graduates who could let her borrow a little money for clothes and transportation. And maybe the police would help now that she had some information. Now that Christine had been missing for way longer than twenty-four hours.

Her stomach clenched at the thought and she picked up her pace, ignoring the fact that her feet were freezing. Where could Christine be? She must have been taken to the training center for uncooperative candidates. Her heart sank. Or she'd already been bought and had been taken out of the country. Or worse.

"Miss Winfree?" a man said from behind her.

Hilary's heart slammed into her rib cage and she bolted, a tiny scream escaping her throat. She didn't know who it was, but whoever it was, he probably wasn't on her side. She ran across a grassy median strip.

"Miss Winfree! Stop! You're not supposed to be out here," the man called, still behind her.

She continued running. *Head for traffic.* Maybe she could get a ride. In her pajamas, she reminded herself dryly, but still kept running.

She felt his breath on her neck and panicked.

"Miss Winfree—"

The man captured her arm and pulled.

Hilary rounded on him, blindly hitting him with one of the stiletto heels as the other shoe fell from her hand. It was the chauffeur, Jensen.

He swore, but hung on to her. She continued to pummel him and he finally let her loose. She jumped out of his reach.

She took two breaths and an arm encircled her waist. The shoe was jerked from her hand and another arm encircled her like a straitjacket.

She kicked impotently.

"You're not getting away," Juan said. "But it was a damn good try. You're going to pay for the headache I'll have tomorrow."

"I wish I had hit you harder. Hard enough to knock you out," she said breathlessly, frustration and fear rushing through her.

He laughed. "But not hard enough to kill me, right, Hilary? You couldn't go quite that far. You should be ashamed of yourself. You almost put poor Jensen's eye out."

"That's nothing," she said, even though she felt a twinge of guilt about Jensen. He'd been nice and polite to her so far. "I won't cooperate with you. I'll be the biggest pain in the butt you've ever experienced. If you take me anywhere, you'd better sleep with one eye open, because I'll do whatever I need to get away from you unless you help me find my friend."

"You need to let the police handle finding Christine," he said, lifting her and tossing her over his shoulder.

"The police are taking too long," she protested in disgust. She'd known Juan was going to be a problem. He was just too tall and too strong and now his shoulder was digging into her gut. "She'll be out of the country by the time they realize she's missing at all. And then it will be too late and—" She stopped when his words sank in. She bounced against his shoulder. "How did you know it's Christine? I never told you her name."

He sighed, holding her legs to keep her from kicking him again. "Because your parents told me." He paused. "You okay, Jensen? I can get you some ice for that eye."

"Thanks," Jensen said.

Hilary glanced at the chauffeur who cast a wary, accusing glance at her. "Sorry," she couldn't help saying at the same time that her anger built. "My parents hired you. I should have known. How financially inefficient. I ask for their help to find Christine, but will they help me? No. So they end up spending the same money or more to rescue me. And I'm still going back to find Christine."

"As long as it's not on my watch," he said, swiping the hotel's backdoor entry with his key.

"I'll scream," she threatened. "I can still get away from you."

He hauled her up the steps like a sack of potatoes. "If you scream and someone actually gives a damn, I'll show them papers you signed describing your mental incompetence and your agreement to voluntarily commit yourself to a mental health facility in order to prevent you from hurting yourself and others."

Hilary gasped. "I didn't sign anything like that."

"Sure looks like your signature," Juan said. "Notarized and everything."

"So you're not a good guy," she said, unable to keep the contempt from her voice. "You're crooked," she said. "There's no difference between you and the human traffickers."

"There's a big difference between me and that white slavery gang," he retorted, carrying her inside the room and putting her on her feet. "I won't rape you, beat you, drug you, or kill you. My job is to get you home for Christmas."

She met his dark gaze, wondering how she could persuade him to help her. If he was on her side, then she *knew* she would succeed. He would be the brawn and she would be the brains. "Then we have time to get Christine."

He shook his head. "Not my job," he said.

"But it would be so easy for you. You're already here. You could call Mr. Harris and ask if he had any girls matching Christine's description. Maybe they would bring her to the estate. Or prison," she corrected.

He stepped closer to her. "You're not hearing me," he said in a low voice. "I'm not going after Christine. My job is to get you home safely to Mommy and Daddy for Christmas."

His closeness and her lack of choices sent fear and desperation running through her. She bit her lip. "I could try to hurt you again. A lot more this time," she whispered.

"I don't want to have to tie you up, but I will."

Nausea rose in her throat. "Or I suppose I could hurt myself."

The barest alarm flickered in his eyes. "You're not that type."

"No," she said. "I'm not, but I guess I could lie and say you hurt me. You look like you could hurt someone a lot."

"You'd have a hard time sustaining the lie. You're too honest," he said.

She resisted making a face. "Or I could offer to pay you."

"You can't afford me."

"I could take up a collection among the sorority sisters and I know we could raise enough money to pay you. We do fund-raisers all the time."

"Bake sales and wet T-shirt contests," he said in a doubtful tone.

"It's an academic sorority," she said in a frosty voice. "And you would be amazed at how much we earn for charity."

"My assignment is to deliver you to your parents' home by Christmas."

"Deliver," she mocked. "You make me sound like a Christmas package."

"Your words," he said with a shrug.

She bit her lip. "She's only nineteen and her boyfriend just dumped her. You could take care of this in no time. If you don't, she could be dead."

"How do you know she's not out of the country already?" he asked.

"We have to find out."

"What's with this 'we,' Tonto?" he asked.

She looked at his tough jaw and stubborn chin. His unflinching gaze disheartened her. He was rock hard in both body and mind. How could she change his mind?

"I've threatened you. I've offered you money. I've tried to explain how dire this situation is. I don't know what else to do. I'm at your mercy," she said. "Please help me."

Rick looked into Hilary's pleading eyes and swallowed an oath. She'd been a lot easier to resist when she'd hit him over the head with that lamp. A lot easier when all she could do was argue. But looking into her honest gaze and hearing the complete lack of manipulation in her voice, he felt like he was looking down a double-barreled shotgun at point-blank range.

Rick could brush aside threats, anger, tears, bribes, even lamps, but he had a tough time with Hilary's flat-out honesty and simply worded request.

"You know it could be hell getting truthful information out of anyone connected with John Harris Slavinsky," he said.

Her eyes widened in realization. "So that's his real last name. I knew Harris couldn't be his real name."

"He's been in business for years. When the authorities close in on him, he just goes underground for a while and reappears in another state."

She curled her mouth in distaste. "It's really disgusting how he misleads the women. I'm pretty sure he was giving drugs to some of them. I think the only reason they didn't drug me was because I played dumb and didn't eat anything." She shook her head. "I hate to think what might be happening to Christine right now."

"Whatever it is, it isn't pretty," he said.

"So will you help?" she asked. "I'm perfectly willing to go back to the estate. I'll do whatever it takes."

He hesitated, remembering the occasions when he'd worn a uniform and the rules had kept him from catching a criminal in time. Working for a private agency meant he could break a few of those rules if necessary.

"We still have a chance if we move fast," Hilary said.

Rick recalled a time when there'd been no chance and felt the dull squeeze of guilt in his gut. Different situation, he told himself, but the sensation gnawed at him.

He sighed. "I'm not promising anything, but I'll make a few calls."

"Thank you." She hesitated. "Juan isn't your real name either, is it?"

"No."

"What is your real name?"

He considered her question for a moment then stuck to policy. "Maybe after this is over, I'll tell you."

"Why won't you tell me now?"

"For a number of reasons, but the first is if for some reason we both have to appear in front of traffickers again, I don't want you to panic and get confused."

"I wouldn't panic," she told him. "I'm not the type to panic. I refuse to be a victim. I have to take action."

"Right," he said, thinking for the tenth time that this could turn into a helluva mistake.

"You're not going to tell me your name, are you?" she said.

"That's right."

"Okay," she said. "Michael."

He looked at her in confusion. "Michael?"

"If you're not going to tell me, then I'll have to guess."

"Just call me Mr. Castillo."

Fifteen minutes later, he spoke with Harris Slavinsky again. Hilary had been so anxious he'd told her to go to the bedroom while he made the call. He didn't want her voice in the background. He used the extra moments of peace to put together a plan. No need to look at the calendar again. He knew he had just three days to pull it off and get Hilary to her parents on Christmas. Roz was going to kill him. It went against all the Agency's rules. An agent never added to the assignment. The assignment was it. No extras.

He knocked lightly on Hilary's bedroom door and she opened it immediately, as if she'd been poised beside the door. "Did you consider sleeping?" he asked.

"I'm too wired," she said. "What did sleazy Slavinsky say? Is he going to give you Christine?"

She was practically bouncing to get moving. Despite the fact that she was mouthy as hell and jumped from step 1 to step 7 without looking, he couldn't deny she was cute with her pink cheeks, rosebud mouth, and expressive eyes. She might be book smart, but the woman needed to be protected from her enthusiasm. Thank goodness he wasn't her keeper on a regular basis. "I gave him Christine's description and he said he would have a match for me by morning."

She clasped her hands together in excitement. "Oh, thank goodness. We can go to the estate, pick her up, and—"

"We have to get funds first."

Her face fell. "Oh. I forgot."

"Not surprised you'd forget about practical things like money," he muttered. "Since your career is adding college degrees to your collection."

She frowned. "That's not fair," she said. "I could have been teaching, but I didn't want to miss the opportunity for a semester of special study."

"What's the area of special study?" he asked.

She paused a half beat. "Women's studies."

He rolled his eyes. "Do you want fries with that?" referring to the lack of marketability of her specialty.

She lifted her chin and narrowed her eyes. "You know, you could use a little time in the classroom when it comes to women's studies."

"Watch it, sweetheart. You don't know anything about how I handle women."

"Yes, I do. I know how you manhandled me in that parking lot and—"

"After you hit me with a lamp and nearly poked out Jensen's eye," he added.

She opened her mouth then closed it.

"Besides, I talked you into leaving the estate with me without needing to drag you out by your hair, didn't I?"

She took a huffy breath and crossed her arms over her chest. "Do you have a steady girlfriend or wife?"

Rick immediately felt a sticky discomfort. "Not right now," he said. "I'm out of town a lot. If I'm not gone for my job, then I'm out on my boat."

"Uh-huh," she said, disbelief oozing into her voice. "Or you're unable to commit. Or women can't stand being around you longer than a weekend at a time."

Her assessment of him irritated him. He shouldn't care, but she bothered him. "And what about you, Ms. Femi-nazi? Where's your lover boy?"

"I was in a serious relationship in California before I returned to take this postgraduate course," she told him in a cool voice.

"So what happened to that?"

She shrugged and looked away. "We decided it wasn't meant to be."

That answer was too easy. "You or he decided?" he asked, because he knew joint romantic decisions were a myth.

She pursed her lips. "I said 'we.' "

"Okay, who suggested it?" he persisted.

"This is none of your business and it has nothing to do with getting Christine back."

"You're right," he said. "He must have dumped you."

"He did not," she retorted. "I initiated the conversation."

"So maybe the reason you returned to your femi-nazi classes is because you were scared of a real relationship with a man."

She recrossed her arms over her chest and took a deep breath. She met his gaze head-on. "I have one thing to say to that. It takes a scaredy-cat to know a scaredy-cat."

He would die before he admitted it, but she nailed him with that one. "Okay, you need to put on your Santa suit again."

She frowned. "Why?"

"Because Jensen and I looked through your clothes and it's the only sexy thing you have."

She looked offended for a second, then shook her head in a dismissive gesture. "If I was going to get involved in human trafficking, I didn't want to look too inviting or someone might try something."

"You succeeded," he said. "But if you didn't want to look too inviting, why did you bleach your hair?"

"Because I heard they like blondes. Why do I have to dress sexy?"

"If they don't bring me Christine then we have to get in another way. I told him you might need additional training and I want to be present during the training so I can use the same techniques when I take you away."

"Training," she echoed. "How bad do you think—"

"It's not gonna be pretty," he said. "But I'll be there to make sure you don't get hurt. It may be the only way we can find out where Christine is. If you don't have the stomach for it, you better tell me by the time we arrive at the compound."

She squared her shoulders. "I can handle it."

"We'll see," he said, studying her.

The barest hint of uncertainty flickered in her eyes and she crossed her arms over her chest. "What—uh—what do you think they will do?"

His head still throbbed from his close encounter with the lamp. He squeezed his scalp. "I don't know. They might be a little sick. Bondage, whips, beating. But I won't let them hurt you. I'd kill them first," he said.

She winced. "Your head really hurts, doesn't it?" She lifted her hand to gently touch his head.

Her fingers felt like silk against his skin. Soothing, but sexy. His heart thumped harder in his chest. His reaction took him off guard. He looked at her lips and wondered how her mouth would feel beneath his. He dipped his gaze lower to her throat, then to her breasts. Hearing her soft intake of breath, he looked into her eyes and caught the signal of her awareness of him as a man. Her gaze darkened and she bit her lip.

He lifted his thumb to her lip where her white teeth marred the plump bow shape. "No biting or I'll have to kiss it and make it better."

Chapter Four

HILARY GLANCED AT JUAN FOR THE HUNDREDTH TIME AS he snoozed in the limo. When he'd touched her mouth back at the hotel, she'd felt her temperature shoot through the roof. Sure, he was attractive, but she hadn't thought he could make her feel anything sexual. Especially in this situation.

She shook her head. It must have been some kind of weird combination of adrenaline and lack of sleep. Speaking of sleep, how could he possibly sleep at a time like this? She looked at the book he'd bought for her at their last pit stop, to keep her *entertained*, he'd told her. She sighed.

He'd grown irritated with her questions after the first thirty minutes of the drive and ordered her to rest the same way she suspected he would talk to a child. When she still couldn't sit still, he'd given her super glue to repair the heel on one of the red shoes Jensen had collected from the parking lot.

The driver watched her with a wary eye. One wary eye, she thought with a sliver of guilt. His other eye was already swollen shut.

Hilary couldn't stand the suspense. The drive was taking entirely too long. She wanted to find Christine and make sure she was safe. She didn't know how she could look at herself in the mirror if it turned out that Christine was hurt. Or worse.

A lump of dread formed in her throat and she forced herself to swallow. She had to stay positive and focused.

"You need to rest while you have the opportunity," Juan said with his eyes still closed.

"I can't possibly rest until we find Christine," she said. "I don't see how you can."

"It would be easier if you would stop moving and sighing," he said, opening his eyes to slits. "The idea is to rest while you can so you won't be tired when you need all your energy."

She sighed and bit her lip. "That's an excellent theory. I just can't do it."

He closed his eyes. "You haven't told me why you're the only one chasing after Christine. If you two have all these sorority sisters, then why aren't they going after her, too? Or her parents?"

"I'm not as active in a lot of the sorority activities because I graduated a few years ago, so I serve as more of an adviser and leave the door open for any of the girls to come to me in case of emergency."

"Mother hen," he said.

She shook her head. "No. I didn't have enough time to parent this semester."

"So why aren't her parents doing anything?"

"Her mother is dead and her father is in absentia. She was on the verge of being kicked out of the sorority because one of her scholarships was discontinued. The foundation stopped giving scholarships."

"Again, what does this have to do with you?"

"She called me several times before she got involved with the traffickers, but I was busy grading papers. I'm a teaching assistant for one of the professors. When she told me about the position she was considering, it didn't sound on the up and up. I had a rushed conversation with her and just told her not to take it."

"She didn't listen," he said.

"Right, she didn't. And if I'd spent more time talking with her or invited her over for coffee or dinner, then I probably could have prevented this whole disaster."

"Because your words have magical powers, you can convince a headstrong underclasswoman to do the right thing."

She shot him a sharp look. "I don't appreciate the sarcasm."

He shrugged. "I'm just telling the truth. If Christine was determined to go, then you couldn't have stopped her."

"I think I could have persuaded her," Hilary said.

"You tried. You did your part. She made her own bad choice."

"So she's going to have to die because of it?" She shook her head. "Haven't you ever made a bad choice? Have you ever made a bad choice and you *didn't* have to bear the consequences? When you deserved to have something horrible happen, but it didn't?"

He paused and met her gaze. "Maybe, but I've had to deal with plenty of bad consequences for stupid decisions."

She felt guilt squeeze her throat again. "It's just not fair," she said. "Put me in Christine's place. First, I have two parents who love me almost to the point of smothering me. The only reason they wouldn't help me with Christine is because they didn't want me involved in anything that could endanger me."

"So the reason you ran to the opposite side of the country is because it was the only way you could politely get them to leave you alone," he said.

She frowned at him. He was dead on, but her parents had been so supportive that she couldn't admit it. "I've never had to think twice about how my education would be financed."

"But you did earn scholarships?" he added.

"Yes." She met his gaze and felt an odd flip in her belly at how much he seemed to know about her. "Just how much did my parents tell you about me?"

His lips twitched. "You mean did the report tell me that you weighed seven pounds and eight ounces at birth and were balder than a bald eagle until you turned two?"

She groaned. "They didn't have to go back all the way to my birth."

"Before that," he said. "According to the report, it took your parents nine years and seven months to conceive you."

She covered her face, feeling the weight of all her parents' dreams settle on her shoulders. "I've heard that once or twice," she said, unable to hide her frustration. The truth was she'd heard about her miracle conception at least a hundred times.

"Tough being a princess?" he asked with more gentleness than she would have expected.

"There are worse things."

"Ah, the guilt factor returns."

"I do have a lot to be thankful for, although if my father had just let me borrow the money to find Christine, that would have helped. It's one of the rare times he has turned me down."

"He didn't want his angel getting her hands dirty."

She glanced down at her Santa suit and smiled grimly. "If he could only see his little princess now."

Hours later, after Juan withdrew a large amount of cash from a bank and Jensen finished the drive to the estate, Hilary sat on the edge of her seat waiting for him to bring Christine out of the house. She whispered a thousand prayers that Christine would be at the estate, hoping the international language of money would make

Slavinsky produce her. She crossed her fingers and would have waved a magic wand if she'd had one. She begged Jensen to let her outside the car to expend some of her excess energy. He refused.

No surprise, she thought. He wasn't going to forgive her anytime soon for what she'd done to him with that stiletto heel.

Her gaze glued to the front door, she finally saw it open. Her heart jumped in her chest. *Please, please, please . . .*

Juan appeared and shook hands with Harris and walked down the steps. Christine was nowhere in sight.

Her heart sank as quickly as it had jumped.

Hilary stared at the door, willing it to open again. Her mind provided a dozen possibilities. She almost forgot her suitcase. She was in the bathroom. She needed a bottle of water. Anything, she thought desperately, anything.

Juan stepped inside the car and shook his head. "Sorry, she wasn't part of the chick parade. Jensen, head toward El Paso."

Hilary searched his face. "Nothing? Nothing at all?"

Juan tugged his tie loose and raked his hand through his hair. "Not for Slavinsky's lack of trying. He brought me eight girls. Count them. Eight. And I had to find something wrong with all of them.

"I don't think any of them were a day over twenty," he added.

Through her own desperation, she caught a flash of Juan's humanity. "You wanted to bring them all with you?"

He glanced outside the window. "They looked like little girls scared to death but trying to find a way out."

"They probably sensed they could be safe with you," she said. "I did."

He met her gaze. "Really? Why is that?"

"You had a sense of humor."

He leaned toward her. "Plenty of serial killers have a sense of humor."

"You gave the impression of being reasonable, negotiable," she said, and saw him lift an eyebrow of disbelief. "Okay, you could have been a charming monster, but I had to follow my instincts. The thing that bothered me is that you looked stronger than I was expecting. I was hoping for someone much older with a paunch."

"Who, in theory, you could outrun," he said.

"Right," she said, pleased that he could see her logic.

"If not for the old fat guy's young bodyguards," he added.

"I was hoping I would be able to outsmart them."

"Right, Wonder Woman." He rubbed his face. "Okay. Both of us need to get sleep now."

"Where are we going?"

"To the location where they send candidates who need extra training," he said.

Her stomach twisted. "Is that where you think Christine is?"

"It's our best lead," he said. "He was reluctant for me to join you for the training, but I insisted and since he expects me to refer clients, he was willing to bend the rules. But I'm only taking you inside as a last resort."

"Why?"

"This could be rough. These people will threaten your parents' lives. They'll threaten to hurt you and kill you. Sometimes they hurt women, drug them. The entire goal is to demean you and crush your spirit so that you'll do whatever is asked with no protest."

She shuddered at the thought of what Christine might be experiencing. "I wish I could have found her sooner. I feel like every second that passes she could be in more danger than ever."

Juan didn't deny it. "If she's still in the country," he said. "The reason I'm telling you this is because if you go in there with me, you need to be prepared for what you'll see. The traffickers aren't concerned with human rights, let alone equal rights."

"You're afraid I can't handle it," she said.

"This won't be your average femi-nazi seminar," he said.

"Just because I have a concentration in women's studies doesn't mean I can't put what I've learned aside temporarily for the sake of getting Christine." She paused. "I'm tougher than I look."

He looked at her in disbelief. "Yeah. Well, if things go right, I'll get the information and you won't see the inside of the house." He leaned back against the seat. "Go to sleep."

Hours later, Jensen pulled up to another locked gate and pushed an intercom button.

"Señora Catalina's weight reduction spa," a woman's friendly voice said. "May I help you?"

"Juan Castillo," Jenson said.

"I will send an escort for you."

Moments later, a large man strode toward them. He extended his hand through the gate. "Identification."

Assessing the large man, Rick got out of the limo, walked to the gate and showed his ID. "I'd like to bring the limo to the house, but I'd like to talk to Señora Catalina before I bring in—" He paused. "My mistress."

He endured the patting down and waited as the guard insisted on patting down Jensen. The guard motioned for Hilary, and Rick drew the line. "I don't let other men handle my merchandise."

The guard hesitated. "Tell her to stand outside the car and turn around slowly."

With a blank face, Hilary did as instructed, but Rick could practically hear her feminist instincts screaming at top volume.

The guard checked out the limo, then gave a nod. "You may enter. Just follow the drive," he said and opened the gate with a remote device.

Rick returned to the limo. "Pretty sophisticated for a fat farm."

"If it was really a fat farm, wouldn't the guard be trimmer?" Hilary asked with a charming but insubordinate smile as she met his gaze.

He felt a twist of amusement. "Keep your sense of humor hidden if you come in the house."

"Yes sir," she said with a mock salute. "Bring back the goods."

"I'll do what I can," he said as Jensen pulled up in front of a two-story farmhouse with a wraparound porch. With rocking chairs and little tables on the front porch, the house appeared homey and welcoming.

Rick narrowed his eyes at the deceptive sight. He wondered if anyone ever sat in those rocking chairs. He climbed the steps and pushed the doorbell. A woman dressed in a white uniform answered the door.

"Mr. Castillo? Please come this way," she said when he nodded, and led him down a hallway to an office. "Señora Catalina will be with you in just a few minutes."

Rick stood instead of sitting and glanced around the room, noting the spare furnishings. Probably a result of needing to pick up and move quickly and offer no identifying characteristics to nosey, talkative visitors.

The door opened and a beautiful but severe-looking woman with dark hair and dark eyes entered. She wore a black dress that faithfully molded to her amazing curves. "Good morning, Mr. Castillo. I'm Señora Catalina."

"Good morning, Señora Catalina. Thank you for fitting me into your schedule."

She lifted her lips in a smile, but her eyes remained cold. "We try to make sure our clients are pleased. It's very unusual, however, for the client to remain here during extra training. I discourage it."

"I understand, but it would be more efficient for me to learn some of your techniques so there will be consistency." He lifted his hand. "This is a lovely home and so quiet. Perhaps you're not training during the holidays. I apologize if I interrupted your plans."

"I'm training other candidates. We have soundproof walls to eliminate any distracting noise. Now, if you'll tell me what you would like to accomplish with your candidate."

"I would like her to do what I tell her to do, but she startles easily, so I think she may require a gentle touch."

Señora Catalina nodded.

"I notice there's no art on the walls," he said in a conversational manner. "Did you just move in?"

"This is a transitional facility," she said. "We're looking for something better suited to our needs."

"So you'll be moving soon?"

She shrugged. "At one point or another. You may bring your new employee in for training now."

"I'd like to see the training room first," he said.

She paused as if she were going to refuse him, then sighed. "If you must. Come this way."

She led the way down the hall to the back of the house to a room empty except for four chairs, two chests, and a steel contraption with chains that he was certain was used for something to do with S&M.

"This is our beginner room," she said. "We have another room for candidates who are having an especially difficult time."

"Do you find the need to conduct advanced training on many of your candidates?" he asked.

"It depends," she said, then smiled again. "But I have a one hundred percent success rate."

"Everyone's a satisfied customer?" he said, noting the coldness in her eyes again.

"Satisfied when they leave," she said, as if she were touting the company line.

He nodded. "Do you ever get involved in transactions for candidates at this location?"

Rick felt her studying him and remained silent.

"Sometimes," she said. "You seem very interested in the way we conduct business."

"Actually, I was hoping to make another purchase," he said. "But I have very specific qualifications. I asked Mr. Harris to help me, but he didn't have exactly what I wanted. I wondered if you might."

"Tell me the qualifications," she said. "I'll see what I can do."

Rick described Christine without giving her name and Señora Catalina pursed her lips. "We'll see," she said. "In the meantime, bring your employee so we can get to work."

Hilary watched Juan walk down the steps wearing an irritated expression. He opened the door to the limo. "Showtime," he said to Hilary and extended his hand to help her out of the car.

"Does this mean we don't have any information yet?"

"That's what it means." He met her gaze and lowered his head to just a breath from hers. "Say 'yes, ma'am,' and do exactly what she says to do. Don't try anything heroic. If you do, I'll have to get you out of there and we'll have zero chance of finding Christine. Understand?"

She blinked at his hard, curt voice. "Sure."

"That's 'yes, sir,' darlin'," he corrected with a grin that didn't meet his eyes.

Hilary resisted the urge to shiver. "Yes, sir."

"Okay, let's go," he said and escorted her up the steps.

The woman in white appeared at the door and led them down the hall to the classroom. Hilary tried to take in every nuance of her surroundings. She craned to hear any noises and noticed all the closed doors. So many closed doors, she thought, and caught sight of the staircase in the back of the house. She wondered if Christine might be upstairs.

The woman in white knocked softly on a door.

"You may come in," another woman said.

The door was opened and Hilary stared at the hard but beautiful woman who stood so straight she wondered if the woman had a titanium rod in her spine.

"Greetings, Mr. Castillo," the woman said.

"Señora Catalina," Juan said.

Automatically extending her hand, Hilary dipped her head. "Hello, I'm Hilary Winfree."

Señora Catalina skimmed her hand with an expression of disgust. "I will call you Señorita. In the future, you will allow Mr. Castillo to introduce you. Otherwise you are to remain silent. Understood?"

Disconcerted, Hilary nodded. "Yes," she said, then catching Juan's gaze, she added, "Yes, ma'am."

"Then let us practice again. Go out of the room and enter again," she said.

Hilary turned around and left the room. Juan stood in front of her. The door opened.

"Greetings, Mr. Castillo. We're honored by your presence. We understand you've been hard at work on plans for the economic growth of your country. Please tell us more about your projects."

Juan paused a half-beat. "*Gracias,* Señora Catalina. I'm initiating several projects in the areas of agriculture exports and manufacturing. Allow me to introduce my dinner companion, Miss Hilary Winfree."

Well done, she thought and waited expectantly.

"Greetings, Señorita," the *señora* said simply, then

turned back to Juan. "We have several foreign visitors tonight who are looking forward to meeting you. . . . "

Hilary finally got it. She was supposed to be a nobody. An un-person. She could do that. She wondered how she could get the opportunity to explore the house. She wondered what Juan planned to do.

"Señorita."

The *señora*'s sharp voice pulled her back. "Yes, ma'am."

"You were not paying attention. You must pay attention to my every word and to every word of Señor Castillo."

"Yes, ma'am," she said, getting the willies from the way the woman looked at her.

"We will repeat the introduction again," Señora Catalina said. "I do not like to repeat myself more than once. I will use other teaching methods if necessary."

"Yes, ma'am," Hilary said, and swallowed a sigh as she and Juan returned outside the door.

"Focus," Juan whispered.

"It's so boring," she whispered.

"Trust me," he said. "You want it to stay boring."

Her stomach twisted at the expression on his face and she watched him knock on the door.

Hilary finally passed the introduction test and Señora Catalina moved onto new skills. "I will teach Señor Castillo a series of hand motions that he may use in public or private to communicate to you. For example, if you wish Señorita to remain quietly behind you, do this," she said and made a hand motion. "If you wish her to stand beside you, do this," she continued, making another motion. "And if you wish her to speak, do this," she said, making yet another hand motion. "And if you wish her to go to her quarters, do this," she said and made another hand motion.

Hilary stared at the woman in amazement. "Isn't that how dogs are trained? With hand motions?"

Señora smiled, but it seemed an evil-looking expression to Hilary. "Yes. Hand signals provide effective communication with canines. But I did not give you permission to speak. Go stand in the corner for five minutes."

Hilary gasped. She'd never been sent to the corner. She remembered a *quiet chair* used for discipline in her elementary school, but she'd never been sent there. She almost argued, but Juan moved into her field of vision and shot her a gaze that told her to obey.

Mentally grumbling, she went to the nearest corner.

"Not that corner," Señora said and pointed to another. "This one."

Hilary endured the five minutes as she tried to catch every word of the conversation Señora and Juan were holding on the other side of the room. She wondered if Christine had been put through this training and felt sickened at the thought. Impulsive Christine may well have voiced her opinion and refusal.

Hilary couldn't help feeling they were wasting time. One of them should be searching the house. Juan clearly felt he needed to baby-sit her, so she had to do it.

"Class resumes," Señora said. "You may return, Señorita."

"Yes, ma'am. May I use the restroom?" Hilary asked in the most submissive voice she could muster.

"Later," Señora said. "You will go at the appointed time. Back to the hand signals."

Hilary glanced at Juan, but he just shook his head. Feeling like Spot the wonder dog, she aced the hand signals and shifted from foot-to-foot in a giant hint.

"Perhaps it would be best if Miss Winfree used the restroom," Juan finally said.

"We can train her so that she goes on command," Señora offered.

"Perhaps later. That's not my current priority."

"As you wish," Señora said in a voice full of disapproval. She glanced at Hilary. "You may use the restroom. Turn left. It is the second door on your right."

Hilary walked out of the room and turned left. The stairs called to her. Señora was wasting their time. Someone had to do something. She couldn't stand the waiting. Juan would kill her, but she had to try. Instead of going to the restroom, she took off her heels and crept upstairs.

Chapter Five

HER HEART RACING AND HER HANDS GROWING MORE clammy by the second, Hilary pressed her ear against a door and heard nothing. She tiptoed to the next door and listened again.

The muffled sound of weeping wrenched at her. She looked from side to side and knocked gently on the door. The sound stopped. "Christine?" she said.

No response.

"Christine," she repeated, just a bit louder.

A long paused followed. "I'm not Christine. They took her away."

Hilary felt a crashing rush of excitement and fear. This person had heard of Christine. She may have even met her. "I'm a friend of Christine's. Open the door."

"I can't. It's locked."

Hilary swore. She felt at the top of the door for a key, but couldn't find one. "Where did they take Christine?"

"I overheard them say something about driving out of the country through Mexico. The guy who took her looked mean."

Hilary's heart sank. "How long ago?"

"Yesterday. Or the day before. Please help me. I'll do anything to get away from these people. Anything."

The woman's pleading voice stabbed at her. How

could she leave this woman here? How could she leave anyone here? She heard a noise downstairs and stepped into her shoes. "I'll try to leave you something. Check the downstairs bathroom," she said and rushed downstairs.

Halfway down the woman in the white dress greeted her. "What are you doing upstairs?"

"I couldn't find the bathroom. I got confused."

The woman looked suspicious. "I will escort you to the restroom," she said. "This way."

Christine followed the woman to the restroom and looked for a place to hide something in the spare windowless room. She looked up at the ceiling and saw a small dark circle. Was that a camera? She turned out the light and crammed the money that Juan had allowed her to have inside the extra roll of toilet paper placed on top of the toilet. She wished she had a small plastic explosive. While Juan probably carried around that kind of stuff in his back pocket, the closest thing to a weapon that she'd ever had was a dictionary heavy enough to break toes.

She stepped outside the restroom and found the woman in white, Señora Catalina, and Juan waiting outside the door.

"You went upstairs, Señorita," Señora said, shaking her head. Her dark eyes were venomous. "That was very bad. Come back to class."

"Señora Catalina, I'll repeat. I don't want her damaged," Juan said. "Marked merchandise would not be attractive at my public gatherings."

"This is a matter of security," Señora said, and closed the door. A second passed and Hilary felt herself pulled into a death grip by Señora Catalina. "Why did you go upstairs? What were you looking for?" the woman demanded and jerked her hair.

Her eyes watered at the sensation of her hair being pulled hard. "The bathroom," Hilary insisted, although every ounce of air was being squeezed from her lungs. "I got confused. I have a terrible sense of direction when I panic, and I'm scared because I keep messing up. I was afraid to ask and I really needed to go. I tried to pull open the doors and they were locked."

"Señora," Juan said, clearly growing impatient.

The woman's grip loosened a millimeter, but Hilary still couldn't breathe. "Señorita," she said as she stroked Hilary's back. "You must understand that if you do not obey, you could be hurt. There is a place on your back where your kidneys are. You can be beaten there, but the marks won't show when you put on your clothes."

Hilary swallowed.

"You must understand that if you disobey you will not be the only one hurt. Your parents. We know where they are. We know how to find them." The woman dug her fingernails into Hilary's lower back. "I'm not sure you understand. I think we will need to use the bracelets and—"

"Señora Catalina," Juan said, cutting in abruptly. He spoke from behind Hilary so she couldn't see his face. All she could see was the blank wall and Señora's arm wrapped around her. "Bring me the bracelets," he said.

Señora Catalina loosened her grip enough for Hilary to catch a breath. "Bring them to you?"

"Yes, me," Juan said. "Miss Winfree is my property. I'll handle this."

A long pause followed. Seconds ticked past. She felt reluctance ooze from Señora Catalina as the woman swore under her breath. Señora dragged her toward a trunk. Jerked sharply, she craned for a glimpse of Juan.

His face tight with anger, he shot her a quelling glance. He moved across the floor in three swift strides and in a flash, he opened the trunk and pulled out a pair of handcuffs.

"Release her," he said in a deathly quiet voice to Señora.

Señora Catalina looked at him curiously. "I thought you wanted my guidance."

"I did, but her disobedience embarrasses me. Her correction is a matter of honor." He closed the handcuffs over Hilary's wrists.

Señora Catalina immediately released her. Juan pulled her face to his, his expression furious. Hilary's heart pounded in her chest.

"You will never disobey me again," he said and gave her a firm shake. "Do you understand me?"

A lump of fear formed in her throat, preventing her from speaking. She searched his eyes and if his gaze could talk, it would have said, *Trust me.*

This was an act, she realized. A show.

"You are never to embarrass me," he told her in a voice completely at war with the expression in his eyes. "I have bought and paid for you. I can do whatever I want with you." He slid one of his hands through her hair. "I can take you any way, anytime I want. I can beat you. I've paid for your life." He lowered his mouth just a breath away from hers. "I can take it away."

He narrowed his eyes. "On your knees," he muttered.

Hilary gaped at him. "What?"

"Get on your knees," he told her.

Every feminist urge inside her screamed in protest. The impulse to tell him to go to hell was so strong she could barely resist.

"Do you really want to disobey again?" he asked, arching his brow.

Exhaling on a long, uneven breath, Hilary sank to her knees. Juan had a reason for this behavior, she told herself. He was clearly trying to accomplish something for the benefit of Señora Catalina. If she hadn't gotten caught going upstairs, she wouldn't be in this position.

"What do you have to say, Hilary?"

She swallowed her pride. "I'm sorry," she said, lowering her head as if in shame. *In for a penny, in for a pound,* she thought.

"What do you have to say to Señora Catalina?" he prodded.

Her mouth filled with bitter distaste. "I'm sorry, Señora Catalina."

"And will you ever disobey again?"

"No, Mr. Castillo."

"Master Castillo," Señora Catalina interjected. "Address him as your master."

The order grated on her. She took a deep breath and told herself it didn't mean anything. Not a thing. "Master," she said.

"You can get up," Juan said.

"I'm not convinced this silly girl won't disobey you again," Señora Catalina said.

"I'm not averse to some insurance," Juan said casually. "Give me the whip. I'll take it with me. Thank you for the extra training, Señora Catalina," he said.

"My pleasure, and please don't hesitate to request more lessons in this area. It's my specialty," she said, her gaze holding blatant invitation.

This woman was too crazy for Hilary. She cleared her throat and Juan looked at her. She eyed the doorway.

"I think we've had enough training today. Miss Winfree, go use the restroom while I chat with Señora before we leave."

"Don't get lost," the Señora warned.

Rick promised himself antacid and ibuprofin the second he got into the limo. He shouldn't have been surprised that Hilary had gone sneaking around the house. He'd known bringing her in would be a risk. He'd just hoped Hilary would be able to reign in her impulses during their brief visit. He'd known Señora was going to punish someone. He could see it coming when Señora had shown him the contents of one of the boxes—whips, brass knuckles, handcuffs, and other toys designed to cause pain and humiliation. Hilary's curiosity had forced him into taking control.

His request had been a calculated risk intended to divert the woman's attention from hurting Hilary, and it had worked. "Thank you again, Señora Catalina. I can see why Mr. Harris calls you a miracle worker."

She smiled at the flattery. "My pleasure. Is there anything else I can do for you?"

"I mentioned that I'd be interested in acquiring another employee. Can you think of anyone who might fit the description I gave you?"

Señora sat down in her chair and rubbed her lip thoughtfully. "We just placed a girl who sounds like she would have fit your description, although I'm not certain it's going to be a good fit. She had problems with training." She sighed. "I could call the client and see if he's happy with her."

"*Por favor,*" he said, and sat in the chair.

She moved the mouse on her computer and dialed the phone. "This is Señora Catalina. I'm calling regarding your recent acquisition. Are you satisfied with your choice?"

A man's loud angry voice carried beyond the phone. Señora pulled the receiver away from her ear.

Her eyes narrowed. "If you had trouble controlling her before you left the country, you were instructed to contact me."

More screaming followed.

"You have caused a very unfortunate situation. Mr. Harris will be in contact with you soon. And no, we won't replace her," she said, returning the receiver to the cradle. She gave a soft sigh. "I regret I won't be able to assist you with your request. It appears the woman I had in mind is lost somewhere in the desert before the Mexican border." She swore in Spanish.

"Lost?" Rick echoed.

"The client was unhappy with her. He took measures," she said.

Translated, he'd beaten her. Rick's gut twisted. "That is unfortunate."

Señora shrugged. "Mr. Harris will handle it. He always does."

"If you should come across another," Rick ventured because he wasn't supposed to be shocked. He wasn't supposed to feel an ugly sense of dread.

"By all means, we'll contact you," she said, and stood. "It's been a pleasure, Señor Castillo."

"I was thinking of leaving the country via Mexico. Do you have a recommended route?"

"Yes, we do," she said, and pulled out a map with three highlighted routes. "Three actually, and they're color coded. You may choose which you prefer; however, I recommend you avoid the green route as the authorities may show up there due to this latest unfortunate incident."

Green it would be, he thought. *"Gracias."*

Hilary followed Juan to the car and scooted inside. He followed her and closed the door, his jaw stiff.

She felt strange about the whole experience inside Señora Catalina's house. Kneeling and asking forgiveness weren't her style. Neither was putting on an act, and Hilary knew she wouldn't have lasted fifteen minutes with Señora if Juan hadn't been there and if she hadn't trusted him. For a forbidden moment, she wondered what else she would have been willing to do if Juan had requested it of her. What else would she do now? The electricity that raced through her confused her. "Was the kneeling really necessary? And can we get rid of these handcuffs?" she asked, lifting her hands.

"In a minute," he said. "Was the kneeling necessary? Since you could have gotten us both killed by going exploring, yes," he said, and swore under his breath. "You jeopardized your life, mine, and our chance to find Christine."

Guilt rushed through her. "I'm sorry if I messed up the plan," she said. "We weren't getting anywhere with Señora." She shuddered. "She's the scariest woman I've met in my entire life."

She watched Juan shrug out of his jacket. "The objective was to build a little rapport so she would take an interest in helping me find another woman I could buy. Christine," he added.

She bit her lip. "I'm sorry, but I did find—"

"Follow the route highlighted in green," he said as he gave a map to Jensen.

Hilary frowned in confusion. "Where are we going? I got some information about Christine," she told him. "I talked to a girl upstairs. I couldn't unlock her door, so I had to talk through the door and she told me Christine had been taken away yesterday or the day before by someone who looked very mean. This could be bad if we don't find her."

He nodded. "It could be bad if we do," he said.

Her stomach tightened at his black tone. "What do you mean?"

He met her gaze and sighed. "I mean Señora Catalina gave me information that led me to believe that Christine has already been injured."

"What did she say? What did she tell you?"

"Turns out the guy who acquired Christine wasn't happy with her."

"Did she run away?"

He took her hands and unlocked the handcuffs. "I

can't pretty this up for you, Hilary. You need to be prepared. He beat her up and dumped her on the road."

Hilary gasped, a wave of nausea rolling over her. "Oh my God. No."

He nodded. "It's time to call the authorities," he said, and dialed Roz. "Hey, beautiful, Rick here," he said when she answered the phone.

"Rick," Hilary muttered. "I never guessed Rick."

"Beautiful," Roz echoed. "How many rules have you broken this time, Chameleon? You've missed the mandatory check-ins. I almost sent someone after you."

"Not necessary," he said. "I only broke a few rules. Nothing to get your panty hose in a twist. I need you to call in the boys in blue. I've got two addresses for trafficking. If they move fast and they're smart, they can catch some scum and set some girls free."

"You know I could fire you for not sticking to the assignment."

"I took a little side trip. That's all," he said, playing down his efforts to locate Christine.

"She talked you into helping her find her friend, didn't she?" Roz asked.

Rick raked a hand through his hair. Hilary was a huge complication in more ways than one. "No time to hash that out. Miss Winfree's friend has apparently been beaten and dumped on the side of the road."

The silence on the other end of the line brimmed with deathly anger. "Give me the coordinates."

Rick gave them to her.

"I could fire you," she said.

"But you won't because I'm good at what I do," he returned.

"True," she said. "I could dock your pay instead."

Rick saw the upgraded GPS system for his yacht disappearing before his eyes. "Have a heart. It's Christmas."

"Or I could just take you off my cookie list."

"Not that," he said, alarm rushing through him. "Not

the cookies. I don't get home-cooked anything these days. Don't take away the cookies."

Roz laughed. "It's good to know your Achilles' heel."

He shifted as his glance caught on the sight of the high heels Hilary had kicked aside. Her silky legs were spread slightly apart as if she didn't realize he could see almost to the tops of her thighs. The inviting sight distracted him and he forced himself to look out the window. "I've had enough of heels for a while."

"What do you mean?" Roz asked.

"I'll tell you another time. You've got some calls to make."

"And you're delivering a package to California," Roz said firmly.

"Exactly," Rick said, feeling Hilary's curious gaze. "Till later. Thanks, Roz."

"You're welcome. Just deliver the package. Bye for now."

He turned off the phone.

"Who was that?"

"The manager of the Agency. She's got the kind of contacts to get people moving even at this time of year. Police should be swarming this route within an hour."

Hilary's face turned solemn. "But it may not be enough," she said.

"True. I have to take you home by Christmas," he reminded her.

She crossed her arms around her waist. "I don't want to leave until Christine is found."

"Everything that can be done is being done."

She studied him curiously. "Do you have some kind of issues with dominating women?"

"Oh great, now I get a free analysis. Not until I met you," he muttered in a mocking voice. "Señora was determined that you would be punished. I chose the least of the evils."

"Because it was your job to keep me safe," she said, studying him.

He stared at her for a long moment and felt something strange happen in his stomach. "Right. It was my job."

She moved closer to him. "Thanks," she whispered, and pressed a kiss against his jaw. "How's your head?"

"I'm fine. It's no big deal," he said, caught off guard by the quick caress but not moving away. He liked the way she smelled. He liked the way she felt.

She lifted her hand to his head and she winced. "That's a huge knot."

"It probably looks worse than it is," he said.

"I don't know," Hilary said, lightly running her fingertips over the swollen place. "It's what my mom used to call a goose egg. I bet you wish you'd never taken this job."

"Maybe," he said, thinking the soft touch of her hands felt good. He closed his eyes. "Or I could have already dumped you off and been on my yacht for my Caribbean Christmas."

"You have a yacht?" she asked.

"Uh-huh," he murmured.

"Caribbean Christmas," she echoed. "That sounds wonderful. Were you taking any family with you?"

"No family. I never met my father and my mother died of cancer a few years ago," he said, feeling a pinch at the memory of his mother. "Just me and my yacht."

"I'm sorry about your mother."

"Yeah. She wasn't much for going to the doctor, and they caught it too late." He paused, struggling with the sense of helplessness he felt whenever he thought about his mother. "She didn't tell me before she died. I nagged her to go see the doctor and was ready to take her in myself." He sighed. "She left a note for me to read after she died, telling me she hadn't wanted me to worry. It was just her time."

"Bet you wanted to wring her neck if she hadn't already passed away," Hilary said.

A dry chuckle rose from his throat. "Yeah, I did."

"So you kinda knew how I felt about wanting to try to find Christine, didn't you?"

He opened his eyes. "Yeah, I did," he said because he'd struggled with his guilt for years.

"What did you do before you worked for this private agency?"

"A specialized branch of law enforcement," he said, figuring that was vague enough. "I was invited to join the Agency when I was put on probation by my administrator. The rules frustrated the hell out of me."

"Why doesn't that surprise me?" she said more than asked with gentle amusement in her voice. "How much trouble are you in because of me now?"

"Nothing I can't handle."

"Exactly what *can't* you handle?" she asked.

He liked the kick of challenge mixing with admiration in her eyes. "You can be damn sure I won't be asking for any assignments that include a dominatrix like Señora Catalina."

"So you're not into bondage or S&M?" she asked.

The self-consciousness in her voice amused him. "No more than the average man," he said. "What about you?"

"Not at all," she said and was silent. "What do you mean 'no more than the average man'?"

His amusement grew. "I mean there's a certain thrill in the idea of being in charge and taking a woman to a new high, or reversing the situation. The pleasure is what we do with out bodies together." He closed his eyes and an image of Hilary, naked in heels, filled his mind. He argued with the mental picture. She wasn't the type to dress for a man. She would be one uptight little princess in bed, he told himself, and the definition of a clinging vine. Not his kind of woman.

Chapter Six

BY THE TIME THE LIMO CROSSED INTO THE AREA WHERE Christine was most likely located, it was dark and late. Although Hilary was starting to feel the effects of lack of sleep, she couldn't imagine accepting Rick's offer of a nice hotel bed when she knew Christine was still out there.

Using information from Rick's agency, they stopped at a crossing where several police cars were parked. In the distance, Hilary saw flashlights alongside the road.

"It's going to be very difficult to find her at night," Rick warned her. "The only thing we've got going for us is a full moon."

"That's enough for me," Hilary said. "But I want to change into some jeans and a sweatshirt and some different shoes."

Rick glanced at her red heels and the vision of her naked in those heels rolled through his mind again. "Good idea," he muttered. "I'll get your suitcase out of the trunk."

"I'll give you some room to change," he said when he returned with her suitcase and started to close the door.

"Wait," she said. "If you want to take a break, maybe Jensen could stay with me," she suggested, then thought of what she'd done to the man's poor eye. "If he's not afraid of me."

Rick gave a rough chuckle. "Nice of you to be concerned," he said. "But I'm okay. You're stuck with me until Christmas in California."

She felt a twist at the prospect of not seeing him anymore and immediately told herself that was a bizarre thought. Surely due to lack of sleep and the tension of the situation. She turned her focus to her suitcase. Hilary felt as if she'd been given a treasure chest. They'd been in such a hurry once they'd left Señora Catalina's house, they'd made only one pit stop and Hilary had forgotten to ask for her suitcase.

Thrilled to ditch her slutty Santa suit once and for all, she stripped it off along with the strapless underwire push-up bra. She decided to skip wearing a bra and pulled on a T-shirt, sweatshirt, and jeans. She'd almost swear her feet began to sing when she pulled on a pair of snuggly socks and tennis shoes. Pushing open the limo door, she stepped outside, where Rick and Jensen talked with a man in a uniform.

She walked toward them. "Where do we start?"

All three men looked at her. "We were just discussing that," Rick said. "We're going to drive farther down the road and search there."

Hilary glanced at the flat horizon and wondered how bad Christine's injuries were. She wondered how long she'd been left. She wondered if they could possibly find her, and if they did, would she be alive.

Rick searched the scrubby Texas ground for signs of Christine at the same time that he kept an eye on Hilary. She walked for hours without one complaint. When she periodically called out for Christine, the pleading sound in her voice did something to him.

The first sliver of dawn broke and he saw Hilary begin to weave. She stumbled and he caught her against him. "Okay, sweetheart, I think you're about done."

"No, no," she protested. "I just need some coffee."

"Hilary, there comes a point of diminishing returns."

"I'm not ready to give up," she said, her voice breaking. She sobbed and the sound wrenched at him. "I don't want them to stop looking. I have to stay—"

"Whoa," he said, turning her in his arms, surprised at the tears welling in her eyes. "I'm not saying we stop searching. I'm saying you need to take a break."

She closed her eyes and buried her head in his chest. "Do you think we'll find her? Do you think she's alive?"

He lifted his hand to touch her and caught himself. The urge to comfort her overwhelmed and shocked him at the same time. He held his hand in midair for several seconds. Despite her lack of resources, she'd acted fearless from the first time he'd laid eyes on her. Now she was afraid. He could hear it in her voice, feel it in her body.

He lowered his hand to her head and cradled it against him. "We've still got a shot, and it helps that we aren't the only ones looking for her."

She sighed into his chest and it gave him the oddest pleasure-pain he could remember feeling.

Pulling back slightly, she swiped her eyes and looked up at him. "Sorry. Wuss moment. It won't happen again."

"It will if you don't get something to eat and take a breather. A shower and a nap would do you a world of good."

She shook her head. "Coffee and food, but I can do without sleep." She shot him a half smile. "You forget I'm a professional student, so I'm an expert at dealing with sleep deprivation to study and finish papers."

He frowned in frustration. "The problem with you professional students is that you might be able to stay awake, but you're used to sitting on that gorgeous rear end while you do it."

She blinked. "I didn't know you'd noticed my rear end."

"I'm trained to notice everything."

"So it's nothing personal," she said.

"Right," he said, but his gut told him that was a lie.

He called Jensen to bring the limo and it arrived within a few moments. After helping Hilary inside, he instructed Jensen to head back to the main road where he'd seen a couple of fast-food restaurants.

Hilary looked so tired he feared she would collapse if she remained standing, so he stuffed her in one of the booths and ordered extra coffee and juice along with everything on the breakfast menu.

"Do you always order everything?" Jensen asked, helping to carry the food to the booth.

"I didn't know what she would want. I figure you and I can take the leftovers."

Jensen shrugged. "Works for me. Does this woman ever sleep?"

"I think she's getting close," Rick said, glancing at her and shaking his head. "She looks like a zombie."

He slid into the booth and set the food in front of her. "What's your pleasure? Biscuits, eggs, pancakes, or breakfast burritos?"

"No to the breakfast burrito," she said, reaching for the coffee with an unsteady hand. "Yes to everything else."

Swallowing an oath, Rick saw a disaster waiting to happen. "Let me help with that. Cream or sugar?"

"Both," she said, pulling her hand back and closing her eyes.

He fixed her coffee and moved beside her on her bench, lifting the cup to her lips. "Here, drink a little."

Hilary took a few sips. Rick felt Jensen's curious gaze and felt a ripple of discomfort. Jensen was still in training and this assignment had been unusual from the get-go. He held the cup for Hilary to drink more and fished in his pocket for his wallet. "Take ten and get whatever you want."

Jensen nodded slowly. "Okay. You want me to get something for you?"

"No, the burrito is mine."

Jensen left and Hilary met Rick's gaze. "Steel-plated stomach to go with the steel-plated muscles?" she said with a little smile.

He felt a ridiculous relief at the sight of that smile. "Yeah. Give me an antacid and I can handle just about anything."

"Even me," she said, and unwrapped a biscuit.

The odds were better with the breakfast burrito, he thought. He watched in amazement as she devoured the biscuit and eggs and plowed through most of the pancakes. She downed her coffee and juice and finally paused, meeting his gaze.

"Why are you staring at me?" she asked.

"Just wondering where it all goes," he said, cocking his head toward the food wrappers.

"I have the metabolism of a hamster running in a wheel that never stops."

"High-strung," he said, sipping his coffee.

She made a face. "I wouldn't have described it that way. I—"

His cell phone beeped and she broke off. He pushed the button to answer the call and lifted it to his ear. "Rick Santana."

"This is Sergeant Cox," a man said. "Our search team has located Christine Gordon."

"What's her condition?" he asked, feeling Hilary's gaze searching his face.

"Serious," Sergeant Cox said. "She has multiple fractures and is dehydrated. She's being taken to County Hospital."

"Thank you, sir."

"You're welcome."

Before he could punch the off button, Hilary pulled on his arm. "What'd he say? Is she okay? Where is she?"

"She's at County Hospital and she's in bad shape, but she's alive."

Hilary shot to her feet. "Oh, thank God. We have to go right now."

He rose. "I'll take you, but she's in serious condition. They probably won't let you see her."

"We'll see about that," she said, gathering the food wrappers and tossing them into the trash. She grabbed Rick's hand and dragged him toward the door. "Come on, Jensen," she called to the driver who was sipping his coffee as he sat at the other end of the room and watched a television hung in the corner. "Get the lead out."

Jensen shot Rick a questioning glance and Rick nodded. "They found Christine."

"Wow," Jensen said, and immediately rose. "Tell me where you want to go. Is she alive?"

"Yes," Hilary said.

"For now," Rick muttered under his breath. "County Hospital," he added.

They left the fast-food restaurant and climbed into the limo. Hilary clung to his hand. He wondered if she realized it.

Biting her lip, she turned to him. "I have to thank you for this. Who knows what would have happened if you hadn't agreed to help me."

"I didn't find her. The search team did."

"But you stuck with me," she said. "And you got the information from Señora Catalina. And you broke Agency rules to do it."

He felt a mixture of warmth and discomfort at the fierce gratitude he saw in her eyes. "Don't thank me yet. I told you she's in bad shape."

"She's gonna be okay," Hilary said. "I feel it. I know it." She dropped his hand and put both her arms around his neck. "She wouldn't have been found without you. Thank you so much."

With Hilary pressed against him like there was no tomorrow, Rick felt an odd lump in the back of his throat. He could feel the honest relief in her hug and a swarm of emotions buzzed through him, bouncing against doors he'd kept shut for years. He couldn't resist the urge to lift one of his hands to her head and her hair felt silky and sweet in his fingers.

She lifted her head slightly and met his gaze. At that moment, he could have drowned in her eyes. Her expression gradually changed from grateful to something that combined feminine curiosity and hunger for more than pancakes. He felt her gaze hover on his mouth and she lifted her lips to his, pressing, searching, asking.

A stinging surge of arousal whizzed through him, taking him by surprise. Off guard, he acted on instinct, taking her mouth more fully, tasting the flash-fire edge of her passion. His heart pounding in his chest, he felt the burn for more.

But he knew he shouldn't even have this much. He broke away. "Whoa," he said, and the dark wanting in her eyes felt like a soft seductive stroke. He sucked in a quick breath of air to clear his head.

"Why whoa?" she asked in a husky voice.

"We—uh—" He cleared his throat. "I've already broken enough Agency rules. I don't need to push this one."

"What? No kissing the client?" Her mouth tilted in a sexy half smile. "No problem. I'll just kiss you instead."

She moved toward him and he stopped her by gently holding her shoulders in place. He shook his head. "You're confused. You're grateful. You're redirecting your emotions. Trust me. As soon as I leave you with your parents tomorrow, you'll forget me by the new year."

Her eyebrows furrowed in irritation. "That's really

arrogant of you to think you know what I'm feeling better than I do."

He shrugged. "I've been through this a few more times than you have."

Recognition slowly dawned. "So women are always throwing themselves at you at the end of a job?"

"It's happened more than once. I made the mistake once of getting involved and I'm not doing that again."

"Why?"

"Because it didn't work out well."

"Why?"

He sighed in frustration. "Because she was a rich daddy's girl who decided she wanted someone who fit her lifestyle better than I did."

"And you think I'm no different?" she asked, clearly insulted.

"Not much," he lied, and mercifully the limo slowed. "We're almost at the hospital. Do you want to go in?"

"Yes," she said, her head whipping around to look out the window.

He breathed a sigh of relief at switching her attention away from him. It must be Christmas, he thought. All this schmaltzy music and dealing with a firecracker of a woman like Hilary was getting on his nerves. He needed to get back on his yacht and forget about the way Hilary affected him. He needed to head out to sea so he didn't get confused by a kiss.

Jensen stopped the car and Hilary turned to look at Rick. "I can't tell you how surprised I am that a man as strong as you are is so frightened of little me."

Blinking, he watched her unlock the door and get out of the car. Her accusation stung. It wasn't true. He wasn't afraid of her. He just knew better and she didn't like it that he knew better. He swore under his breath. He was *not* afraid.

Rick proved he wasn't afraid of Hilary by sitting with her in the waiting room for hours. He gave her coffee and goaded her into eating a sandwich. Despite her best efforts, Hilary fell asleep on his shoulder. And he was still not afraid.

He might want to hold her in his arms and inhale her into his system, but he wasn't afraid of her. After all, he told himself, he wouldn't see her after tomorrow. He ignored the twist that thought caused him while his arm fell asleep.

A weary-looking doctor approached them. "Mr. Santana? Miss Win—" He broke off and gave a slight smile when he saw that Hilary was asleep.

Rick jiggled her gently. "Hilary," he said. "Wake up. Doctor's here."

"What?" She bobbed her head and blinked. "Oh. Doctor," she said, rising to her feet. "How is Christine?"

"She's suffered several bruises, fractures, dehydration, and a concussion, but I think she's going to be okay. It will be a couple of days before she's released from the hospital and she'll need a place to go. The staff told me the phone number for her emergency contact isn't in service."

"Her father," Hilary said. "And he hasn't been of much service to his daughter. She'll come to my house."

Rick lifted his eyebrows but didn't say anything. Hilary sounded extremely confident given the way her parents had brushed off her initial request for help.

"Good," the doctor said. "You can see her for a few minutes, but she's resting, so don't expect her to talk."

"Thank you," Hilary said. "Thank you for taking care of her."

The doctor just smiled. "It's what I do. She's in room three-two-two. Just a few minutes, okay?"

Hilary and Rick took the elevator to the third floor and entered Christine's room. Rick saw a tumble of red curls and a patch over one of her eyes. Christine's young face was black, blue, and green with bruises and one of her arms was wrapped in a cast. She probably had a few broken ribs, too, he thought. "Poor kid," he said.

Hilary turned away from Christine and lifted a hand to cover her eyes. "Oh, God," she whispered, clearly unprepared for Christine's injuries.

His heart twisted at the sight of the tear that streamed down her cheek and he stuck his fists in his pockets to keep from taking her into his arms. For three seconds.

He pulled out his hands and tugged her against him. "She's gonna be okay," he told her. "She just looks like hell right now."

"But if I could have just talked to her before she left—"

"You gotta stop with that. She's alive because you hounded the daylights out of me and put yourself at risk. She's alive. That's what's important. Besides, she doesn't need your guilt now. She needs your friendship."

She took a shaky breath. "You're right."

"Of course, I'm right. Do you want to leave now or—"

She shook her head. "No. Just give me a minute."

He watched her walk to Christine's side and smooth her hair the same way a mother would comfort a child. "You're gonna be just fine, sweetie. Just fine," she said.

Rick dragged Hilary to a nearby hotel to crash for a few hours before their six A.M. flight to Malibu. This time, for his own sanity, he put her in her own room and avoided conversation the next morning by sitting several aisles away from her on the jet.

After waiting for her luggage, he hailed a cab. During the ride to her parents' home the silence between them felt more oppressive than the humidity on an August day in Miami.

"You can talk to me. I won't force myself on you," she said, her lips twitching.

He shot her a dark glance.

"You were a lot more fun when you had a sense of humor," she told him. "How's your head?"

"Fine."

"Let me see."

"No," he retorted.

She shrugged. "Okay, if you think it would be good public relations for your agency for you to have to drag me into my parents' house screaming at the top of my lungs—"

He swore and dipped his head for her to look at it.

She made a *tsk*ing sound and the touch of her fingers was so gentle it reminded him of a cool breeze. "You have some nasty bruises."

"I'll live," he said, lifting his head away from her.

"Tell me something," she said. "Are you afraid of me because my parents have a certain standard of living? Or are you afraid of me because of how you feel about me?"

"I said I'm not afraid of you."

"I don't believe you."

"Then you're wrong," he said and realized he would need to be brutal. He didn't like it, but it was necessary.

As the cab pulled up in front of a large house with a well-tended lawn and a Bentley in the driveway, he met her gaze without wavering. "I don't want to bust your ego, princess, but you're no different than ten other women I've rescued. You don't do anything for me." He gave a wry smile. "Don't worry. You'll forget me by the new year."

Epilogue

"DELIVERY FOR RICK SANTANA," HILARY CALLED, DROP-ping her backpack on the dock and stepping onto Rick's yacht with her heart beating a mile a minute.

"Just a minute," Rick called from belowdecks. "I'll be—" He broke off just as his gaze landed on her. "What are you doing here?"

"Delivering a package," she said, distracted by the sight of his naked chest.

He gave her a hungry look from head to toe then nar-rowed his eyes. "What's in it?"

"Cookies," she said, nervous, but trying not to show it. "Your supervisor gave me her recipe."

His jaw dropped. "How did you get in touch with my supervisor?"

"Daddy helped. I told him everything you did and he was impressed."

He raked a hand through his hair and looked at her as if she were a pain in the butt. "Okay," he said, reaching for the package. "Thanks for the cookies."

"And here's your check," she said, giving him an en-velope holding the money she'd raised to pay him.

He opened the envelope and raised his eyebrows. "Your dad?"

She shook her head. "Sorority sisters."

He tapped the envelope against his palm thoughtfully. "How's Christine?"

"She's staying at my house and my parents are thrilled to have someone to fuss over." She smiled as she remembered how both her mother and father had taken Christine under their wings at first sight. "It's almost like I have a real sister now."

He nodded. "I'm glad it turned out well. I'll enjoy the cookies."

Now came the hard part. "The cookies are actually for a specific purpose."

"For me to eat," he said.

"Well, yes, but you're supposed to only eat them when you're with me."

"Why?"

Her heart felt as if it crawled into her throat. She swallowed hard. "Because it's the new year and I didn't forget you, and I don't think you forgot me." She braced herself for his denial.

He shrugged. "So?"

"So I think there was something special that got started between us and I think we owe it to ourselves to get to know each other in a different environment."

"*We* do?" he echoed, full of skepticism.

He wasn't budging, and Hilary was starting to feel self-conscious and stupid. What if this had been a huge mistake? What if she'd misread him?

Her stomach twisted. She felt a rush of anger at herself. At him. "You know, you could notice the fact that I had to beg for your address from your supervisor and I've flown across the country and baked these damn cookies because I feel something for you. Something strong with lots of possibilities. Possibilities I've never experienced before. But if you don't feel the same way or if you just want to be a jerk about it, then I'm not going to beg. You can have the check and the cookies, but you just remember that I packed in a backpack everything I need to exist for the next week in the Caribbean with the right guy and that guy could have been you. But you missed out."

She spun around to leave the yacht. Feeling like an idiot, she snatched up her backpack.

"I don't believe you," Rick said.

She was so frustrated she almost didn't look at him, but she did. "You're not giving me much of a chance to prove it, so—"

"I'm talking about the backpack," he interrupted, his hands on his lean hips. "I can't believe a woman would be able to pack everything she needs for a week in a backpack."

She stared at him for a long moment. Why was he talking about her backpack? Had she misjudged his intelligence? Was he dense?

"Why don't you show me what's in it?" he asked.

She sighed but bent to unzip it.

"No, here on the yacht," he said and stepped forward to extend his hand.

Feeling a trickle of hope, she accepted his hand and he helped her onboard. She tried desperately to read him.

"You got quiet," he said.

"I did all the talking," she said. "Your turn."

He inhaled and raked his hand through his hair. "I missed you," he said. "I didn't like that."

"I missed you, too," she said, seeing the same powerful emotions in his eyes that she felt inside her. "What do you think we should do about it?"

"Spend some time with each other. See if you get tired of me." He slid one of his hands through her hair.

"And what if I don't get tired of you?" she asked.

He met her gaze. "Then I'll be the luckiest guy on the planet."

She slid her hands around his neck. "Prepare to get lucky."

He finally smiled and took her mouth in a kiss that made the world spin and somehow, she knew that this was just the beginning for her and Rick.

·Big, Bad Santa

Pamela Britton

Chapter One

"DR. KAITLYN LOGAN?"

Kait Logan looked up from the paperwork she'd been studying on her desk and her muttered "Yes" turned into a yelp of surprise when a huge giant of a man stomped forward and grabbed her by the arm.

"Hey," she cried, trying to pull away.

"Come with me," he said.

But she couldn't move. One, the man had hands the size of catcher's mitts. Two, he blocked her path, and that was saying a lot. Six-foot-two of pure muscle, by the looks of it, all clothed in black. Black eyes. Black hair. And black . . . chaps? What was this? An early Halloween prank arranged by one of her staff?

"Look, mister," she found herself saying, shoving the glasses up on her nose before remembering she didn't wear them anymore. "I don't know who you are, but if you have an animal injured, you don't need to order me around. I'll come with you without the use of force."

"Animal?" he asked, black brows pushing together. Then he shook his head, as if trying to dislodge her silly words from his ears. "I don't have an animal."

"Then what—"

"Come with me," he ordered again, trying to pull her up.

"I'm calling nine-one-one."

He ducked down, and the hand she'd used to reach for her phone was suddenly batted away. His big fingers closed around her wrist and tugged her up.

"Ouch!"

"Down," he said, shoving her to the floor.

Boom!

She tried to scream again, her cheeks so firmly pressed into the polyester carpet her skin stung. Glass fell around her with a wind chime–like tinkle that made her shudder as she tried to cover her head—except that her arms were pinned by the man's body.

What the—

"Don't breathe," he said.

Don't breathe—

And then she saw why.

Smoke began to pour out of a tin-can thing. Her eyes widened, then began to water, sulfur-scented gas causing Kait to choke.

"I told you not to breathe," the man growled. And then he shifted off her. Kait thought he had to have cut himself on broken glass. In the next instant he lifted her off the ground; warm air from outside momentarily cleared the smoke so she could see. A man wearing a black ski mask came toward them. Her tear ducts went into overdrive and she had to close her eyes. Her rescuer, or whoever he was, must have noticed because he pressed her face against his chest, big arms wrapping around her.

He scooped her up.

This couldn't be happening, Kait thought, wondering who the heck the man outside was. This couldn't be happening.

But it was, because in the next instant she was being carried away, and for a second . . . but, no, he wasn't giving her a hug, he was running, fast. She tried to wrap her arms around his neck, but he was too darn big. Besides, the minute he got her out of her office he set her on her feet, put a big hand at the small of her back, and muttered the word "Run."

Kait didn't need to be told twice. The dogs kenneled in her clinic began to howl. Even the cats screamed in protest. She darted past her operating room, past the buff-colored walls with framed pictures of dogs and kitty cats on the wall, heading for the door at the end, the framed posters rattling as she passed.

The exit door burst open.

The man behind her jerked her toward the OR just as something popped. Through tear-filled eyes she had a brief glimpse of something that snaked toward her, something attached to long wires, but then the OR doors swung closed, the automatic return causing them to fan back open again.

What the hell *was going on?*

"Move."

And by now Kait had reasoned that whatever else might be true, obviously he wasn't a bad guy. She rolled to her knees and pushed herself up.

The OR doors burst open. Kait heard herself scream as she wrenched open yet another door, this one leading to a long, narrow lab with microscopes and a centrifuge on the counter. Another pop. She knew enough to duck down. So did the man, both of them falling to the tile floor. He kicked the door closed. She lurched to her feet, blinking to soothe her burning eyes as she turned the lock, then twisted toward an exit door off the lab.

"Hurry," he barked.

She hurried; her heart was beating so hard she couldn't hear her feet on the hard floor, couldn't hear anything other than her own breathing and the persistent sound of the question that ran through her mind.

What the hell *was going on?*

They burst outside. Sage-scented air erased the acrid

stench of sulfur, but it didn't help her eyes. They still felt as if grains of sand rubbed against them.

"This way," the man said, jerking her toward the narrow alley that ran between her business and the one next door. It was early evening, late November, but you wouldn't know it, the desert air unusually warm. Garbage cans clattered when her foot accidentally brushed one. She almost fell. He-man kept her upright.

Someone blocked their path.

One moment bright light marked the end of the alley, the next someone in a ski mask stood there.

Holy shi—

"Down," her rescuer said.

Kait ducked right as the big man grabbed an aluminum lid.

Pop!

Ping-ping-ping.

She looked up; metal prongs were sticking through the lid. But she caught only a glimpse of them because the next second Terminator man threw the lid aside, then pointed a pistol in their assailant's direction.

A pistol?

Poof.

That was all the sound it made when he pulled the trigger. Kait had seen enough movies to know that the long, skinny thing at the end was a silencer, but, really, what else would it be? This was, after all, a scene right out of a B movie.

"Run," the man said again.

She ran. Right. Past. The dead man.

Oh, Lord. He was dead. He really truly was dead. Kait almost stopped, almost started to see what she could do, her instinct to heal causing her to slow.

"Don't," he ordered, jerking her by.

No. Yes. Of course. That man had just shot something at her.

The man had *shot* at her.

She almost fell to her knees.

He-man held her up, all but dragging her down the access road behind her office. A motorcycle sat behind the neighboring business, a chrome-and-steel monstrosity that Kait immediately identified as a Harley Davidson.

Well, that explained the chaps.

"Get on," he ordered.

Her eyes had begun to clear, enough to notice the pistol he pointed back the way they'd come, his big shoulders tense as he waited for her to do as instructed while he watched her back.

She hesitated.

"Lady," he growled out of the side of his mouth, just as they did in the movies, "get the fuck on."

"I don't know if—"

He stepped toward her.

"If you don't get on that bike you'll be dead."

She believed him.

She got on the bike. He hopped on in front of her, tucking the pistol God-knew-where before he started the thing. Kait wrapped her arms around him automatically, feeling sinew and corded muscles that grew harder as he leaned forward and stabbed the gas.

They took off. The big engine roared down the back alley, the sound drowning out the barking dogs. Gravel slid out beneath the back tire, pinging the rear doors of other businesses. Kait ducked, her back muscles tensing as she waited for those . . . those things to be shot at her and to penetrate her skin.

He was dead. That man back there was dead. She'd seen the blood oozing out from beneath his back.

And the man in front of her had done it.

Suddenly, she wanted to hop off, but they were taking a corner, the big bike leaning toward a wedge of shrubs that framed the alley. Her reddish brown hair, pulled back in its customary ponytail, began to whip at her cheeks as they roared onto the main road, the smell of desert sage, unusually strong in the winter, doing nothing to mask the scent of tangy man in front of her.

"Take off your lab coat," he yelled back at her.

And any thoughts of escape died a swift death as they picked up speed. At this rate, she'd break her neck if she jumped off. Besides, where would she go? Reno, Nevada, didn't exactly have a lot of terrain where she could hide. The rock-covered hills behind her practice would give him and the bad guys an easy time of finding her.

"What?" she called back at him.

"Take off your lab coat."

Her lab coat. Why the heck did he want her to—?

"They'll be looking for a motorcycle with a white-coated female on the back. Take it off."

Oh, yeah . . . well. That made sense. She unbuttoned the coat, screaming, "Who are you?" as she peeled the thing from her shoulders, the sleeves hitting her in the face as warm wind caught it, took it, and flung it high in the air.

"Name's Chance. Chance Owens. Here's a helmet. Strap it on."

Chance Owens. Who was Chance Owens? And why had he come to her rescue?

But then she couldn't think because she was fumbling with her helmet straps, wondering how he'd managed to quickly pull his own on and then strap it down with one hand. Her own helmet was too big, but she didn't care. It'd protect her head from bullets.

Or . . . other things.

They slowed only to take a corner, still at breakneck speed, Kait's body sliding toward his, her thighs clenching tighter. If they kept this up, she wouldn't need to do her Thigh Master for weeks. They took off again, and Kait had a brief moment of clarity, one followed by the thought that the bad guys could likely find them just by sound, and then they were turning yet another corner, the brown horizon dipping and falling. She clutched him, her stomach clenching so hard she thought she might be sick.

Dear God, don't *let me die.*

She had animals to take care of. A parrot to feed back home. *A* life *to live.*

It wasn't until the fourth or fifth turn that she thought to look around. They were still in a commercial area, storefronts and the occasional supermarket whizzing past. Wind pressed against her eyes, making them tear and whipping reddish strands against her face. But a quick glance back revealed nothing but the stunned faces of drivers as they shot past in a burst of speed and noise.

"Hang on," he called out.

The back wheel locked up. Kait bit back a scream as they skidded to a halt, then tipped sideways, the man turning into a crowded parking lot. A Ralphs supermarket.

"What are you doing?"

"Camouflage," he called back.

"We're going to camouflage ourselves? With what? Ralphs brand toilet paper?"

"No," he shot back, racing past a startled mother who jerked on the hand of her child. Chance Owens didn't give them a second glance, just guided his bike past her and the child, then turned in front of the store before making yet another turn toward the back. They passed a less crowded parking area, went down a narrow access road, and then turned again, Chance heading toward a loading ramp. A short cement wall grew taller and taller, the big bike echoing around them as he came to a stop at the base of the six-foot-deep dock.

"Get off," he told her.

She glanced at the closed roll-up door, wondering if she should make a run for it.

"And take off your shirt."

The words made her straighten. "I beg your pardon?"

"Take off your shirt," he repeated, swinging his leg over the side of the bike. He turned to face her and took off his helmet. He said, "Don't give me that look, Dr. Logan. If I wanted to rape you I wouldn't have taken you to a crowded supermarket."

"We're not near a crowd."

"No, but if you scream, I guarantee you someone will come running."

"Who are you?" she said, the question just popping out of her mouth.

He crossed his big, beefy arms, the black T-shirt he wore seeming to bind around his biceps, causing them to bulge. He was handsome, if square-jawed jocks were your thing—which they weren't.

"I told you. Chance Owens."

"No," she said, shaking her head, the end of her ponytail brushing her ears. "Who are you?"

He darted a glance right and left. "Look," he said. "I'll explain later. Right now, we need to get a move on it."

"Someone tried to kill me."

"No," he said quickly, sharply, black eyes as hard as the galvanized metal railing that lined the pit of the dock. "They weren't going to kill you. Those were tasers they were using. They're meant to knock you out."

"Knock me out? Why the heck would someone want to knock me out? And—" Oh, Lord, she felt suddenly queasy. "You killed that man."

"Kait," he said softly, the look in his eyes fading to gentleness. That surprised her. Hulking men dressed in black chaps should not, as a rule, look so—so . . . nice. "Someone wants to kidnap you because they know about the migratory chip."

Migratory chip? "Wha—I don't—"

And then she straightened. The migratory chip. Her pet project. The one she'd been working on for years.

"How the heck does anybody know about that?"

"Two weeks ago you wrote to Senator Prescott about government funding. With that letter you set into motion a chain of events culminating in today's attack. The agency I work with reasoned that you might attract attention from nonfriendlies. I've been watching your place for about a week."

"A week?" He'd been watching her a week?

"That microchip you invented, the one that sends electronic pulses to the frontal lobes of a bird's brain? Well, it didn't take a rocket scientist to reason that if you can control the direction a bird flies, you might be able to arm that bird with cameras. Or maybe turn it into a biological weapon. The possibilities are endless. And what are foreign governments going to do? Shoot every bird out of the sky?"

"Oh, my Lord."

"In short, Dr. Logan, you've created the world's first avian weapon."

Chapter Two

SHE DIDN'T TAKE THE NEWS WELL.

Fuck it, Chance thought. She'd needed to hear the truth. Maybe hearing the kind of trouble she was in would make her more malleable.

Except he felt sorry for her. And concerned. Crap, he couldn't believe that when he'd picked her up for a moment there he'd actually hugged her. And then a moment ago, when she'd asked him who he was, he'd had to cross his arms to avoid touching her face in a consoling way. What the heck was wrong with him?

"Look. I know this is a shock," he said, tempted to cross his arms again because he couldn't seem to stop the urge to touch her. "But we really need to get moving. The longer we're out here, the more time they have to get a bird up in the air. And motorcycles are about as easy to spot from the air as white cars. In other words, we need to move."

"I—"

Her mouth opened and closed a couple of times. He felt that strange softening sensation again. Maybe he was coming down with something.

"Shouldn't I go to the police?" she asked.

"Negative," he said. "All they'll do is send an officer to check out your story."

"And they'd find a dead body. One that *you* shot." She looked him square in the eyes, a hint of accusation glittering in her blue ones. Good. That was the spirit. Fight, Kaitlyn, he privately told her.

"I doubt that body is still there," he said, hating to dash her hopes but knowing his words were true. He had enough experience with these types of bastards to know they covered their tracks.

"What?" she asked, blue eyes widening. "How can a body just disappear?"

"They'll pick it up."

"There'll be blood on the ground."

"They'll have picked that up, too."

"Impossible."

"Look. You want to go to be police, fine," he said. "Go. Don't blame me if you end up dead by the end of the day."

"You said they don't want to kill me."

"They don't, and that should scare you even more."

And it did. He could tell. She looked exactly like someone at the top of a roller coaster—right before it skidded over the edge. Good. Maybe she'd wise up, because if she put her fate in the hands of local law enforcement—

He didn't want to think about it.

"Who are you?" she asked again, chin flicking up.

"I'm someone who wants to keep you alive. And I promise, if you come with me, I'll keep you alive—and deliver you to people who will keep you safe until the danger has passed."

"Are you with the military?"

"Negative," he said. "I'm better than military."

It wasn't the answer she wanted to hear, that was for sure. And it was equally clear that she had more questions, but then she straightened her shoulders, her head lifting in a show of bravado.

"What do you need me to do?"

Good girl, he almost said. And then came the urge to touch her again, to flick her chin up and smile at her. Except he couldn't. God help him, he had a feeling touching her would be a very bad, bad idea.

"Strip," he said curtly, more curtly than he'd meant.

"I beg your pardon?"

He gave her the same look he used to give to his privates, one meant to tell them without words that they needed to listen. "Get out of your clothes. We need to disguise ourselves."

She looked like a woman who was trying to decide if running a yellow light was worth the risk. "You have clothes for me?"

"Standard biker babe attire."

"Oh, great."

And that almost made him smile. She held out her hand. "Give it over."

Damn, but he liked her spirit. By this point most women he'd rescued were sobbing into their hands, or his shoulder.

He turned, opening a saddlebag on the side of his bike. Inside were a pair of chaps for her, a T-shirt, a leather jacket for him with the words BORN TO BE WILD on the back, and a red bandana—hers or his—he didn't care.

"Put the chaps on," he said. "And take your hair down. They'll be looking for a woman in a ponytail."

"Turn around," she asked.

Whatever. It wasn't like he'd take a peek, however tempting that might be.

A couple of seconds later she said, "How do I put the chaps on?"

He turned around, and Chance Owens, ex–military man and agent of Brown and Donahue, otherwise known as BAD, felt his jaw drop open.

Hole. Lee. Shit.

Dr. Larson was stacked.

She wore the shirt, the black one, the word BOOBA-LICIOUS scrawled across the front. Where the hell had his agency gotten that from? The shirt was small, too small. What she needed was a large. An extra-large.

"Here," he said, clamping down on sudden unwanted and unprofessional thoughts.

Crap, Chance, you're on *a frickin' mission. Get your mind out of the gutter.*

He crossed over to her. "The zipper's at the top, up by your thighs."

"I can't see it," she said, trying to peer behind her.

"It's right there," he said, pointing to the leather panel with the zipper sewn into the side.

He didn't want to touch her. *Please God, don't let me have to touch her.*

"Where?" she asked again.

He bent and took a deep breath, his fingers brushing her thighs.

Okay, that wasn't so bad.

"Match it up with the other side," he told her, flexing his fingers.

Why was he reacting like this? Why?

He watched her connect the two ends, then start to pull the zipper down, which meant she had to turn her body. That gave him a view of her rear end, which got him thinking about how long her legs were, which made him start to think about—

Stop, he told himself. Just, stop. Stop. Stop. Stop.

When she straightened again, she had a puzzled look on her face.

"What?" she asked. "Did I do something wrong?"

No. The thought jumped into his head. *You've done everything right.*

"Nothing," he said, turning away from her, jerking the jacket out of the saddlebag and tugging the thing on. It was seventy degrees outside. The sun was still pretty high even though it was technically early evening—dusk in the desert seemed to last forever, only to suddenly disappear in a blaze of glory. Still. He might look out of place wearing a jacket.

But suddenly he needed the damn jacket.

It would cover the woody in his pants.

She felt like Biker Barbie.

Fugitive Biker Barbie.

Loose brown hair streamed out behind her; her arms were around a guy who could easily have been first runner-up at the Mr. Olympus competition; and that man was driving her to "someplace safe."

How had this happened?

It was a question that repeated itself through her head over and over again. It seemed odd that just a few short hours ago she'd been in her office, poring over her charts, the small practice quiet after her staff had gone home, and now suddenly—blam—here she was on the back of some bike being whisked away because of her Bird-Brained Project—as her ex used to call it.

This couldn't be happening.

Unfortunately, it was.

Less than an hour later they pulled up to a restaurant. No, scratch that, not a restaurant—a biker bar.

"This is your safe house?" Kait asked, peering at the faded wood façade, the single-story building with the tar and gravel roof. It looked like a good wind might blow it over. A wooden sign hung in the front, one of the old-fashioned, British pub–type signs. HOG HEAVEN it announced. "This is where you propose to keep me safe from bad guys?"

He nodded. "They won't be looking for you here. They'll be looking for you at outlying hotels. Maybe figuring you got away with the help of a friend and that you're lying low. The last place, and I do mean the last place, they'll think to search for you is here."

"So . . . what? You leave me here until the police look into matters and I can go home?"

"Affirmative. It's not safe to be on the road right now. Who knows how many people they have canvassing the highways. By now I'm almost certain they'll have air support. It's better to lie low and head out tomorrow."

"And where, exactly, will we go then?"

"To a secure government facility."

She slapped her forehead. "Of course. I should have figured. Is that before or after I swallow the secret microfilm?"

He looked at her as if he'd taken a swig of milk only to find out it was orange juice. "You have a better idea?"

She nodded. "I want to call the cops. I'm not comfortable with the whole 'secret mission' thing," she said, making quotes in the air with her fingers. "Frankly, I'm not so certain running away is a good idea."

A truck went by, grit rising up from the road to sand-blast her face. Kait squinted. The sun had started to sink below the horizon, turning the heavens into a colorful piñata. From inside the bar she could hear the bass boom of music. And all he did was stare down at her, looking like nothing more than a black-clad Mr. Clean. With hair. Minus the earring.

"Look," he said. "I'll tell you what. When we get inside, you can use the bar's phone to call the police. Don't tell them where you are, just tell them what happened and that you're scared and hiding out somewhere and can they please send an officer to your clinic."

"Why don't I just use your cell phone?"

He shook his head. "No signal."

"No signal—" But then she realized where they were, aka: off the beaten path. She weighed her options. For a moment she thought about insisting he take her to the police. But, really, when it came right down to it, there was a part of her that worried he might be right. As far-fetched as it seemed, as surreal as this might be, she couldn't deny that men had been shooting at her with strange . . . things. She didn't want them shooting at her again.

"Okay," she said as a big rig rushed by. His air brakes as he slowed down were so loud that she all but jumped into Chance Owens's arms.

He smirked. She flicked up her chin. He motioned with his hand that she should precede him, and so she did.

Kait had never been in a biker bar before, although she'd always been a little curious about them. That said, she wasn't expecting much based on the outside. That turned out to be good because compared to the inside, the outside was the Taj Mahal.

It looked as if a million fistfights had beaten the place down. Chairs with missing arms stood around wobbly Formica tables, a few of those tables occupied by leather-clad bikers, most of whom preferred metal chains and steel-toed boots to other accoutrements. It was the kind of bar with a long counter on one side and a jukebox to her right, the source of AC/DC (or some other rock band). A pool table sat in the back; a stained-glass bar light with many, many missing pieces of glass hung over it. Two men played pool—both wore NBA-sized rings, only theirs were made out of sterling silver and were skulls instead of diamonds, and both had hair longer than her own. They looked up when she walked in, one man's pool stick shooting skyward in a very phallic way.

She wasn't naïve enough to think that he wasn't checking her out. His friend must have noticed the expression on his face because he suddenly turned toward her. His pool stick stabbed skyward, too.

"Hot damn," he said.

Obviously, they didn't get much action if they were gawking at her.

Chance stepped in front of her. Kait thought the move tantamount to lifting his leg and peeing on her. Really. But it worked. The two men looked away.

It wasn't that she didn't know she had a hot body. She'd always been dramatically shaped. It had happened late in her life—when she was seventeen. She liked to tell her friends it took her a lot longer to develop because there'd been *a lot* to develop. But her body was something she tended to hide. Oh, there was the odd occasion when she let her hair down and let her breasts out. But doing so always made her feel uncomfortable—men constantly gawking, women continually glaring. It was easier just to cover the damn things up.

"Over here," Chance said, grabbing her by the elbow and leading her to the bar. A woman stood behind the counter, her face looking like an apple that'd been left out in the sun too long. She was supposed to have blond hair but the bleach hadn't taken, and so it was the yellow of a cheap doll, the ends as frayed as a scrub brush.

"Stan here?" Chance asked.

The woman flicked her chin to the left. Kait assumed Chance must know where she was pointing because there was no one at the bar, just a bunch of empty wooden stools that had seats worn smooth by chaps and jeans and who knew what else.

She followed Chance, bracing herself for the lascivious stares of the pool players. She wasn't disappointed. Lord, what she wouldn't give to be able to flick them on the nose like one of her canine patients and give them a stern *Bad dog.*

They stopped before a door. Chance knocked.

"Come in" came from the other side.

Inside a bunch of men played poker, and if the front room patrons of Hog Heaven hadn't scared her, the four men playing poker surely would have. She would bet not even a shark would take a bite of those four, all of them looking like escapees from Sing Sing complete with tattoos, earrings, and water-balloon beer bellies. One of them had gray hair, which made Kait think he should be long past the age of playing with motorcycles.

"Well, if it isn't Stonewall Owens," the gray-haired man said.

That made Kait's brows rise. Stonewall? Granted, the man had a chest wide as a Mack truck, but Stonewall?

"Need the room out back," her rescuer said.

"How long?" The man's eyes flicked to her.

"A night. Maybe two."

The old man thought about it for a second or two, then looked back at his cards. "You know where the key is. Just clean up after yourself."

"C'mon," Chance said, heading toward an exit sign.

The room, as it turned out, was a shack out in back of the bar, where the smell of rotting garbage and old beer filled the air. Overhead, the sky had gone black in typical desert fashion, suddenly and completely black. A fluorescent light on a large pole bzz-bzz-bzzed as it tried to come on. Chance retrieved a key from under a worn and frayed fake-grass mat with WELCOME pressed into the middle. The door looked as if it might come off the hinge when he pulled it open. Air at least twenty degrees warmer than outside drifted toward them.

"Go inside," he said, flicking a switch. "I'll go get the phone."

"You mean there's no phone out here?"

"No," he said sharply. "Bathroom's in the back, that door to the left there."

And when he turned and left her standing there sweltering in the too-warm air, Kait had a sudden moment of panic. What was she doing here? But the strangest thing was that she felt . . . safe. That man out there. Chance "Stonewall" Owens. He made her feel safe. And, obviously, he was on her side. If he was a bad guy, he wouldn't let her call the police.

Closing the door, she took stock of her surroundings. A single bulb spilled burnt ocher light around the interior of the room, revealing walls painted white, the stucco missing or cracked in numerous places. Dead flies coated the bottom of the fixture, causing Kait to grimace. In the center was a bed with a chipped and rusted brass frame and a black comforter over the top, the orange Harley Davidson logo in its middle faded to the color of a peach. The place had been a storage shed at one point; she was certain of it because there were no windows, and the only way in or out looked to be through that front door.

"Here," her rescuer said a moment later, causing Kait to start. He handed her a phone so chipped and battered it looked like it'd been used as a hockey puck. "Don't call nine-one-one," he said. "The owner doesn't want a rescue crew showing up. Bad for business. And don't call anyone else. They might be tracing your boyfriend's line."

"I don't have a boyfriend."

"No?" he asked, and did she imagine the flicker of interest she saw in his eyes?

Nah.

"No."

"Don't call any friends, either. When you're done, I brought you your clothes. You can change back into them." He held up the black saddlebag.

"Thanks," Kait said. She couldn't be certain, but she thought his eyes darted down, thought they lingered for a second on her breasts before she took the bag from him.

Not him too?

"Here's the bar's phone number," he said. "Give it to them in case they need to call you back."

"Aren't you worried about a trace?"

"Why would the police trace your call?"

She supposed he had a point, and so Kait took the piece of paper, setting the saddlebag down just inside the door. First things first.

Chapter Three

IT TOOK LESS THAN A MINUTE TO GET THE NONEMERgency number to the police station; then she waited another second or two while being transferred around. When she'd been connected to the officer in charge, it took considerably longer to explain everything that had happened, and even more time to make the man understand that she wasn't doing drugs, and then a moment or two longer to explain why she hadn't immediately called 911. She knew she'd muddled it even before she gave the officer the bar's phone number.

"I sounded like an idiot," she said when she hung up, handing the phone back to Chance.

"You're upset. It's understandable."

"That man probably thinks I'm a crackpot."

"No. He probably thinks you're *on* crack."

Which made her look up. He gave her a teasing smile. *Be still my heart.*

He had razor stubble covering a truly square chin, the type of chin you only ever saw on action figures. There was a dent in the middle. His lips looked too pretty to belong to a man. Eyes as dark brown as well-worn leather peered down at her gently. Despite his size she found herself thinking he had kind eyes, maybe even gentle eyes.

She looked away. "Maybe I should go to the police station."

"No," he said. "Bad idea. They'll have someone watching for you."

And that made her shiver because she couldn't deny that someone had shot at her today. And while she had a hard time swallowing the reason why, she was smart enough to realize she'd best err on the side of prudence.

"I'll wait until they call back."

"Good," he said. "In the meantime we'll hang out here."

"*We'll?* Where will you stay?"

"I'll be outside, watching for bad guys."

"Oh. Well. Okay. Do you, um, do you have a weapon or something I could keep nearby?"

"Do you know how to shoot a pistol?" he asked, his eyes clearly curious.

"No, but I know how to pull a trigger."

He smiled again. And there they were, those dents on either side of his mouth. *My, my, my.*

"I don't like the thought of being in here alone."

"You won't be alone."

And as she looked into his dark brown eyes, she believed him. This man cared. For some reason, he wanted to keep her safe.

"Thank you," she said.

"You're welcome."

"Will you tell me now what organization you work for?"

"No."

"Why not?"

"In the event you're captured."

That had her forgetting what a handsome hunk of a man he was. Well, at least for a moment or two. "Is there a chance of that?" she asked after forcing moisture back into her mouth.

"No," he said firmly, emphatically, the brown flecks

around his pupils seeming to go black. "You'll be taken to safety tomorrow. Nothing's going to happen to you."

"Then tell me who you work for."

"Negative," he said. And then the look on his face softened. "I can't risk someone getting their hands on the microfilm."

"What micro—" But then she realized he was teasing her about the comment she'd made earlier, when they'd been standing outside the bar. She shivered, and before she could label her reaction as illogical, her body began to . . . to *tingle,* her pulse rate rising the longer he held her gaze. And he held it a long time, long enough for her to know he felt something, too.

And then he straightened, his big body backing out of the doorway like a squirrel down a hole. "Lock the door after I've gone."

He closed the door.

What *the*—?

Kait pressed her hands against her cheeks, feeling the heat in them, the unmistakable evidence of her body's reaction. She stood there for a full two minutes before she remembered to do as he asked and lock the door. And then she turned, aimlessly heading for the bed, which creaked like a trampoline as she sat down.

What the heck was wrong with her? It wasn't as if she found big, burly men attractive. Usually she favored the intellectual types, definitely not guys who rode Harleys.

She lay back on the bed, arms splayed out, staring up at a ceiling coated with spiderwebs and spotted with something else, something that she didn't want to think about. Maybe she'd reacted the way she had because he'd rescued her. Yeah. That must be it. She'd heard of that happening before. A woman got carried off by some handsome guy, and the next thing she knew, she wanted to have his babies. It was biological, she reasoned. Some preprogrammed response women were wired to feel when a male specimen arrived to protect her from prey.

Then why didn't you feel that way when Frank Draper chased that bear out of your tent when you went camping?

And why didn't you feel that way when that Timothy Johnson stopped you from falling off that roof?

Granted she'd only been twelve years old when Timmy rescued her, but she remembered very clearly turning her head when he'd tried to kiss her later.

She heard a light knock. Kait sat up. "Chance?" she called out.

"I brought you something to use as a weapon," he said.

Oh. Okay. She went to the door, unlocked it. He held out his hand, Kait noticing absently that he had little round scars on them.

"Here," he said softly.

A beer bottle.

And for some reason she wanted to laugh. "What am I supposed to do? Clout the bad guys over the head?"

"No. You break it first, then use the jagged edges as a knife."

"Oh."

Their eyes met. She froze.

This was ridiculous, she told herself. *You just met the man. Sure he's hot, but not that hot.*

Yes, he is, a voice insisted. *Oh yes, oh yes, oh yes, oh yes. And c'mon, Kait, when are you ever going to meet a man this hot again?*

"Thanks," she said, taking the bottle from his hand. Their fingers brushed.

She looked up, couldn't stop her eyes from darting to his.

Black lashes narrowed, giving him a gunslinger's glare.

"You know, I think I need to—"

He pulled her to him.

She felt her head snap back. She opened her mouth to protest, but his lips covered hers so fast there wasn't time. It was a hard kiss. A punishing kiss. A kiss meant to show her he wanted her.

Lord help her, she wanted him, too.

Her arms wrapped around his neck. He was big, so big, and her nipples peaked in instant desire. His tongue slipped into her mouth, swiping against her own tongue, stroking it over and over again until she decided she could stand there all night.

Stop him, Kait. This is out of line. Way out of line.

But the whole damn day had been out of line and bizarre and strange. Oddly enough, this didn't feel strange. This felt . . . right.

And then his hand touched her side, his hand slipping beneath her T-shirt and cupping her breast. That made her go weak. When he pinched her nipple, rolling it between his thumb and forefinger, she just about fell. He held her up.

You shouldn't let him do this. You shouldn't, you shouldn't, you shouldn't.

His hand dropped and suddenly cupped her.

Never mind.

Oh, Lord. Never mind.

She groaned, her legs parting as he stroked her. His finger found the perfect spot, the spot that grew flush with heat and moisture as he pressed against it.

Somehow they moved as one, the back of her legs coming up against the wall. His hand left her for a second to clasp her left side, his right hand doing the same on the other side. Before she could blink, he'd lifted her, bracing her against the wall with his body, her legs automatically wrapping around his hips, arms doing the same around his shoulders. Then his hand slid inside her jeans. She wondered how he'd gotten them open. But she didn't care how because he was spreading her, opening her. . . .

Oh, jeez. Oh, jeez, jeez, jeez. She shouldn't let him do it, but she did anyway, encouraging him to dip his fingers inside, even as a part of her said no. No, no, no. It was wrong, wrong, wrong. . . .

He unsnapped his own jeans.

She let him go, one arm hanging around his neck like a monkey, the other sliding down. . . .

No. *You are not going to stroke him. You are* not *going to touch him.* . . .

She wrapped her hand around him.

They both arched, Kait wanting to position her body on top of him. But he was stroking her again and it felt so good. They kissed, his hand down her pants, her hand stroking him. She wanted to suck on his tongue. No. She wanted to suck on him. She wished he'd throw her down on the bed and replace his fingers with his tongue.

As if he read her mind he turned, and Kait felt the dizzying sensation of being spun around. There was a moment of sanity as he all but threw her down on the bed, his big erection jutting out toward her.

What was she doing? What was she *thinking*?

And then he pressed his hot mouth against her.

"Oh, God," she moaned.

She wanted him. She wanted this. She wanted sex. Now. With him. Hard and fast. Sex, sex, sex.

"Yes," she moaned.

Yes.

She was having a wet dream.

Chance stared down at the writhing woman on the bed and realized she was having a wet dream. Thank God, he told himself, his heart still pounding in his chest. When he'd heard her moans he couldn't open the door soon enough, couldn't flick on the light fast enough.

Only in some respects what he found was worse. Much, much worse. She was having an f-in' wet dream.

About him?

God, wouldn't that be some—

Totally out of line, Chance.

He knew that. But damn it, he couldn't move as she lay there, moaning, her head thrashing from side to side, the word "yes" being hissed from between her lips.

His dick got hard. He went back to the door, firmly telling himself to step out of the room. But he paused, deciding to take one last look.

That was when she opened her eyes.

She froze. So did he.

And he couldn't resist. He really couldn't resist. "Pleasant dreams?" he asked.

She scrambled up like he'd pulled a gun on her.

"What the hell?" she asked, her nipples so hard beneath her BOOBALICIOUS shirt that she looked like a walking advertisement for a porn flick.

"I was . . . I was . . . ." She pulled the pillow out from behind her, shielding her face with it. "I was dreaming about horses," she said suddenly, the pillow dropping, her chin flicking upward.

"You were dreaming about riding something, all right."

She threw the pillow.

He laughed. *Laughed.*

While on a mission. With a woman who, if he didn't miss his guess, had just had a wet dream.

About him?

He spied the blush on her face.

Oh, yeah—about him.

"You always have such an active fantasy life?"

The look she gave him was filled with humiliation.

"Go away," she said. "Just go away."

"Look," he said. "If it makes you feel any better, I've been imagining what you look like without that top of yours all evening."

And now why'd he go and do that? Why'd he try and make her feel better? She didn't need to know that. God, all it'd do was cause friction between them. Sexual friction.

"It doesn't make me feel better. Not at all."

He crossed his arms. He had to cross his arms because if he didn't, he had a feeling he'd touch her—and that was bad.

"We're attracted to each other, Dr. Logan. It's nothing to get upset about."

"Easy for you to say," he heard her mumble. "You didn't just have the wet dream."

And suddenly she looked adorable, and it took so much effort not to go to her, not to place a hand on her head and tell her it was all right, that he was flattered.

And turned on.

"Look. Obviously you're exhausted. That's why you're reacting to me the way you are. I'm exhausted, too. I've been watching your place for days."

And fantasizing about her the whole time.

Shut up, Chance.

"You should get some rest."

Wanna share the bed?

"Yeah. I think you're right."

What the hell is wrong with you, Owens?

But he knew. He'd watched her for days. Watched her walk clients out to their cars. Watched her lavish love and affection on the animals she cared for. Watched how great she was with people, especially kids. They were alike in so many ways. She had no family, very few friends. In fact, the woman seemed to devote herself entirely to her four-legged friends, just as he did, only his four-legged friends were all horses. She was adorable, he'd realized on the second day. That had mutated to gorgeous by the third. And now that he knew there was a hot body beneath the lab coat he was truly fascinated.

Cripes.

"I'll be outside."

She didn't answer.

"Pleasant dreams."

But as he slowly closed the door, he couldn't resist teasing her one last time.

"About me," he added.

He had a feeling she would have thrown another pillow at him, if she'd had one. And as the door closed behind him, Chance felt a chuckle vibrate up his throat, emerging into a full-fledged laugh.

Holy crap, she was beyond adorable.

Yeah, a voice said. *And since* when *did assignments become* adorable?

The answer to that question came sure and fast.

Never.

Chapter Four

IT WAS NOT A RESTFUL NIGHT. THEN AGAIN, CONSIDER-
ing the fact that she jumped at every sound, that was to
be expected.

Worse, the police never called back.

At six in the morning she got up the nerve to call them
back. Once again she was transferred around. This time
she was connected to a woman.

"Dr. Logan? Oh, yeah, I see a report filed right here,"
the woman said. "What can I help you with?"

Kait's heart pounded like a stereo cranked on high.
"Did an officer go by my place of business?"

"Hmm," the woman murmured. "Yeah. It looks like
someone did. Around twenty-two-thirty," she said, and it
took Kait a moment to convert that into nonmilitary time.

Ten-thirty P.M.

"Everything normal, the report says."

"*What?*"

"Everything appeared fine, Dr. Logan. Probably a
passing car kicked up a rock and broke your window.
These things happen."

"A car—" Kait said, breath catching. But then it came
out in a rush. "It was not a rock. Someone shot at me.
With . . . with . . . things. They shot tear gas inside my
office. Things were very definitely not 'fine.' "

"Are you sure you gave the officer the right address?"

"Of course I'm sure. Do you think after eight years of private practice that I don't know my own office address?"

She was beginning to sound hysterical. She knew it and the woman on the other end of the phone knew it. Kait could tell the moment she said, "Ma'am, maybe you should just calm down—"

"I'm not crazy."

"I never said you were."

"Or on drugs."

"I never said that, either."

"But you're thinking it."

"No. I'm thinking if you're really upset about this, come down to the police station and give us a statement."

"Are you sure you had the right address?" Kait asked.

The woman read her the numbers. It wasn't wrong. Kait would have hung up if the door suddenly opening hadn't made her shriek.

"Ma'am?" she heard from the other end of the line. "Ma'am? You all right?"

It was Chance, his wide body blocking the doorway. He didn't come into the room. Well, not all the way. He stood by the door, his tall form framed by white light that turned his body into a dense shadow.

"I'm fine," she told the officer.

"Come down to the police station," the woman said.

"I'll think about it," Kait said before hanging up, the phone beeping as she rang off.

"What'd they say?" he said, his tree-stump arms crossed in front of him so that they bulged.

"That everything looked fine."

He didn't move, just stood there, his silence all the "told you so" she needed.

"It has to be a mistake," she murmured.

"It's not a mistake," he said, chin swinging left and

right once. "These are professionals, Dr. Logan. They probably had a cleanup crew out there the moment we left."

"Cleanup crew?"

"People whose job it is to mop up crime scenes like yours. They'll replace broken glass. Clean up the mess. Mop up blood."

She looked away at the mention of blood, the image of that man on the ground forever burned into her mind. Her stomach rolled. "But how can they do that?"

"Simple. They arrived prepared. They knew a window would be broken, probably had one ready to slip into the old frame. They might have figured on casualties, might even have had a way of getting the body out unseen. These are scary people, Dr. Logan. Anything is possible."

"Why?" she asked. "And who?"

"We think it's a militant faction out of Libya, but we can't be certain. Frankly, it could be anybody, including Al Qaeda. As to why, you have something they want. A biological weapon such as the world has never seen before. Better than any drone plane, better than any unmanned anything, because it's completely innocuous. Nobody will suspect a bird flying in the sky."

"But all my birds do is fly in a straight line. That's it. Nothing more."

"That's enough," he said grimly. "They're probably hoping to perfect the technology, probably thinking they might be able to program birds to do exactly what they want, in which case the possibilities are endless. Tiny cameras could make the birds the ultimate eye in the sky. An airborne virus could be given to them. With enough birds and enough virus, you could wipe out an entire city. Or how about turning the bird into the avian equivalent of a suicide bomber—"

"Stop," she said, holding up a hand, her stomach tightening to the point that she felt ready to throw up.

"Make no mistake, these people mean business. Like as not they searched your office for your research and, failing to find anything of use, decided to go directly to the source. If they'd caught you they'd have taken you, tortured you, then dumped your body so it would have looked like a senseless crime."

And all because she'd wanted to help an endangered species. What type of sick human beings took her idea and twisted it? And what would they have done if they'd found her research? Luckily, it had been at Dr. Grey's house, Kait having asked her colleague to review her work and check it for errors one last time. What would have happened if she'd kept it instead? She shivered.

"What do we do now?"

"You call your office manager from a pay phone on the road. You tell her you're sick. Then I'm going to take you to Fallon Naval Air Station. You'll be in good hands there."

She nodded, feeling a sudden urge to go home, to crawl into her bed and pull up the covers.

Don't *cry*, a stern voice warned her. Do not cry *in front* of *him*.

But the edges of her vision blurred anyway. Damn it all.

She heard him move, heard him because she'd closed her eyes, and it was funny because she knew intuitively where he was. She knew that he stopped near her left shoulder. Knew he stared down at her, not touching, not daring to do that because there was still this . . . this thing between them.

"I had a sister in your shoes once."

That made her eyes spring open, made her look up at him.

She knew in an instant that what he admitted was difficult and deeply personal, and that he only did so because he thought it might help.

He wanted to help.

Why did her heart melt at that?

"Is that why you do what you do? Work for this—" She shook her head a bit, trying to put a name to what he did. "—organization?"

"It is."

Eyes gone dark with a need for understanding stared down at her. She noticed then that he wore his chaps, his shirt as black as his eyes, his dark hair looking wet, shadows painting the damp strands blue.

"Did she die?" she found herself asking, not really wanting to know, but knowing she needed to hear the answer just the same.

The way his eyes flickered was all the answer she needed. "I'm sorry," she said.

"It was an accident, one that won't be repeated. I made sure of that when I went after the bastards who killed her myself." And though he didn't straighten away from her, it felt as if he withdrew. Gone was the softness; in its place came the steely-eyed look of a warrior.

She shivered.

"We should head out," he said. "I had a friend bring you something else to wear. I'll wait outside while you change."

She emerged fifteen minutes later wearing a black shirt that covered considerably more of her than yesterday's. She'd brushed her hair, too, obviously having found the toiletries in the bag.

And damn it all, Chance had to stop from going to her, from tipping her chin up and telling her everything would be all right.

"Thanks for the clothes," she said, blue eyes blinking against the sunlight. She handed the empty duffel bag back. And when he moved away, she stopped him with a hand, her fingers landing on his skin, fingers shockingly cold. That's why he flinched. Not because he felt any sort of jolt.

"Look," she said softly. "I just wanted to say thank you. I don't know who you work for. I don't know why you're helping me, but *thank you*."

His gaze caught on her lip, Chance wondered what she'd do if he bent down and lightly grazed her lips with his own.

He'd been dying to do that since last week.

"You're welcome," he said, having to fight the urge to do exactly as he fantasized. "Come on."

Last night he'd moved his bike out behind the bar, out of sight. This morning sunlight glinted off the spotless chrome, sending a beam of warmth across his face. He slid onto the black leather seat, pulling his helmet on at the same time he tipped the bike up. He pretended to be busy with his helmet, but the truth of the matter was, he had to brace himself for the feel of Kait's thighs clasping his own. And when at last he felt that warmth, when at last her thighs pressed into him, he almost gasped.

He wanted her.

And it was time to admit that his attraction to her was beginning to border on obsession.

Son of a—

"Ready?" he asked, hands dropping to the handlebars.

"Ready," she answered, those tiny fingers of hers slipping under his arms and clasping his side.

She'd had a wet dream about him last night.

He'd be having wet dreams about her for the next several nights.

The bike roared to life after a wheezy chugalug, Chance pushing the thing off the kickstand so fast he almost tipped them over. He felt her thighs clasp him even harder and almost groaned.

Okay, best to get this over with. PDQ.

The drive to Fallon would take less than an hour. With any luck, she'd be off his hands in fewer than two.

He gunned it.

She clutched him harder. His jaw muscle began to ache; when he shifted gears and her upper body pressed against his back, he just about closed his eyes.

Son of a—

"Loosen up," he told her, turning onto a side road that'd take them to 80. "We're not going to wreck."

"I don't like motorcycles," she yelled into his ear.

"You didn't mind them yesterday."

"Yesterday some guy was shooting cattle prods at me."

He felt his teeth dry as he momentarily smiled. "We'll be there soon, Dr. Logan. Just try to relax."

Maybe you should take your own advice.

But it was hard. She held on to him like a kitten on a ball of yarn. His teeth ground together. To be honest, he almost wished the bad guys would spot them. At least then he'd have something to focus on.

They arrived in record time, mostly because Chance pushed the speed limit as much as he could. As they approached the base's guardhouse, his mood began to improve. Desert scrub sent up the sickly sweet smell of sage, sand, and rocks stretching on for miles and miles around them, flat, nothing but blue-gray mountains in the distance.

Chance saluted the SP on duty, his front tire nudging the red-and-white crossing arm that blocked the drab brown base from entry.

"Name?" the man asked.

"Chance Owens."

"Nature of business?"

"I'm delivering one Dr. Kaitlyn Logan to the base commander," he motioned behind him.

"ID?"

Chance fished inside his front pocket, pulling out his Nevada license.

The white-helmeted guard gave the chopper and his passenger an arch look. "Does he know you're coming?"

"He does."

The man went back into his bulletproof booth. Kait leaned toward Chance to say, "Look, Chance. I just want to say thank you once again. I'm grateful the American public has people like you around."

"Just doing my job," he said, even though inside the words were *Don't suppose you'd like to show me just how grateful you are?*

"Sorry, sir," the SP said a minute later. "I spoke to the base commander and he doesn't know a thing about you or a Dr. Logan."

"*What?*"

"You'll have to pull through the gate then back around while we check this out."

"There's nothing to check out. I was told to bring Dr. Logan to Fallon and deliver her to the base commander, whoever that is. Maybe you should talk to the battalion commander."

"Already did. He's never heard of you either."

And to be honest, the guard looked a little testy, likely because a black-clad Hell's Angel look-alike wasn't exactly someone who garnered sympathy.

Okay. He needed to think this through. Maybe someone had failed to deliver the message up the chain of command.

But fifteen minutes later, that notion was dispelled, too, and by then a Hummer full of SPs had arrived, their fifty calibers looking mighty serious.

Not good. Not good at all.

"You know," Chance said as Kait stood anxiously off to the side. "Why don't I call my commander and ask what this is all about?"

"It would help if you could tell us what branch of the military you're with."

"Look, Seaman First Class . . ." Chance's eyes shot down to the man's brass name tag, which was hard to read with sunlight arcing off of it. "Rodgers," he finally made out. "I can't tell you that."

"Oh, really?"

"Really," Chance said. "So we'll just be on our way."

"On our way," he heard Kait echo, obviously flummoxed.

"Get on the bike."

"Wait a minute," she said. "What about leaving me here?"

He pinned her with a glare. "Kaitlyn," he said softly. "Please get on the bike. I need to make a few phone calls, and I can't do that here."

"Can't I stay with them while you do that?" She pointed to the men with the fifty calibers.

"Negative," Chance said. "They won't let you."

And when she glanced at the SP for confirmation, he only nodded. "Security."

"Maybe you should just call the police instead?" she said.

"We already tried that, remember? Let me just make a call and try to find out what happened. It could be the base commander hasn't gotten the communiqué from my commander. It shouldn't take but a few minutes to sort things out."

But he could see the indecision floating through her eyes. He'd be indecisive, too, if someone promised him something and then didn't deliver.

Son of a—

But then she said, "Okay." And when he looked into her eyes, he saw acceptance—acceptance and something else that made his insides go jiggy.

He saw trust.

Chapter Five

HE TOOK HER TO A SPOT WITHIN SIGHT OF THE GUARD-house just in case there was trouble. Kait didn't want to know what "trouble" might be and so she appreciated the precaution.

So far, she could tell his conversations hadn't gone well. Actually, there hadn't been any conversations at all. She could see him a few hundred yards away, dialing one number, then another, stabbing the off button with more and more force. Finally, she heard his raised voice, but he must have been leaving a message because he walked toward her less than ten seconds later.

"What's wrong?"

"I don't know," he said, his eyes as dark as the scrub that surrounded them. "I can't get ahold of anybody."

"Maybe you're dialing wrong?"

He gave her a look.

She lifted her hands. "Just a thought."

He squinted as a car approached. Every time someone came near them his hand hovered near his waistline. The shirt he wore didn't have any obvious bulges and pro-trusions, but she assumed he had a gun tucked some-where.

A gun.

To protect her.

"So what do we do now?" she asked, hating that she sounded worried and maybe even a little scared. Amazing how quickly she'd come to rely on him.

"We regroup."

"And where do we do that?"

"Maybe back at Hog Heaven."

"No offense," she said, "but I'd really rather not go back there."

"And I'd really rather not take you there. Better to keep on the move. Less chance of someone ambushing us that way."

"So how about a hotel?"

"Negative," he said. "They'll be keeping an eye on them."

Kait felt her brows lift. "There must be a hundred hotels in Reno. They can't watch them all."

"Yes, they can."

That took her aback for a moment. "So where do we go?"

He put his hands on his hips, the look in his eyes changing for a second to something that made her want to gulp.

"My place," he said.

"Your place?"

"It's only an hour away. It's remote. Security system. My place."

"But, um, don't you think it'd be easier if we hung out here?"

"Negative," he said, and she could tell the more he thought about it, the more he liked the idea. "They won't let us. In fact, I'm surprised those SPs haven't come by to boot us out. My place."

His place. Oh, dear.

Stop it, Kait. It's not like the man's going to jump you. You wish *he'd jump you.*

She was a vet. The most excitement she'd had in recent months was a Pomeranian mistaking her leg for its mate. Sad. Really, really sad. Obviously, she was desperate for some action.

But he was right. She wanted to go someplace safe. She was tired of the back of her neck continually tingling. She felt as if she had a big red target painted on her shoulders.

"Let's go," she said.

He looked relieved, and then . . . perturbed? No. that wasn't it. He looked concerned. For her safety, obviously. Well, that made two of them. And that nervousness only increased when she climbed aboard his bike a moment later. Every time a loud noise rang out, she jumped, clutching at Chance Owens's sides as if he could spin around on his bike and protect her. She hated it.

The feeling lessened a bit when they left the city. The freeway climbed through low-rolling hills, the bright hues of civilization fading like an old photograph until all that was left were sepia browns and grays. They climbed to a higher elevation. Desert scrub faded to oak trees and then pines. They drove through small towns, former boomtowns in gold rush days, but now nothing more than a few crumbling storefronts with poverty-stricken residential areas around the perimeter. The pine trees grew taller—older—the smell of them something an air freshener company would likely give a mint to capture. She began to relax after about an hour.

"Not much farther," he called back.

Kait wished they could go on riding. With no one following, it was easy to forget that someone had tried to abduct her yesterday.

He turned off the main road. Sunlight flickered through the trees, strobe-lighting the road in front of them. Less than a mile later the trees began to thin a bit, opening into a grass-covered field, the blades so many shades of green that Kait thought it the prettiest meadow she'd ever seen.

"It's gorgeous," she said, the sound of the Harley echoing through the countryside.

"It's secluded," he said, as if that was all that mattered. And maybe it was. He struck her as the type who valued his privacy, who didn't want people knowing where he went and when he left. But he hadn't struck her as an animal lover, and so when she spotted the horses grazing alongside a white fence that backed right up to his house, she straightened in surprise. Draft horses, Kait realized.

"They're huge," she said as he slowed down.

"They're Friesians," he said, coming to a slow stop. One of the horses was curious enough to stick his nose toward them, the roman-shaped nostrils flaring.

"I know," she said.

He leaned sideways, cocking his head. "You know?"

"Well, I am a vet. And I love horses," she said. "When I opened up my own practice, I promised I'd get one. Hasn't happened."

"Too bad," he said. "There's nothing like riding to calm your mind."

And he would need a horse that size, she realized, because even when sitting on the bike the top of her head barely cleared his shoulders. And then she caught sight of his house. She didn't know what she expected. Okay, maybe she did: a log cabin in the woods. Maybe a one-story ranch house, not a gorgeous multistory contemporary home with angled glass, redwood siding, and green trim. Everything, from the landscape to the angle of the roof, made it look as if it were part of the pine tree–studded scenery.

He roared to a stop in front of a three-car garage, while Kait thought that his house was nicer than anything she'd ever hoped to own. Granted, now that she could stop investing her own private funds into her research project she could likely afford something a little better than her modest two-bedroom home, but this . . . this was in a different league altogether.

Just how well did rescuing damsels in distress pay, anyway?

It was a question that repeated itself as he opened an ornate double door, lead glass distorting her image as she walked by. Inside, a vaulted ceiling swept upward, and dark-oak beams formed upside-down Vs over her head. To her left, just beyond the front door, stood a suit of armor.

"You know," she found herself saying, "if you'd worn this when we'd first met, it might have saved a lot of confusion."

She smiled. Their gazes met, and for a second, just a moment, really, she thought he stilled, though he might have drawn back a bit. But she chalked it up to imagination because what came to his face was a smirk.

"If I'd worn that when we'd first met, I'd have been a tin can for target practice."

She smiled again.

He looked away, a big hand sweeping through his tousled black hair. "Look," he said. "I'm going to go in and make a few calls. Make yourself at home. There's a shower upstairs and a bedroom right next door if you want to take a nap. This might take a while."

Kait nodded, watching him walk to the end of the short hall, turn left, and disappear around the corner. But while a shower sounded great, she didn't feel comfortable stripping.

Not after her dream last night.

Humiliation painted her cheeks red. Thank God he didn't see her blush. Shaking her head at herself, she followed him, until she turned right instead of left, stepping into a sunken living room about the size of her backyard. Okay, maybe not that big, but it was so spacious she felt like a ladybug trapped inside a glass jar. A set of bay windows—two stories high—overlooked the meadow, the white fence with the horses on the other side rolling away from the home.

Beautiful.

And for the first time in twenty-four hours, Kait took a deep breath. How could anything bad happen out here? They hadn't been followed. No one had spotted them leaving Reno—she was certain of it, having kept watch along the way. No strange men pointed tasers in their direction. No nothing but peace and quiet. She walked toward the window, stopping before the glass, turning to look around the room. Warm sun poured over her back. She sat down in a comfy armchair, the beige fabric forming to her body. Heaven. How long she sat there, eyes closed, the quiet of the house settling over her, she had no idea. When at last she opened her eyes a giant fireplace with large, flat stones surrounding it caught her attention. It looked like the perfect place to spend a winter night, maybe on a fur rug, with a few candles—

Kait!

But that was part of the reason why she couldn't drift off to sleep. She couldn't stop thinking about him. She'd spent more than an hour clasping his big body and it had done things to her insides. He smelled good, too. That might seem like a strange thing to notice, but he really did. Like the outdoors, she realized. Sweet, with a hint of pine and earth.

She got up and walked to the fireplace. There were pictures on the mantel, four or five of them. Two were of a family, a boy and girl of about six and seven trying to squirm out of their smiling parents' grasp, the father in uniform. Was that the sister who'd died? There was another picture, this one when the kids were older. In it they were all posed, the girl standing next to her obviously proud papa, his military uniform spotless, as spotless as the young man's who stood next to him.

Chance.

She could tell immediately. He might have been younger, but he was still just as tall and just as honed as he was now, and he was obviously very proud of his sister. He had his arm around her. The whole family was standing in front of a mosque, the four towers with their balloon-shaped tops glinting in the afternoon sunshine.

"We were in Turkey."

She jumped but didn't turn because the girl was so full of life, so darn pretty, it seemed somehow wrong that she was dead.

"She was twenty-one," he said, coming up behind her. "We'd just had a birthday party for her the night before."

"How . . . ?" But she couldn't finish the question. She didn't have the right to know. When she glanced up at him, she was glad she hadn't asked. The look in his eyes. Oh, Lord, it just about broke her heart.

"How did it happen?" he finished for her.

"No, I . . . really. I don't need to know."

He shrugged. "I don't mind telling you. My dad was head of security for the embassy. One day terrorists attacked."

"I'm sorry."

"No need to be."

"Chance—"

"Actually, I should thank the marine commander who fucked up and got them killed. Because of him I started to help people like you."

No. It wasn't okay. It would never be okay. She could see that. "What—what do you mean?" she asked.

"They discharged me after I beat him to a pulp."

"Oh, Chance."

"Because of him people died. I vowed then and there that I'd never let what happened to my sister Samantha happen to someone else."

She went to him, picking up his hand, noting the scars

again, round areas of discoloration. He didn't seem to realize she was touching him.

"What are these?" she asked.

"What are what?"

"These."

Chance followed her gaze and his teeth ground together. "Nothing," he said quickly, trying to pull his hand away.

"They're burn marks, aren't they?"

He told himself not to react. Told himself not to give anything away. "They're nothing," he said again.

"What happened?"

"Nothing," he said, forcing himself to look down at her.

And that was when it happened. That was when he saw her mouth drop open. "My God," she said. "When you went after them, they captured you and tortured you, didn't they?"

He didn't answer.

"Oh, Chance."

She stepped up to him, placing her arms around him. Hugging him.

"I'm so sorry," she said softly.

"Don't be. It was a long time ago."

Her hands captured his own, thumbing one of the scars. "But it's still here," she said, "right here with you."

It always would be.

"Is that why you do it?" she asked, her fingers lightly stroking him. "Is that why you ride off rescuing damsels in distress?"

"In part, but also because of my sister."

She smiled, her look one of admiration. "You're a good man, Chance Owens."

"That's not what that commander said after I beat his ass."

"You had a right to be angry."

He was still angry. He'd closed himself off to feeling for anything and anyone. And then he'd been sent to watch over her and he'd felt a stirring of . . . something.

She kissed his hand, and suddenly Chance wanted more. He wanted a hell of a lot more.

He pulled her into his arms, kissing the mouth he'd been fantasizing about for days.

The reality was far better than the fantasy.

She was every bit as warm and wonderful to kiss as he'd thought she would be. And then she opened her mouth. He took a chance and slipped his tongue inside, thinking she might withdraw, surprised and yet not surprised when she didn't. She wrapped a hand around the back of his neck, pulling him down, pulling him nearer.

She tasted good. So good. And so sweet.

His hand found the underside of her breast, her bra the type that didn't have any of that padding. Oh no. He could feel her in all her glory, her size substantial enough that he couldn't cup all of her.

"Wait," she said, trying to pull her lips away. But he followed her mouth with his own. "Just wait," she said after turning her head. But that was okay, because he found her ear, wondered for a second how it would taste, then probed the inside with his tongue.

"Oh, man," she moaned. "Oh man oh man. I wish you wouldn't do that." And her words were nearly a whisper.

He swirled his tongue around the inside, then drew back so he could nibble her lobe.

"And I really, really wish you would do that," she said, melting into him. She was so damn tiny. So damn petite. It made him want to pick her up. Made him want to carry her away. To take her to safety.

She was safe. As long as she was with him.

"Touch me," he whispered in her ear. "Touch me, Kait."

"Chance. I don't think—" She gasped as he slid his hand down from her breast and to the mound of flesh perfectly cupped by her jeans. "Oh, man."

He slid his fingers between her legs.

"I don't— Oh."

"I think I could kiss you for hours," he said just before he wrapped his arms around her tighter, kissing her deeply. Some women might shy away from such a bold assault, but not Kait. Not his Kait. She seemed to want it as much as he did.

"To hell with it," he heard her murmur.

And then she kissed him back. She shifted a little so her legs could slide open, encouraging him to touch her there. And he did. Her woman's mound radiated heat, so hot. He could feel dewy moisture seep from her jeans. But he didn't want to feel fabric, he suddenly realized. He wanted to feel flesh. That soft flesh.

His hand shifted. She knew what he was about to do because he dragged his fingers up her fly. But she didn't stop him when he undid the first button. Didn't say no when he worked the pants open, then slipped his hand—

Ahh.

She moaned. He could feel the sound vibrate from inside of her mouth. She moaned and he probed deeper, both with his hand and his tongue, sliding his fingers over her silky mound, fiddling with the slit between her lips, gently inserting a finger . . .

"Chance," she hissed.

He drew back. He watched her. Watched as this beautiful woman, a woman he'd been fascinated with since the moment he'd seen her rush to aid an injured dog that first day he'd been doing surveillance, watched as her mouth dropped open, her lips beestung swollen from his kiss. Her head lolled back, her legs sliding farther apart so he could explore deeper, and then deeper still.

"Oh, Chance."

He rubbed her faster, playing with her, watching the play of emotions on her face as he brought her closer to an orgasm. Watched as her eyes closed, her hips starting to follow the motion of his hand. He wanted to bring her pleasure. For some reason, he needed to please her, wanted to make her happy.

Her eyes opened.

"Stop," she ordered.

He instantly removed his hand.

"I want you to make love to me."

They weren't the words he'd been expecting, and the delight he felt upon hearing them made him think there was more to his feelings for her than seemed logical.

"I do," she said, her blue eyes wide and utterly trusting.

"Good," he said, a part of him thinking, Bad idea. He shouldn't. He really shouldn't. . . .

He carried her upstairs. She clung to his neck the whole time, her head resting in the crook of his neck.

She felt good there.

She felt right.

He didn't have time to analyze his thoughts because the minute they were in his room, he laid her on the black bedspread and pulled his shirt off his body in one quick motion, his jeans coming off next. His erection fought against his briefs. He set it free, meeting Kait's gaze as he did so. She didn't look surprised or uncomfortable. Her eyes went soft, the look in them one of such sexual intensity that his whole body tingled in anticipation. She made him feel just like he had the first time he'd had sex. Aroused. Excited. Nervous.

Yes, he admitted. Nervous.

She sat up and pulled her shirt over her head.

Nervous.

Her bra came off next, her hair sliding through the neck hole so that it fell to her shoulder in static disarray. Her hands moved to the waistband of her jeans, pushing them down at the same time she flicked her tennis shoes off, the things landing on the carpet with a muffled *thud-thud*.

And then she lay back, naked, waiting, her body sprouting goose pimples from the cold—or arousal.

She had a hell of a body.

Her full breasts spilled over the sides of her rib cage, light brown nipples puckered with desire. Her body was tan, her abdomen flat, her long legs cocked to one side as she waited for him to join her on the bed.

He wanted to cover her right then, like one of his stallions. But something held him back. Something caused him to simply stare. She was beautiful. Not just because she had the perfect mixture of curves and valleys. No, she was beautiful because when she looked up at him there was no fear, no anxiety, just trust. She wanted him and she wasn't afraid to let him know it.

"Kait," he said softly.

"Make love to me, Chance," she said, holding out her hand.

He sank down on the mattress, the brush of her skin like the sting of hot water. His erection nudged her thigh as he lay on his side, facing her. His hands shook as he supported his weight on one elbow, his free hand lifting to stroke the line of her jaw. Such a feminine jaw for such a strong woman.

She clasped his hand, drawing it to her, kissing the burn marks that spotted the top of his hands. She hadn't seen the rest. He didn't want her to see the rest, and so he kissed her.

She helped him forget. As their tongues touched he realized he'd found something special, something unique. It made him draw back.

"Chance?" she said to him, seeming to ask the same question that was on his mind.

How could *this be?*

How could he be in bed with a woman he just met, whom he was pledged to protect, and yet feel so connected to her?

"This could be serious," he heard himself murmur.

"I know."

"I don't usually bed women I've just met."

"No?" she asked.

"No," he said.

"Good."

Kait slid her hands around him, pulling him on top of her as she'd fantasized about doing from almost the first moment she'd met him. It was a brazen move, but she had a feeling if she didn't do something fast he might change his mind. He had honor, this man, and she could tell he was about to have an attack of moral conscience. She didn't want that. Oh, no. Having decided to bed the man, she wanted him. Now.

Only she wanted to go on kissing him forever, too. Lord help her, she couldn't get enough of his tongue brushing her own.

His hand lowered, and she shivered in anticipation as his fingers drifted down her body, pausing near her breast so he could circle her nipple with his thumb. She'd known her breasts were hard, but she'd never felt them so sensitive before, never felt such a keen urge to press into a man's hand as he began to tease her, his mouth pulling away and then lowering to the sensitized tip. He sucked her into his mouth.

She arched as his other hand found the spot he'd teased earlier, the spot that made her body heat with sexual excitement. She gasped, spreading her legs apart, wanting him to keep going this time. He did, and Kait lost herself to the pleasure. His mouth teased her nipples, sucking them, nipping at them, his tongue flicking the sensitive tip in the same way his fingers teased her toward an orgasm.

"Chance," she moaned, trying to encourage him to slip between her legs, to push his erection inside her. That's what she wanted. Him. But he didn't move, and so she did, capturing him in her hand, just like she had in her dream. Only this was better than a dream. He was bigger in life than he'd been in her mind. She glided her hand up his staff. This time he moaned, his mouth moving back to her as he kissed her, his tongue slipping inside her at the same time his fingers slipped inside her down there.

Yes, she silently moaned, cupping her lips around his tongue, her fingers mimicking her mouth.

They both groaned. They both grew more and more aroused. But it was perfect, their teasing of each other. So when she felt her climax growing too near, she suddenly pulled away.

He growled.

She moved quickly, still holding his erection, her mouth lowering to take the place of her hand. She paused just before taking the engorged tip inside her.

"Lady, you're playing with fire," he warned.

"I like fire," she said, slipping her mouth around him.

He gasped. She cupped him, her hand working him at the same time she sucked him into her mouth.

"Kait," he hissed.

He tasted good. She went back for more. He arched his hips after one or two strokes. She took as much of him as she could, loving the way controlling him made her feel. So utterly female. So perfectly a woman.

That she could make his big body tremble filled her with power, and need. She wanted him to lose control completely, just as she wanted to lose control. She felt him swell, tasted the salty evidence of his near-release touching the tip of her tongue.

"Kait," he gasped.

She shifted, lowering herself atop him.

"Condom—"

"Shh," she ordered, kissing him. She trusted this man. She didn't know why, but she did. She loved how he tasted in her mouth. Reveled in the way he kissed her back. Trusted that what they did together was right and that he wouldn't let anything happen to her.

"Kait—"

She took him all the way in, only to slide back up his shaft. His hands clasped her hips, pushing her back down. She rocked, her breasts thrusting out; Kait caught a glimpse of her hard nipples.

She wasn't going to last long.

Neither was he.

She lifted, not wanting to climax. Not yet. She wanted to savor her time with him, wanted the moment to go on and on and on.

He tipped his hips up, finding the core of her, pressing against her in a way that made her whole body tighten with a pleasure so great she thought for sure she'd slip over the edge. She didn't. Like her, he seemed to know intuitively how to maximize her pleasure. And like her, he knew exactly how much to touch her so that within seconds, she was almost begging him to let her come.

Jesus Lord, what was this? How could it be so completely perfect with a man she'd only just met? How—?

And then she came.

She heard herself cry out, another surprise because she didn't usually. But she did then, her cries echoing each throb of pleasure. She moaned and rode him, tightening around him right as he began to pulse inside her, his own moans mixing with hers.

Kait tipped forward, unable to hold herself up. She landed against his chest, the ridges of muscle so hard it felt like resting her cheek against warm marble. Her body continued to contract; so did his, until all that remained was languid satisfaction.

She didn't want to move. She never wanted to leave the protection of this man's arms, but as she held him and stroked him, she noted the myriad of scars on his body.

"Did they give you these, too?" she asked, still holding him. There was no need to explain who *they* were. There was only one *they* in Chance's life.

"Some of them," he said.

"Bastards."

He drew back, a half smile on his face as he said, "I made them pay. When I escaped, none of them were left standing." And then his smile faded. "I just wish I'd been in time to save my family."

"Oh, Chance," she said, stroking a hank of hair off his face. "I'm so sorry."

"Don't be. It's why I do what I do. Why I am who I am. And if I hadn't been booted out of the Marines, I'd never have started to work for the Agency. I'd have never met you."

Her heart melted all over again. Funny how she'd always heard the cliché expression before, but she'd never realized people used the term because it truly did feel as if your heart turned to mush in your chest. That's the way she felt when she stared into Chance's eyes.

"This wasn't very smart," he said, stroking a hank of her hair off her face.

"I know, but I don't regret it."

They looked into each other's eyes, and in his Kait could see the same wonder she felt.

"I might have just gotten you pregnant," he said.

"Would you marry me if you did?"

"You know," he said, swiping a lock of her hair away from her face. "I think I just—"

The window broke.

Kait gasped. Chance immediately shoved her aside, protecting her.

"Don't breathe," he told her.

But Kait didn't need to be warned. She recognized the sound of spraying gas.

They'd been found.

Chapter Six

.

Somehow Chance scooped up his clothes, grabbing Kait's along the way.

Fucking A—how the hell had they gotten past his security?

But there was no time to think. He pulled Kait up and toward his closet.

"Get dressed," he ordered the minute the door had closed behind them.

"Chance, what are—?"

"Shh," he said, locking the door. And when he'd finished, he pulled on his jeans at the same time he shoved aside a row of suits, finding the crack in the wall with little trouble and pressing against it. He turned back to her right as his secret passage opened.

"It'll take them thirty seconds to figure out where we've gone," he whispered. "Less if they've got infrared trained on us."

Someone kicked at the closet door.

"They have infrared," he said. "C'mon."

She'd pulled on her jeans and the black T-shirt, inside out. "Where does this lead?"

He urged her to take the steps two at a time. "Just follow me," he said, worried that if the bad guys had infrared, they might have a Sonic Ear trained on them, too, and he didn't want them knowing that this led to an underground basement where it would be impossible to see their heat signature. From there they'd exit his house through a tunnel, one that ran beneath his driveway and opened to a path less than a hundred yards away. He only hoped there wouldn't be men out in the woods, though something told him there would be.

And they didn't have shoes.

He should have been expecting this. And if not expecting it, watching for it. Instead he'd been having sex.

It made him almost as bad as the major screwup who'd gotten his family killed.

They hit the basement running, Kait following behind him. He left the light off, but there was enough sunshine filtering in through the narrow windows that they could see the way. Not much farther.

The tunnel was at the opposite end of the basement. They'd have to squat as they ran through it, and their eyes would be blinded by sudden sunlight when they got to the other side. That would make it hard to see bogies, but it couldn't be helped.

He opened another hidden panel, helping Kait through and then closing it behind them.

"Chance," Kait cried as they were plunged into darkness, the smell of dank earth filling Chance's nostrils.

"I'm right here," he said, placing a hand against the side of the tunnel, using the other one to pull her forward. He knew the way, had practiced it at least a hundred times. You never knew when bad guys might blow your cover. That moment appeared to be now.

Would they be waiting? Had the bad guys been here when they'd arrived? Was that why his perimeter alarms hadn't gone off?

He could smell fresh pine-scented air long before they got there, the tunnel slanting up on a gradual incline that would take them to a natural outcropping of rock made to look like an animal burrow—a large animal burrow. He'd be able to see the surrounding area once his eyes adjusted, but not the area behind them. And if the others had already infiltrated the tunnel . . .

He refused to think about that. The temperature went from muggy to cool. He held Kait back, whispering, "Stay here," as he went to reconnoiter the area.

So far so good.

He let his eyes adjust.

He could hear voices, but they sounded faraway, as if the bad guys were calling out to one another. Searching for them. They'd have to make this quick or else the enemy might spot the motorbike.

"C'mon," he ordered Kait. He heard her harsh breaths, knew she followed behind, the occasional "Ouch" thrown in. No shoes. It would make crossing to the dirt bike more difficult. But if he had to, he'd pick her up. Pain could be ignored. They didn't call him Stonewall for nothing.

His head was the first thing to emerge, the back of his neck tingling as he listened for a sound that might save his life, such as the cocking of a gun or the snap of a twig. All he heard was the voices in the distance. He motioned Kait forward.

"Here!" They heard someone yell.

"Go," Chance yelled, urging Kait toward the bike. "Go, go, go."

Something crashed through the underbrush. Chance didn't need to look behind him to know what it was. Somehow he flung himself aboard, the two-cylinder engine *p-p-pop*ping to life. Kait slipped on behind him and they were off.

There was a nearly inaudible thud. He felt pressure whiz by his ear. Probes snaked by, their metallic tethers twanging like high-tension wire.

"Keep down," Chance called.

They crashed through underbrush, around pine trees. His bare foot worked the gears, first gear, second—

Something black came at them from his right. Chance leaned left just as another pop sounded. One of the pines saved his ass.

Third gear.

By now he was having to take the path faster than was safe with two riders. But they were almost away. Almost to the part where the path straightened out.

Fourth gear.

"Hold on," he called out.

They were going to make it. He took the last turn.

Fifth gear.

He heard it before he saw it.

Helicopter.

The path opened up. A black PAV-low hovered in front of him.

Shit!

Chance swerved off the path, but pine needles made the ground slick, and the bike's back end pitched wildly. He tried to hold on to it, but with Kait's weight on the back, there was no hope. He could feel the bike begin to fall, could hear Kait's gasp. He let go, twisted. Kait fell partly on top of him, and the two of them tumbled across pine needles like a frickin' rolling pin.

"Kait," he said when they finally stopped.

But she didn't answer, maybe because she couldn't hear him over the sound of the chopper. "Kait. We've got to get up."

"Not so fast, soldier," a voice called out.

Chance's head jerked up.

Someone stood over him. Someone dressed all in black. Black face paint, black hat, black flak jacket. Someone who looked an awful lot like—

"Chameleon," he said, his relief so great he almost bowed his head. Instead he turned to Kait. "You okay?" he asked again.

"Chameleon?" she asked, eyeing the man with black hair peeking out beneath a black cap.

"That's me, ma'am," Chameleon, aka Rick Santana, said. "I work for the same agency as Stonewall."

"How the hell—?" Chance asked.

"It was all part of the Agency's plan," Rick said. "We knew Stonewall would bring you here, but we couldn't risk telling him without alerting the bad guys. Seems we had a mole." Rick looked him in the eye. "But we've got him now."

"You could have told me."

"Honestly, we couldn't trust anybody." Rick turned to Kait. "Ma'am, you'll need to come with me. We need Chance's help mopping up the bad guys. You need to be taken to safety."

"But I—" She looked at Chance helplessly.

"Kait," Chance said.

They'd used them as frickin' bait.

But he'd dwell on that later. Right now he needed to get her out of here. "Go," he said. "I'll catch up with you."

"But Chance, I—"

"Go," he said again.

She didn't move. Chance bent down and kissed her softly, gently, his lips lingering, a part of him wondering if this would be the last time he'd ever see her.

"Go," he said after drawing back. "Go for me."

She held his gaze the longest time, something in the depths of her eyes making Chance's heart contract.

"Okay," she said.

He hated to let her go, but he did. Rick caught his eye. And even though he knew it was unprofessional, even though he knew he'd never hear the end of it, he mouthed the words, "Take care of her."

To his surprise, Rick mouthed the words, "I will."

Chapter Seven

SHE WAS TAKEN TO A TOP-SECRET MILITARY BASE. KAIT listened with dawning relief as she was debriefed. They'd caught the Libyans and the mole, thanks to their little trap. Kait was free to go home.

But where was Chance?

He didn't meet with her at the military base. Didn't pick her up as she half-thought he would. Didn't even call. He must have been held up. Unless he was—

She asked if he was okay. They reassured her that he was. But then why didn't he come to her?

It seemed surreal to be dropped back off at her vet clinic. Everything seemed exactly the same. No broken glass. No dead bodies. All was as it should be, the dogs in her kennel just as glad to see her as they always were.

Unreal.

She went home, waiting for Chance. She waited that whole night, and when her worry and fear got the better of her, she called the number on the business card she'd been handed. That was all it was, a phone number—no agency name, no nothing. Just the number.

Someone answered on the first ring.

"May I speak with Chance Owens?" she asked.

"I'm sorry," a sexy female voice said. "He's not available."

Jealousy reared its ugly head. "Can you tell him Kait Logan called?"

"Certainly, Dr. Logan."

Kait almost hung up, but at the last moment she said, "Wait."

"Yes?" the voice replied.

"Can you tell me . . . Do you mind letting me know . . . Is he okay?"

"He's fine, Dr. Logan."

Kait sighed in relief, then hung up the phone after an embarrassed good-bye. She wondered if the woman had to deal with calls like hers all the time. Did agents make a habit of jumping into bed with their clients? Was that what she was? A fling. It didn't feel like a fling, no matter how short a time they'd known each other.

But he didn't call.

One day faded into two. By the third day she was calling herself a fool for jumping into bed with him. Obviously it was all part of the game for him. A little danger. A little excitement. Some woman offering her body. No wonder he rescued women for a living.

By the fourth day the sting of embarrassment had faded into hurt, because no matter what she told herself, no matter how many times she called herself a fool, she'd felt something for him. And yet he didn't call.

She couldn't stop thinking about him. She couldn't stop reliving every moment they'd shared, every look, every touch, wondering if she'd succumbed to that mythical thing called love at first sight.

Lust at first sight, she quickly corrected herself. At least for him.

But not for her. For her it had been more than that. She didn't jump into bed with men who turned her on. This had been special. And unique. Only apparently he didn't feel the same way.

So she took deep breaths. Eventually the pain faded

into a dull throb. She wasn't pregnant. That was good. And the senator she'd contacted about her research finally returned her call. She learned she'd been given a special grant that would allow her to put her theory into practice next spring. That should've lifted her spirits— only it didn't.

November turned to December and before she knew it, Kait faced her annual Christmas party. Usually she closed the office down early and met with her half-dozen or so employees at a restaurant. But this year she decided to do something a little different. This year she held a party at her house, throwing herself into the planning as if there was no tomorrow. She did it as a way of forgetting Chance. Only she could never forget Chance. Never.

And so three days before Christmas her guests arrived. She dressed in a red-velvet Christmas dress, one with a pretty bow at the back. She'd decorated her single-story house with twinkling white lights that wrapped all around the porch and her landscaping. Inside she'd hung ribbons and bows and the occasional sprig of mistletoe, with her tree sitting in a corner of the cozy family room. She didn't live lavishly. She would never live lavishly. But she was proud of her little home and happy to show it off.

At least she wouldn't be alone tonight.

Stop it, she warned herself. It was over between her and Chance, not that there'd ever been anything between them. At least not on his part.

"It looks great," Abigail, her office manager, said as she arrived, her short blond hair intersected by reindeer antlers, her blue eyes shining with pleasure. "You've gone all out."

"I have, haven't I?" Kait asked, following her gaze. They both stared at the Christmas tree. Kait loved old-fashioned lights, the bright blues and greens and reds.

She loved tinsel and had tossed plenty of it on the boughs of her tree, so that the sweet-scented pine glittered like a casino.

"That poor tree," Abigail said, her sequined Christmas sweater sparkling as she turned back to Kait. "I'm surprised the branches haven't broken."

"I spent a fortune at Wal-Mart."

"Well, better you than me packing it all up a few weeks from now."

Which made Kait smile, a smile that faded. A part of her had been hoping to show the tree to Chance.

She threw herself into her party then, making sure there was plenty of eggnog to go around. And then, later, she had fun handing out presents, each of the gifts chosen personally. No generic gift baskets for her. She loved her employees as much as she loved the animals she helped.

"Good Lord, who is that?" Abigail gasped.

Kait followed her gaze, jerking upright so fast she sloshed eggnog over the rim of her glass.

"Chance," she gasped. Chance wearing faded blue jeans and a bright red jacket and hat—a Santa outfit. If she hadn't been so damn mad at him she would have laughed. She turned away, myriad emotions filling her. Humiliation. Embarrassment. Anger. She wasn't ready to face him. If she did, she might just sock him.

He caught up to her right at the entrance to her kitchen. "Kait," he said, catching her hand, turning her back to him.

Every one of her employees knew something was up. Silence settled over the room.

"Chance," she said softly, sharply.

"You're mad."

She flicked her chin up. "Why should I be mad that you finally got around to seeing me?"

"The First Noel" was playing in the background;

wrapping paper from the presents was strewn about. He looked so damn silly standing there with a Santa hat cocked off the side of his head.

And so damn good.

"I'm sorry."

"You should be."

"I told myself a hundred times to leave you alone. That what happened between us was all imagined."

"Yeah? That's what I told myself, too."

"No, it wasn't. You knew it was special. That's why you're so mad."

Her heart stopped in her chest, then beat so hard that adrenaline rushed through her body.

"Oh, yeah?" she asked.

"So I decided to test out a theory of mine."

"Oh? What's that—"

He kissed her.

Someone gasped. It wasn't her, though that's exactly what happened in her mind: She gasped and then drew back and tried to push him away.

Only she didn't do it. That feeling had overcome her, that feeling that surfaced when they'd touched—a feeling of coming home.

But at last sanity returned. She jerked her lips away. "Why the heck didn't you call me?"

"Because I didn't want to get involved with anybody. I told myself I didn't need the complication. Because I'd convinced myself the Agency needed me more than I need you."

"And does it?"

"No, Kait. It doesn't. I need you."

Her heart stopped again.

"I don't know what this is between us, Kait," he said softly. "I don't know where it will lead, but I don't want to ever let you go again."

Oh, Chance.

"Can you ever forgive me, Kait? Can you give us a second chance?"

Could she? Dare she? He'd left her high and dry. Would he do it again?

But as she stared into his eyes she knew the answer: In his eyes was the soul of a very special man, one she knew without a doubt she could love.

And in truth—they needed each other.

"Chance, I—"

He kissed her again, and Kait realized that he was afraid of her answer. And so she kissed him back, his big body softening, and the moment their lips touched she knew she'd made the right choice.

I love him, she found herself thinking. As bizarre and unbelievable as that might sound, she'd fallen for him.

And the most amazing thing of all, he'd fallen for her. It was there in his eyes for all the world to see. When he drew back her employees saw it. She saw it. She had a feeling their families up in heaven saw it.

And then he bent and whispered the words in her ear. Kait closed eyes that suddenly had tears coming out of them. This couldn't be happening. This really, truly couldn't be happening.

But it was.

She didn't know where it would lead, but it was real. *He* was real. And he was here, in her arms, where she hoped he would stay forever.

Epilogue

"DR. KAITLYN LOGAN?"

Kaitlyn suppressed a grin as she pretended to study the charts in front of her.

"Are you Dr. Kaitlyn Logan?" the man repeated.

At last she looked up, meeting the gaze of the man who stood in the doorway. "Actually, I'm not. I'm Dr. Kaitlyn Owens, so if you're about to shoot me with meat tenderizers, I'm afraid I'm not your girl."

The man came into the room as Kait leaned back in her chair, her hand resting against her protruding belly.

"You look like Dr. Kaitlyn Logan—except for the belly, of course."

"Yeah, well, some man knocked me up. Can you believe that?"

He came to her side, Kait's teasing smile turning to one of happiness as she stared up at him.

"Lucky man," he said.

"No," she answered. "Lucky woman."

"Oh, yeah? Why's that?"

"Because not only did I find a man willing to dress up in a Santa suit for me, but he has the most amazing job."

"Yeah," Chance said, drawing her into his arms. "Making you happy."

"You *do* make me happy. Even if you do have to go off and rescue damsels in distress on a regular basis."

"It's not just damsels."

"Was it a man this time?"

He shook his head. "A couple."

"But you helped them."

"Don't I always?"

"Yes," she said, turning sideways so she could snuggle better. "But I wish you didn't have to."

"Kait—"

"Shh," she said, leaning back to place her fingers against his lips. "Don't say it. I know."

"I'm taking fewer missions, staying closer to home—"

"I know," she said.

"But you still worry."

"I still worry."

"You know why I do it."

"I know why you do it," she said. Chance watched as her eyes filled with warmth, the planes and angles of her face softened by her pregnancy. "And how can I stop you from doing something that ultimately brought you to me?"

He smiled down at her. "You've always understood."

"I do. But I miss you. Especially on days like today, when I have an ultrasound and the doctor asks me if I want to know what sex our baby is."

He felt his heart quicken, felt his whole body tense as he waited to hear whether she'd found out or not.

"Do you want to know?"

"I'm not sure I do," he surprised himself by saying.

"Well, if you change your mind . . . ?"

She slipped out of his arms.

"Wait a minute," he said, smiling and laughing a bit as he pulled her back. "Okay. Go ahead. Tell me."

"Are you sure?"

"I'm sure."

She smiled, but it was a smile unlike the ones that had

come before it. A soft smile full of tenderness and love.
"We're having a—" Her chin tipped down. She looked
up at him through suddenly teasing eyes.

"Kaitlyn—"

But then the teasing look faded. She reached up and
placed a hand against his cheek. "We're having a girl,
Chance. A beautiful baby girl. You should have seen
her. She was perfect." And then her eyes were full of
tears. Her lips wobbled a bit. "So completely perfect,"
she said softly.

"Oh, Kait. I'm sorry I missed it."

"No," she said, her nose sounding clogged. "Don't
be sorry. You were doing what you should be doing—
helping people. Saving lives. Little Samantha will be so
proud of her daddy."

Sam. His sister's name.

"Kait," he said softly.

"We always said—"

"But you don't have to do it."

"Yes, I do. Samantha Amanda Owens. After your
mom and sister. It's a fitting name for a little girl whose
father—"

He kissed her. She kissed him back immediately, her
taste just as sweet and wonderful to him as it'd been the
first time their mouths had touched.

God, he loved this woman.

He'd been so damn lucky to find her. She was his gift
from heaven. His miracle. Sometimes he even thought
she was his reward for the horror he went through all
those years ago. She and the baby were his family, his
only family, and he vowed to protect them like he'd
vowed to keep other innocents from harm.

She pulled back, murmuring, "I love you."

"I love you, too," he said softly. And then his eyes
caught on the computer monitor on her desk. Red dots
were sprinkled across a map of Northern California.

"How are they doing?" he asked.

She half-turned, peering down at the screen. "So far not a single one of them has strayed from their migratory path."

"In other words, it's working."

She looked up at him. "Did you ever doubt it would?"

"Never," he said, about to kiss her again when something stopped him. "What is it?" he asked.

She glanced back at the screen. "I just worry someone will take what I've done—"

"—And turn it into something bad," he finished for her. "I know. And it's a possibility. I won't lie. But that's what I'm here for, Kait. That's what all of us are here for. To make the world a better place. You're doing it with your birds, and I'm doing it with my military background. Together the two of us are a hell of a team."

She grabbed his hand. "Together the three of us are a hell of a team."

And when she reached up on tiptoe and placed a kiss against his jaw, Chance felt tears come to his eyes. He'd never thought to have this. Never thought to have the love of a woman like Kaitlyn. He loved her with a fierceness that took his breath away. And now that she was pregnant, he figured it wouldn't hurt to slow down a bit, maybe take even fewer missions.

They kissed. Chance pulled her closer. Yeah, he found himself thinking. It wouldn't hurt at all to stay closer to home.

"I love you," she murmured again.

"I love you, too." And just in case she doubted his words, he tried to show her just how much without using words. And then he showed her again later than night, and the next day, too. Chance vowed to prove his words every day of his life.

And he did.

KILLER CHRISTMAS

Kelsey Roberts

Prologue

"OH SHIT! SANTA'S DEAD."

Although Meghan Beckham's heart jumped into her throat, she forced herself not to look up from the semi-cluttered desk in spite of her assistant's panicked tone. Terri Smith—as she'd learned in the past six months—panicked easily and often. Calm was Meghan's watch-word. Since her brother's death it seemed everyone was either counting on her to exhibit the serenity of a Madonna or shatter into a million pieces. No middle ground was acceptable. She took a long, deep breath and exhaled slowly.

"Not possible," Meghan said, affixing her signature to a memo that would authorize her gaggle of attorneys to begin buying the buildings on either side of the store.

"Santa died yesterday." Meghan paused to shove her reading glasses back into place. "We sent flowers to his widow, and you were right here when I called his wife and offered the whole family our condolences and anything they wanted from the store, remember?" The man had worked for Beckham's for two seasons, and his death had shaken her, reminding her of her own long-denied need to mourn her brother's death. But there hadn't been time. There still wasn't time. Everyone was counting on her. "So, yes, Terri, I'm aware he d—"

"No, ma'am!" Terri cut in.

That got her attention. Meghan peered up to find the girl she'd inherited from her brother looking even more pale and flustered than usual. It wasn't that Terri was unattractive, though a trim and a few highlights would do wonders for her hair. New clothes were easy. Beckham's was *the* landmark store in Palm Beach—had been since 1924.

"He's dead, ma—Miss Beckham."

"Got that yesterday," Meghan insisted, feeling her stomach begin to churn. *Where is my antacid?* "He had a heart attack on his coffee break. The agency was supposed to send a replacement this morning."

"Dead too."

"The *replacement* Santa?"

Terri nodded. "As a carp."

Meghan shot to her feet. "This is not possible," she repeated what was becoming her mantra de jour. "This is horrible," she gushed on a rush of air. "Has someone called nine-one-one? Notified next of kin? Called the police?"

"Miss Beckham?" Terri interrupted. "He's not just dead. It's *worse*."

"What could possibly be worse than dead? Very dead?" Meghan was losing her grip.

"A knife. Sticking right out of his belly that no longer jiggles like a bowl full of jelly." Terri spread her arms. "A really *big* knife. A *seriously* big knife."

A knife—God help her—was *not* death by natural causes. Not by any stretch of the imagination. "Back up. Have the police been called?"

"Yes."

She rounded the desk, catching the pocket of her vintage Chanel suit on the corner. She heard the *riiiip* of fabric and didn't care. Employees and customers would be arriving and she didn't want them traumatized, nor did she want to compromise the dignity of the poor dead

Santa. "Please, Terri. Please tell me he isn't propped up in the middle of the Christmas display where everyone can see him."

"No, ma'am. I mean, no, Miss Beckham."

Relief washed over her. That was something, at least.

"He's in the front window."

Chapter One

"NOT GOING TO HAPPEN," MEGHAN SAID EMPHATI-
cally as she scribbled her nearly illegible signature on a
check. She ignored the dismissive snort from Barrett
Trent, who relaxed in the chair opposite her desk.

Terri was sitting on a sofa in the outer office. Meghan
knew this because she could see the scuffed heels of
her assistant's shoes through the crack in the door. Terri
should have been at her desk, but she obviously had
moved to the small settee, not even bothering to conceal
the fact that she was listening in on the conversation.

Barrett had lost weight in the two years since a serious
heart attack and accompanying quadruple bypass had
grudgingly forced him into early retirement. He was still
a dashing man, even though he'd traded his hand-
tailored Italian suits for crisp, colorful golf attire. The
canary yellow shirt and pleated navy shorts revealed
skin tanned by lazy afternoons at the club. At sixty-two,
his light brown hair was just beginning the transition to
gray at the temples.

"It's already happened," he stated with the same
authority he'd wielded during his long tenure as Beckham's in-house counsel. "He'll be here in a few minutes."

Meghan's hand stilled, poised above the neatly typed
check to Yardly Investigations. She didn't recognize the

vendor, but was so distracted by Barrett's announcement that she tossed the check aside momentarily to glare at the older man. "You don't get to make decisions around here anymore," she reminded him gently. "Especially not bad ones."

Barrett smiled patiently and looked at her in that I-know-what's-best-for-you, fatherly fashion that made it almost impossible for her to stand her ground. Almost.

"No, Barrett. It's the height of the Christmas season. How would it look for me to be walking around the store with some muscle-bound, gun-toting, minimum IQ, moronic bodyguard glued to me? It would scare the customers who aren't already too scared to shop here because of the . . . *incidents*."

"It's—"

"Oh . . . wow," Terri gushed loudly from the outer office.

Meghan glanced toward the partially opened door and frowned. "Excuse me for a moment," she apologized, standing and straightening the wrinkles from her just-a-tad-too-short Lilly Pulitzer skirt to the most appropriate length she could manage given the small amount of fabric she had at her disposal. "I need to have a few words with my assistant."

You're and *fired* would be good. And, in spite of the fact that she couldn't function without an assistant at this time of year, she might have said them.

One glimpse of the tall, dark, incredibly gorgeous man sucked every bit of oxygen from her lungs. *Wow?* Wow didn't even begin to cover it! It took her a few seconds to recover.

"This totally hot guy says he's here to see you, ma'am," Terri announced. It was as close to an appropriate introduction as the young woman ever ventured.

Meghan forced a smile and tried to recall how to speak . . . aloud. Not a simple task given that the man was looking at her with the most intense green eyes she'd ever seen. He wasn't just looking. His gaze roamed freely from her head to the tips of the hyacinth pink toenails peeking out from her Jimmy Choo patent slides. The fact that he'd scanned her like a document wasn't the worst part—nope. It was his lack of reaction. Nothing. Nada. Zero. Zippo.

Her vanity was seriously wounded, but she managed to keep the smile from slipping completely off her face.

Her spine stiffened as she extended her hand and summoned every measure of aloofness in her being. "I'm Meghan Beckham. And you are?"

He didn't take her hand. Instead he nodded a cursory acknowledgment, then brushed past her as if she were invisible.

"He's hot as sh—" Meghan shut the door to her office before Terri could finish her comment.

Mr. No Name–No Interest was inspecting her office. *Right!* her little voice screamed. *My office!*

She stepped forward and was all set to tell him to leave when Barrett rose and said, "Meghan, meet Jack Palmer."

His back was to her as he looked out the picture window behind her desk. "First thing we do is relocate her. Is there another office available?"

She was fuming. "Actually, in polite society, the *first* thing we do is introduce ourselves."

His broad shoulders strained the soft cotton fabric of his snug black polo shirt. So he had a great body. So what? He had the manners of a toad. "But feel free to speak *about* me instead of *to* me."

He moved quickly and with a stealthy quiet that belied his size. In what seemed like the blink of an eye, he was standing in front of her. Well, not standing so much as towering, and not in front so much as over her. Meghan didn't like that. She didn't like the intimidation this man radiated. Or his chiseled features. Or the deep lines etched around his mouth and eyes. She didn't like that he smelled faintly of soap and coffee. Mostly, she didn't like that she noticed all those things. Or that noticing them made her tingle all over.

"I'm not really concerned about polite society, Miss Beckham. That's not what you're paying me for."

She nearly choked on that one. "I didn't hire you, so—"

Barrett placed a hand on her forearm, silencing her before Meghan could think of a good way to tell Palmer a) that she wasn't paying him and b)where he could find the very fastest way to hell.

Jack stared down into eyes as volatile as a thundercloud. It took a substantial amount of willpower to maintain his bland expression. Meghan Beckham was not at all what he'd expected.

When he'd learned from Roz that his next assignment was a single woman who ran a department store in Florida, Land of Retirees, he'd pictured an older woman in a tailored suit with blue hair and one of those big broach thingies pinned on her shoulder. Not this. Definitely not her.

His pulse increased just being close to her. The only thing blue about Meghan was her eyes. Well, not blue, exactly, more like blue flecked with brilliant silvery specks. The effect was stunning, as was her face. If she had a flaw, he sure couldn't see it. Not in her high cheekbones, delicate jawline, or that mouth that practically begged to be kissed.

"I don't know what you've been told, Mr. Palmer."

Man, she made his name sound like a vile curse.

"But I have no need of your . . . *services*."

She scooted around him—which was just fine, because it gave him another opportunity to check out her tanned, toned legs—and went to her desk. She went to the checkbook and tore the next one out of the book, scribbled on it hurriedly, then held it between her fingertips and arched one perfectly shaped brow. "Your services are not needed. But thank you, this should cover your inconveniences for the day. Have my assistant validate your parking receipt on your way out."

"I hear differently," he replied easily, shifting so that he was half-leaning against her credenza. "Two dead Santas can't be a good thing for you or your business."

"The police department is investigating. I'm sure they'll do their civic duty and find whoever is responsible," she informed him.

"With time, probably," he agreed, absently raking his fingers through his hair. "Maybe faster if they had your cooperation."

Her cheeks colored slightly, offset completely by the almost arrogant tilt to her chin. "I *am* cooperating."

He drew in a deep breath and let it out slowly. "You were told the best course of action would be for you to close the store, right?"

"Not best for me," she promised him, tossing her long, blond hair off her shoulders. "Not best for the thirty-five employees at Beckham's—some of whom have been with us for nearly half a century. And definitely not the best thing for our customers just three weeks shy of Christmas."

"I passed a lot of overpriced stores on my way here. I'm sure your customers could find four-hundred-dollar blouses in any number of them."

The smile she offered didn't reach her eyes. "They could," she readily agreed. "But why would they when ours are thirty percent off?"

"I spoke with Cerventes, the detective assigned to the case. They have no leads and nothing tying the victims together. Nothing but you and your store." She faltered for a second but recovered nicely. While she did look like a decent breeze could blow her the couple of blocks into the ocean, he sensed a distinct strength about her.

"Not me, Mr. Palmer. The common denominator is

Santa." She waved the check as if it was a red flag to his bull and turned to the mute older man sitting in the chair wearing a bright smile. "This was obviously a mistake. So in fairness, I'm paying for your time, Mr. Palmer. I'm swamped, so we're done here."

Jack didn't move a muscle. "That isn't how this works."

"Pardon me?"

"I get paid when the job is done."

"It is done, Mr. Palmer. It won't get any *doner*." She put the check on top of the files on her desk. "I'm too busy to waste any more time on this. If you're unwilling to accept this check, send a bill here to the store and I'll see that you're appropriately compensated."

The corners of his mouth twitched. He really wanted to laugh at her. Did she actually think that dismissive, big-deal-executive tone would work on him?

"Be reasonable, Meghan," he heard Barrett plead. "Jack here is the best. He'll keep an eye on you until the cops find out who's killing your Santas and why."

"Because there's a Christmas-hating lunatic on the loose?" she suggested.

"It's not about Christmas," Jack offered reasonably.

She sighed her irritation. "You've been here all of—" She paused to check the pricey watch decorating her slender wrist. "—ten minutes and you've already solved the case?"

"Something like that." He pushed off the furniture, hearing it squeak a bit in the process. As he approached her desk, he noted challenge brimming in those pretty eyes. "While I was at the police station, I had a look at the files."

She had a cute little mole on her right cheek. Distracting little sucker, too.

"Santa Number One was most likely poisoned. That usually means a woman perpetrator."

She shrugged. "I could have gotten that bit of insight from Court TV."

December in Florida meant lots of bare skin. Jack liked that about the state. Miss Meghan Beckham's arms, as well as her pretty legs, were bare. Another distraction. Obviously, Miss Beckham avoided the sun. No leathery, beach-baked skin for her. Nope. "But Santa Number Two was stabbed; that's pretty much a guy thing."

"Are you insinuating there are two Christmas-hating lunatics running around Palm Beach?"

"Depends."

He could almost hear a flurry of questions racing through her mind. Eventually, she settled on the obvious. "On what?"

Chapter Two

"IT DEPENDS ON YOU, MISS BECKHAM. MORE SPECIFI-
cally, on whether or not you buy the illogical concept
that there could be two killers who just happened to target your store inside a week."

Okay, so any reply would make her look like a fool.
Meghan opted to remain quiet. It wasn't that she wasn't
scared—who wouldn't be in the aftermath of two
murders in such close proximity? It was admitting that
she was scared. And having Jack—disturbing, intriguing Jack—around twenty-four hours a day, seven days a
week for the foreseeable forever was terrifying. It would
mean she'd lose those precious moments she reserved to
grieve for her brother. She'd lose what little time she had
to draw on her reserve of strength to face the next day as
the sole heir to the Beckham legend. It would mean depending on someone. Something she had never done
with anyone but Michael. She wasn't at all sure she was
ready or even able to take that kind of risk again.

At Jack's request, over Meghan's strong objection,
and as if choreographed, Casey Trent-Beckham appeared. Meghan greeted her brother's widow with a
hug, then watched as Casey whisked her father out of
the office. Meghan was fairly certain that the old guy
had prearranged his departure. Barrett was thorough

like that—left nothing to chance. And what better ruse than Casey? Everyone knew that Casey could barely stand to set foot in the store since Michael's death, in spite of the fact that she had practically grown up as a Beckham before marrying one.

Meghan watched as Jack sauntered over and fell comfortably into the chair vacated by Barrett—*that manipulative coward.* She'd speak to the cowardly one later, but for now, her attention was totally and completely on the man flipping through the small notepad he'd pulled from the back pocket of his slacks.

It wasn't fair that the first man in, well, forever, to pique her libido's interest had to be *this* man. This guy wasn't even a possibility. He was everything she didn't want in a lover. He was arrogant, stoic, controlling— too bad, because he was downright toe-curling. *Not,* she pointed out to herself sternly, that she was considering him as a lover.

Meghan reminded herself that she wasn't interviewing for a lover. Or a husband. Or, even, God help her this temptation, a sperm donor. Unfortunately, and annoyingly, like most women on the ugly side of thirty, she was hearing the faint *tick-tock* of her biological clock. A spouse would be nice, children were in her probability column, but at this juncture, she'd probably have to settle for the fantasy of sex on a regular basis and keep all that other stuff on the back burner.

It had been a while since her last meaningful interpersonal relationship imploded. Just a few months back, she'd been thinking she was ready to try again, but until half an hour ago there'd been no one who floated her boat. Meghan reminded herself of her brother's favorite cliché: "Careful what you wish for."

"I'll need some additional information in order to set a schedule for you to follow."

Sighing loudly, she sat down behind the protection of her large desk, lacing her fingers and resting her forearms on the smooth surface of her desk. "You aren't going to go away, are you?"

"No."

Damn Santa killers and damn Barrett. "My schedule is chaotic at this point. In fact, my hours can be grueling."

He cocked his head and she saw a twitch of amusement at the corners of his mouth. "Really?"

"Yes. You look like you're in decent shape, but it is a hectic pace."

"Put your mind at ease, Miss Beckham. In my former life I occasionally had to run alongside cars, so I think I can handle whatever you've got going on."

She cocked her head. "Did you, indeed?"

"Former Secret Service." All business—*her* business—he gave her a cool look. "This isn't about me, so can we continue?"

Sure, 'cause I want to spill my guts to a stranger. "I try to arrive by six and I rarely leave before ten."

He scribbled something, then lifted his chin so those brilliant green eyes met hers. "Step one is to vary your routine."

She smiled stiffly while gritting her teeth so hard her jaw started to hurt.

"Step two is relocation."

"I'm sorry, but that isn't possible."

"None of this is open for discussion, Miss Beckham."

"I beg to differ." She hated that she could almost imagine herself begging for a few other things as well. Did he have to be so damned attractive?

"Beg all you want. These are the rules."

"What makes you think your rules have any meaning around here, Mr. Palmer? Maybe you missed the sign out front. This is Beckham's, and as *the* Beckham, Barrett's meddling aside, I generally have the final word on things." At one time it would've been her brother Michael sitting behind this giant desk. He and their grandfather before him had left enormous shoes for Meghan to fill. But Michael had died in the car accident six months ago, the accident that had done nothing more than give her an already fading scar on her knee and a slowly healing hole in her heart.

"Have a lot of experience with murder, do you?"

Point in his favor. "No. But I am hopeful the police will apprehend—"

"Hope all you want. Hope is good. But in my experience, you won't have a lot of luck hoping away someone hell-bent on killing you."

"Killing Santa," she corrected, as a shiver of real and tangible fear slipped the length of her spine. "This is Palm Beach, Mr. Palmer. We don't have serial killers and, more specifically, I don't have enemies like the kind you're describing. Hell, I barely have time for friends. It doesn't make any sense that someone would want to kill me."

His brow furrowed into deep, distinct lines. "When was the last time you spoke to Detective Cerventes?"

She felt a small pang of guilt. "I talked to him for a few minutes the day Santa Number Two was killed. Since then we've been playing phone tag and—"

"You didn't think he might have something important to tell you?"

"No. I assumed he was simply calling with a courtesy update."

She watched as he blew a breath in the direction of his forehead. "Jeez, lady, we'll back up. *Now* step one is getting you up to speed."

She bristled slightly at the open annoyance in his tone. "You've told me everything you learned from the police, so let's go right back to negotiating step two. I can't vary my arrival time, but I'm willing to discuss my departure times."

He laughed. Not a toss-your-head-back belly laugh,

more like a short chuckle that managed to aggravate her to the edge of reason.

"Discuss? Negotiate?" he mockingly repeated as if they were new words she'd invented on the spot. "You don't get it, do you?"

"Sure I do." She met and held his gaze. "I'm sensing that due to the nature of your work you're probably a control freak who either doesn't respect women or just doesn't like working for them—too soon to tell. I get that you're used to people jumping when you bark orders. I get that you were under the delusion that you could walk in here and I'd be so blinded by your looks that I'd tow the line no questions asked. I get—"

"Blinded by my looks?" he asked with a far too self-satisfied grin. "I wouldn't have pegged you as the kind of woman to admit something like that."

"Get over yourself, Mr. Palmer. I'm sure you've got mirrors at your place. You know you're attractive and I'm fairly sure you use that to full advantage when the need arises. Don't try to be coy; it doesn't suit you at all."

"No, it doesn't," he agreed quickly.

Too quickly, the little voice in her head warned.

"We aren't negotiating or debating here, Meghan. It's my job to keep you from getting killed and I'm very good at my job as long as the client understands the . . . parameters of the situation."

"Believe me, I understand that someone has killed two seasonal employees in my store." *When did I become 'Meghan'? And why does it sound so good when he says it?* "Not the kind of pre-Christmas publicity I wanted, to say nothing of the poor families who are dealing with their grief at a time when the rest of the world is festive and celebrating all around them."

Jack heard the words as well as the conviction behind them. He filed away the revelation that compassion slipped into empathy somewhere along the line. Death was personal to this woman. Was it her father? Mother? A lover, maybe? He reined in those thoughts, dropping his gaze and rubbing the back of his neck, hoping all of his actions camouflaged the fact that he was mildly disturbed thinking about her with a lover. "Due respect, Meghan, you're not seeing the big picture."

When he glanced up, he saw a kaleidoscope of raw emotion swirl in those silvery blue eyes of hers that knotted his gut. To her credit, she regrouped almost immediately, slipping back into seasoned-executive mode. "And I can tell by your tone that you're dying to tell me something you think has slipped my grasp."

Leaning forward in his seat, he flipped the pad closed. "I don't have a tone. Look." He paused to rake one hand through his hair again. "Let's start over, okay?"

She shrugged or nodded—didn't matter. What counted was that she didn't tell him to leave again, so he assumed that was his cue to continue. "The killer wasn't after the Santas. He or she is working their way to you."

Scoffing, she shook her head. "Not possible. There isn't a person on the planet who dislikes me enough to kill me."

"I'm pretty certain there is. If not, he or she would kill Santas all over the island and not just here at Beckham's."

"I don't have enemies, Mr. Palmer. If someone really wanted to kill me, why waste time on innocent men in Santa suits? I'm not convinced."

"After I spoke with him, Detective Cerventes isn't completely convinced either. He told me he'd been trying to talk to you. Said you brushed him off for meetings or whatever. I guess Barrett figured you'd have a harder time brushing me off."

Meghan rubbed her face, soaking in all the information. She was playing the past few days in her head in fast forward. She was dodging people—anyone, everyone—except vendors, customers, and all things Beckham's.

Her sole focus had been on posting a killer Christmas season but she'd never meant that *literally*. Fifty percent of the store's annual revenues came between Thanksgiving and Christmas. With the deals pending for the expansion, she needed the cash flow. It had been her focus—apparently a blinding one.

"So what are you suggesting, Mr. Palmer?" Her mind was working in hyperdrive. "Wait! Did you talk to the detective or go see him? I'm confused. How long have you been involved in this little investigation?"

"I spoke to him by telephone after the first Santa incident. I went to his office on my way here."

"And Barrett found you how?"

"We worked together on another project," he said.

Meghan wasn't too keen on his evasive answer, but something told her that was probably the best she was going to get. Still, persistence was one of her strong suits. "Mr. Palmer, I'm going to need a little more than that."

"First, try calling me Jack. 'Mr. Palmer' seems a little formal given that we'll be glued together for the foreseeable future."

"I know Barrett is worried about my safety and the safety of everyone who works in this store. So are the Palm Beach police. We're all being careful. I've posted additional guards at the entry and exit doors and—"

"All good baby steps, Meghan," he concluded. "But you're forgetting the really important thing."

"Which is?"

"Someone already tried to kill you once."

Chapter Three

"NOT YOU, TOO," SHE SNAPPED. "BARRETT IS WRONG. IT was an accident. A senseless, unfortunate accident. I know. I was in the car. I can assure you, there was nothing malicious about it. Nobody was out to get us."

"Your brother is dead."

"Yes," she returned crisply, her eyes filled with deep sorrow. "And his passing isn't something I discuss."

"Maybe he was the target and you were just collateral damage. An acceptable loss. After all, he was the heir to the Beckham empire."

"Something he never wanted," she assured him quickly. "How do you know all this?"

"Barrett," he supplied, keeping Roz and the Agency out of it for now. He was dumping a lot of information on her at once. "He also told me what would have happened had both you and your brother died in that car crash."

"Did he tell you that his fears stem from his loving devotion to his daughter?" Meghan challenged. "If his theory was correct—and that's a huge if—and if I had died as well, then Casey, as Michael's widow, would have inherited, making her the next target. Barrett worships Casey and I think his completely understandable adoration has clouded his judgment in this instance."

"Or not," he said with a shrug. "You're the one with the iron-clad family trust documents. So answer me this one, if you die now, who gets all this?"

She sighed heavily. "Technically . . . Casey. I don't have any other family. Apparently my father had planned on Michael or me producing the next generation of Beckhams a little faster than we managed. Or didn't manage, as the case may be."

"So Barrett's concern for his daughter isn't without merit."

"Yes, it is," she insisted, tenting her fingers on her desktop as she leaned forward. "The accident was an accident. You're a self-proclaimed expert on murder, so you tell me. If someone had been trying to kill us both that night, why wait six months to try again?"

"Opportunity," he suggested. "Maybe the killer had to regroup after the first attempt failed."

"Maybe it's more likely that there's someone out there with a real hatred for Santa." She shook her head. "I don't know, Mr. Palmer. I just have a hard time believing any of this is a possibility. You didn't know Michael. I did. He didn't have enemies either."

"None?"

"None," she answered quickly. "He was a very laid-back guy. Much to the disappointment of our father, Michael didn't have a competitive bone in his body. That's why he hated all this. He was more than willing to delegate anything and everything to Sam or me."

"Sam?"

She nodded and he noted that her expression softened. "Sam Shelton came to work at Beckham's as a clerk. Worked his way up the ranks and is the executive vice president. He was hand-picked by my father. Over Casey's minor objection, Sam served as best man at Michael's wedding.

"After Dad died, Michael felt so guilty that he made an honest attempt at running the store. Sam spent hours in here trying to teach Michael all the things he needed to know to step in as CEO. He was making headway, then the accident happened and . . ." Her voice trailed off.

"You survive the *accident*, end up as CEO, and Sam gets what?"

Her eyes narrowed to angry gray slits. "I don't appreciate your implication, Mr. Palmer. Sam Shelton has been an important and trusted member of the Beckham's family for twenty years, knowing full well that this was, is, and will be a family-owned and -operated business. Sam's never asked for or expected anything more than the generous salary and bonuses he receives."

"Then he's either a saint or as dumb as a stick," Jack mumbled.

"No, you're a cynic," she tossed back at him. "Are you so jaded that you can't appreciate or even recognize loyalty and commitment?"

"Normal people tend to be loyal to themselves first."

"Oh, for—Sam was Michael's *best friend*. There's no way he would have hurt him."

"And you?"

"Not a possibility," she insisted. "He's like a brother to me."

"But Casey doesn't like him?"

She shrugged. "Casey and Sam vied for Michael's attentions. Don't get that look," she warned. "Not like *that*. Michael didn't bat for both teams. I'm just saying that until Casey and Michael got together, it was always Sam and Michael. I'm sure deep down Casey and Sam don't really hate each other or anything."

"You're telling me that Sam didn't want control of the store. And Casey didn't want control of the store. So who did?"

"Me."

"Are you going to stop calling me Mr. Palmer anytime soon?" He asked a few hours later as he watched her bundle spreadsheets into her briefcase.

Realizing nothing shy of a nuclear explosion would get him off his assignment, she relented. "So, Jack, how exactly does this work? I mean, how close do you have to be?"

He shrugged and flashed her that melting smile. "I don't have to see you naked. Not that that would be a problem, if it comes up."

"Nothing is going to come up." Meghan felt a smile tugging at the corners of her mouth. *Man, can this guy diffuse tension, or what?* "I think I can safely promise you that you may cross seeing me naked off your list of duties."

"You never know. I like to be prepared. Seriously, Meghan, we do need to revamp your life. Every aspect of it, from the time you wake up until the minute your head hits the pillow."

While logic and common sense promised her he was absolutely right, she also knew the ramifications of what he was suggesting. It wasn't just her fiscal duties. She had a responsibility to the employees and told him as much. He didn't take it well.

Temper flashed in his eyes and his mouth pulled into a taut, unyielding line. "The name Beckham is going to mean squat when the only place people will see it is on your toe tag in the morgue. How exactly do you plan to carry on the fine Beckham's tradition when you're dead?"

"Apparently, you're here to prevent that improbable possibility. You do your job so I can do mine." He rolled his eyes at her, something that didn't sit too well. "Look, Jack. I understand that this is a horrible situation that has already cost two innocent, nice old guys their lives. I don't buy that it's about me, but right now isn't a really good time for me to go hide under a rock until this loon is caught. Cozy up to that idea and come up with some sort of plan that works within the parameters of my responsibilities here at the store."

He stood, ramming his fists into his pockets in the process. "Shouldn't your first priority be to stay alive?"

"It is," she assured him, trying not to give in to the intimidation of his raised voice. "If you're as good as you say you are, you should be able to work around my schedule."

"I'm at my best when my client doesn't have a serious case of the stupids." He marched over to the framed collection of diplomas above the credenza. Jack opened and closed his fists inside his pockets. He didn't care about her academic history—hell, he already knew most of it. He ground his teeth, reining in his anger.

The last time he'd been faced with a stubborn female depending on his protection, it had ended badly. The memory of it still caused a knot in his gut. Pushing those thoughts aside, he scanned her achievements—honors graduate of Wellesley and the Wharton School of Business. Impressive, but not as interesting to him as the photographs he spotted.

He knew from the dossier Roz had sent along with the rest of the information on the assignment—and those great oatmeal cookies—that Meghan wasn't anyone's first choice to assume the helm of the store when Beckham Sr. passed. He guessed the identity of the vibrant face of the young man smiling in the picture. So this was Michael Beckham. This was the favorite son and heir apparent.

This was the dead brother. And the only one with a scintilla of a reason to want him out of the picture was Meghan. She was a smart woman. Too smart to have rigged an accident that could very easily have killed her as well and not leave a single fleck of forensic evidence behind. Nor did she impress him as the suicidal type, so who was killing the part-time employees. And why?

She did, however, impress him as annoying as hell as their day progressed. They'd argued about the elevator—he made her use the stairs. About the car—he insisted on using his SUV. And the route to her home—he'd taken a scenic route and driven past the trendy address twice just to be sure.

"Nice digs," Jack remarked almost two hours later when she showed him inside her massive seaside home and he waited while she disabled the alarm.

"It was a lot nicer before the evil stepmother got hold of it," she supplied. "Her redecorating—and that's being kind—has taken a lot of time, effort, and energy to undo."

Jack reached out and took hold of her upper arm. He didn't expect the jolt he felt as his fingertips closed on her smooth, warm skin. "Turn it back on," he insisted, gently turning her back toward the alarm's keypad.

"Sorry," she muttered. "I don't normally have it on when I'm home."

She punched a series of numbers on the keypad but he was distracted by the fact that her hair smelled like fresh flowers. "You do now."

"Right."

Her perfume was subtle and expensive. "You've got to change the code. Using your birth date in reverse order is too easy."

"Not a problem. I'll call the alarm company in the morning."

"Evil stepmother?" he asked, realizing he was still holding on to her arm. "Audrey, right?"

She turned and peered up at him, her mouth curved into a distinct frown. "You're pretty well versed on my life, Jack, and I gotta tell you, it kind of creeps me out since I know just about nothing about you."

"Part of my job," he insisted as he followed her through the arched foyer into an expansive living room that looked more like a gallery than a private home.

What he knew about art could fit inside a thimble, but he'd bet his last dollar that the paintings and sculptures represented big bucks.

"So what's the deal with Audrey?" They passed through a good six thousand square feet of house before ending up in a state-of-the-art kitchen.

Meghan tossed her purse and briefcase on a tiled countertop before she grabbed two glasses from an overhead rack. "Wine?"

He shook his head. "Not for me, thanks. We were discussing Audrey?"

"Anything involving Audrey means I need alcohol." Meghan slipped off her shoes as she went to a glass-fronted refrigerated cabinet and retrieved a bottle of chardonnay.

A fancy opener was mounted on the counter above the cabinet. Jack's brain catalogued all this stuff not because he was awed by the obvious wealth. Money was almost always a viable motive and Meghan seemed to have a fair amount of it. He filed that away as a possible road leading to whoever was so hell-bent on killing her.

Straddling a stool adjacent to the center island, Jack watched as she poured herself a generous amount of wine. He liked the way she moved. She was an intriguing blend of polished breeding and complete lack of pretense. He could easily see her holding her own as a society hostess as well as kicking back on the beach. Secretly, he liked the beach image better. There was something really appealing about the vision of her in a revealing bikini, slathered with glistening sunscreen, an ocean breeze in her hair.

"Hot?"

Jack felt his eyes grow wide at her question. "What?"

"You're flushed—too warm, I'm guessing. I can turn up the air-conditioning. Sorry, I tend to keep the house warm, especially to nonnatives."

"It is a little warm in here," he admitted. He didn't

share that the heat surging through him wasn't completely related to the early-December heat wave. Though it was nearly midnight, the temperature still hovered just shy of eighty.

She smiled. A smile he felt in every cell of his body. "I love the breeze off the ocean at night. Let's go out on the lanai."

"That's not safe."

She rolled her eyes. "It is unless our Santa Slasher has his own navy. The Coast Guard is very attentive and there's a private security company that patrols the streets as well as the shoreline. Lighten up, Jack. This place is a fortress."

"It's fine if you stay close to the house. If not, I might have to resort to tying you to a chair," he suggested, only half-joking. This woman seemed hell-bent on making his job difficult.

She didn't bite at the bondage suggestion. Which was a good thing, Jack reminded himself. "Just for a few minutes," Meghan negotiated. "Then we'll come back inside and darken the shades. Promise."

Watching her flip switches as she went, he felt as if he was watching stage lights come up. *Lanai* didn't seem an important enough word for the place she took him to. It was a large area, complete with a lighted, multilevel pool, at least a dozen thickly cushioned lounge chairs, and what he guessed was a pool house—even though it probably had more square footage than his apartment—before a low retaining wall separating them from the ocean beyond.

A warm, fresh breeze came up from the sand, tousling the strands of her silky hair as he watched her gather the strands into a messy knot. He wondered if she had any idea how incredibly sexy she was when she lounged on the chaise, bared feet tucked off to one side, wineglass in her hand, moonlight reflected in her eyes. Judging by her relaxed features, he guessed the beach was her element.

Waves crashed in the darkness as he sat on the edge of the chair next to hers. "Audrey?" he prompted again.

"You have to understand," she began on a breath. "My father was a fairly great dad but a really lousy husband. Audrey was a lousy wife. They divorced two years before my dad died, but Audrey didn't go quickly or quietly."

"Is she capable of murder?"

Meghan thought about that for all of two seconds. "Hardly. She would never risk breaking a nail." She saw Jack smile out of the corner of her eye and hated that she noticed. Hated more that it mattered. This wasn't a date. This man wasn't interested in her. She should probably write that on her palm in permanent marker because she seemed to have trouble remembering that fact. Meghan's brain seemed more focused on his body, on the way he moved, on him in general.

"Would she pay someone to hurt you?"

"I'm guessing not. Barrett drew up an iron-clad prenup that sent Audrey back over the bridge, as her catty friends would say."

"Over the bridge?"

"An expression," she explained, sipping her wine. "They were only married for five years, so Audrey's divorce settlement wasn't enough to allow her to live on Palm Beach. 'Over the bridge' is snobbish code for insufficient funds to live on the island. Not terribly nice, but Audrey's friends aren't noted for their compassion. West Palm is a lovely area with—"

"Stop worrying I'll think you're a snob. I don't."

Meghan snapped her mouth shut. She was worried about that and relieved to hear he didn't think she was some sort of dilettante. Not that it should matter. How had this gotten so complicated in a matter of hours? Maybe having some lunatic running around had addled her brain.

"So who is Jenna Lewis?"

Meghan was impressed by his thoroughness. "She was my father's 'special friend,' " she said with a grin as she made air quotes around the words. "Jenna and my dad had an on-again-off-again thing for about ten years."

"During his marriage to Audrey?"

She nodded. "Told you he was a lousy husband."

"But that sort of thing is accepted in these social circles, right?"

"For some, but not me," she assured him. "The size of a person's portfolio doesn't make cheating acceptable."

"What about your brother?"

She took a long sip of wine, trying to drown the tightness in her chest. "Michael was devoted to Casey."

"Even when he was atoning for his lack of interest in the store?"

"He worked long hours, but she understood."

"If he wasn't into the store, then why'd he work there all those years?"

"It's a family thing," she explained. "We all worked at the store. Michael and I started in shipping as teenagers. My father was real big on learning by doing. I loved it, Michael hated it."

"Then how come he was the chosen one?"

"Sexism, favoritism, who knows. My father would never accept that Michael didn't have a passion for the store. Everyone knew that Michael delegated almost everything to his assistant, Sam Shelton. I'm sure my dad knew, too, but he just wanted to follow the family tradition of passing the torch from father to son."

"How did Michael handle that?"

"Michael's heart wasn't in it. All he wanted was to marry Casey and—as hokey as this sounds—do volunteer stuff. Michael liked volunteering." Her heart twisted at the memory of her brother's kindness. Why had he died? Why had she lived? "He preferred helping people to selling them things."

"Like four-hundred-dollar blouses."

She blew out an exasperated breath at his wry comment. He managed to amuse her and at the same time force her to defend the store. "Quality and originality cost, Jack. A lot of the merchandise we carry at Beckham's is one of a kind and/or hand-sewn."

"Don't get yourself in a knot," he said, raising his palm in her direction. "I'll admit that my knowledge of couture is limited and take your word for it."

"It's more than the merchandise," she insisted. "Beckham's is a destination. People come to Beckham's for the atmosphere as well. The grand piano plays standards that make people smile as they remember Christmases past, hum along while they're served steaming Christmas treats from polished silver trays. Our staff is trained to do more than simply grab a garment off the rack. We're about personal service and complete accommodation to the needs of the shopper. We want our customers to know—"

He chuckled, cutting her off. "I get it, Meghan, really. Have you always been so into the store?"

Her annoyance melted. "Always. It's a magical place to me. I love every inch of it. I walk in the door and I can feel all the generations of Beckhams—my great-grandfather, my grandfather, and my father. I've seen it grow and change and yet never lose the uniqueness that makes it so special."

"And here I thought all anyone really needed was a Super Wal-Mart."

"A very nice place," she readily agreed. "But a different shopping experience. For the record, Michael felt the same way. Made my father nuts."

"I'll bet it did. Tell me about Casey."

"Sweet person. Completely shattered when Michael died in the accident." Meghan had been shattered as well, but unable to show it. Everyone seemed to be waiting for her to crack, but she allowed tears only in the solitude and safety of her own bedroom. Her eyes began to sting with tears now, so she cleared the lump threatening to clog her throat and continued. "They'd been married four months. She'd been in love with my brother for years and vice versa. I think they started discussing marriage on their first date."

"Judging by the quick look I got today, she's a pretty woman. Where does she live?"

"She and Michael used to live here. After he died—" Meghan shrugged. "It was too painful to stay here with him gone." In that moment, something about Jack made her feel as if he could handle her tears. Dangerous thought. She took a sip of wine and forged ahead. "She has a lovely condo about a mile from here. I know you met on the fly this afternoon. But you'll see her again soon. Casey tends to flit in and out—I think grief keeps her in a state of perpetual motion," Meghan said, thinking that grief kept her in perpetual motion, too, only she chose Beckham's as her escape route. "And she'll be at the annual Christmas party and you can meet her properly then—"

"Excuse me?"

"The annual holiday party," Meghan explained. The prospect of the party filled her with mixed emotions. The celebration would feel so empty without Michael's laughter. Yet she knew he would hate it if the party was cancelled. He always looked at it as a way for the Beckham family to do something for the Beckham's employees. So she'd do a stellar job, pay tribute to the only thing he really loved about the store.

"It's here at the house. A grand tradition begun by my grandfather. It's in three days."

"Not anymore."

She blinked at his rock hard tone. "What do you mean?"

"Consider it canceled, Meghan."

She looked at him in disbelief. "It's a party, Jack."

"No, it's a security nightmare."

A dozen emotional responses bubbled to the surface but she squashed them down. She stood, back rigid. "Well, you're a security expert, so I suggest you come up with something because the party *is* going to happen. I'm not going to disappoint people."

"Would you rather get killed?"

"No. But wringing your unyielding neck is sounding really good right now."

Chapter Four

"WHAT IN THE NAME OF GOD IS THAT?"

"Not a morning person, eh?" Jack asked as he balanced the tray in one hand long enough to shove the spreadsheets off to one side of her bed with the other. Pale streaks of dawn shone through the uncurtained window, painting her lush body in brilliant shades of rose.

Meghan rubbed her face and tousled her hair, her eyes heavy with sleep, giving Jack a voyeur's-eye view of her considerable assets barely covered by a deep pink silk nightgown. He felt an instant heat in his groin that spread through his system in pulsing waves as he sat down on the bed, placing the tray between them.

He was playing with fire here, Jack thought. He wasn't supposed to be in bed with her. Even if it was a giant bed. Even if he was fully clothed. And eating. The plan had been to bring her breakfast because he'd been up for hours and bored silly. He was on the road so often that any chance to cook anything was a thrill.

She frowned down at the loaded plate. "While I appreciate the gesture, I don't normally eat *all* the eggs and *all* the bacon at the same time."

He reached over and took the tray. "I thought you might say that." Hoisting his legs up on the bed, he rested the tray in his lap—glad to be hiding his arousal from her—and began eating. It wasn't easy, since he had to force each bite past the lump of desire in his throat.

She was full of surprises. She stretched and wriggled before settling back against the pillows, then took the communal coffee mug off the tray and took a sip. "It's sweet."

"I happen to like sugar in my coffee."

"Sugar is a big no-no," she sighed, taking another drink.

Jack could think of several bigger no-nos he'd like to do to her.

She raised her arms above her head and stretched unselfconsciously. Her pale skin was a stark contrast to the fuchsia silk that seemed to be painted on her skin. The straps were thin and delicate, and when she dropped her arms one strap slipped partway down one slender shoulder to reveal a tantalizing view of the ample fullness of her breast. Jack imagined himself pressing his lips against the pulse point at her throat, then slowly, purposefully, allowing his mouth to glide along her skin, tasting as he went. Until finally, his mouth closed over the almost visible outline of her pebbled nipple.

He didn't choke on his breakfast. Nope. Worse. He groaned.

She gave him a pointed look, even as her lips curved into a lazy, sensual smile. "Stop frowning, Jack. You crawled into my bed, remember?"

"Not my best idea," he admitted. What else could he do? That ship had sailed. "Maybe it would be a good idea for you to go get dressed."

"I don't think so." Her voice was incredibly deep and sultry. She picked up a slice of bacon and brought it to her mouth. White teeth took a bite.

Jack felt that bite right down to his toes. "I do."

She placed the coffee mug back on the tray, which still

happened to be on his lap. She half-rolled so that she was looking up at him. "I'm not dressed for company." Her eyes glittered. The lady was enjoying his discomfort.

"I agree." His erection was proof of that.

"It's even worse than you think," she remarked, grinning.

"You wouldn't say that if you could read my mind."

"I'm sure I've got a pretty good handle on where your brain is right now. But we have a slight problem."

Jack put the fork down with a clang and prepared for one of her lectures on proper decorum. "Okay, okay. I've overstepped my bounds by entering the sanctuary of your bedroom. In my own defense, I didn't think you'd be wearing a sexy nightgown."

"That's the problem," she said on a rush of breath that washed over his forearm. "It's not a nightgown, it's a camisole."

"If that was supposed to douse my fantasies, it didn't do the trick. A camisole and sexy panties are—"

"Now we've reached the problem. I'm not wearing panties so much as a thong, which means we're fast approaching that part we discussed about you seeing me naked. At least parts of me."

"I take it you'd like me to leave." He put the tray aside and started to stand.

"The jury is still out on that."

Jack's heart skipped. He knew of a million reasons why he should get up and out of there. Problem was, not a single one of them was reaching his brain. All he could think of was the camisole, the thong, and creative ways to peel them from her body.

He ached in places he'd forgotten he had. It took him three deep breaths and every ounce of willpower to shove off the mattress and stride toward the door. His fingers clenched the polished handle and he paused, not turning around. "I'm walking out of here because I should, not because I want to. Make me this offer a second time and 'should' can go to hell."

"Scared, Jack?"

He gave her a hot look, then, without answering, slammed the door shut between them.

Meghan heard him storming down the hallway outside her room.

She grinned. "Check and mate."

She was still smiling as she showered, dried her hair, applied makeup, and dressed. Her pseudosexual encounter with Jack had made her feel alive for the first time in months. "How sick is that?" she asked herself as she slipped the straps of her sandals on her heels. "It's been way too long since I've had sex."

Jack was an attractive man. Meghan liked the way his black hair always looked mussed, she liked the way his emerald eyes went hot and smoldering when he looked at her, she liked his firm mouth—she wanted to feel that firm mouth on hers. She wanted to know what he tasted like, what his skin felt like—the anticipation excited her. The very possibility of having him make love to her was energizing almost to the point of making her giddy.

The attraction was clearly mutual. But really, she had to use a little impulse control here. She did have him at a distinct disadvantage since he'd admitted he was hot for her. He was normally so stoic that seeing him struggling to keep from blatantly staring was just too hard to pass up. Maybe she'd just been getting even for the way he'd intruded into her life. Maybe his presence just reminded her that she needed to feel attractive and appealing once in a while.

"Or . . . I just want him," she whispered as she closed the clasp on her sapphire pendant. She really did have impulse control, right? Right.

Wrong. Wrong, wrong, wrong! Jack castigated himself as he roamed through the house checking the locks on the windows and doors as he listened to the clicks of her heels on the tiled floor. The Agency's operatives had a code. Standards. Rules. One of the biggies was not sleeping with a protectee—never let it get personal. Less than twenty-four hours into the assignment and he was ready to jump into bed with her. Ready? More like dying to. *Shit!*

"Want some?" she called from the kitchen.

Glancing over his shoulder, he saw her lifting the coffee carafe and nodded. He had half-hoped she was still wearing the camisole and that sexy smile and was offering him something more than a second cup of coffee. "Sure. Thanks."

"Cream? Sugar?" she asked when he walked over and perched on the barstool next to hers.

"Sugar." He had to admit that even though in her tailored teal dress she was polished and professional, an underlying sensuality radiated from her. Or maybe he just felt its pull. Didn't matter really, bottom line was—Jack's senses were completely homing in on her. He smelled her perfume as he noticed that her dress fit without being snug. He wondered how the dress skimmed her curves without clinging and yet still inspired any number of fantasies. He watched the way she held her coffee mug in both hands as she brought it to her mouth. Her lips were glossy and slick, tinted with a light pink that matched the splash of color on her cheeks. When she parted her lips and blew slowly on the hot beverage, it was everything he could do not to fall off the friggin' stool.

Suddenly this simple assignment was incredibly complicated. The smart thing would be to find the killer—fast. Then beat a path home to D.C., where he could forget Meghan Beckham. Though something told him she wasn't the kind of woman a man could forget. Ever.

"We'd better go," she said after glancing at the digital clock above the stove. "I've got a seven o'clock meeting with Sam." She hoisted her briefcase onto her shoulder. The sheer weight of it caused her to list slightly as she finished one last, healthy gulp of coffee before heading toward the door.

"Don't you want to know why I don't offer to carry your bag?" he asked as she pressed the series of buttons to give them ten seconds to get out the door before the alarm armed.

"Because you have to have your hands free," she replied simply.

"How'd you know that?"

"Deduction," she answered, allowing him to walk in front of her as they made their way to the SUV. "If I really was in danger, then it would make sense that you'd need your hands to fend off an attack."

"Very good."

"Please tell me you don't stereotype all blondes?"

He smiled down at her as he held the door open. "Me? The muscle-bound, minimum IQ bodyguard?"

She winced. "Heard that, did you?"

He went around and slipped easily behind the wheel of the car. "Yes, and I can't tell you how offended I was at being called muscle-bound. I prefer to think of myself as athletic."

She laughed. "Okay, I was wrong. There, happy now?"

He started the engine and put the car in gear. "Ecstatic."

"What *exactly* do you do?"

"The obvious," he answered easily.

And evasively, she thought as they headed toward trendy Worth Avenue. He was good at evading questions. And more prepared than a flaming Boy Scout. How, she wondered silently, had he managed to change into khaki slacks and a chocolate polo shirt when she hadn't seen so much as an overnight bag?

The irritating chime of her cell phone stole her attention. Probably a good thing, she decided as she reached into her bag and read the caller ID before flipping open the phone.

"Hey, where are you?"

"Hi Sam, sorry, I'm running a little late this morning."

"Everything okay?" he asked, genuine concern in his tone. "You're usually here well before the rest of us."

"I just got a late start. I'm here at—" He snatched the phone from her so fast it startled her. "What was that?"

"Another rule," he stated matter-of-factly. "You don't tell anyone your exact location. Not even your priest."

Grabbing her phone back, she pressed the redial button, glaring at his profile the whole time. "Sorry, Sam, my service dropped for a minute."

"I've got coffee waiting. See you in a few."

"Thanks." She closed the phone and placed it back in her bag. "That was really rude," she told him sternly.

"Necessary," he said unapologetically as he drove past the entrance to the store's garage.

"I'm late," she told him, hearing the internal clock ticking louder and louder with each passing moment.

"Get used to it."

"Technically, I'm your employer. Doesn't that mean I'm the one who should be determining the rules?"

"Not so much, no."

"Jack, be reasonable. I have responsibilities."

"So do I."

"You can be very annoying, do you know that?"

"So I've been told."

Her mood didn't improve as he made no fewer than five trips up and down the street before he finally pulled into the garage. Meghan's patience was hanging by a thread as she leaped from the car and hurried toward the elevator. She got maybe a dozen paces before Jack's fingers encircled her arm.

She stopped abruptly, causing his large body to press into hers. The feel of his solid form sent shock waves pulsing through her system, short-circuiting her annoyance. It was hard to be angry with someone when every fiber of your being was electrified. Meghan lifted her hand, fully intending to simply give him a gentle nudge backward. That was, of course, until she felt the solid ripple of muscle beneath the fabric of his shirt.

Her brain took an immediate detour into curiosity land and she was almost overwhelmed with a desire to leisurely explore his body.

Focus! she commanded her addled mind. She was a professional with a meeting, not some hormonal teenager with no control over her libido.

"What now?" she snapped, more exasperated with herself than with him.

"No elevators. We walk up."

"Easy for you to say," she grumbled as she turned toward the stairs adjacent to the elevator shaft. "You don't have to climb three flights of cement steps in heels."

"I didn't choose the shoes," he returned easily as he placed a hand at her elbow. "We're changing everything about your routine, Meghan. Told you that yesterday."

Her heels clicked and echoed a staccato rhythm as she made her way up to the office. Her mood wasn't helped as she listened to the sound of the elevator just inside the concrete housing. She secretly blessed strict building codes on Worth Avenue that banned high-rises. At least it was only a three-story climb.

Sam was waiting at Terri's desk and greeted her with a pleasant if surprised smile as she emerged from the stairwell with Jack in tow. Quickly, he came toward her, lifting the briefcase from her shoulder as he gave Jack one of those hey-pal-you-could-have-carried-this-for-her looks.

"Jack Palmer, this is Sam Shelton. Sam, Jack."

Sam fell into step next to her. "And he is?"

"A temporary pain in my ass."

Leaning closer, Sam's breath tickled her ear when he said, "More like a *big* pain. The guy's like granite. Is he the one Barrett hired?"

"Guilty," Jack said from behind them. "Just pretend I'm not here."

"That'll happen," Meghan muttered as she entered her office.

Five hours later, she was still acutely aware of Jack's presence. Mainly because he was so friggin' still. How *did* he do that? It was creeping her out and making it almost impossible for her to concentrate on the information Sam was sharing regarding the purchase of the adjacent building. Terri popped in and out, pointless interruptions that Meghan guessed were to grab a quick look at Jack and/or to accept the flirtatious looks Sam had been giving her assistant from day one.

"Should we order in?" Sam asked.

"Yes," Jack answered for her.

Meghan had her favorite bistro on speed dial. She requested the usual salads for herself and for Sam, then glanced over at Jack.

"Burger and fries."

"Heart healthy," she commented before giving his order.

She and Sam worked out a few more kinks in the expansion plans before the delivery arrived. As usual, Terri was not at her desk, where the petty cash was kept, which meant Meghan had to hunt through the disheveled desk to find the envelope.

Jack moved up and sat next to Sam as they cleared space for the food. His fries smelled heavenly and it was everything she could do not to reach over and grab a small wedge of fried heaven.

"So," Jack began, looking at Sam, "I didn't know Barrett was telling people about me."

"I'm not people," Sam responded easily.

Touché, she thought, taking a bite of lettuce.

"I encouraged Barrett to hire someone. It's the prudent thing to do. Meghan *is* Beckham's now."

"You're a traitor, Sam."

"No, I'm your friend and I care what happens to you."

"How much do you care?" Jack asked.

Meghan nearly choked on her tasteless salad as she tried to swallow quickly. "For God's sake, Jack! Sam and I aren't romantically involved."

Jack turned his gaze on her and calmly stated, "You were."

Chapter Five

"YOU'RE OUT OF LINE," SHE CHIDED.

Jack noted the faint stain of color on her cheeks.

She continued in a genuine huff, "This isn't an inquisition and that is ancient history."

"Is it?" he pressed Sam.

"Very," Sam replied affably. "Not that we didn't try," Sam said, winking at her before looking in Jack's direction. "Truth be told, Meghan and I nearly screwed up a great friendship by trying to turn it into a romance. Luckily for the two of us, we figured that out quickly. No harm done."

"So, it was an amicable breakup?" Jack asked.

"There was nothing to break up," Meghan insisted. "It was a short fling, fueled mostly by Father's desire to pair the two of us. Geez, Jack. It was two weeks like, um, five years ago. Let it go."

He shrugged. Honestly, he wasn't picking up any chemistry between the two of them at all. "So why do you dislike Casey?"

Sam smiled patiently. "Dislike is a little . . . strong. We just never jelled," he responded diplomatically. "I respect her, though. She was my best friend's wife and my boss's daughter. She's devoted to Barrett and she adored Mike."

"I thought Meghan's father was your boss."

Sam nodded. "He was. Before Mr. Beckham was my direct boss, I reported to Barrett. In fact, Barrett was the one who insisted Mr. Beckham move me up the corporate ladder."

"But you don't like his daughter."

Sam made a noise that sounded a lot like a snort to Jack. "She's spoiled, okay?"

"Cherished," Meghan corrected.

Sam gave a humorless chuckle. "Self-absorbed."

"Sheltered," Meghan countered.

"I'm sure Meghan can give you a lengthy list of her positive qualities," Sam suggested tactfully.

"They're like small children," Meghan informed Jack as she tossed Sam a reproachful look. "Always have been. They've been sniping at one another for the better part of ten years. Made Michael crazy."

"I never start it," Sam defended.

"Neither does Casey. And Michael would want the two of you to be helping each other now. He loved both of you."

Jack was getting the picture and it wasn't a pretty one. He wondered how often Meghan had refereed moments between her brother's wife and his best friend. In his experience, it was never good to be in the middle of that kind of triangle.

"So, Sam," Jack began, pushing away his plate, "any thoughts on who might be killing off the Santas?"

"Not a clue. But the guy downstairs is pretty brave. He took the job knowing we've lost two Santas so far."

"So far?" Meghan choked, apparently still unwilling to accept the possibility that this wasn't over.

"I didn't mean it like that," Sam backpedaled. "And don't look so horrified, Meghan. I've got two plain-clothes security guards on him. He's safe. Nothing will happen."

She dropped her head into her hands and Jack felt

genuinely sorry for her. He felt a few other things as well—none of them part of his duties or reflective of the code by which he'd agreed to live under the terms of his employment with the Agency. Still, he couldn't seem to help the tractor beam drawing him to this woman. He was a trained observer, normally limiting his observations to those necessary to do his job. But with Meghan, he couldn't seem to keep his mind from wandering down paths that were clearly marked *off-limits* and *dead end.*

If he'd been playing it cautious, he'd get on the phone and insist Roz send someone else to watch over the stunning blonde with the Santa crisis. The mere thought of bailing on her now wasn't working. It would include admitting that for the first time in ages, his interests weren't strictly work related.

Okay, so he'd just make sure he kept everything on a purely professional level—no more trips into her bedroom, nothing that wasn't strictly necessary for him to protect her from whoever had her in their sights.

His little mental pep talk was interrupted by the poorly timed arrival of another guest.

A tall young woman waltzed into the room and he was reaching for the weapon concealed in his ankle holster when he recognized her from yesterday. Ten seconds in the presence of Casey Trent-Beckham and Jack had to admit he was coming down on Sam's side. The smile she offered didn't feel genuine and he'd never seen such an expertly made up woman in his life. She was perfect— *too* perfect.

Offering a small, well-jeweled hand in his direction, she gushed, "It's so lovely to formally meet you. Daddy explained how he hired someone to look after Meghan after we left here. He had to, since his only instruction to that point was to tell me to show up and drag him out."

"I got the feeling that was orchestrated by your dad. And for the record, Santa's probably the one who needs looking after," Meghan inserted, coming around her desk to give Casey a quick hug. She noticed instantly that Casey looked tired. More tired than usual. Apparently she still wasn't sleeping. Brushing a few strands of chestnut-colored hair from her friend's face, Meghan couldn't help but frown. "Great makeup, but I know there are dark circles under there. You really should see someone, Casey."

"I will," Casey promised, appeasingly. "Forget me, how are you doing?"

Sam stood then, tossing what was left of his lunch into the trash. "I've got some calls to return. Let me know when you're free." He left abruptly and without even so much as acknowledging Casey with more than a nod of his head.

As soon as he exited, Casey leaned forward and whispered, "Can't you send him on a buying trip to the Antarctic?"

"Be nice," Meghan pleaded. "Can I have Terri get you something? Coffee, tea? Something to eat?"

Shaking her head, Casey shifted her Prada bag to the opposite hand. "I can't stay. I really just dropped in to make sure you were okay. Besides, Mother has decided that staying busy will keep me from thinking about Michael. So, I'm off to some pointless gathering of the Something-Something-Something Library Something to volunteer my services to do . . . *something.*"

Meghan smiled. "I'm sure your mother has your best interests at heart."

"Impossible," Casey said with a small wave of her hand. "My mother doesn't know what my interests are."

"True. Maybe you'd like to take Jack with you? He's probably bored out of his mind just sitting here watching me."

"No," Jack insisted, leaning back in his seat in order

to make eye contact. "And to quote you, feel free to talk *about* me instead of *to* me."

The warm stain on her cheeks remained even after Casey left the room, leaving nothing but the ghost of her perfume behind. Meghan returned to her seat and slipped her shoes off. "I'm sorry about before. I'm usually not rude; I'm just unaccustomed to having someone in my space at all times."

He shrugged. "Get used to it. At what point are we going to cancel your party?"

She pretended sudden and intense interest in the paper in front of her. "When hell freezes over."

"Meghan," he groaned on a breath of exasperation. "I'm the security expert and I'm telling you, a party right now is a stupid move."

Part of her knew that and part of her was seriously pissed at having her intelligence called on the carpet. Easier and less scary to go with the second part. "Stupid?"

"Very," he replied bluntly. His eyes bore into her from across the short distance. "Two days isn't long enough to do complete background checks on the guests. Then I'm assuming we're talking caterers and waiters and—"

"I know virtually everyone attending and I've used the same caterer for years."

"Is there some reason you're going out of your way to make my life difficult and yours optional?"

She opened her mouth, then snapped it shut. He had an amazing ability to make her feel like a fool. After what felt like an eternity of silence, she tried a different tack. "What steps can I take to make the party more secure?"

"Cancel it."

She silently counted to ten. "Short of that? Look, Jack, in reality, we don't even know *if* the Santa killer is a threat to me. It's not like there's anything concrete so far."

"Two dead bodies in your store and a fatal automobile accident that killed your brother and should have killed you are pretty good indications."

She drew her lower lip between her teeth and released it slowly. "The crash *was* an accident. The police said so, and the accident reconstruction company said as much, so move on. I have to—"

"What accident reconstruction company?"

She shrugged, feeling uncomfortable under the glaring intensity of his gaze. "I sent the accident report to a private company that specializes in reconstructing car accidents. I only did it because Barrett made me paranoid. Which, by the way, is exactly why he hired you. Barrett has never believed it was an accident." She reached into her bottom desk drawer and pulled out the large manila envelope, then passed it across to him. "Read for yourself. The tire blew out and debris from the tire ruptured the gas line. That's why the car exploded when it hit the barricade."

She sat quietly as Jack poured over the pages she had barely managed to skim. She didn't want to know all the details. *Couldn't* was more accurate. She didn't want to think about Michael's last moments.

Her stomach clenched. "So, can we forget Barrett's theory that the accident was some sort of failed attempt to kill off the Beckham heirs?"

"Hardly," Jack said, looking up from the documents. "If anything, this report makes me more suspicious than ever."

"Why?"

"Because it doesn't feel right."

"I'm not following you," she admitted. "The cover letter very clearly states that their computer reconstruction of the crash proves it was an unfortunate accident."

"I see that."

"So what's the problem?"

"I'm not sure," he said. "I know what it says, but I'd like to send it off to a friend of mine to review, okay?"

She nodded, all too happy to have a reason to rid herself of the report.

He put the report back into the envelope and, as he was disposing of the last bit of his lunch, said, "Tell me about the first Santa."

"He was a nice guy," she recalled fondly, shifting one grieving memory for another. "Worked for Beckham's for several seasons. The day he died, he'd come in early."

"Why?"

Meghan thought back. "He had to fill out payroll forms, get a locker—usual stuff."

"Nothing out of the ordinary?"

She shook her head. "I only saw him for a minute or two. We happened to be in the employee lounge at the same time."

"Why?"

"I was getting coffee and I teased him for using the last packet of artificial sweetener."

Jack stroked his chin and she noted his brow furrowed into deep lines before he spoke, suggesting, "Could have been how he was poisoned."

"That would have made the killer very, very lucky, don't you think? I mean, it's a communal room."

"Take me there," Jack instructed.

Slipping her shoes back on, Meghan led him past Terri's still-unoccupied desk, down the corridor, toward the etched glass doors marked PRIVATE.

As they walked, Jack glanced into the open offices and read nameplates on the closed doors, confirming his memory of the schematic Roz had provided. The executive offices included Meghan's, Sam's, Human Resources, Legal, a conference room, and a small kitchenette. The administrative assistants all had space outside their respective bosses' offices. Fairly standard.

Once outside the restricted executive area, there was a second conference room and a series of offices for the buyers for each department as well as a long, narrow locker room, restrooms, and then finally the lounge area.

"Where do the hallways lead?" he asked.

"Storage," she replied as they entered the lounge.

The room was small—a half-dozen round tables and chairs—and smelled like coffee and popcorn. There were two people seated at the far table. One was a woman Jack put in her late fifties, who immediately snapped closed her compact and stopped touching up her lipstick when she saw Meghan. The other was an African American man about half that age in a tan uniform.

"Afternoon, Miss Beckham," they said in unison.

The security officer's chair legs scuffed against the polished tiled floor as he stood in polite acknowledgment.

"Relax and finish your drink, Darius," Meghan insisted, waving him back into his seat as she moved to the table, smiling as she addressed them. "When are your grandchildren coming, Harriett?"

The woman beamed, answering quickly, "They'll be here the twentieth. Break's over. I've got to get back to the floor."

"I'll go down with you," Darius added, quickly gathering up his soda can and tossing it into the garbage can. "Have a nice day, ma'am."

Jack was glad the room had emptied; it gave him an opportunity to look around without spectators. Meghan started for the door as he was reaching for the refrigerator's handle. "Where do you think you're going?"

"I have work to do," she reminded him, placing her hands on her hips.

Nice hips. Nice legs. Nice everything. He gave himself a little mental slap. "In a minute."

Nothing out of the ordinary in the refrigerator. Sodas,

coffee creamers in a variety of brands and flavors, half-eaten takeout, a few fruits and vegetables, and some general-purpose condiments. The cabinets were equally unremarkable.

"Seriously, Jack," she said, her words a tad more insistent. "I've got things to do."

He didn't need to turn around to know that her eyes had narrowed slightly and her pretty lips were pursed. It was her irritation face.

He began opening the cabinets, finding an eclectic assortment of items, mostly grab-and-run foods—power bars, energy bars, candy bars, granola bars, and diet bars. Most things were labeled with the owner's name or initials. In the last cabinet, above the well-utilized coffeepot, he found supersized boxes of sugar packets and artificial sweeteners. Taking them down, he opened them and discovered that one was less than half empty. The other nearly full.

Turning, he met her impatient eyes and asked, "Who buys these?"

"We get them with our other office supplies," she explained. "Terri is supposed to check them and restock as needed—which is probably why we ran out the day Santa Number One died."

"Were you out of sugar or just the artificial stuff?"

She sighed. "Both. I remember he apologized to me and said he normally used sugar but since there wasn't any—what?"

Jack grabbed her by the hand and hurried her back down the hallway. "I think it's time we had a little chat with your assistant."

Chapter Six

"You're not making any sense, Jack!" Meghan insisted as she tried to keep up with his long strides. Forget the strides, most of her attention was fixed on the feel of his large hand holding hers. Or more accurately, on memorizing the feel of his callused palm and the warmth of his skin.

Forget him making sense! I've totally gone off the deep end. Here I am with the possibility of a killer in my midst and all I can think about is how it would feel to have his callused palm pressed against me. Now who isn't making sense?

"Sure I am," he remarked when they arrived at Terri's still-empty desk. "Is this woman ever where she's supposed to be?"

Jack dropped her hand, which was more disappointing than Terri's complete lack of work effort. "I'm not sure what you think she might have done. How can you think she masterminded some sort of grand scheme—"

"Can you just get her here?"

Be happy to, because I take orders from you and I don't have anything else on my plate right now. One thing Meghan knew was how and when to pick her battles. This wasn't one of them. The sooner Jack got whatever it was out of his system, the sooner she could get back to work. "I'm sure she's in the building," she said, grabbing the phone off the desk and pressing the button for the operator. Quickly, Meghan asked that Terri be paged. Just as quickly, Terri appeared in the hallway, slipping out of Sam's office.

"Sorry," she said without so much as a hint of regret. "Mr. Shelton needed me."

"Mr. Palmer wants to talk to you."

Terri shrugged. "Whatever."

Terri walked into Meghan's office. Jack followed next, which was just fine because it gave Meghan a completely unobstructed view of his broad shoulders, tapered waist, and muscled thighs. The guy had a body to die for. Apt, since if he caught her gawking, she'd die of humiliation. Not a bad way to go, she decided as she plastered a bland expression on her face and took her place in her chair.

Jack moved to the edge of the desk, half-sitting, half-leaning, fully glaring. It took maybe a second for him to realize what Terri had been "helping" Sam with. Her hair was mussed, her pupils were dilated, and he could see the pulse at her throat still beating faster than it should.

"We're going to talk about the employee lounge, Terri. Do you normally have to order sugar and sweetener at the same time?"

She shrugged. "Why?"

"Both boxes look relatively new."

"I just reordered like a week ago. We go through the fake stuff pretty quickly, but I guess someone snagged all the sugar to bake or something because we ran out."

He glanced over at Meghan and saw most of the color had drained from her face. Turning back to Meghan, he asked, "When did you realize the sugar was gone?"

"Miss Beckham put a note on my desk."

"No one complained the day before?"

Terri shrugged. "No, which is freaky, because they always bitch—er—complain if something isn't right."

"Can you get me the purchase orders for the last six months?" he asked.

"Sure. They're on my computer. It'll take me a few minutes." She got up and went toward the door.

"Close the door on your way out," Meghan instructed.

Jack moved from the desk to the chair, then looked into Meghan's troubled gray-blue eyes. "To quote your eloquent assistant, there's something freaky going on."

"I get where you're going. You think someone managed to get into the break room and dump the sugar, forcing Santa to use the artificial sweetener—which was actually poison—killing him, right?"

"Something like that."

He watched as she raked her fingers through her hair. Deep lines of concentration appeared on her forehead. "That's a pretty elaborate scheme to kill a Santa, don't you think?"

"Yes. Unless it wasn't meant specifically for Santa but rather the first step in a fairly complicated plan."

"I know retail, Jack, not this." She pressed her fingertips into her temples. "Start at the beginning and walk me through it step by step."

Since he wasn't sure, he should have kept his suspicions to himself. For the first time, he read real fear in her eyes. A pang of guilt knotted his gut. He'd wanted her to take her personal security seriously, not scare her shitless. "I'm just sounding out a theory here, Meghan," he said. "It might be nothing."

She started to say something when the intercom buzzed. She smashed the button harder then necessary. "Yes?"

"Ms. Lewis is on line two. Do you want to talk to her?"

"Put her through, Terri."

"Oh, and I have the stuff printing. Do you want me to bring it in?"

"Please," Meghan answered as she lifted the receiver. "Hi, Jenna, how are you?"

While she was on the phone with her late father's mistress, Jack kept working the hypothesis in his brain. Intuition told him the store was the key. It was the only thing that made sense. Assuming the accident was meant to get rid of Meghan and her brother, then the killer needed to finish the job without detection. But then his theory fell apart. How could the killer be assured that Santa would be the next person to go to the break room and use the tainted sweetener?

Unless Santa wasn't the intended victim. He let out a breath and ran his palms over his eyes. His theory was falling apart even before Terri brought in the purchase orders he'd requested. Jack knew he was missing something—a crucial piece of the puzzle.

It didn't help that the purchase orders confirmed his suspicions. Not once in the previous six-month period had Beckham's ordered sweetener and sugar at the same time. He didn't believe in coincidences, so he was back to someone staging the poisoning. "So what does that get me?"

"What?" Meghan asked as she placed the receiver back on its cradle.

"Just thinking out loud," he replied, hoping he'd put a lightness in his tone that he wasn't anywhere near feeling. "Problem?" he questioned, reading her expression.

"I've got a late dinner tonight." She paused and flipped through the calendar on her desk. "Right here," she indicated, tapping the page. "I forgot all about it. Will it be a problem?"

"Depends. Where? When?"

"City Place with Jenna at ten. I'd cancel but she sounded pretty depressed."

"Jenna? Yeah, right, your father's mistress. Can you have her go to your house instead?"

"I'm a really bad cook," Meghan admitted.

He was surprised he didn't get the expected argument from her and wanted to reward her newfound cooperation. "I happen to be a great cook."

"That may be true, but the only thing in my refrigerator since you cooked all the bacon and eggs is a jar of mustard dying of loneliness, in case you didn't notice."

"I noticed, but it's not a problem," he assured her. "I'm assuming you can get a grocer to deliver?"

She nodded. "Terri can call in the order."

"Let's keep everyone else out of the loop," he cautioned.

She turned the phone toward him after scribbling a phone number on a small sticky note. She called Sam back into her office and continued her meeting while Jack stepped out and faxed the accident report to his friend, then tried—in vain—to work through his theory.

Eight hours of contemplating mergers, buy outs, and potential zoning issues had pretty much fried Meghan's brain by nine-thirty. Terri had vanished at the stroke of six. The store had closed almost half an hour ago and she could hear the faint chatter of the employees filing out of the locker room and the gentle, distant hum of the public elevator taking people down to the garage.

Sam stuck his head in to say good night on his way out to join Barrett and his wife for drinks. Soon it was quiet enough that all she was conscious of was the even sound of Jack's breathing.

Her powers of concentration were nonexistent, so she tossed her pen on the desk and sighed loudly. "I'm ready to call it a day," she told him.

"Fine with me."

He rose and stood near the door while she gathered up her purse and stuck a few things in her briefcase. After slipping her shoes on, she walked into the hallway, stopping so Jack could precede her out into the corridor.

They had reached the stairway when Meghan heard the sound of voices in the locker room. Jack instantly plastered her against the wall with his body.

Air rushed from her diaphragm as she was smashed between the cool, hard wall and his warm solid body. It took several seconds for her to realize that he had a gun in his hand.

Dropping her briefcase and purse, she placed her hands on his shoulders as soon as she recognized the voices. "It's Darius and my Santa," she said, wondering why she was nearly yelling. Then she realized it was because her heart was pounding in her ears as adrenaline surged through her.

Jack lowered the gun as the two men appeared in the hallway. Their boisterous conversation stopped abruptly as soon as they caught sight of Meghan and Jack.

"Sorry, Miss Beckham," Darius offered. "We got to talking and time got away from us. I hope we didn't disturb you."

"No," she insisted, slipping out from behind Jack. "Is everyone else gone?"

Darius nodded. "Sure are. We'll get out of your way now."

"You're not in our way," Meghan insisted. "Take the executive elevator," she offered. "It's already up here so you won't have to wait."

"Thank you," the men replied, stepping past her to get into the normally restricted area. "Aren't you joining us?"

Jack stepped forward, reached in, and pressed the button. "You guys go ahead; Miss Beckham forgot something in her office."

"Night," they said as the decorative metal gates closed and the elevator began to descend.

"What did I forget?"

Before Jack could answer, there was a loud creak, then a snap, then sparks and horrible screams as the elevator cable snapped. As if in slow motion, Meghan listened in horror as the elevator box scraped and tumbled down the shaft before landing with a loud thud. Followed by nothing but a deadly silence.

Chapter Seven

DETECTIVE CERVENTES WAS A HANDSOME MAN WHO'D made the newspapers when he'd become the first Cuban immigrant to join the Palm Beach Police Department twenty years ago. He was efficient, talented, and standing in Meghan's office as the grandfather clock in the hallway chimed in a new day.

Her horror had turned into shock. Now she was just numb. She was numb knowing Santa was dead—*again*. Numb knowing Darius probably wouldn't survive his injuries. And numb knowing that she and Jack should have been the ones in the elevator.

"I'm going to have a patrol car follow you home. It's my recommendation that you stay there for your safety and the safety of others until we find out who is responsible for this."

"She will," Jack answered, taking her arm and helping her to her feet.

Meghan grabbed her purse on her way out of the office as the detective added, "I'll post men here in the store around the clock as well."

"Thank you," she mumbled as Jack placed his arm around her shoulders and led her toward the stairs. The burden of her guilt weighed heavily on her. "Darius is still listed as critical, and another person died because of me," she said as she and Jack reached the second floor landing.

"No," Jack corrected, squeezing her shoulder, "you aren't responsible. You're a target, Meghan. You can't hold yourself responsible for the actions of a lunatic."

"I should have listened. Closed the store. I should have—"

"Wouldn't have mattered," he cut in. "A determined killer doesn't care who gets in his way. No one could have predicted the guy would tamper with the elevator."

"But *I* told them to use it," she argued, swallowing the bitter taste of regret.

"I hope you don't mind. I had Terri call Jenna and cancel your dinner after the thing with Darius. You need to get some sleep," Jack suggested. "You're exhausted and the memory is too fresh."

They reached the underground parking garage where half the police department milled around apparently waiting for her. Three marked cars escorted them back to her house, then parked and took root out front.

"Why don't I fix you something to eat," Jack offered as she reactivated the alarm system once they were inside, "then you can get some rest."

Meghan shook her head. "Thanks, but no thanks. I couldn't swallow a thing right now." While Meghan appreciated Jack's offer, she wasn't up to it. Right then, all she wanted was to be alone with her raw emotions.

"I'm still waiting for a call back from the accident investigation people," Roz told Jack. "Are you absolutely sure the accident was staged?" she asked.

"Positive," Jack said. Then he wished her well before hanging up, mildly distracted as his brain splintered into several different directions.

Again Jack tried to picture the boss he'd never met. Roz's voice betrayed nothing and all he really knew about her was that she coordinated the Agency assignments and sent him homemade cookies. The cookies said kindly grandma. The voice said buttoned-down executive in a pinstriped suit, with stiffly lacquered hair and sensible shoes. They didn't mesh. The rest was all supposition and conjecture. Pretty much like what he had in the Beckham case.

The sun had been up for a couple of hours and he'd yet to hear Meghan stirring in the bedroom. Just as well. He figured she probably needed more than a decent night's sleep; she needed her space. Not that he didn't want to go to her. That had been pretty much an all-night battle. One he'd very nearly lost a time or two. The knowledge that she was mere feet away seemed to spark strong feelings in him.

Hadn't he learned his lesson all those years ago with Laura? He'd sworn after that disaster that he'd *never* get attached to a protectee again. His love for Laura had been strong but brotherly in nature. She was young and reckless, and he should have made sure the agents he'd assigned to her that night kept a vigilant watch on the headstrong twenty-year-old who was hell-bent on going to that party. But he hadn't and Laura had slipped out on her detail.

A week later it had been his job to tell the vice president that Laura's body had been found in a shallow grave.

Yet here he was—two days into the assignment—thinking of this protectee in ways he knew were a bad idea. A very bad idea. And not just because it might cloud his judgment. He was too much of a professional to be blinded by lust. Hell, of the two, that was the easier one to control. Well, not so easy when his brain flashed a quick and vivid image of her to taunt him. Oh, he wanted her. That was a given. It was the other thing that was driving him nuts. The feeling of being . . . *connected*. That was weird.

Meghan managed to raise his blood pressure and make him feel comfortable all at once. The raised blood pressure he could deal with—no problem. The comfort level, he thought as he held his head in his hands, that was an unexpected kink.

"Damn it!" He stood and began to pace the spacious living room. As if . . . *feeling things* for her wasn't enough of a monkey wrench, he was also frustrated to hell and back trying to anticipate the lunatic's next move. Three store Santas were dead. What was the connection? The fact that all three murder victims were Santas? All three were employees of Beckham's? All three incidents could just as easily have happened to Meghan? None of the above? Jack raked his fingers through his hair as he paced from one end of the large space to the other.

He needed to know the connection if he had a hope in hell of unraveling this and anticipating the killer's next move.

Not only was it imperative to resolve this before the killer struck again, but, to be honest with himself, doing his job was a hell of a lot less complicated than trying to decipher the reasons why he was so drawn to Meghan.

"So what am I missing?" he asked the morning quiet. "What's the common thread?" Annoyed when answers didn't come on command, Jack gabbed the accident reconstructionist's report and reread it for the tenth time. Not the summary cover letter, but the actual pages of the report. The company had been thorough. They had checked and rechecked everything, then created a computer model of the incident that mirrored everything from confirmed witness statements to police photographs to factoring in the wind speed that night.

Jack might not be a physicist, but he grasped the concepts contained in the pages as he read them over and over. Slowly, he began to formulate a scenario that didn't precisely match the cover letter. But it sure as hell matched the reports and photographs. At least he thought so. He'd have to wait for Roz's call to confirm his suspicions.

Moving back to the kitchen, he poured himself another cup of coffee, then started a fresh pot, his third one this morning. Meghan liked it strong enough to grow hair on her ch—Jack rubbed a hand across his face. His frustration was fueled by more than just a healthy dose of physical longing. Though when he heard the shower, his groin stirred. Lust was easy to dismiss.

Liking Meghan Beckham was a lot more complex. And considerably harder to write off.

He *liked* her. Liked her strength. Liked her tenacity. Liked that she gave a damn about her employees, even the two she'd never met. She didn't just care because these men had worked for her. She cared on a deep personal level that made her more human. More fallible than she liked to portray.

He took a long swallow of coffee, hoping his brain would focus on the hot liquid searing his throat. No such luck. The only thing that burned was his fierce need to be with her. Pictures of Meghan, naked and wet, standing under the stream of the shower, slipped in and out of his mind. He groaned aloud and suffered in silence as he heard her hair dryer, then the drawers, then finally the sound of her bare feet as she came down the hallway.

Normally, he would have been impressed by the display of inner strength. By the way she'd put the previous night's incident in proper perspective. But this wasn't normal. Not by a long shot.

Normal didn't include the smell of floral shampoo that arrived a split second before she came into the room wearing a plain white robe that seemed anything but plain when wrapped around the outline of her incredible body.

He allowed his eyes to roam freely and happily over her upturned face. He knew he should offer some sort of greeting but he was afraid that if he opened his mouth at that moment, it would be to insist that they go back into her bedroom.

As if reading his mind, Meghan stood still, her thickly lashed eyes focused on him. Her lips parted slightly, allowing each breath to ease in and out of her pretty mouth.

A moan of strong, urgent need rumbled in Jack's throat. He felt a seizing in his gut and a tightness in his groin as his gaze dropped lower to her long, delicate throat and then lower still, to the hint of cleavage just above the V formed by the neckline of her robe.

Banishing rational thought from his brain, Jack took the two steps necessary to reach her, wrapped his arm around her waist, and dragged her against him. The feel of her body against his was like finding the true meaning of life.

He wanted to take it slowly, intended to, in fact. But intentions were a memory the minute he dipped his head to brush his lips to hers. He felt the warmth of her mouth and tasted the cool mint as his tongue teased her lips apart.

With his mouth on hers, Meghan flattened her hands against his chest, enjoying the strong beat of his heart beneath her touch. She felt his reluctance as he loosened his grip and she stepped back ever so slightly. Her own heart was beating so hard she couldn't think straight. After the events of last night, something inside her had shifted. A door had opened. She wanted this man.

She allowed herself to look at him boldly, taking in the vast expanse of his shoulders, drinking in the sight of his shirt where it was pulled tightly across the contours of his impressive upper body. His strength tugged at something deep inside her and the primal urge to get as close to him as possible surprised her, knocking her normal defenses aside. She openly admired the powerful thighs straining against the soft fabric of his jeans. The mere sight caused a fluttering in the pit of her stomach.

"So," she said, her voice sounding husky in her own ears, "what are we going to do about this since my self-control seems to have gone right out the window? I'm thinking it would be stupid for us not to sleep together."

"I agree." His voice was shallow, his breathing uneven. "I want you. But we're not kids. We can't have everything we want."

"Does that mean you want me as badly as I want you?" Meghan held her breath waiting for his reply.

He met her gaze. "Right now, your *safety* is my prime concern."

She threaded her arms around his neck. "I hear a 'but' in there."

"Not a 'but.'" The slightest grin lifted the corner of his mouth. "An 'on the other hand.' There are three armed police officers outside a secured location. I'm here to guard your body. I need to stay close to you. Very, very close."

"I think we could get a lot closer in the bedroom, don't you?" she said, biting her lip. She looked up at him, enjoying the anticipation fluttering in her stomach.

The clock on the mantel showed six fifteen. Meghan was safe here with him. Nowhere they needed to be for at least another hour or more. There was nothing new to act on. "You shouldn't make these kinds of offers, Meghan. Not unless you mean them."

She got up on tiptoe to kiss his chin. "I rarely say anything I don't mean."

"We have that in common," he muttered as he brushed his lips against her forehead.

It would be wonderful to forget everything. Just for a few hours. No memory of the accident, the Santas.

Nothing but the magic of being with him. She felt his hesitation at the same time she saw the need stamped across his features.

Meghan took a deep breath and went for it. "Look, Jack. I'm asking you to go to bed with me. Nothing else. No strings, no histrionics. If you want to, great, if not, okay, but stop debating the idea because I gotta tell you, it's wreaking havoc on my self-esteem."

"Sorry," he said as he moved and pulled her into the circle of his arms. "But I wasn't expecting this."

"Me either," she admitted, adding, "I haven't been able to think of much of anything but you since we met."

Protected in his arms, Meghan closed her eyes and allowed her cheek to rest against his chest.

His fingers danced over the outline of her spine, leaving a trail of electrifying sensation in their wake. Like a spring flower, passion flourished and blossomed from deep within her, filling her quickly with a type of frenzied desire she had never felt before. He ignited feelings so powerful and so intense that Meghan fleetingly wondered if this was possible or merely a product of fear and a restless night. Then he slipped the tip of his finger inside the neckline of her robe for a split second and she couldn't think anymore. Except maybe to consider begging when he stopped.

Jack moved his hand in a series of slow, sensual circles until it rested against her rib cage, just under the swell of her breast. He wanted—no, needed to see her face. He wanted to see the desire in her eyes. Catching her chin between his thumb and forefinger, he tilted her head up with the intention of searching her eyes. He never made it that far.

His eyes were riveted to her lips, which were slightly parted, a glistening shade of pale rose. His eyes roamed over every delicate feature and he could feel her pulse rate increase through the thin fabric. A knot formed in his throat as he silently acknowledged his own incredible need for this woman.

Lowering his head, he took another tentative taste. Her mouth was warm and pliant, and so was her body, which now pressed urgently against him. His hands roamed purposefully, memorizing every nuance and curve.

He felt his own body respond with an ache, then an almost overwhelming rush of desire surged through him. Her arms slid around his waist, pulling him closer. Jack marveled at the perfect way they fit together. It was as if Meghan had been made for him. For this.

"Meghan," he whispered against her mouth. He toyed with a lock of her hair first, then slowly wound his hand through the silken mass and gave a gentle tug, forcing her head back even more. Looking down at her face, Jack knew there was no other sight on earth as beautiful and inviting as her smoky blue eyes.

In one effortless motion, he lifted her, carried her to the bedroom, and carefully lowered her onto the bed. Her light hair fanned out against the pillow.

"I think you're supposed to get on the bed with me," Meghan said in a husky voice when he perched at the edge of the mattress.

With a single finger, Jack reached out to trace the delicate outline of her mouth. Her skin was the color of ivory, with a faint but warm flush.

Sliding into place next to her, he began showering her face and neck with light kisses. While his mouth searched for that sensitive spot at the base of her throat, he felt her fingers working the buttons of his shirt.

He waited breathlessly for the feel of her hands on his body and he wasn't disappointed when the anticipation gave way to reality. A pleasured moan spilled from his mouth when she brushed away his clothing and began running her palms over the tight muscles of his stomach.

Capturing both of her hands in one of his, Jack gently held them above her head. The position arched her back, drawing his eyes down to the outline of her erect nipples.

"This isn't fair," she said as he slowly untied the belt cinching her waist.

"Believe me, Meghan, if I let you keep touching me, I'd probably last less than a minute," he reassured her.

Meghan responded by lifting her body to him. The rounded swell of one exposed breast brushed his arm. He began peeling away the single layer covering her. He was rewarded by the incredible sight of her breasts spilling over the edges of a lacy bra that was sexy as sin. His eyes burned as he drank in the sight of taut peaks straining against the lace. His hand rested first against the flatness of her stomach before inching up over the warm flesh. Finally, his fingers closed over the rounded fullness.

"Please let me touch you!" Meghan cried out.

"Not yet," he whispered as his thumb and forefinger released the front clasp on her bra. He ignored her futile struggle to release her hands as he dipped his head to kiss the raging pulse point at her throat. Her soft skin grew hot as he worked his mouth lower and lower. She gasped when his mouth closed around her nipple, then called his name in a hoarse voice that caused a tremor to run the full length of his body.

Moments later, he lifted his head only long enough to see her passion-laden expression and to tell her she was beautiful.

"So are you."

Whether it was the sound of her voice or possibly the way she pressed herself against him, Jack neither knew nor cared. He found himself nearly undone by the level of passion communicated by the movements of her supple body.

He reached down until his fingers made contact with a wisp of silk and lace that almost constituted enough to be labeled panties. The feel of the sensuous garment against her skin very nearly pushed him over the edge. He whisked the thong over her hips and legs, until she was finally next to him without a single barrier.

He sought her mouth again as he released his hold on her hands. He didn't know which was more potent, the feel of her naked body against his, or the frantic way she worked to remove his clothing. His body moved to cover hers, his tongue thrust deeply into the warm recesses of her mouth. His hand moved downward, skimming the side of her body all the way to her thigh. Then, giving in to the urgent need pulsating through him, Jack positioned himself between her legs. Every muscle in his body tensed as he looked at her face before directing his attention lower to the point where they would join.

Meghan lifted her hips, welcoming, inviting, as her palms flattened against his hips and tugged him toward her.

"You're incredible," he groaned against her lips.

"Thank you," she whispered back. "I want you. Now, please?"

He wasted no time responding to her request. In a single motion, he thrust deeply inside of her, knowing without question that he had found heaven on earth.

He caught his breath and held it. The sheer pleasure of being inside her sweet softness rocked him from head to toe. He wanted her just as crazy, just as hot, just as out of control as he was. He slid his hand between them and teased her hot spot. She wrapped her legs around his hips as he pushed inside her in a primal, building rhythm. Her gasp gratified the hell out of him as he felt her body convulse and tighten around him. He felt her body splinter in an intimate squeeze, then allowed explosive waves to surge from him. One after the other, ripples of pleasure poured from him into her. Satisfaction had never been so sweet.

With his head buried next to hers, the sweet scent of her hair filled his nostrils. Jack reluctantly relinquished possession of her body. It took several minutes before his breathing slowed to a steady, satiated pace.

Rolling onto his side next to her, Jack rested his head against his arm and glanced down at her. She was sheer perfection. He could have happily stayed next to her in the big soft bed until the end of time.

The telephone rang just then, disturbing the lazy tranquility of the moment. Meghan flinched at the strident sound. "I don't want to answer that."

Jack knew how she felt. It might be Roz with news— "You'd better."

"I know," she reached for the receiver. "Hello?" Every vestige of postcoital pink drained from her cheeks. "*What?*"

Instantly alert, he read the absolute shock and horror in her eyes.

Meghan cupped one slightly trembling hand over the receiver and said, "She's dead."

"Who?"

Chapter Eight

"SHE WHO?" JACK ASKED AS HE FOLLOWED HER LEAD and scrambled out of bed.

"Jenna," Meghan said as she struggled to dress. "That was Detective Cerventes. He said Jenna committed suicide and . . ." She paused and pressed her hands to her mouth, shaking her head as her eyes filled with tears that never fell. He watched as she sucked in a deep breath, then continued. "He said she left a note claiming she was responsible for the Santa murders."

"Jenna?" he repeated. "Dad's mistress, Jenna? The one who was supposed to come over here for dinner?"

She nodded. "The same one who would never, ever kill herself or anyone else."

After pulling on his jeans and shirt, Jack helped her button the blouse she grabbed from the closet. Her hands were trembling, as was her bottom lip, yet she managed to keep it together.

He reached up and grasped her shoulders, then looked directly into her eyes. "Are you absolutely sure, Meghan? I mean you can never really know everything about another person."

She shrugged out of his hold. "We're not talking about a secret pill habit, Jack. I've known this woman for years," she insisted as she tugged the bed covers into a version of order. "Yes, she's been unhappy—even depressed—since my father died. And yes, she occasionally drinks too much. But there's no way anyone could convince me that she killed the Santas, injured Darius, or intended to hurt me. Note or no note. Cerventes is on his way over here. He said he has some questions."

"Maybe you should listen to him before you decide that Jenna couldn't have done it. Maybe the evidence—"

"Is a big pile of bullshit." She glared at him. "Trust me, Jack. I don't know how, but I know this is totally wrong."

"Fine."

She stopped in midstride and turned toward him. "*Fine?* That's it?"

He shrugged and rubbed the tension beginning to knot at the base of his skull. "I didn't know the woman. I'm willing to wait and see Cerventes's evidence before I debate the possibilities—pro or con—with you."

Cerventes arrived fifteen minutes later carrying an evidence bag. Jack greeted him and showed him into the living room where Meghan stood by the tinted window, staring out at the ocean beyond.

His heart felt heavy as he watched her automated movements as she tried to smile at the detective. She offered the detective a seat on one of three sofas, then sat opposite Cerventes. Jack moved to join her, sitting close enough to elicit a nonverbal response from the other man.

"We recovered this at the scene," Cerventes stated gently as he paced the bagged note on the table separating the sofas.

The single page was splattered with what Jack recognized as high-velocity blood splatter. He heard Meghan's sharp intake of breath on seeing the note and put his hand on her knee as he leaned forward and took a closer look.

As promised, the note contained a full confession for the killings as well as an explanation. According to the suicide note, Jenna's goal had been to destroy Beckham's as punishment for Beckham Sr. not leaving her anything when he died. Jack had to admit it was plausible. Revenge and money were two pretty popular motives in his experience.

"Is it Jenna's handwriting?" he asked, tilting the encased letter in Meghan's direction.

After studying it for a moment, she nodded reluctantly. "But I don't care what it says. Jenna did not do this."

Cerventes cleared his throat. "There's more, Miss Beckham. We recovered bolt cutters in her apartment. Initial testing indicated the tool marks match those on the elevator cables."

Meghan didn't flinch. "I don't care if they match the rifle Oswald used to shoot Kennedy. Jenna was not a killer."

"We also recovered the same poison used in the sweetener packets for the first slaying."

Meghan was unwavering in her conviction. "There has to be some other explanation, Detective. Keep investigating."

Cerventes stood. "I'm sorry, Miss Beckham, but as far as the Palm Beach Police Department is concerned, this matter is closed."

She shot off the sofa like a rocket. "You can't do that! Somehow, *someone* forced Jenna to write that note and planted evidence in her apartment."

"There's no indication of that, Miss Beckham. With your identification of the handwriting, this investigation is closed. It's over, Miss Beckham."

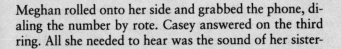

Meghan rolled onto her side and grabbed the phone, dialing the number by rote. Casey answered on the third ring. All she needed to hear was the sound of her sister-in-law's voice and Meghan burst into tears. Given the events of the previous twenty-four hours, she deserved a good cry.

"Jenna was bitter," Casey said cautiously.

"I never dreamed she was *that* bitter," Meghan admitted now that she'd had some time to absorb the truth of the facts presented by Cerventes. "Not enough to hurt complete strangers, me, *and* herself. At least I never thought so. Maybe it does make sense—kind of. I didn't want to believe it at first, but there really is no way to explain away her handwriting."

"This is shocking news, Meghan. I'm going to come over. I have to cancel a few things, but I can be there in thirty minutes or so."

She rolled onto her back and watched the blades of the ceiling fan spin. The pillow still held the memory of Jack's scent. It brought Meghan an odd comfort. But one she knew was merely borrowed. "No, that's not necessary, really. I'm going to hang out here for a little bit longer then go into the store for a while."

"You *aren't* going to the store," Casey insisted.

Meghan took a deep breath and relaxed it slowly. "I need to. Habit. Besides, I don't know what else to do," she admitted. What were her other options? Run out and beg Jack to stay and . . . what? Case over. Closed. Jenna had confessed. Evidence didn't lie. Much as it pained her, she was coming around to accept that.

Saying good-bye to Jack was part and parcel of acceptance. Even if she didn't want to.

"Well, you are going to stay home. At least for today. Get rid of your bodyguard and we'll hang out and then later I'll go grab dinner and we can watch old movies. I'll even spend the night. How's that?"

"Good, but I really hate to impose on you," Meghan admitted, wiping the remnants of her tears away. "Really," she sniffed. "I'll be okay."

"I'm coming over, Meghan. I insist," Casey offered

without hesitation. "What about the cute bodyguard? When is he leaving?"

"I'm about to send him on his way."

"You must be relieved. I know how much you like your privacy and how much you didn't want him around."

Meghan was a lot of things, but relieved wasn't one of them. Confused, scared, angry, sad, frustrated. And for the first time in forever, *alone* sounded really lonely. Still, she needed to get Jack out of her life before she did something really pathetic—such as beg him to stay.

"I'm really sorry about Jenna," Casey offered.

Me too, Meghan thought. "Thanks, Casey. And thanks for caring."

"What's family for?"

She was pondering that question after she hung up the phone. She lingered, knowing what she had to do and dreading it all at once. Still, she knew putting it off would only make it worse. It was time to face reality.

Jack was out on the lanai, standing near the retaining wall. He turned the minute he heard her at the door. She looked vulnerable, but the determined tilt of her chin brought a feeling of dread to the pit of his stomach.

"Feel better?" he asked.

She shrugged. "Numb actually. I came out to thank you."

"Listen, Meghan," he began, reaching for her. She edged back, leaving him no choice but to let his hand slap down to his side. "I've been thinking about—"

He went silent when she raised her hand. Her gaze fixed off in the distance. Never a good sign when a woman didn't meet your eyes. Painful when the woman was Meghan.

"You should go, Jack."

"I don't have to, Meghan. Hear me out."

"You do have to, Jack."

He placed his finger beneath her chin, forcing her to meet his gaze. "Why do I have to?"

"B-because it's what I want."

"You aren't very convincing."

"I left a check by the front door. Please leave."

"Meghan, we need to talk. I have a theory."

"No more theories." She stepped away from him as if he had the plague. "Go, Jack. Please? Don't make this harder than it already is. Your work here is finished."

"What about—"

"Please don't say 'us,' " she groaned as she crossed her arms. "There is no *us*. 'Us' requires more than forty-eight hours. 'Us' requires more than a physical connection."

Frustration, hurt, rejection, every emotion he could think of rolled through him. He felt his temper flare and balled his hands into tight fists. "I know that. All I'm suggesting is that I hang out here while we—"

"No, Jack. Thank you, but no. There's nothing to investigate or protect. Jenna confessed."

"And you believe that now?" he scoffed.

"Yes."

"Then you're a fool."

Chapter Nine

"IT'S OVER, JACK," ROZ SAID WHEN SHE CALLED HIS CELL phone. "Barrett Trent called earlier and told me all about the Lewis woman. I would have preferred to hear it from you."

Jack rubbed his face and rolled his head around on his shoulders. "You would have if I thought the Lewis woman was the killer. I don't." He should've listened to Meghan when she'd been so positive Jenna Whatever couldn't have done it. That her father's ex-lover was incapable of killing herself. Instead he'd used his own considerable arrogance and swayed her into believing something that he was now sure he'd been dead wrong about.

"The police are convinced," Roz said in her no-nonsense tone. "Mr. Trent is convinced. So what's the problem?"

"Meghan," he said on a frustrated breath.

"Meghan?" Roz repeated, none-too-subtle curiosity hanging on each syllable. "Is there something else you want to share, Jack? If this is personal, then I think—"

"Not personal," he lied. "Just wrong, Roz. Did you get the report back from the accident guy yet?"

"Yes."

"And?"

"And it confirms your suspicions."

Jack cursed. "Well then, that proves Jenna isn't our killer. If she was, she'd have admitted to rigging the car wreck, too, don't you agree?"

"Yes," Roz agreed. "But we've been removed from the case. Time for you to go home."

"Not yet," he said, gripping the steering wheel as he pulled over so he could keep Meghan's driveway in his rearview mirror. The cops were gone. But he'd made her promise to reactivate the alarm system as soon as he left.

"You know the rules," Roz cautioned.

He raked his fingers through his hair. "I also know this doesn't *feel* right." He saw the red Mercedes convertible pull up to the drive and recognized Casey as she made the turn toward the house. He was glad Meghan wouldn't be alone. Although he'd rather it was himself, not her sister-in-law, there to keep her company.

"Okay, so it has to be someone who would have had access to Michael's car as well as unfettered access to the store."

"Who is that?"

"I can think of four people off the top of my head," Jack admitted. He ticked them off to Roz.

"You can cross Barrett Trent off your list," she told him.

"Why?"

"Because I did a complete background check on him when he first contacted me after Michael's accident. He was on a cruise ship in Greece when the car crashed. I verified it with the cruise line as well as the passenger manifest from the emergency flight he used to get back here to be with his daughter."

"The daughter just went into Meghan's house."

"You're still there?" Roz asked.

"Outside," he admitted. "I was afraid she'd call the cops on me if I didn't leave. Hang on." He turned to watch Meghan and Casey speed out of the driveway. "I've got to go, Roz. Keep digging on the others. I'll call you back."

"I really don't feel like being with people," Meghan grumbled as Casey drove—a tad too fast—over the bridge into West Palm Beach.

"It'll do you good," Casey insisted.

"Holy shit, Casey, the train is coming!" Meghan yelled when Casey did a slalom around the caution bars lowering to warn people off the tracks.

"Sorry, necessary detour," Casey remarked.

Meghan's heart was in her throat. "You're scaring me," she said firmly, in hopes of getting the other woman's attention. "Please slow down."

Casey checked the rearview mirror, then marginally slowed the car. "Don't worry, Meghan, you won't be scared for long."

"Thank you."

"Don't thank me," Casey said calmly. "I'm going to kill you once and for all."

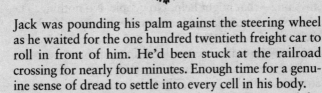

Jack was pounding his palm against the steering wheel as he waited for the one hundred twentieth freight car to roll in front of him. He'd been stuck at the railroad crossing for nearly four minutes. Enough time for a genuine sense of dread to settle into every cell in his body.

Tapping the redial button on his cell, he waited for Roz to answer. "I've got an idea," he said. "Can you check real estate transactions for me?"

"Sure. What am I looking for?"

"Anything in Sam Shelton's name. It has to be him."

"Hang on." He heard the click of the keys on her keyboard. "Nothing for Sam," Roz told him, clearly distracted as she spoke. "Wait—"

"What?" Jack demanded watching the rail cars speed by. Would this damn train never end?

"I may have something. Two somethings, actually."

Meghan couldn't believe she heard correctly. Shock and disbelief ricocheted through her. The only logical explanation was that Casey had gone off the deep end. It had to be grief over losing Michael. Something. *Anything* to explain the venom and hostility oozing from the woman. "I don't understand, Casey," Meghan said when they entered an industrial park just west of the city. "What's gotten into you?"

"You're as dense as your brother. You just don't die as easily," she said, pulling a small-caliber gun and pointing it at Meghan's head. "Get out."

Her brain was swimming in waves of confusion. "Jesus, Casey! What are you think—ouch!" Meghan felt the sting of the gun smacking against her temple. She touched her fingers to the spot and they came away damp with blood. "Okay, okay! I'm going."

Exiting the car, she glanced around for something—anything—that might help. No people. No nothing. The place was deserted save for one other car. One she knew well.

Casey shoved her toward the door of the warehouse, jabbing the gun into her ribs as they crossed the ten or so yards. Meghan was fairly certain that if she went inside, she wouldn't ever come out—at least not alive.

Pretending to stumble, she reached down, gathered up a handful of gravel, and tossed it into Casey's eyes. Then she bolted.

But she didn't get far. One second she was running and the next Sam had her by the waist and was dragging her inside the warehouse. It was dark and dank, smelling faintly of motor oil and insecticide. Sam tossed her onto the cement floor.

"Bitch," Casey cursed, punctuating the remark with a kick in her ribs.

Meghan moaned as the air rushed from her lungs. She saw bright white flecks as she rolled on the floor, writhing in pain.

"Enough," Sam said, dragging her to her feet and depositing her in a metal chair. It was surreal to look into their faces knowing they were going to kill her. "I don't get it," Meghan croaked out, holding her sore ribs. "Why?"

"You owe us, Meghan," Casey supplied, her voice tainted with venom. "We're tired of waiting to collect."

Meghan blinked, still confused. "Collect what? My brother loved you. He married you."

"No one ever thought to ask if I loved him," Casey retorted. "I didn't. Not ever. I wanted to marry Sam. I told my father and he hit me. Can you believe it?"

"Right now?" Meghan asked smartly. It earned her another solid whack with the end of the gun barrel. She cried out but realized that as long as they were causing her pain, she wasn't dead. If she wasn't dead, she had hope. "Sorry. Okay. So all this has been about you wanting to marry Sam? Jenna, the Santas—all this?"

"You're forgetting Michael," Sam injected. "That's actually where it started. You were both supposed to die in the accident. I rigged the tire to blow and the gas tank. All traces of the explosives were supposed to be destroyed. But what are the chances that you'd be thrown clear before the explosion? Jesus, I couldn't believe it!"

"So you could have the store?" Meghan guessed.

Sam shook his head. "It's more than the store, Meghan. It's the prestige, something your do-gooder brother always took for granted. Your father handed him that store and he couldn't have cared less."

"But I do, so why are you doing this?"

"We earned it," Casey insisted. "The original plan was for me to marry Michael, then you and Michael would die together, then I'd inherit. I'd marry Sam and there'd be nothing my parents could say."

"Only you didn't die," Sam continued. "And I had to suck up to that moronic assistant of yours so I could keep tabs on you. Thanks to Terri's eagerness to share everything with me, I was able to switch the report from the accident reconstruction company so you wouldn't get suspicious. I came up with the poisoning idea. Santa wasn't the target per se, but we figured three or four murders would be enough to convince the cops that a serial killer was on the loose. But Barrett got concerned and hired that Palmer guy, so we had to adjust the plan.

"The hardest part was getting Jenna to write the note. I had to play a little game of Russian roulette with her before she finally took pen in hand."

Meghan saw a flash of movement pass outside the window. If there was someone outside, she needed to get his attention. She needed noise. Bracing herself, she said, "The two of you are nuts. Cruel, disgusting—ouch!"

This blow toppled her to the floor. She actually saw stars and flashes, heard grunt and groans, then a pop of gunfire and the acrid scent of smoke. She felt a burning sensation in her arm, saw a gush of blood. Then nothing.

Meghan blinked against harsh, bright light. She smelled antiseptic and slowly tried to process the scene around her.

White. It was very, very white. White-tiled walls,

white sheets, white everything. "I'll be damned, there is a heaven. Who knew you could be dead *and* thirsty?"

She heard a gentle laugh and turned her sore head in the direction of the sound. Blurred at first, it took a few seconds before Jack's face came into full focus.

"You aren't dead," he promised her, lifting her hand and kissing her knuckles. "A little silly from the pain-killers, but you're fine."

"You stayed?"

He nodded. "I'm hard to get rid of. Which is good, because as it turned out, you needed me."

"I never said I didn't."

"Not in so many words," he countered. "But you did fire me and you pretty much tossed me out of your house on my ass."

"Not possible. Anyone that stupid should be shot." Her lips curved. "Oh, wait! I *was* shot."

He laughed again as he kissed her forehead. "I'm staying, Meghan. We can go slow, whatever you want."

"I want you, Jack."

"For how long?"

This was a trick question. "Ah—"

"Let's make this simple," Jack gave her a penetrating look. Clearly he hadn't slept in forever. His eyes were shadowed, his jaw needed a shave. He been worried and stuck around to keep her safe. He'd gone over and beyond the call of duty.

He looked so dear to her as he said gruffly, "Should I go and buy a spare toothbrush? Or should I sell my condo in D.C. and have my furniture shipped?"

Meghan's smile bloomed from her heart. "I have the number of a great moving company in my address book. We'll call them *after* you've kissed all my aches and pains better."

Pillow Talk

Carnival Pride℠
April 2-9, 2006

7 Day Exotic Mexican Riviera Itinerary

DAY	PORT	ARRIVE	DEPART
Sun	Los Angeles/Long Beach, CA		4:00 P.M.
Mon	"Book Lover's" Day at Sea		
Tue	"Book Lover's" Day at Sea		
Wed	Puerto Vallarta, Mexico	8:00 A.M.	10:00 P.M.
Thu	Mazatlan, Mexico	9:00 A.M.	6:00 P.M.
Fri	Cabo San Lucas, Mexico	7:00 A.M.	4:00 P.M.
Sat	"Book Lover's" Day at Sea		
Sun	Los Angeles/Long Beach, CA	9:00 A.M.	

ports of call subject to weather conditions

TERMS AND CONDITIONS

PAYMENT SCHEDULE:
50% due upon booking
Full and final payment due by February 10, 2006

Acceptable forms of payment are Visa, MasterCard, American Express, Discover and checks. The cardholder must be one of the passengers traveling. A fee of $25 will apply for all returned checks. Check payments must be made payable to **Advantage International, LLC and sent to: Advantage International, LLC, 195 North Harbor Drive, Suite 4206, Chicago, IL 60601**

CHANGE/CANCELLATION:
Notice of change/cancellation must be made in writing to Advantage International, LLC.

Change:
Changes in cabin category may be requested and can result in increased rate and penalties. A name change is permitted 60 days or more prior to departure and will incur a penalty of $50 per name change. Deviation from the group schedule and package is a cancellation.

Cancellation:
181 days or more prior to departure	$250 per person
121 - 180 days or more prior to departure	50% of the package price
120 - 61 days prior to departure	75% of the package price
60 days or less prior to departure	100% of the package price (nonrefundable)

U.S. and Canadian citizens are required to present a valid passport or the original birth certificate and state issued photo ID (drivers license). All other nationalities must contact the consulate of the various ports that are visited for verification of documentation.

<u>**We strongly recommend trip cancellation insurance!**</u>

For complete details call 1-877-ADV-NTGE or visit www.AuthorsAtSea.com

---

For booking form and complete information
go to **www.AuthorsAtSea.com** or call **1-877-ADV-NTGE**

Complete coupon and booking form and mail both to:
**Advantage International, LLC,
195 North Harbor Drive, Suite 4206, Chicago, IL 60601**